Harvest of the Heart

Willow Creek Second Chances - Book Two

by Les Dupuy

Copyright Page

Harvest of the Heart
Willow Creek Second Chances Series: Book Two

Copyright © 2025 by Les Dupuy
All rights reserved. No part of this publication may be reproduced, distributed, or transmitted in any form or by any means, including photocopying, recording, or other electronic or mechanical methods, without the prior written permission of the author, except in the case of brief quotations embodied in critical reviews and certain other noncommercial uses permitted by copyright law.

This is a work of fiction. Names, characters, places, and incidents are products of the author's imagination or are used fictitiously. Any resemblance to actual events, locales, or persons, living or dead, is purely coincidental.

Published in the United States of America.
Scripture quotations are from the King James Version (KJV) of the Bible.

Visit the author at: https://amzn.to/4j8bWfm

Table of Contents

Copyright Page
Table of Contents
Dedication
Acknowledgments
The First and Forever Friends
About the Book
ACT I
Chapter 1 - Booths, Blessings, and Butterflies
Chapter 2 – Faith, Firelight & First Glances
Chapter 3 – Left Behind
Chapter 4 – When Yesterday Won't Stay Buried
Chapter 5 – When Joy Feels Far Away
Chapter 6 – Storm Clouds Over the Co-Op
Chapter 7 – The Belle Comes Home
Chapter 8 – Pies & Pickles
Chapter 9 – More Than Just a Bed
Chapter 10 – Second Chances, First Steps
Chapter 11 – Buried Battles & Bitter Truths
Chapter 12 – The Cost of Legacy
Chapter 13 – When the Truth Won't Stay Buried
ACT II
Chapter 14 – Tree Fort Promises - Room to Soar
Chapter 15 – Tree Fort Roots - Belonging Begins
Chapter 16 – Tree Fort - Between the Branches
Chapter 17 – Growing Things
Chapter 18 – Tending What's Broken
Chapter 19 – Storm Shelter Prayers
Chapter 20 – Storms Bring the Good Stuff
Chapter 21 – Whispers & What-Ifs
Chapter 22 – Fences Mended, Seeds Planted

Chapter 23 – Forgiveness & Faith
Chapter 24 – Ghosts, Gossip & God's Plan
ACT III
Chapter 25 – Ben's Table
Chapter 26 – The Deed Revealed
Chapter 27 – The Aftermath
Chapter 28 – Table for Three
Chapter 29 – The Spaces Between
Chapter 30 – The Boys' Prayer
Chapter 31 – Porchlight Apologies
Chapter 32 – Sunday Dinner Proposal
Chapter 33 – When the Rain Falls
Chapter 34 – A Sunday Kind of Love
Chapter 35 – Butterfly Moments
Epilogue – The Treehouse and the Promise
Coming Soon: Book 3 – Truth Begets Light
    Where It All Began: An Excerpt from Book 1 of the Willow Creek Second Chances Series Tennessee

Second Chances in Middle Tennessee

Chapter 1: No Place Like Home
Chapter 2: Refuge Found
Chapter 3: Unfinished Business
The Willow Creek Second Chances Series (Christian Romance)
About the Author

Dedication

To God be all the glory. Thank you, once again, for the words. I pray this work honors You.

To everyone who has been betrayed by broken promises, remember: God never breaks His promises. He never fails us. His timing is perfect in His plans.

"Trust in the Lord with all thine heart; and lean not unto thine own understanding.
 In all thy ways acknowledge him, and he shall direct thy paths."
— Proverbs 3:5–6 (KJV)

Acknowledgments

Getting older is not for the weak at heart. For all those who are joining me on my journey, keep your sense of humor and your lidocaine roll-on close, and buckle up. It is a proven fact that someone presses the gas pedal harder for every trip around the sun.

To all those who have been brewing an idea for years like a fine wine, time to open the bottle and let it breathe.

To my family who tolerate my dirty laundry, dirty floor, and messy flower beds, I am sorry to tell you I have a few more chapters practically writing themselves.

To our Father in Heaven, thank You for finally giving me the words to tell these stories I've been carrying in my heart for decades. I pray they do You justice and that one of my readers becomes interested in Your Word.

The First and Forever Friends

They grew up beneath the oaks, built forts out of scraps and dreams, and learned that when life falls apart, you go home to God and your people. Always.

Meet the First and Forever Friends:

- ★ Clara Sharp Walker
- ★ Maggie Cunningham Reeves
- ★ Ethan Walker
- ★ Wade Beaumont
- ★ Harry Spinnaker Sr.
- ★ Greg Whitlow

About the Book

Return to the fictional town of Willow Creek, Tennessee, nestled in the rolling hills about an hour south of Nashville, where faith, family, and second chances run deeper than the roots of the oldest oaks.

Maggie Cunningham is a single mother of two boys, working two jobs just to keep a roof over their heads after being betrayed and abandoned by a man who promised them forever. She never expected to find love again, and she certainly never expected it to come in the form of Ben Reeves.

Ben is a fourth-generation farmer trying to hang on to his heritage through one of the worst droughts he's ever seen. Love isn't something he's had time to look for—but when Maggie enters his life, he finds himself rethinking everything, including his faith.

Can Maggie find the strength to trust God's timing and risk her heart again? Can Ben make room for love amid the dust and debt?

It takes deep roots to survive the dry seasons. It takes stronger ones to weather the storm. Will their love lead them back to each other—and to the God who never left?

Harvest of the Heart

By Les Dupuy

ACT I

Seeds of Change

Chapter 1 - Booths, Blessings, and Butterflies

"Remember ye not the former things, neither consider the things of old. Behold, I will do a new thing; now it shall spring forth; shall ye not know it? I will even make a way in the wilderness, and rivers in the desert." - Isaiah 43:18-19 (KJV)

Maggie Cunningham darted between booths at Willow Creek's Town Square Park, clipboard clutched against her chest, checking vendor names off her list. Managing the Memorial Day festival while keeping an eye on her boys was like juggling flaming torches—one slip and everything would come crashing down. But she'd mastered the art of appearing in control, even when her heart raced with the familiar worry that she wasn't enough. Not as a single mother, not as a committee chair, and certainly not as a woman who'd been abandoned with two young sons and a mortgage she could barely afford.

"Mom! Ralph's trying to eat all the samples at the pie booth again!" Alan called.

Maggie took a deep breath, plastered on her everything's-fine smile, and turned toward her eldest son's voice. Another day, another chance to prove she could do this alone—even when her arms ached for someone to share the load.

Maggie scanned the crowd for Alan and Ralph and caught sight of Ava Walker weaving through the booths, her ponytail flying like a festival banner. Little Noah trailed behind her, clutching a handful of tickets in one hand and his dignity in the other.

The sight made her smile. Ava and Noah weren't her family by blood, but Maggie loved them like they were her own niece and nephew. They were the children of her best friend, Clara, her life-long sister from another mother.

Watching them now—Ava commanding the scene like she owned it, Noah huffing behind her—it was like seeing a rerun of NoBoots and Giggles, the nickname Maggie and Clara had earned as kids for always losing their shoes and laughing too loud.

Some things never changed. Some things did.

Ava Walker darted between the colorful booths lining Willow Creek's Town Square Park, her blonde ponytail bouncing with each excited step. She glanced back to make sure Noah kept up, his smaller legs working double-time.

"Hurry up, slowpoke! We gotta try everything before the lines get too long!"

Noah clutched his tickets, knuckles white with determination. "Which one first?"

"Crown Him with Many Rings!" Harry Jr. shouted, already sprinting toward the booth where golden rings glinted in the May sunshine.

Emma Collins squeezed between them. "No way! Aim for the Ark is way better. My mom says I have the best arm in third grade."

Ralph Donahue-Cunningham tugged at Alan's sleeve. "Can we do the dunking booth? I wanna see Principal Grayson get soaked!"

Alan rolled his eyes but couldn't hide his grin. "Later. Let's start with something we can actually win."

The children converged on the ring toss, jostling for position as Ethan Walker called out encouragement from behind the booth.

"Step right up! Three rings for two tickets! Crown the bottles and win a prize!"

At the Bullseye for the Bible booth, Ben Reeves knelt beside Alan, adjusting the boy's aim. "Little higher—steady now."

"Like this?" Alan squinted, tongue poking from the corner of his mouth.

"Perfect." Ben stepped back, hands hovering nearby without touching.

Across the festival grounds, Maggie Cunningham paused mid-sip of sweet tea, watching the interaction. Something fluttered in her chest as Ben patiently demonstrated the proper throwing technique for Ralph, who bounced on his toes with excitement. Ben's weathered hands were gentle, his smile genuine when Ralph's dart hit the outer ring.

A small smile tugged at her lips. Ben glanced up suddenly, catching her gaze. Maggie quickly looked away, pretending to find the church pamphlet in her hand fascinating.

"Maggie, honey, you want another sandwich?" Lorraine Cunningham appeared at her daughter's side, plate piled high with potato salad.

Henry Cunningham followed, grease-stained hands recently wiped on a napkin. "Your mama's worried you're not eating enough."

"I'm fine, Daddy." Maggie tucked a strand of hair behind her ear. "Just watching the boys."

"Those your little ones?" Sara Dawson asked, approaching with a shy girl around Ava's age. "I'm Sara. This is our foster daughter, Charnise."

"Nice to meet you," Maggie smiled warmly at the child. "My boys are over there—Alan and Ralph."

"Uncle Wade!" Emma Collins barreled into Wade's legs, followed by twin toddlers waddling behind. "Brett and Bert want cotton candy but Mama said ask you first!"

Wade chuckled, ruffling Emma's hair. "One small cone between the three of you, and that's my final offer." He winked at Mary Beth, who mouthed a silent "thank you" over her nephews' heads.

Maggie found herself drawn back to the ring toss booth where Ralph now stood on tiptoe, tongue poking out in concentration. Ben stood behind him, keeping a respectful distance but ready to help. When Ralph's ring clattered against the bottles without catching, his shoulders slumped.

"Almost got it," Ben encouraged. "Try holding your wrist like this." He demonstrated the motion without touching Ralph.

Ralph mimicked the stance, took a deep breath, and tossed again. The ring spun around the neck of a bottle before settling into place. Ralph's eyes widened.

"I did it! Alan, look! I did it!"

Ben's face lit up with a smile that reached his eyes, crinkling the corners. Something warm and unexpected bloomed in Maggie's chest. She hadn't seen that kind of gentle patience with her boys since—

She looked away quickly when Ben glanced in her direction again, busying herself with digging through her tote bag. Her fingers brushed against a thick envelope, and she pulled it out, momentarily confused. The law firm's letterhead brought it all rushing back.

Final divorce decree. Termination of parental rights. Deed transfer.

The memories crashed over her—Roger signing each document without hesitation, not even asking to say goodbye to the boys. His girlfriend waiting in the car outside the attorney's office, engine running. The way he'd handed over his house keys without meeting her eyes.

"Beautiful day for a festival, isn't it?"

Maggie startled as Clara settled onto the bench beside her, tucking the envelope hastily back into her bag.

"It sure is." Maggie forced brightness into her voice. "The kids are having a blast."

Clara's eyes were gentle. "And how about you? Having a blast too?"

"Oh, you know me." Maggie waved dismissively. "Happy when they're happy."

"Maggie." Clara's voice softened. "It's been five years. You're allowed to be happy for yourself too."

"I am happy." Maggie pointed toward the dunking booth. "Look—Ralph's about to soak Principal Grayson!"

Chapter 2 – Faith, Firelight & First Glances

"Thy word is a lamp unto my feet, and a light unto my path." - Psalms 119:105 (KJV)

"And second place in the Memorial Day Pie Contest goes to..." Hattie Beaumont paused for dramatic effect, her reading glasses perched on the end of her nose. "Maggie Cunningham for her strawberry-rhubarb masterpiece!"

Applause erupted from the crowd gathered around the pavilion. Maggie's eyes widened in surprise as Clara squeezed her arm.

"Go on up there!" Clara whispered, giving her a gentle push.

Maggie tucked her hair behind her ear and made her way to the front, accepting the red ribbon with a shy smile. She scanned the crowd, momentarily locking eyes with Ben Reeves standing at the edge of the gathering. His face broke into a warm smile that lingered just a beat too long.

Maggie felt heat rise to her cheeks and quickly looked away, focusing instead on Hattie's congratulations.

"Your best one yet, dear," Hattie said, patting Maggie's hand. "Though you've got a ways to go before you knock Francie Sharp off her throne."

Francie beamed from her spot at center stage, blue ribbon pinned proudly to her apron.

When Maggie returned to Clara's side, her friend's knowing smile made her squirm.

"What?"

"Ben Reeves couldn't take his eyes off you," Clara whispered, nudging Maggie with her elbow. "Still wanna tell me there's nothin' there?"

"Oh, hush," Maggie muttered, but couldn't help glancing back toward Ben, who was now helping a customer at his produce stand.

Clara linked arms with her. "Come on, let's go collect your winnings. I bet the Momma Twins are already there, collecting their spoils."

Across the square, Ben counted the day's earnings with a satisfied nod. The Crop 'Til You Drop booth had done well—better than he'd expected. Folks had snatched up his early strawberries and spring greens, even paid premium for his heirloom tomato seedlings.

Not enough to make up for what the drought would cost him, but every dollar helped when the bank was breathing down his neck.

"Good haul today?" Walt Beaumont asked, helping Ben load empty crates into his truck.

"Can't complain," Ben replied, though the weight on his shoulders said otherwise.

As he folded the last table, he noticed an envelope tucked under his truck's windshield wiper. Ben plucked it free, recognizing the bank's logo in the corner. His jaw tightened as he tossed it onto the passenger seat without opening it. He already knew what it said.

Instead, he grabbed a cold sweet tea from one of the remaining coolers and twisted off the cap.

"Heading to the bonfire?" Wes called, hauling trash bags toward the dumpsters.

Ben nodded, forcing a smile. "Wouldn't miss it."

He locked his truck and headed toward the growing crowd at the far end of the park, where flames were already licking skyward against the deepening twilight.

The bonfire crackled, sending orange sparks spiraling into the night sky. Ben found Ethan and Wade near the edge of the gathering, away from the main crowd.

"There he is," Wade nodded, handing Ben a folding chair. "How'd the stand do today?"

Ben settled between them. "Better than expected. Sold out of everything but the kale."

"Nobody likes kale," Ethan chuckled. "Not even the health nuts pretend anymore."

They sat in comfortable silence, watching the flames dance. The weight of the unopened bank letter pressed on Ben's mind.

"You doing alright?" Wade asked quietly. "Saw you toss that envelope in your truck earlier."

Ben stared into the fire. "Just another friendly reminder from the bank." He took a long swig of tea. "Drought's hit hard this year. Third generation trying to keep that land going, and I might be the one who loses it."

Ethan leaned forward. "Have you thought about leasing out some of your land? Might ease some pressure."

"Thinking's all I do lately." Ben ran a hand through his hair. "That land's been Reeves soil since my granddaddy cleared it. Hard to let even a piece go."

Wade clapped him on the shoulder. "Whatever you decide, you've got folks in your corner."

"Speaking of which," Ethan said, "Clara and I are heading out Tuesday for that cabin in the Smokies. Mind keeping an eye on the house while we're gone? Just drive by occasionally?"

"No problem," Wade nodded. "Though I suspect Ms. Francie will be over there watering plants twice daily whether Clara wants her to or not."

They laughed, and Ben felt a genuine smile break through his worry. These were good men. Good friends. The kind who built lives worth living— Sheriff Wade out there protecting and serving, Ethan with Clara and the kids.

Ben wondered if such happiness was in God's plan for him.

Across the field, Maggie sat on her truck's tailgate, Ralph and Alan on either side of her as they waited for the fireworks to begin.

"Ten more minutes!" Ralph bounced excitedly.

Clara approached, wrapping Maggie in a tight hug. "I almost forgot to tell you—when Ethan and I get back from our honeymoon, we want to take the boys for a sleepover. Give you a night to yourself."

"You don't have to do that," Maggie protested.

"We want to." Clara squeezed her hand. "Everyone needs a break sometimes, Maggs."

Maggie watched Clara's face glow with happiness. Her friend had found her way back to love after so much pain. Maggie wondered if such a path existed for her.

"Well, look who won second place," Ben's voice startled her from her thoughts.

He stood beside her truck, hands in his pockets, looking more relaxed than he had all day.

"Just lucky, I guess," Maggie smiled. "Rhubarb's plentiful this year."

"From your mama's patch?"

She nodded. "Can't beat Cunningham rhubarb."

Ralph scrambled to the edge of the tailgate. "Mr. Ben! Did you see me win at the ring toss?"

"Sure did, buddy." Ben stepped forward to help him down. "That was some fine throwing."

As Ralph jumped, Ben steadied him, and Maggie reached out instinctively. Their hands brushed, lingered. Their eyes met over Ralph's head.

"Congratulations on the pie," Ben said softly. "Wish I could've tasted it."

"Maybe next time," Maggie replied, surprising herself.

Ben's smile deepened. "I'd like that."

The first firework exploded overhead, bathing them in golden light. Would there be a next time? Only God and tomorrow knew.

Chapter 3 – Left Behind

"My God, my God, why hast thou forsaken me? why art thou so far from helping me, and from the words of my roaring?" Psalms 22:1 (KJV)Chapter 3

Dew glistened on the grass as Clara and Ethan pulled up to the Sharp family farm. The sun had barely crested the horizon, painting the sky in watercolor strokes of pink and gold. Ava and Noah tumbled out of the backseat, their excitement at spending a week with their uncles overshadowing any sadness about their parents' departure.

"You'll be good for Uncle Luke and the boys, right?" Clara knelt to straighten Noah's collar, her hands lingering a moment too long.

"We'll be fine, Mama," Ava assured her, arms wrapped around her mother's neck. "Uncle Caleb's gonna show me how to build a birdhouse!"

Ethan hoisted their bags from the truck bed. "And what did we say about climbing trees?"

"Only with an uncle watching," Noah recited, fidgeting with anticipation.

While Clara and Ethan took the kids inside to go over final instructions with Francie and Burle, Luke Sharp motioned to his younger brothers from behind the barn.

"They're inside. Quick, before they come back out." Luke produced a bag of decorations from his jacket.

Eli grinned, pulling out streamers and a hand-lettered "JUST MARRIED" sign. "Ethan's gonna kill us."

"Worth it," Caleb laughed, tying empty cans to the truck's bumper with fishing line.

Inside, Clara hugged her parents, fighting the unexpected tightness in her throat. "You have our number at the cabin. And the emergency contacts are—"

"Clara-Fair," Francie interrupted gently, using Ethan's nickname for her. "These children will be loved and spoiled and returned to you in one piece. Now go enjoy your husband."

23

Clara nodded, swallowing hard. She'd never been away from Ava and Noah for more than a night—not since escaping Truman. The thought of a whole week made her stomach twist.

"They'll be fine," Ethan whispered, his hand warm on her back. "This is good for all of us."

When they stepped outside, the kids had already disappeared with their uncles. From somewhere near the old oak tree came shrieks of laughter.

"Last one up's a rotten egg!" Caleb's voice rang out.

"Not fair! Your legs are longer!" Ava protested.

Clara took a step toward the sound, but Ethan caught her hand.

"Let them go, sweetheart. That's what this week is about."

She nodded, forcing herself to turn toward their truck—and gasped. Streamers fluttered from the side mirrors, tin cans dangled from the bumper, and "JUST MARRIED" was emblazoned across the back window in shaving cream.

"LUKE!" Ethan bellowed, but he was laughing.

Three guilty faces peered around the barn, grinning widely.

"Gotta give the newlyweds a proper send-off!" Eli called.

As they climbed into the decorated truck, Clara caught a final glimpse of her brothers leading the children toward the house, Eli with Noah on his shoulders and Caleb already pulling candy from his pockets.

"They'll be okay," she whispered, more to herself than to Ethan.

He squeezed her hand. "Better than okay. They'll be loved."

Sunlight streamed through the kitchen windows, catching dust motes that danced in the warm beams. Maggie curled her fingers around her coffee mug, savoring the warmth against her palms. From the living room came the muffled sounds of Alan and Ralph playing with their Lego sets, their voices rising and falling with the drama of whatever world they were building.

The church bells chimed in the distance. Nine o'clock. Service would be starting soon.

Maggie glanced at the boys' Sunday clothes, still hanging on the laundry room door where she'd placed them last night. She'd ironed Ralph's little button-up and laid out Alan's good shoes. But this morning, when she'd woken to their laughter, something in her had crumbled.

"Not today," she whispered to her coffee. "Maybe next week."

Her mother would be disappointed. Lorraine Cunningham never missed church, not even when she had the flu. She'd call later, voice tight with concern. "Didn't see y'all in the pew today. Everything alright?"

Maggie sighed, reaching for the manila folder on the table. The attorney's letterhead stared back at her, cold and official. She skimmed the contents again—Roger had left behind a mess of unpaid taxes on the rental property they'd bought together. Property she didn't even know existed until after he'd gone. Now the IRS wanted their money, and somehow it had become her problem.

The memory surfaced like a bruise being pressed. Roger standing in their bedroom, suitcase in hand. "I can't do this anymore, Maggs. This life—it's suffocating me."

Alan and Ralph huddled in the hallway, faces streaked with tears. "Where are you going, Daddy? When are you coming back?"

Roger hadn't even looked at them.

"Lord," Maggie whispered, eyes burning, "I did everything like you say to do it. I saved myself for marriage. I made sure we went to church every Sunday. I had my kids baptized. I did everything right." Her voice caught. "Why did it all end up like this? What did I do to deserve this? God, why?" She pressed her palms against her eyes. "Please tell me what to do."

The only answer was Ralph's laughter from the next room.

Her shoulders slumped. She shoved the letter back into the folder and pushed it aside, reaching instead for her planning book. The leather cover was worn at the edges, the pages filled with recipes, cost calculations, and sketches for Kneadful Things Bakery.

They needed a building to bake in. Somewhere to make this dream real. Somewhere to start over.

Dawn broke over Reeves Farm in shades of amber and gold. Ben heaved another hay bale onto the flatbed, sweat already darkening his shirt despite the early hour. Ms. Pickles trotted behind him, her white coat gleaming in the morning light as she inspected his work with solemn dignity.

"What do you think, girl? Good enough?" He scratched behind her ears, earning an appreciative grunt.

The farm had been quiet since his parents passed. Too quiet sometimes. Ms. Pickles nudged his leg, reminding him there was still work to be done.

"Right. Feed's not gonna spread itself."

As he climbed into his truck, the white envelope caught his eye again, sitting on the passenger seat where he'd tossed it yesterday. The bank's logo glared at him through the thin paper. Ben picked it up, turning it over in his calloused hands.

Not today.

He yanked open the glove compartment and shoved the envelope inside, slamming it shut with more force than necessary. Ms. Pickles tilted her head, watching him.

"Don't you start," he muttered.

His phone buzzed with a notification. Missed call. The bank. Again.

Ben pressed play on the voicemail, jaw tightening as the message filled the cab.

"Mr. Reeves, this is Vernon Tuttle from First County Bank. You are behind on your loan payment. Please call us back as soon as possible to make arrangements to catch up on your payments."

He deleted it. What was he supposed to tell them? That drought had withered half his crops? That feed prices had doubled? That his irrigation system had broken down twice this season?

An hour later, freshly showered and dressed in his one decent button-down, Ben slipped into the back pew at Willow Creek Baptist. His eyes scanned the congregation, searching for a head of auburn hair and two fidgeting boys.

No sign of them.

"Morning, Ben." The usher, Harold Mason, handed him a bulletin. "Good to see you."

Ben nodded his thanks, settling into his usual spot. The wooden pew felt hard beneath him, familiar in its discomfort. The choir began the first hymn, voices rising in harmony around him.

He bowed his head, not even pretending to follow along in the hymnal. Lord, I need some help here. The farm, the bank... His thoughts drifted to Maggie's empty seat across the aisle. And them.

He caught himself and frowned. That wasn't what he should be praying about. The farm was what mattered. Not the way Maggie's eyes crinkled when she laughed. Not how her boys had taken to Ms. Pickles. Not how empty the church felt without them.

Chapter 4 – When Yesterday Won't Stay Buried

"Will the Lord cast off for ever? and will he be favourable no more? Is his mercy clean gone for ever? doth his promise fail for evermore? Hath God forgotten to be gracious? hath he in anger shut up his tender mercies?" Psalms 77:7-9 (KJV)

Ben's phone buzzed against the kitchen table as he stared at the farm ledger, the columns of red numbers blurring before his eyes. Ms. Pickles lifted her head from her spot near the back door, ears perking up at the interruption.

"Reeves," he answered, already knowing who it would be.

"We need to talk." Walt Beaumont's voice came through sharp and clear. "Today. About the accounts."

Ben pinched the bridge of his nose. "I'm working on it, Walt."

"Working on it ain't cutting it anymore." In the background, he could hear Wes muttering something. The twins had always operated like two halves of one mind. "Wes says we've extended more credit in the last six months than in the two years before that."

"What am I supposed to do? Half these folks have children to feed."

"And we have a business to run." Walt's voice hardened. "We can't keep floating credit to half the county. You said you could handle this. At least Mr. Brewer knew when to cut people off."

The comparison to the Co-Op's previous owner stung. Old man Brewer had never turned anyone away at first, but he had been ruthless at cutting them off when he felt they were taking advantage of his generosity.

"Fine. I'll come by this afternoon."

After hanging up, Ben walked out onto the porch, the ancient boards creaking beneath his boots. The fields stretched before him, parched and thirsty. Three years of drought had turned the soil to dust. The farmstand barely broke even most weeks.

How could he demand payment from folks facing the same struggles? The Millers with their five kids, the Hendersons with their medical bills, the Carters who'd lost their oldest boy overseas last spring.

Ms. Pickles nudged his hand with her snout, eyes solemn.

"I know, girl." He scratched behind her ears. "Ain't your problem."

Ben tilted his face toward the cloudless sky, a bitter laugh escaping his throat.

"I don't know what else to do, Lord. I've tried everything I know. I go to church every Sunday. I've remained pure. I don't swear. I take care of my animals and the land." His voice cracked. "Why won't you just make it rain? Why do we have to suffer so?"

Only silence answered him, stretching across the barren fields.

"Easy there, Sadie-girl. Almost done." Maggie gently stroked the border collie's head while checking the healing wound on her hind leg. The dog whimpered but stayed still, dark eyes watching Maggie's every move.

"Good news, Mr. Peterson. The stitches are holding beautifully." She smiled at the elderly farmer who'd been pacing the small exam room. "Just keep the cone on for another three days, and she'll be back to herding in no time."

"That's my good girl," Mr. Peterson cooed, his weathered face softening. "Don't know what I'd do without her."

After they left, Maggie leaned against the counter at the desk, rolling her shoulders to ease the tension. She'd been up since 4:30 AM—Ralph had another nightmare, and by the time she'd calmed him down, it was time to start breakfast, pack lunches, and get everyone moving.

"Coffee refill?" Lila, the vet tech, appeared with a steaming mug.

"Bless you," Maggie murmured, accepting it gratefully. "Is our fearless leader in yet?"

"Running late. His truck wouldn't start." Lila glanced at the waiting room. "Three more walk-ins just showed up."

Maggie nodded, taking a long sip. The caffeine hit her system like a lifeline.

Her phone buzzed. A text from Clara—a photo of her and Ethan on a mountain overlook, sunlight catching their faces. Miss you! The cabin is PERFECT.

Maggie smiled, genuinely happy to see her friend so radiant. Clara deserved every moment of this happiness after everything she'd endured.

Gorgeous! Enjoy every second. We're fine here. She added a heart emoji before sending.

The ache rose in her chest, familiar and unwelcome. Clara had found her second chance. Ethan had found his. They'd both walked through fire and come out stronger, together.

"Lord," she whispered, tucking her phone away, "I'm trying to be patient. I know you have a plan. But some days..." She swallowed hard. "Some days it's hard to believe there's someone out there for me. For us."

The clinic door chimed as another patient arrived. Maggie straightened her shoulders, painted on a smile, and pushed away from the counter. No time for self-pity. The boys needed new shoes for school, the electric bill was due, and she still had to finalize next week's cookie orders for Kneadful Things.

"Good morning," she called, voice steady despite her exhaustion. "How can we help you today?"

Dusk settled over Reeves Farm, painting the sky in deepening shades of purple. Ben sat in his truck, engine off, staring at the white envelope on the dashboard. He'd avoided it all day—during his tense meeting with the Beaumont twins, while fixing the irrigation pump, even when he'd stopped by the diner for a quick dinner.

But now, in the growing darkness, there was nowhere left to hide.

Ms. Pickles watched from the passenger seat, her intelligent eyes following his every move. She'd sensed his mood all day, staying closer than usual, as if her presence might somehow shield him from what was coming.

"Can't put it off forever, can I?" he murmured, reaching for the envelope.

His fingers trembled slightly as he tore open the seal. The bank's letterhead seemed to glow in the dim light of the cab. He unfolded the paper, scanning the cold, formal language.

Notice of Foreclosure Proceedings.

The words blurred as he read further. Ninety days to settle the debt. Tax liens. Loan default. Four generations of Reeves family history, about to be auctioned off to the highest bidder.

Ben's chest tightened, a vise squeezing around his lungs. He'd known it was coming, had felt it approaching like a storm on the horizon. But seeing it in black and white—official, inevitable—made his stomach drop.

Ms. Pickles whined softly, nudging his arm with her nose.

"It's over, girl," he whispered, voice rough.

Hanging his head in his hands, shoulders drooped in shame.

"Everything my great-grandfather built. Everything my daddy worked for. Gone."

He let the papers fall to his lap and leaned his head back against the seat, staring up through the windshield at the first stars appearing in the night sky.

"Lord," he said, the words barely audible even to himself, "I'm at the end. If you're still listening..." His voice caught. "I need help. I don't know what else to do."

The only answer was the chirping of crickets and the soft breathing of his loyal companion beside him.

Chapter 5 – When Joy Feels Far Away

"My tears have been my meat day and night, while they continually say unto me, Where is thy God?" Psalms 42:3 (KJV)

Maggie closed Alan's bedroom door, pausing to listen for his steady breathing. The glow-in-the-dark stars she'd stuck to his ceiling cast faint green pinpoints across his sleeping form. Down the hall, Ralph had finally settled after another round of reassurances that no, Daddy wasn't coming back, but yes, they were going to be okay.

She padded to her bedroom, the floorboards creaking beneath her bare feet. The house felt too quiet, too empty. Five years, and she still hadn't gotten used to being the only adult under this roof.

Sinking onto her bed, Maggie reached for her phone to set her alarm. Another notification from Clara—a sunset photo this time. Ethan had his arms wrapped around Clara from behind, both of them silhouetted against brilliant orange and pink clouds over some mountain vista. Best honeymoon ever. God is so good.

Something inside Maggie cracked.

She set the phone face-down on her nightstand, her vision blurring. The dam she'd built to hold back her emotions—the one that got her through parent-teacher conferences alone, through birthdays where her boys watched the door for a father who never came, through endless nights of bills spread across the kitchen table—finally broke.

A sob tore from her throat, harsh and primal. She curled into herself, clutching a pillow to muffle the sound. Her shoulders shook with the force of her weeping.

"Why?" she gasped between sobs. "Why wasn't I enough?"

The tears came harder now, years of bottled grief pouring out. She cried for the marriage that had died so suddenly, for the betrayal that still burned, for the frightened boys who'd watched their father walk away without a backward glance.

"I did everything right," she whispered to the empty room. "I loved him. I trusted him. I believed in our vows."

Her fingers clutched the pillow tighter as another wave of anguish washed over her. Five years of pushing down this pain, of brave smiles at parent-teacher conferences and cheerful birthday parties where everyone pretended not to notice the empty chair. Five years of "Mommy can fix it" and "Daddy's just busy" until the lies felt like stones in her throat.

"We were a family," she choked out, rocking slightly. "We were supposed to be forever."

The moonlight cast long shadows across her bedroom floor—the same bedroom she'd once shared with Roger, before he'd decided their life together wasn't worth fighting for. Before he'd traded their history for someone new, someone who hadn't carried his children or known the sound of his laughter on quiet Sunday mornings.

Her Bible sat on the nightstand, its leather cover worn from years of faithful reading, pages dog-eared at verses that had once brought her comfort. The gold leaf on the edges had tarnished in places where her fingers had lingered during midnight prayers. Tonight, it remained closed, a silent witness to her breakdown, the promises within feeling as distant as the stars visible through her bedroom window.

Maggie wiped her face with the back of her hand, her breath coming in ragged gasps. Her gaze fell on the photo of Clara and Ethan again, their happiness like a physical blow.

"You gave her a second chance," she whispered, the words sharp with bitterness. "Clara went through hell with Truman, and You brought her back to Ethan. You healed them. Where's mine, Lord? What about me and my boys?"

The silence of the house seemed to mock her. Outside, a distant roll of thunder echoed her turbulent thoughts.

"I gave everything I had." Her voice grew stronger, anger threading through the grief. "I followed all the rules. I was faithful. I waited until marriage. I put my family first. I forgave when he stayed out late. I prayed when things got hard."

She stood up, pacing the small bedroom, hands clenched at her sides.

"And he still left. He still chose her. He still signed away his own children like they were... furniture." Her voice broke on the last word, remembering the cold, clinical meeting with the lawyers where Roger had surrendered his parental rights without hesitation.

Maggie stopped at the window, staring at her own reflection superimposed over the darkness outside. She hardly recognized the woman looking back at her—hollow-eyed, shoulders curved inward as if to protect a wound.

"What's the point of faith if it doesn't protect you?" The question hung in the air, dangerous and raw. "What's the point of believing in Your plan when it feels like You've abandoned us?"

Lightning flashed, illuminating the fields beyond her property for a brief moment. The sudden brightness made her flinch. A storm without rain dangerous in this drought.

"Everyone at church talks about Your love, Your protection. But where were You when he packed his bags? Where were You when I had to tell my boys their daddy didn't want them anymore?"

The storm passed sometime in the night, leaving nothing but brittle grass and dust clouds. Maggie stood before her bathroom mirror, applying concealer to the shadows under her eyes. The woman staring back at her looked composed, put-together—nothing like the broken creature who'd sobbed into her pillow for hours.

She twisted her hair into a neat bun, straightened her blouse, and practiced her smile. It didn't quite reach her eyes, but it would have to do.

"Mom! Ralph used all the syrup!" Alan's voice carried up the stairs.

38

"Did not! There's still some left!"

"Boys," Maggie called, her voice steady despite the pounding in her temples. "Let's not start the day with fighting."

She descended the stairs, stepping over a toy truck and sidestepping a backpack. The kitchen was a whirlwind of half-eaten toast, spilled milk, and bickering children. Just another Tuesday.

A knock at the door cut through the chaos. Maggie glanced at the clock—6:45 AM.

Her father stood on the porch, a paper bag in his grease-stained hands. "Mornin', sugar. Brought you some of your Mom's biscuits. She made extra."

"Daddy, you didn't have to—"

"Grandpa!" The boys abandoned their breakfast dispute, rushing to the door.

Henry Cunningham's weathered face lit up. "There's my boys!" He handed Maggie the bag and scooped Ralph into a bear hug. "How's school? You keepin' those teachers on their toes?"

While the boys chattered, Henry studied his daughter over their heads. His smile faded.

"You look like your mama used to when she was tryin' not to cry," he said quietly.

Maggie busied herself with the biscuits, arranging them on a plate. "Just tired, Daddy."

"Boys, go finish your breakfast," Henry said, his voice gentle but firm. "I need to talk to your mama a minute."

When they'd scampered off, reluctantly abandoning their biscuits, he took Maggie's hands in his weathered ones. The calluses on his palms were familiar and comforting. "Well, even Jesus took a nap in that boat during the storm. Let yourself rest, sugar. You're carryin' too much on those shoulders."

Maggie pulled away, reaching for her coffee mug to hide the tremble in her fingers, fearing that accepting the comfort daddy offered right now might just break her. She took a long sip, avoiding his concerned gaze. "I don't have time to rest, Daddy. Single motherhood is not for the weak. The laundry doesn't wash itself, and those boys need somebody steady." She forced a smile that didn't reach her eyes. "I'll be alright. Always am. It's how you and mama raised me to be."

Henry's eyes held hers a moment longer, seeing more than she wanted him to. "Call me if you need anything. I mean it."

After hustling the boys to school, Maggie drove through town toward the veterinary clinic. Morning sunlight glinted off storefronts, the world moving forward despite her sleepless night. She slowed at a four-way stop, watching a young couple cross the street, their toddler balanced on the father's shoulders.

The little girl's laughter floated through Maggie's half-open window.

She gripped the steering wheel tighter, that familiar ache spreading beneath her ribs. The family disappeared into Hattie's, the father holding the door, his free hand resting on the small of his wife's back.

A horn honked behind her. Maggie startled, realizing she'd been sitting at the stop sign too long. She waved an apology and continued down Main Street.

The white steeple of Willow Creek Baptist Church rose against the blue sky ahead. Maggie had driven this route thousands of times, but today the sight of it made her breath catch. The morning sun hit the stained glass windows, sending prisms of colored light dancing across the lawn. So much of her life's story happened there.

For a disorienting moment, the building seemed to pulse with life—not just wood and stone, but something alive and waiting. The bell tower, the arched doorway, the worn steps where she'd sat as a teenager, Bible in hand, heart full of certainty about God's plan for her life.

Come home.

The thought wasn't words so much as a feeling, a tug beneath her breastbone.

Maggie swallowed hard, turning her head away from the sight. She pressed her foot to the accelerator and drove past without slowing, eyes fixed firmly on the road ahead.

Not today. She couldn't face those walls, those memories, that silent invitation. Not when her faith felt as fragile as spun glass, ready to shatter at the slightest touch.

The clinic sign appeared around the bend. Maggie pulled into her parking space, took a deep breath, and reached for her professional smile.

Another day. Another chance to prove she could handle it all alone.

Chapter 6 – Storm Clouds Over the Co-Op

"Have mercy upon me, O LORD, for I am in trouble: mine eye is consumed with grief, yea, my soul and my belly. For my life is spent with grief, and my years with sighing: my strength faileth because of mine iniquity, and my bones are consumed." Psalms 31:9-10

The spigot dripped steadily—a mocking rhythm in a land desperate for water. Ben crouched in the dusty corner of the barn, adjusting the wrench with hands that bore the evidence of a lifetime working this land. Calluses, scars, dirt embedded so deep no amount of scrubbing would remove it.

"Come on, you stubborn thing," he muttered, putting his weight into the turn. The metal groaned, then finally gave. The dripping slowed, then stopped.

One small victory in a war he kept losing.

Ms. Pickles nudged his leg, her warm snout leaving a damp spot on his worn jeans. The old Kuvasz looked up at him with eyes that somehow understood more than most humans. Nine years old and still following him everywhere, her white coat collecting burrs and dust as she patrolled her domain.

"At least you're still on my side, girl." Ben scratched behind her ears, earning a contented sigh from the loyal dog.

He straightened, his back protesting the movement. At thirty-five, he shouldn't feel this worn down. His father hadn't started stooping until his sixties. But then, his father hadn't faced three years of drought, a mountain of debt, and the slow death of everything he'd built.

The chickens clucked impatiently as Ben emerged from the barn. The feed bucket scraped against the worn floorboards as he dragged it toward their pen. Even they seemed listless in the relentless heat, pecking without enthusiasm at the grain he scattered.

"Don't you all start giving up on me too," he warned, counting heads out of habit. Twenty-three. Same as yesterday.

Ben lifted his gaze to the horizon. The sky stretched endless and blue above him, not a single cloud to break its perfect, cruel emptiness. The fields beyond the chicken coop had faded from green to a sickly yellow-brown. Crops withered, soil cracked. The irrigation pond had shrunk to half its size, revealing a ring of cracked mud around its edges like a wound.

"Three years. No real rain, Lord." The words came out rough, somewhere between a prayer and an accusation. "Not a drop when we need it, then a flood when it's too late for the seedlings."

Ms. Pickles pressed against his leg, sensing his mood. Ben absently stroked her head, his eyes still fixed on that empty sky.

Back at the farmhouse, Ben settled at the kitchen table, bills spread before him like a losing hand of cards. The old rotary phone sat heavy in his palm as he dialed the number he'd come to dread.

"Willow Creek First National, this is Patricia speaking. How may I assist you today?"

"Morning, Patricia. It's Ben Reeves again." He tried to keep his voice steady, professional.

"Oh, Ben." Her tone softened immediately. "How are things out at the farm?"

"Hanging in there." The lie came easily after so much practice. "Is Mr. Johnson available? I need to discuss my loan situation."

A pause. "I'll see if he's in. Hold please."

Ben drummed his fingers on the faded tablecloth, counting the water stains and coffee rings. The hold music played thinly through the receiver—some classical piece that seemed to mock his mounting anxiety.

"Benjamin." Johnson's voice was crisp, businesslike. "What can I do for you today?"

"I'm calling about my payment extension. I was hoping we could discuss refinancing options."

"I see." Papers shuffled on the other end. "Mr. Reeves, we've already extended the terms once. Your next payment is due at the end of the month."

Ben swallowed. "I understand that, sir, but with the drought—"

"Every farmer in the county is dealing with the drought," Johnson cut in. "I'm afraid my hands are tied. Mr. Tuttle, the CEO, has established a new policy regarding agricultural loans. No more extensions without substantial collateral."

"My family's worked this land for four generations," Ben said, heat rising in his voice. "Surely that counts for something."

"I'm sorry, Ben. I truly am." Johnson's voice dropped, almost to a whisper. "But it's out of my control. The bank is under new management, new priorities."

The line went dead before Ben could respond. He stared at the receiver for a long moment before hanging it up.

"Well, Lord..." he muttered, pushing back from the table. "That's strike three."

Ms. Pickles whined softly from her spot by the door, sensing his distress.

The Co-Op's bell jangled as Ben pushed through the door, Ms. Pickles staying dutifully at his side. The familiar smell of feed, leather, and motor oil usually brought him comfort. Today it just reminded him of one more thing he stood to lose.

Walt and Wes Beaumont looked up from behind the counter, their identical faces showing different expressions—Walt's concerned, Wes's guarded. The twins had partnered with Ben three years ago, bringing fresh capital to the struggling farm supply store.

"Morning, Ben," Walt offered. "Coffee's fresh."

Ben shook his head. "Just came to talk about the Anderson account."

Wes sighed, sliding a ledger across the counter. "They're six months behind, Ben. We can't keep extending them credit."

"They lost their entire east field to that brush fire," Ben countered. "They need time."

"We're bleeding cash," Wes said, tapping the books. "Can't keep floating neighbors who can't pay."

Walt shifted uncomfortably. "Ben, we understand loyalty, but—"

"But what?" Ben's voice rose. "Folks around here are drowning. The Andersons, the Millers, the Pattersons—they've been buying from this Co-Op for decades."

"And we appreciate that," Wes said evenly. "But sentiment doesn't pay our suppliers."

Ben slammed his hat on the counter, startling an elderly customer browsing seed packets. He took a deep breath, trying to rein in his temper. "We're not vultures, circling while folks are down."

"Nobody's saying—" Walt began.

"Seems like that's exactly what you're saying." Ben's control finally snapped, his voice echoing through the store. "This Co-Op was formed by local farmers to serve local farmers. We've always taken care of each other in hard times and it will always be the right choice to offer grace. In fact, if you read our partnership papers, you'll find it listed as a required business practice. We agreed, and you both signed on the dotted line, to let this place go under before we take more than a man has to give."

The store had gone silent. Three customers stood frozen in the aisles, watching the confrontation unfold. Even old Pete Lowe, who'd been examining pipe fittings, stared open-mouthed.

Ben snatched his hat from the counter, jammed it on his head, and stormed toward the door, Ms. Pickles on his side. "Figure it out," he growled over his shoulder. "But we're not calling in the Andersons' debt. Not today."

The bell jangled violently as he pushed through the door, Ms. Pickles barking out agreement, leaving stunned silence and shocked stares in his wake.

Ben's truck rattled and protested as he pulled into the church parking lot, the engine coughing twice before falling silent. He sat there, hands still gripping the wheel, knuckles white with tension. The church stood silent before him, its white steeple reaching toward that empty, mocking sky.

Ms. Pickles whined from the passenger seat, upset at having her snooze interrupted.

"Sorry to wake you old girl," Ben muttered.

His chest felt tight, like someone had wrapped barbed wire around his lungs and pulled it taut. The anger that had propelled him out of the Co-Op drained away, leaving nothing but bone-deep exhaustion in its wake.

He leaned forward, resting his forehead against the steering wheel. The plastic was warm against his skin, the truck's interior stifling in the midday heat. Sweat trickled down his temple, but he didn't bother to wipe it away.

"God," he whispered, voice cracking on that single syllable. He cleared his throat and tried again. "God, I'm trying. I swear I am."

The words came easier now, tumbling out raw and unfiltered.

"But I can't see a way through. The bank's closing in. The crops are dying. I'm losing partners faster than I'm losing money, and that's saying something."

He squeezed his eyes shut, fighting the burn behind his lids.

"Please help me. I'm drowning here." His voice dropped to a ragged whisper. "I can't do this by myself anymore."

The confession hung in the stifling air of the truck cab, more honest than any prayer he'd offered in months.

Ms. Pickles gave another whimper and shifted to rest her muzzle on his thigh, her front paws folded beneath her jaw, gaze locked on him with steadfast devotion.

Ben extended his hand to rub behind her ears, and she responded with a consoling lick against his palm, as though communicating, I've got your back, Ben.

Her coarse tongue scraped across his flesh, genuine and tangible and immediate. That uncomplicated gesture—undeserved allegiance—dislodged something tight within his ribcage.

The cell phone in Ben's pocket buzzed, startling him from his prayer. He wiped his eyes with the back of his hand before fishing it out. Clara's name flashed on the screen.

"Hello?" His voice came out rougher than intended.

"Ben! It's us!" Clara's voice bubbled through the speaker, bright as sunshine. "We're calling from the cabin. You wouldn't believe this place—the forest is practically at our doorstep!"

Despite everything, Ben felt the corner of his mouth twitch upward. "How's married life treating you two?"

"Well," Clara lowered her voice dramatically, "I've discovered Ethan can't dance to save his life. Two left feet and no rhythm. Nearly knocked over a waiter last night."

"That's a lie," Ethan's voice came from somewhere nearby. "I was avoiding a puddle."

"A puddle on a dance floor?" Clara laughed, the sound so carefree it made Ben's chest ache with something like envy.

"Hey, we've got a load of light fixtures arriving Friday for the retreat," Clara continued. "Could you possibly sign for them if we're not back?"

"Sure thing."

"Oh, and Ben—" Ethan's voice now, having apparently wrestled the phone away. "Clara slept the whole first day here. Snores something awful. Like a chainsaw cutting through oak."

Clara's indignant "I do not!" carried clearly through the line.

Ben found himself chuckling. "Glad somebody's got good news."

There was a brief pause before Ethan spoke again, his tone shifting. "Heard about the dust-up at the Co-Op today."

Ben's smile faded. "Word travels fast."

"Small town," Ethan replied simply. Then, more quietly: "What can I do to help?"

The question caught Ben off guard. Not because Ethan had offered—that was just who he was—but because Ben couldn't remember the last time someone had asked. He'd been carrying everything alone for so long.

"Just keep praying God provides an answer," Ben said finally. "I'm running out of both time and ideas down here."

Later, as evening shadows stretched across the porch, Ben settled into the ancient rocking chair his grandfather had crafted decades ago. The wooden slats creaked beneath him, a familiar complaint that had soundtracked countless evenings on this very spot. Ms. Pickles flopped at his feet with a contented sigh, her white coat turned golden in the fading light.

Before him, the sun hung low and heavy, a molten disc sinking behind fields that should have been lush with summer growth. Instead, row after row of stunted corn stood like soldiers fallen in battle, brown and brittle where they should have been green and vital.

"Another day, another disappointment," Ben murmured, his voice barely audible above the evening chorus of cicadas.

No rain again. The weatherman had promised a thirty percent chance—might as well have promised gold falling from the sky. Ben had watched those clouds build on the horizon all afternoon, dark and promising, only to slide north and deliver their precious cargo to someone else's parched land.

The evening air hung thick and still, pressing against his skin like a damp cloth. Even the breeze had abandoned Willow Creek, it seemed.

Ben reached for his father's Bible, its leather cover worn smooth by decades of handling. The spine cracked softly as he opened it, the pages falling naturally to Psalms 31, where he'd left his bookmark earlier that morning.

"Have mercy upon me, O LORD, for I am in trouble," he read aloud, the words catching in his throat. "Mine eye is consumed with grief, yea, my soul and my belly. For my life is spent with grief, and my years with sighing..."

He stopped, the words blurring before him. He'd tried to read this passage three times now, seeking comfort in the ancient lament, hoping to find some echo of his own struggle that might point toward hope.

But the words refused to penetrate the wall of exhaustion and worry surrounding his heart.

With a sigh, Ben flipped the Bible shut and rose from the chair. Ms. Pickles lifted her head, questioning.

"Come on, girl. Nothing out here but dust and disappointment."

He turned and walked inside, leaving the darkening fields behind.

Chapter 7 – The Belle Comes Home

"And when he came to himself, he said, How many hired servants of my father's have bread enough and to spare, and I perish with hunger! I will arise and go to my father, and will say unto him, Father, I have sinned against heaven, and before thee, And am no more worthy to be called thy son: make me as one of thy hired servants." Luke 15:17-19 (KJV)

The silver Audi kicked up a cloud of dust as it rolled down the gravel drive toward the farmstand. Brittany Reeves gripped the steering wheel, her knuckles white against the leather. She'd circled the property twice before working up the nerve to pull in.

The Crop 'Til You Drop sign hung crooked from its post, the once-bright paint now faded and peeling. The farmstand itself—a sturdy wooden structure her father had built the summer before her tenth birthday—looked smaller than she remembered. Less grand. The red paint had weathered to a dull rust color, and one of the shutters dangled precariously from a single hinge.

Brittany cut the engine and sat motionless, air conditioning still blasting against the Tennessee heat. Through the windshield, she studied the landscape around the Farmstand. It needed a woman's touch. Some landscaping and signage, some picnic tables and maybe a pathway lined with decorative pavers to add a pop of color.

"Come on, Britt," she whispered to herself. "You've faced down health inspectors and restaurant critics. Your brother can't be scarier than that. Maybe you'll get lucky and Ben won't be here."

Still, she didn't move.

A bark startled her from her thoughts as a large white dog trotted around the corner of the farmstand. Ms. Pickles. The dog paused, head tilted in curiosity at the unfamiliar vehicle.

The screen door of the farmstand creaked open, and Ben stepped out onto the porch. He had a towel slung over his shoulder, his t-shirt damp with sweat and water. He'd been fixing something—probably the temperamental water line that had plagued the property since they were kids.

He squinted against the sun, recognition dawning slowly across his face.

Brittany finally pushed open her car door and stepped out, forcing a bright smile. "Surprise!"

"Well, look what the wind blew in." Ben's voice carried across the yard, flat and unreadable.

"Thought I'd grace the homestead with my big-city presence," Brittany called back, aiming for lightness. "Bet you missed my charming personality around here."

Ben didn't smile. His eyes flicked from her designer sunglasses to her impractical shoes, then to the expensive car behind her.

"You here for a visit or a handout?"

The words hit like a slap. Brittany's smile faltered, her carefully rehearsed speech evaporating in the summer heat.

After closing the Farmstand, the Reeves siblings headed for home in their separate vehicles. Ms. Pickles bounded across the yard, her loyalty to Ben momentarily forgotten as she recognized an old friend. She circled Brittany, tail wagging furiously.

"At least someone's happy to see me," Brittany murmured, kneeling to scratch behind the dog's ears.

Ben uncrossed his arms and grabbed one of her suitcases. His mom raised him to always be a gentleman first. "Let's take this inside."

The farmhouse kitchen hadn't changed in the five years since Brittany had last set foot in it. The same faded yellow curtains framed the windows. The same ancient refrigerator hummed in the corner. Even the wall calendar—though the year had changed—featured the same breed of horses her mother had always loved.

Brittany stood awkwardly by the kitchen table while Ben filled two glasses with tap water. He slid one across to her without a word.

"I lost everything, Ben." The confession tumbled out before she could dress it up. "The restaurant. The investors pulled out."

"And now you remember where home is?" His voice was quiet but cutting.

"That's not fair." She gripped the edge of the counter. "I called. I sent money when I could."

"Christmas cards and birthday checks don't make up for disappearing, Britt."

Tears pricked at her eyes. "I didn't come back to mooch. I came back to start over."

Just six months ago, she'd been on top of the world. Her restaurant, Sage & Salt, had been the toast of Nashville's food scene. Write-ups in Southern Living. Lines around the block. Brittany Reeves, the farm girl turned culinary star, bringing "elevated country cuisine" to people who'd pay thirty dollars for fancy grits.

She remembered the night everything changed. Standing in her gleaming kitchen, surrounded by copper pots and marble countertops, when Marcus—her business partner and the man she'd foolishly trusted—handed her the paperwork.

"We're underwater, Britt. The investors are pulling out."

The rest unraveled with terrifying speed. The lease, gone. The equipment, repossessed. Her apartment, unaffordable without the restaurant income. And Marcus, vanished with what remained of their operating capital.

Yesterday, she'd packed what she could fit into a rented U-Haul, gave away what remained, and headed toward home. Willow Creek wasn't a far drive, only about an hour and a half, but she spent the entire trip questioning every mile whether she was making another mistake.

"I didn't know where else to go," she admitted, her voice small in the quiet kitchen. "When I left, you told me I always had a home here. Did you mean it?"

Ben's shoulders slumped. The anger that had been fueling him drained away, leaving only exhaustion in its wake.

"Course I meant it." He sighed, running a hand through his hair. "Your room's still there. Ain't touched a thing."

Brittany nodded, not trusting herself to speak. She gathered her smallest bag and headed down the familiar hallway, past the family photos still hanging crooked on the wall. Their parents smiling from wooden frames, frozen in time before God called them home within two years of each other.

She paused at her bedroom door, hand trembling slightly on the crystal knob that had looked like a giant diamond fit for a princess when she was younger. With a deep breath, she pushed it open.

The room stood exactly as she'd left it. Moonlight filtered through the faded blue curtains she'd sewn in Home Ec class, casting golden rectangles across the quilt her grandmother had made. The walls were a time capsule of her younger self—posters of Julia Child mid-whisk, Justin Wilson with his trademark grin declaring "I gar-on-tee!" A signed 4-H barrel racing ribbon, faded but still proudly displayed on a cork board alongside ribbons from the county fair's baking competitions.

Her bookshelf sagged under the weight of dog-eared cookbooks, some borrowed from the library and never returned. Her mother's old copies of Southern Living magazines, pages folded to mark the recipes that had most interested her, stacked neatly beside trophies from horse shows and debate club. Fond memories of pouring over the pages and discussing ingredients and methods with mom rushing through her.

Brittany ran her fingers along the spines of the books, stopping at her favorite—a battered copy of Mastering the Art of French Cooking that she'd saved up for months to buy. She'd spent countless nights under these same ceiling stars, dreaming of culinary school and leading a team of sous chefs and prep cooks in the world's best kitchens while the rest of Willow Creek dreamed of football championships and church socials.

She sank onto the edge of her childhood bed, the springs creaking in familiar protest. Her fingers found the blue ribbon from her first cooking competition—age twelve, peach cobbler, first place. She'd been so proud, so certain that she was destined for greatness.

The ribbon blurred as tears filled her eyes.

"God," she whispered, her voice breaking in the quiet room. "I had it all figured out. Why does it all feel like it was for nothing?" She traced the frayed edge of the blue ribbon, remembering how her hands had trembled with excitement when the judge pinned it to her apron. Back then, the future had seemed so clear—culinary school, prestigious kitchens, her name in glossy food magazines. Now here she was, back where she started, with nothing but memories and a drawer full of faded dreams to show for all her striving.

In her eyes, this was what failure looked like. In God's plan, this was him resetting her in preparation of unimagined blessings.

The cicadas' symphony filled the night air as Brittany slipped onto the front porch. The ancient swing creaked under her weight, a sound so familiar it made her chest ache. She'd spent countless summer evenings on this swing—planning her escape, dreaming of the day she'd leave Willow Creek behind.

How ironic that she now found comfort in its familiar embrace.

The screen door squeaked, and Ben's silhouette appeared. He paused in the doorway, then stepped forward, two mason jars of sweet tea in his hands. The ice clinked against the glass as he handed one to her.

"Figured you might need this."

Brittany accepted it with a grateful nod. The first sip transported her back—summer evenings watching fireflies with their parents, the sweetness of childhood preserved in sugar and mint.

Ben settled beside her, and the swing groaned in protest. For several minutes, they sat in silence, rocking gently, the only sounds the chorus of night insects and the occasional distant bark of a neighbor's dog.

"I'm sorry about earlier," Ben finally said, his voice low. "We've all lost things lately. But it's good to see you. I've missed you, Sis."

The simple admission broke something loose inside her. The wall she'd built—the sophisticated chef persona, the woman who didn't need her small-town roots—crumbled a little.

"Missed you too, big brother." She leaned her head against his shoulder, just as she had when they were kids and thunderstorms frightened her. "Adulting is hard. I wish mom and dad were here to give us all the answers."

Ben's arm came around her shoulders, solid and steady. "Yeah. Dad would've known what to do about the north field. And Mom would've had that kitchen of yours up and running again before you could blink."

Brittany smiled against his shoulder, remembering their mother's boundless energy and their father's quiet wisdom. The grief was still there, a dull ache that never quite went away, but somehow sharing it made it easier to bear. "I don't know how to do this without them, Ben." she admitted quietly.

"I'm struggling with the same thing, Britt. We're on the verge of losing the farm, and I'm not getting any answers from anywhere. I just keep praying and reading dad's bible, searching for solutions, hoping dad's still around. Wishing he and God would just give me the answer, or at least point me in the right direction. I feel like I'm letting them down. I've no idea what to do next."

In his mind, this was the end of the road. But maybe in God's hands, it was just an uphill switchback, leading him to the top of the mountain.

Chapter 8 – Pies & Pickles

"Then was our mouth filled with laughter, and our tongue with singing: then said they among the heathen, The LORD hath done great things for them." Psalms 126:2

Maggie pulled her SUV alongside the weathered farmstand, wincing as she checked her watch. The morning had started with Ralph spilling orange juice across his math homework and Alan forgetting his baseball glove. Now she was running late for work with a trunk full of pies that needed delivering first.

She popped the hatch and spotted Ben trudging up from the direction of his truck. His shoulders slumped forward, jaw clenched tight enough to crack walnuts. Whatever business had taken him into town that morning hadn't gone well.

"Morning," she called, trying to sound cheerful despite her own exhaustion.

Ben barely glanced her way. "Morning." The word came out clipped, distracted. He fumbled with the farmstand door key, his movements stiff and mechanical.

Maggie pulled out the first box of pies, watching him from the corner of her eye. He moved with a slight hitch in his step, favoring his right leg as he pushed through the screen door.

"You wrestle a goat and lose?" The words tumbled out before she could stop them.

Ben froze mid-step, turning slowly. For a moment, his face remained stone-still, then a reluctant smirk tugged at one corner of his mouth.

"Goat started it."

The absurdity of their exchange hung in the air between them. Maggie bit her lip to keep from grinning too widely.

Ben's eyes drifted to the stack of pie boxes she was juggling. Something in his expression softened.

"Where are my manners? Let me help you with those." He crossed the gravel lot in a few long strides.

Their hands brushed as he took the top boxes, and Maggie felt that strange flutter in her chest again—the same one she'd been trying to ignore for weeks. She busied herself with grabbing more pies while her cheeks cooled.

Together they carried the boxes inside, arranging them in the display case. Ben lifted the lid on a peach pie, inhaling deeply.

"Your peach pie might win next year," he murmured, not quite meeting her eyes.

Maggie blinked, surprised by the unexpected praise. "That almost sounded like a compliment." She glanced at her watch again. "Thanks for the help. I gotta get going. I'm late for work."

She hurried back to her SUV, feeling oddly light despite her rushed morning. A smile stayed fixed on her face all the way to the vet clinic.

Behind her, Ben practically bounced back into the Farmstand, a grin spreading across his face for the first time in days. He looked back in time to catch her looking back at him. Their eyes catching, sending a zing through his whole body. One of these days, he might be brave enough to do something about that. God willing. For now, he shoved it back, he had more pressing puzzles to solve.

Three hours later, Maggie looked up from the reception desk to see Ben pushing through the clinic's front door, a large white dog trotting beside him. Ms. Pickles, the semi-retired livestock guardian dog, moved with the dignified air of royalty despite her advancing years.

"Well, look who's here," Maggie said, brightening at the sight of them. The morning's brief interaction at the farmstand had lingered pleasantly in her mind all day.

Ms. Pickles recognized Maggie immediately. Her tail swished once, twice, and she pulled ahead of Ben, leading him straight to the reception counter.

"Hello there, beautiful girl." Maggie leaned over the counter to scratch behind the dog's ears. Ms. Pickles closed her eyes in bliss, leaning into the touch. "What brings you in to see the doc today, Ms. Pickles?"

Ben adjusted his cap, a hint of amusement playing at his lips. "Pickles, tell Maggie that you are a lady aging gracefully. We're just here for a check-up."

Ms. Pickles woofed softly as if confirming his statement.

Maggie laughed, typing their information into the computer. "Well, she looks wonderful for nine. Dr. Peterson's running about fifteen minutes behind, but I'll get y'all settled in Exam Room 2."

She grabbed a clipboard and led them down the hallway, conscious of Ben's footsteps behind her. Ms. Pickles padded alongside, her nails clicking rhythmically against the linoleum.

The hallway was just long enough to give Ben a good look at Maggie's backside. The electricity sparking between them almost powerful as that zing shot through him again. He was so affected, he almost tripped into the room. Cutting his eyes quickly, clearing his throat to regain control, he settled Pickles to avoid looking at Maggie.

"Doc will be with you shortly," Maggie said, holding the door open. "Can I get either of you anything while you wait?"

"We're fine, thanks." Ben settled into a chair while Ms. Pickles sniffed every corner of the small room.

Back at her desk, Maggie glanced at the clock. Her lunch break had started five minutes ago, and her stomach growled in protest. She gathered her purse and headed for the breakroom.

The small space was mercifully empty. Maggie pulled her lunch bag from the refrigerator and settled at the table. She unwrapped her turkey sandwich and pulled out a crisp dill pickle spear wrapped in wax paper—her favorite part of lunch.

Maggie took a satisfying bite of her sandwich, savoring the moment of quiet. She'd just raised the pickle spear to her lips when the breakroom door burst open with a bang.

A white blur shot through the doorway. Before Maggie could process what was happening, Ms. Pickles lunged forward, her massive head darting toward Maggie's hand. With surgical precision, the dog's teeth closed around the pickle spear and yanked it away.

Maggie sat frozen, hand still suspended in mid-air, empty except for a tiny bit of pickle skin. Ms. Pickles retreated to the corner, crunching her prize with obvious delight.

The absurdity of the situation hit Maggie all at once. A laugh bubbled up from deep in her chest, growing until she was doubled over, tears forming at the corners of her eyes.

Ben appeared in the doorway, slightly out of breath. "I am so sorry. She bolted the second Dr. Peterson opened the door to grab something."

"She—" Maggie gasped between fits of laughter, pointing at the dog who was licking her chops. "She stole my pickle!"

Ben's worried expression melted into a sheepish grin. "Guess she remembers you."

Ms. Pickles, mission accomplished, trotted over to Ben's side, looking entirely too pleased with herself.

"You little thief," Ben muttered, though his tone held nothing but affection. He hooked a finger through her collar and pulled up a chair across from Maggie. "Mind if we join you? I think someone owes you an apology."

Maggie wiped her eyes, still chuckling. "Please."

Ben reached into his pocket and pulled out a treat for Ms. Pickles, who took it with ladylike delicacy—a stark contrast to her pickle-thieving behavior.

"That's how she got her name, you know," Ben said, his voice softening. "I used to sneak pickles outta Mama's crock when I was a kid. She'd sit beside me and wait her turn. Patient as could be, but those eyes—" He glanced down at the dog with unmistakable love. "She'd guilt me into sharing every time."

Something about the simple story touched Maggie deeply. She looked at Ben—really looked at him—and saw beyond the gruff farmer to the boy he'd once been, sharing stolen pickles with his faithful companion.

Something inside Maggie shifted. She felt it like an earthquake. She silently asked "God, why are you shaking me?" Confusion intensified by the butterflies fluttering in her stomach. In a moment of pure feminine joy, she decided to go with whatever this was for now. Enjoy the moment.

A genuine smile spread across her face, warming her from the inside out.

Dr. Peterson poked his head into the breakroom. "There you are! I've been looking everywhere."

"Sorry, Doc. Ms. Pickles had a pickle emergency." Ben stood, dusting crumbs from his jeans.

"So I see." The vet smiled. "Let's finish up that exam so Ms. Pickles can get back to her farm duties."

Ben hesitated, glancing at Maggie. "Sorry about your lunch."

She waved him off. "Worth it for the entertainment."

After they left, Maggie finished her sandwich in peaceful silence. The break room felt emptier somehow, as if Ms. Pickles had taken some of the energy with her when she left. Maggie found herself replaying Ben's story—the little boy sneaking pickles, sharing them with his pup. Such a simple memory, yet it had softened something in her.

Twenty minutes later, the bell above the clinic door chimed. Maggie looked up to see Ben and Ms. Pickles heading out. The big dog paused, turning her head to give Maggie one last look, tail swishing against Ben's leg.

"Clean bill of health," Ben called, adjusting his cap. "Thanks for your help."

"Anytime," Maggie replied, surprised by how much she meant it.

She watched through the window as they climbed into his truck. Ms. Pickles sat regally in the passenger seat, white fur catching the afternoon sun. Ben leaned over to scratch her ears before starting the engine. The simple gesture of affection made Maggie's heart squeeze.

As they pulled away, she reached for her phone and opened her grocery list app. She tapped the screen, adding "Extra dill pickles" to her list, then paused, smiling to herself.

"There's still good in this world, Lord," she whispered. "Even in pickles."

For the first time in months, Maggie felt a flutter of something she'd almost forgotten—hope, small but persistent, like a seed pushing through soil after a long winter.

Chapter 9 – More Than Just a Bed

"Behold, I will do a new thing; now it shall spring forth; shall ye not know it? I will even make a way in the wilderness, and rivers in the desert." Isaiah 43:19

The newlywed Walker's pickup truck kicked up a cloud of dust as it rolled down the gravel drive toward the farmhouse. Clara leaned forward in her seat, eager for the first glimpse of home, and Old Trusty, after a week away. Beside her, Ethan's tanned hand reached over to squeeze hers, his wedding band catching the afternoon light.

"Ready to face reality again, Mrs. Walker?"

Clara turned to him, her smile bright despite the exhaustion of travel. "As long as I'm facing it with you. Gatlinburg may only be three hours away, but it was too far for this momma's heart."

The front door of the farmhouse burst open before they'd even parked. Ava shot out like a rocket, Noah trailing behind her, both children practically vibrating with excitement.

"Mama! Daddy!" Ava called, bouncing on her toes as the car stopped.

Clara barely had the door open before Ava crashed into her, nearly knocking her backward. Noah hung back, waiting his turn with uncharacteristic patience until Ethan scooped him up in a bear hug. "Hey, daddy", Noah whispered with newness.

"Did you bring us anything?" Ava asked, peering around Clara toward the luggage.

"Ava Ruth," Clara scolded gently, though her eyes danced with amusement.

"What? Uncle Luke said that's what people do when they go on trips."

Treva appeared in the doorway, Harry beside her carrying a large casserole dish. "Welcome home, lovebirds. Hope you're hungry."

Inside, the kitchen table overflowed with comfort food—fried chicken, mashed potatoes, green beans, and three different pies. The scent of home wrapped around Clara like a familiar blanket.

"Y'all didn't have to do all this," she protested weakly, already eyeing the blackberry cobbler.

"Course we did," Treva said, shooing her toward a chair. "Can't have you cooking on your first night back."

Maggie entered with Alan and Ralph, carrying a chocolate cake. "Thought you might need something sweet to ease the transition back to reality."

Clara hugged her friend tight. "I missed you."

"It was only a week," Maggie laughed, but hugged back just as fiercely.

Over dinner, the children regaled them with stories of their week with "the uncles." Noah's eyes grew wide as he described helping Uncle Eli with a sick calf, while Ava dramatically recounted how Uncle Luke had taught her how to make bank selling her friendship bracelets through Hatties General Store and Percolating Grace .

"Did you know money doesn't just appear in the bank?" she asked, completely serious.

Clara choked on her tea, and Ethan patted her back, fighting his own laughter.

"What about you two?" Treva asked, passing the basket of rolls. "How were the mountains?"

Clara and Ethan exchanged a private smile, sun-kissed and glowing.

"Perfect," Clara said simply. Ethan nodded in agreement.

After the meal, as they sat around the living room with dessert plates balanced on their knees, Clara pulled out her phone and scrolled through the calendar.

"I hate to break up the homecoming, but we've got three days to turn the retreat into a camp suitable for kids," she said, laughing despite the enormity of the task ahead.

Ethan groaned good-naturedly, leaning back against the couch. "Vacation's over, y'all. Back to real life and all those half-built cabins waiting for us."

Maggie watched them, happiness for her friend warring with a pang of longing. She pushed it away, focusing instead on the verse Preacher had shared on Sunday: "Behold, I will do a new thing; now it shall spring forth; shall ye not know it? I will even make a way in the wilderness, and rivers in the desert."

New beginnings were happening all around. Maybe someday, one would happen for her too.

Everyone pitched in cleaning up dinner dishes and then left the new family alone to settle into everyday life as a new family.

As Clara put the kids to bed, Ethan looked around his old bachelor pad and recognized a family home taking shape. A wave of appreciation for God's miracles washed over him as he saw little touches of his new family sprinkled in with his old. Clara, Ava, and Noah were blending their things in with his. He was filled with gratitude and prayed that everyone in his life could come to know this feeling.

The next morning, Willow Creek Retreat buzzed with activity. A small army of volunteers swarmed over the grounds like industrious ants, transforming the newly renovated space into a functioning summer camp.

Clara and Maggie worked side by side in the dormitory bathrooms, rubber gloves up to their elbows as they scrubbed away the construction debris, stocked the bathrooms with toilet paper and towels, and laid out the shower mats in the shower stalls.

"Tell me again why we didn't hire professionals for this part?" Maggie asked, blowing a strand of hair from her face with a puff of air.

Clara laughed, spraying another tile with cleaner. "Because professionals cost money, and we're saving every penny for the kids."

With all the sarcasm she could muster, Maggs said "I can't figure out why we couldn't get more volunteers to help with this part."

Clara snorted and rolled her eyes at her best friend. It felt good to laugh again with her. They both had been through such difficult times, but things appeared to be looking up for them.

Down the hall, they could hear the rhythmic thump of mattresses being dropped onto newly assembled bunk beds. Beds waiting to be made ready for their first use with all those sheets and blankets they had spent 2 days washing and drying.

In the dining hall, Brittany directed Treva with the precision of a five-star chef, despite the humble surroundings. "No, the serving utensils go on the right of each dish. And we need to organize the pantry by food groups, not just shove everything in."

Treva rolled her eyes but complied. "Yes, Chef. Anything else, Chef?"

Outside, the men's work was equally intense. Ben and Greg wrestled with the frame of a tiny home while Guy and Peter worked on the electrical and plumbing connections. Luke, Caleb, and Eli assembled furniture for the counselors' quarters, their tools creating a symphony of construction.

Paul Grayson moved between groups with his clipboard, checking items off his meticulously organized list. "Windows are in, Greg? Excellent. Guy, how's the wiring coming along in cabin three?"

Luke Sharp sat at a makeshift desk under a tree, checkbook open, calculator in hand. "At this rate, we'll be eating beans for the next decade," he muttered, writing another check for supplies. "Do we really need premium mulch for the garden beds?"

Back in the kitchen, Brittany paused her organizing to watch Clara pass by with an armload of fresh linens.

"Clara, wait. I had a thought about the camp activities," Brittany called out.

Clara stopped, raising an eyebrow. "Another one? We're already packed to the gills."

"What about cooking classes? Farm-to-table lessons for the kids and counselors. We could use the garden harvest, teach basic nutrition, meal planning, budgeting."

"You sure about that? These kids have barely cooked anything beyond microwave meals."

Brittany straightened her shoulders. "I may be broke, but I'm still a chef. And every kid should know how to feed themselves properly."

Paul, who'd been passing by with his clipboard, stopped. "That's actually a great idea, Brittany. Self-sufficiency skills are exactly what these young people need."

By mid-afternoon, a dusty blue sedan pulled up the gravel drive. Four young adults emerged, squinting against the Tennessee sun, duffel bags slung over their shoulders. They stood awkwardly at the edge of the activity, clearly unsure where to go.

Clara spotted them first and nudged Maggie. "Our counselors are here."

Maggie wiped her hands on a towel and followed Clara to greet them. Up close, they looked even younger—barely adults themselves.

"Welcome to Willow Creek Retreat," Clara said warmly. "I'm Clara Walker, and this is Maggie Cunningham."

A tall young man with close-cropped hair stepped forward first. "Anthony Graves, ma'am. Just aged out last month." His handshake was firm, but his eyes darted around, taking in the surroundings like someone who'd learned to map all exits.

Beside him, a muscular young man with a faded high school football t-shirt nodded. "Hector Rodriguez. Coach said this might be good for me." His voice trailed off, and Maggie caught the hint of disappointment—dreams interrupted.

A petite young woman with intricate braids stepped forward next. "Rosita Carter. Thank you for having me." Her smile seemed practiced, like armor.

The last counselor shifted her weight, adjusting a sleeping toddler on her hip. "Winona Juarez. This is Oscar." She gestured to the boy. "He's two. I hope that's okay."

"More than okay," Clara assured her. "We have childcare arranged."

Maggie watched them—these four young people with old eyes. Each carried invisible burdens, stories written in the cautious way they held themselves, in their wary smiles. They reminded her of herself after Roger left—shell-shocked, trying to figure out who they were supposed to be now.

Something shifted inside her chest. A purpose, maybe. These kids needed more than just a paycheck and a place to sleep for the summer. They needed someone who understood what it meant to rebuild from ashes.

"You're going to be great," Maggie heard herself say, surprising even herself with the conviction in her voice. "And we're here to help, every step of the way."

Clara dropped a quick text in the group chat "Everyone, come meet our counselors!" She waved the team over, her smile wide and welcoming.

The makeshift construction crew set down their tools and wiped dusty hands on jeans as they gathered in a loose circle. Ben hung back slightly, his cap pulled low, but Maggie noticed how his eyes carefully assessed each newcomer.

"Everyone, this is Anthony, Hector, Rosita, and Winona with little Oscar," Clara introduced, gesturing to each in turn. "They are our first crew of summer counselors in training. We have about two weeks to give them enough information to make camp a success and keep everyone safe at the same time." She turned to the counselors and winked as she said, "but no pressure."

Handshakes were exchanged all around. Guy Nelson's enthusiastic pump nearly pulled Anthony off balance, while Treva offered Winona a gentle smile and immediately made faces at the sleepy toddler on her hip.

Ethan stepped forward, his carpenter's hands rough but his expression kind. "We're just finishing up your quarters—tiny homes with all the basics. Should be move-in ready in about an hour. Each one has a kitchenette, bathroom, and bedroom. Nothing fancy, but they're solid."

"Better than my last three places," Anthony murmured, earning understanding nods from his fellow counselors.

Paul Grayson cleared his throat and moved to the center of the group. His button-down shirt remained remarkably unwrinkled despite the day's heat and work.

"I'm Paul Grayson, principal at Willow Creek High School. Somehow that made me the unofficial team lead for this project." He chuckled, gesturing to his clipboard. "I'll be your main point of contact for any questions or concerns. And I'll be handing out the next day's agenda every evening at supper. Let's gather around for a moment before we continue."

The circle tightened as Paul bowed his head. Everyone followed suit, even the counselors, though Hector glanced around first before lowering his eyes.

"Lord, we thank You for bringing these young people to us safely," Paul prayed, his deep voice steady and sure. "We ask Your blessing on the work we're doing here. May the lessons we've prepared be adequate for these counselors, and may they in turn guide the children who will come. Keep everyone healthy and safe throughout this summer. In Your name we pray, Amen."

"Amen," echoed through the group.

Chapter 10 – Second Chances, First Steps

"For I was an hungred, and ye gave me meat: I was thirsty, and ye gave me drink: I was a stranger, and ye took me in." Matthew 25:35 (KJV)

As evening approached, the retreat board members gathered near the dining hall, eager to welcome the counselors properly. Clara stood at the front, her face flushed with excitement and exhaustion.

"Before we eat, let's give you all a quick tour," she said, handing out maps and gesturing for the counselors to follow. "This is your home for the summer, so you should know your way around. We're behind on putting up all the directional signage but for now, everything is close and visible so you shouldn't have too much trouble getting around."

The group moved together through the main buildings—the dining hall with its long wooden tables, the activity center with shelves of craft supplies and games, the small chapel with windows that caught the setting sun. Wade pointed out the security features he'd installed, while Francie explained the garden layout with animated hands.

Maggie explained where all the outdoor fire extinguishers and water hoses were located and briefly explained lockdown and emergency response procedures. "The emergency response devices are listed on your map, and the procedures are listed on the back. We'll review these in more detail during training but we want you to always be prepared. As you all have learned in your short lives, you never know when the unexpected will happen."

"And that bell," Ellie said, pointing to a large brass bell mounted outside the dining hall, "is our emergency signal. Three rings means everyone gathers here."

By the time they returned to the dining hall, delicious aromas filled the air. Treva and Brittany had prepared a welcome feast—fried chicken, mashed potatoes, fresh vegetables from Francie's garden, and Treva's famous blackberry cobbler for dessert. Harry, Ava, Alan, Noah, and Ralph had joined them and were setting up the buffet station.

"Before we eat," Clara said, "we always say grace. Ben, would you lead us tonight?"

Ben looked startled for a moment, then nodded, removing his cap. Everyone bowed their heads as his deep voice filled the room.

"Father, thank you for bringing these young people to us. Bless their time here and the work they'll do with the children that come. Help us guide them well. Thank you for second chances. For this and all your bounty we are about to receive, make us truly grateful, Lord. For it is in Jesus' name, we pray. Amen."

Around the table, conversation flowed more easily with each passing minute. Anthony described his passion for woodworking, which caught Ethan's interest immediately. Rosita mentioned her experience with younger foster siblings, and Hector shared his dreams of coaching someday. Winona spoke softly about her grandmother's illness while little Oscar dozed in a portable crib nearby.

Maggie ended up sitting beside Ben at the table, and she was on edge from all the incidental brushes with his leg and his arm. She could feel the heat blooming in her cheeks so she took a drink of her sweet tea to cool off.

Beside her, Ben was having an inconvenient equal reaction. Of all the places to lose control. This had never happened to Ben. He took a drink of his sweet tea and started reciting produce prices in his mind to cool off and regain control. Feeling confused and vulnerable, Ben hurried to finish his meal, needing a break from the very enticing Maggie Cunningham.

"Tomorrow we'll start your training," Paul explained, passing a basket of rolls. "CPR and First Aid first, then conflict resolution, activity planning, and basic counseling skills. Pick up a copy of the schedule from that basket by the door as you leave."

When dinner ended, Clara stood again. "At camp, everyone pitches in with cleanup. That's our rule here—we all work together."

The counselors joined in without complaint, clearing tables and washing dishes alongside board members. Wade showed Hector how to properly load the industrial dishwasher, while Maggie and Rosita wiped down tables, chatting about favorite books.

Finally, Ethan and Clara led the tired counselors to their tiny homes, nestled in a semi-circle near the edge of the property.

"These are yours for the summer," Ethan said, handing each a key. "We tried to stock it with as many basics we thought you might need. We'll arrange a shopping trip to town in the next few days and we're working on regular transportation to and from."

"You each have a small coffee maker and toaster oven for quick meals if you need a break from the crowd, but we will provide breakfast, lunch and dinner in the dining hall every day."

"It's been a long day, so for now, go on in and get settled in your new home. Let us know if you have any trouble. If something breaks, it's Greg's fault. Everybody have a good night."

Inside each cabin, the counselors found welcome baskets filled with snacks, drinks, and toiletries. Bathrooms were stocked with towels, soaps, and other necessities. The refrigerators held milk, eggs, bread, and other basics.

"One more thing," Paul said, presenting each counselor with a smartphone. "These are programmed with all our numbers. Day or night, someone will answer if you need help."

Winona's eyes filled with tears as she looked around her cabin. "This is more than just a bed for the summer."

"That's right," Clara said softly. "It's a second chance, a new beginning."

"Call me in the morning, Winona, and I'll help you get Oscar settled in the daycare. And let me know if you need anything for him, or your Grandmother, before we are able to get you all to town for a shopping trip." Francie said as she held Winona's hand.

The next morning arrived with a soft pink sky and the promise of another busy day. Paul had set up chairs in a circle in the activity center, first aid dummies positioned at the center.

"CPR certification first," Paul announced as the counselors filed in, rubbing sleep from their eyes. "Our town's medical experts have graciously offered their time."

Nurse Lila Brooks entered with a confident stride, carrying a large duffel of supplies. Dr. Sam Hargrove followed, his usual tired eyes brightened by the morning coffee in his hand.

"Morning, everyone," Lila said cheerfully. "We're going to make sure you can save lives today."

In the kitchen, Brittany stood surrounded by inventory lists and recipe cards, her chef's brain calculating portions and nutritional requirements. Her fingers drummed nervously against the stainless steel counter as she surveyed the industrial kitchen.

"What am I even doing here?" she muttered, pushing a strand of hair behind her ear. "These kids need a real nutritionist, not some failed chef who couldn't hack it in Nashville."

She stared at her meal plan for the campers—simple dishes she could prepare in bulk and teach the campers to prepare at home. Nothing like the intricate plates she'd dreamed of creating. Nothing that would impress anyone.

Brittany picked up a potato and turned it over in her hand. In culinary school, she'd learned fourteen ways to prepare a potato. Here, she'd be lucky if the kids ate them mashed without complaint.

"You look like that potato insulted your mother," Treva said, appearing in the doorway with a pie carrier.

Brittany set the potato down. "Just wondering if I'm the right person for this job."

"Having second thoughts about those cooking classes?" Treva set her pie on the counter and crossed her arms.

"Maybe." Brittany sighed. "These kids don't need fancy knife skills. They need basic nutrition and survival cooking. I'm trained for fine dining, not..." she gestured around the kitchen, "camp food."

Treva laughed. "Honey, you think I was born knowing how to make pie? My first crust was so tough you could've used it as a frisbee."

Brittany smiled despite herself. "I just don't want to let these kids down."

"Then don't." Treva opened her pie carrier, revealing a perfect golden crust. "Teach them what they need, not what you think impresses people."

Brittany looked at her lists again, suddenly seeing possibilities rather than limitations. These kids didn't need a celebrity chef—they needed someone who could show them how to feed themselves on a budget, how to make healthy choices with limited options.

"You know what?" Brittany said, straightening her shoulders. "I'm going to rewrite this curriculum. Less gourmet, more life skills."

"To start with, we'll need more protein options," she muttered as Luke Sharp entered with his ever-present calculator.

"Need help with inventory? Is the dining budget all set?" Luke asked, peering over her shoulder.

"Kids eat more than you'd think," Brittany replied. "And these kids especially—we don't know what life is like for them at home, but while they are guests at the Retreat, we can make sure they have what they need."

Luke grimaced. "I'll see what we can do to shift things around so you have more in your budget. You're right. Our food purpose is to offer optimum nutrition and teach them as much about the food chain as possible."

"And until we reach sustainability, we will need to supplement our food items. I know a guy who can get us local eggs at half price," Brittany offered.

Handing Luke a stack of business cards, Brittany added "And Ben mentioned extra produce from the Farmstand. Oh, we could check with Walt to see if he knows of any local meat producers who would give us a discount. The WC Dairy has reached out looking to partner or barter. They will provide classes on livestock and dairy production if we agree to buy their products, and they are offering a steep discount."

"Now you're speaking my language," Luke said, pencil already adjusting figures.

Meanwhile, in the girls' bunkhouse, Maggie stood precariously on a stepstool, measuring tape in one hand, pencil tucked behind her ear.

"These windows need some privacy," she called over her shoulder. "The sun hits right on the beds at dawn."

She hadn't expected Ben to appear in the doorway, toolbox in hand.

"Ethan sent me to help with the curtain rods," he said, his voice a low rumble that seemed to fill the empty room.

Maggie nodded, suddenly aware of her old t-shirt and work jeans. "Great. I've marked most of them."

Ben moved beside her as she wobbled slightly on the stepstool. Without comment, his hands found her waist, steadying her with a gentle pressure.

"I've got you," he said quietly, not able to help the flexing of his hands around her waist.

The touch sent warmth spiraling through her. She froze, pencil mid-mark, acutely conscious of his calloused hands, the clean scent of his soap mixing with honest sweat.

"Thanks," she managed, voice uncharacteristically soft.

She soaked in the pleasure of his hands on her body despite hating how vulnerable that made her feel.

Their eyes met when she glanced down—his steady gaze holding questions neither was ready to ask. The moment stretched between them, fragile and full of possibility. The spell broke when Maggie dropped her pencil.

Later, as the day's work wound down, Ben found himself on the retreat's main path, watching the sunset paint the buildings in gold. The row of tiny homes, the chapel with its simple cross, the garden beds waiting for tomorrow's planting—it all seemed both finished and beginning.

He sensed Maggie before he saw her, coming to stand beside him, arms crossed against the evening chill. The now familiar feeling of peace her presence brought warming his insides and calming his spirit.

"It's almost something," she said, amazed, surveying their handiwork.

Ben looked at her profile, gilded by the fading light, then back to the retreat spread before them.

"Give it a minute," he replied softly. "Might become everything."

Chapter 11 – Buried Battles & Bitter Truths

"Have mercy upon me, O LORD, for I am in trouble: mine eye is consumed with grief, yea, my soul and my belly. For my life is spent with grief, and my years with sighing." Psalms 31:9-10 (KJV)

Dust motes danced in the thin shafts of sunlight filtering through the basement windows of the library. Maggie sneezed, then wiped her sleeve across her forehead, leaving a smudge of grime. Three hours she'd been down here, surrounded by the musty smell of old paper and forgotten history.

"Records this old should be digitized," she muttered, carefully turning another brittle page in the ledger.

Grace had shown her to the town archives with an apologetic smile. "Sorry about the mess. Been meaning to organize these for years."

Maggie didn't mind the solitude. Today was her off day at the vet clinic, and with Alan and Ralph at school, she welcomed the quiet focus of research. The bakery project had given her a goal, a purpose beyond just surviving day to day. Something that could provide for her family comfortably. With being a single mother to two growing boys and paying the mortgage by herself, times had been tough since Roger's abandonment.

Her finger traced down another column of property transfers from the 1980s. The building they were eyeing had once been a five and dime store, then a fabric store, before sitting vacant these past eight years. She needed to confirm there were no liens or restrictions before they sank their savings into it.

Flipping to the next volume, Maggie paused. A folded document had been inserted between pages—a land survey map with familiar boundaries. Her heart quickened as she recognized the creek that bordered Ben's property.

"That's odd," she whispered, carefully unfolding the yellowed paper.

The map showed the Reeves farm, but divided differently than she'd seen on the map Ben has hanging at both the Co-Op and the Crop 'Til You Drop. A thick red line cut through the property drawing, slicing the plot into an east and a west section. The West side, which ran along the highway was highlighted. That's where he grows his produce for the farmstand. What in the world?

Attached to the map was a deed transfer, dated fifteen years ago. Maggie's eyes widened as she read the fading type.

"This portion hereby transferred from Samuel J. Reeves to..." She squinted at the signature, her stomach dropping.

Samuel—Ben's father—had signed over nearly half the farm. Not sold it. Transferred it. For one dollar.

"But Ben said..." Her voice trailed off as she remembered his fierce words about keeping every inch of his family's land.

With trembling fingers, Maggie slid the document into the library's ancient copier. The machine groaned to life, casting green light across her face as it captured the evidence of a secret Ben clearly didn't know.

She folded the copy carefully, tucking it into her research folder, her mind racing with questions she wasn't sure she wanted answered.

Maggie sat motionless in her car, parked in the library's small lot. The folder lay open on her lap, the copied document staring back at her like an accusation. Outside, life in Willow Creek continued—Mrs. Pickens walked her poodle past the window, waving cheerfully. Maggie managed a weak smile in return, then slumped back against the headrest.

"What am I supposed to do with this?" she whispered to the empty car.

The weight of knowledge pressed on her chest. Ben had no idea. She was certain of it. His fierce pride in that land, the way he spoke about keeping his father's legacy intact—there was no way he knew half of it wasn't legally his anymore.

Maggie ran her fingers over the signature. Samuel J. Reeves. Ben's father had signed away half his son's birthright, and Ben was working himself to exhaustion trying to save it all.

What if he doesn't know? The question echoed. Of course he didn't. But who was the recipient? The name was smudged on her copy, nearly illegible.

Wouldn't you want someone to tell you? Maggie closed her eyes. Yes. No. Maybe. Finding out Roger had betrayed her had nearly broken her. The pain had been unbearable—but living in ignorance while he made a fool of her had been worse in retrospect.

Her hands trembled as she folded the paper again. She'd lived betrayal before. The memory of that gut-punch moment when she discovered Roger's affair surfaced unwanted—the phone call, the woman's voice, the sickening realization that her life was built on lies.

"I can't be the one to bring that pain to someone else," she whispered. "Not to Ben."

Not when his eyes had finally started showing something besides exhaustion when they looked at her. Not when his calloused hands had steadied her with such gentle care.

The dashboard clock ticked forward. She had to pick up the boys soon. Life demanded she keep moving, even with this terrible knowledge burning a hole in her pocket.

Chapter 12 – The Cost of Legacy

"A good man leaveth an inheritance to his children's children: and the wealth of the sinner is laid up for the just." Proverbs 13:22 (KJV)

Ben slammed the ledger shut, the sound echoing through the empty barn. His shoulders ached from hunching over numbers that refused to add up, no matter how he arranged them. Outside, the first hints of dawn crept across his fields—fields he'd been working since before sunrise yesterday.

"This ain't working," he muttered, rubbing his bloodshot eyes.

Ms. Pickles nudged his leg, her warm weight a small comfort. He scratched behind her ears, grateful for the company in these pre-dawn hours when the weight of the farm pressed heaviest.

The barn door creaked open. Wes Beaumont's lanky frame appeared, two steaming cups in hand.

"Thought I'd find you out here." Wes handed him a mug. "You look like hell warmed over."

Ben accepted the coffee with a grunt. "Thanks for the compliment."

"Tractor's fixed. Parts cost more than we budgeted." Wes leaned against the workbench, studying Ben's face. "Walt's worried about you. So am I."

"I'm fine."

"Liar." Wes nodded toward the ledger. "Those numbers talking back yet?"

Ben took a long sip, letting the bitter warmth fuel his depleted reserves. "I'm working every acre, doing the books at midnight, praying for rain—and it still ain't enough."

The silence stretched between them, broken only by Ms. Pickles's contented snuffling as she settled at Ben's feet.

"You need to let some land go," Wes finally said, his voice gentle but firm. "The north section's been nothing but trouble. Soil's poor, drainage is worse. Sell it off, focus on what's productive."

"Ain't happening." Ben shook his head, the mere suggestion cutting deep. "Every inch of this land has my family's blood in it."

Wes sighed. "Just think about it. That's all I'm asking."

After Wes left, Ben walked to the barn's open door, watching pink light spread across his fields. The morning dew caught the sunrise, turning ordinary grass into a sea of diamonds. His grandfather used to say that was God's way of reminding farmers that their work, however humble, was precious.

The memory washed over him unbidden—he couldn't have been more than twelve, gangly-limbed and eager to prove himself a man. His father had taken him to the north field, the very one Wes suggested selling. The summer heat had been relentless that day, sweat soaking through his T-shirt before they'd even started.

"This soil right here," Dad had said, crouching down to scoop a handful of dark earth, letting it sift through his fingers. "Your great-great-granddaddy Thomas bought it with gold coins he'd saved working other men's land for fifteen years."

Ben remembered how his father's eyes had softened, looking not at the dirt but through it, into the past.

"When the drought of '53 came, your granddaddy Pete dug that irrigation ditch by hand. Took him three weeks. Saved this whole section." Dad had pointed to the tree line. "Your grandmother Ruth planted those oaks as saplings, carried water to them every day for a summer."

They'd walked the property line together, his father's hand heavy but gentle on his shoulder.

"This land ain't just dirt and crops, son. It's your history. Every Reeves for four generations has put their mark on it. Their sweat. Their dreams." He'd looked Ben square in the eyes then. "One day, it'll be yours to tend. To pass on. That's what makes it special. That's what makes it home."

Ben blinked back to the present, the weight of those words heavier now than they'd been then. How could he sell even an acre, knowing what it had meant to his father? To his grandfather?

The land wasn't just his livelihood. It was his legacy.

Ben's hands tightened around the mug. The mere suggestion felt like betrayal.

"That land is all I have left of my dad. My mama. My name." His voice dropped to barely above a whisper. "My daddy made me promise not to sell any of it."

Chapter 13 – When the Truth Won't Stay Buried

"For nothing is secret, that shall not be made manifest; neither any thing hid, that shall not be known and come abroad." Luke 8:17 (KJV)

"Look at these crown moldings," Francie said, tipping her chin up and pointing it at the ceiling edge. "They sure don't make 'em like this anymore."

The five women stood in the dusty interior of what had once been Willow Creek's five and dime. Sunlight streamed through the grimy front windows, illuminating decades of neglect—and possibility.

"The electrical needs updating," Treva noted, tapping a defunct light switch. "But the bones are good."

Maggie nodded absently, her folder clutched against her chest. She'd arranged the bakery documents on top, burying Ben's deed deeper where it couldn't accidentally fall out.

"Maggie, you're a million miles away," Clara touched her arm. "What'd you find in those archives?"

"Oh!" Maggie startled, forcing herself to focus. She laid the folder on an old counter and spread out the building's history. "The property's clear—no liens or easements. It was originally built in 1938."

Hattie peered over her reading glasses. "My grandmother talked about buying penny candy here."

"We could keep some of that vintage charm," Clara suggested. "Maybe a display case with old-fashioned treats alongside our signature pies."

Francie's eyes sparkled. "Those test batches at my kitchen have been selling out. Tina said three Nashville folks who stopped at Hattie's asked if they could order whole pies for pickup next time they pass through."

"That's what I'm talking about!" Treva clapped her hands. "From Francie's kitchen to Kneadful Things Bakery. We're turning dreams into dough, ladies."

The women laughed, the sound echoing in the empty space.

"Think what this could mean," Hattie said softly. "Jobs. Income. A reason for folks to come downtown again."

"A fresh start," Maggie murmured, more to herself than the others.

Clara squeezed her shoulder. "For all of us."

As the others continued planning—where the ovens would go, how many tables they could fit—Maggie's thoughts drifted back to the folded paper hidden in her folder. The bakery represented hope, a way forward. But that deed... that deed could destroy everything Ben had worked for.

"Maggie?" Francie's voice broke through her thoughts. "You with us, sugar?"

"Sorry," Maggie smiled weakly. "Just imagining how beautiful this place will be when we're done."

But her mind remained split—half present with these women who'd become her support system, half buried with a secret she didn't know how to share.

The Willow Creek Town Council chambers were a far cry from the dusty old five and dime. Polished oak benches faced the raised dais where five council members sat beneath the town seal. The room buzzed with quiet conversation as townspeople filled the seats.

Maggie smoothed her skirt, grateful she'd changed out of her jeans before coming. Beside her, Treva clutched a leather portfolio containing their business plan, her knuckles white with tension.

"You'll do fine," Maggie whispered. "Just like we practiced."

Ellie Jernigan called the meeting to order with three sharp raps of her gavel. "Item four on tonight's agenda: proposed business permit for Kneadful Things Bakery. Ms. Walker, you have the floor."

Treva approached the podium with squared shoulders. Gone was the woman who handed out pies with a smile and a wink. This Treva was all business, her voice steady as she outlined their vision.

"Kneadful Things will revitalize a vacant building, initially create six jobs with the potential to expand to 30-50 employees, and bring foot traffic downtown. Our projections show..."

Maggie watched the council members' faces. Paul Grayson nodded encouragingly. Sheriff Wade jotted notes. But Mavis Holbrook's thin lips remained pressed in a bloodless line, her eyes narrowing as Treva described their financing.

When Treva finished, Mavis leaned toward her microphone.

"Well now, isn't that just precious." Her smile didn't reach her eyes. "But I have concerns about parking capacity. Section 12 of our zoning ordinance requires one space per hundred square feet of retail area."

"We've addressed that on page eight," Treva replied, flipping pages in her portfolio.

Mavis waved dismissively. "And have you considered the impact on traffic patterns? Main Street already backs up during shift change at the warehouse."

"The bakery would primarily operate during off-peak hours—"

"Then there's the matter of financing." Mavis adjusted her glasses. "In these uncertain economic times, the council must ensure new businesses have adequate capital reserves. We can't have another empty storefront six months from now."

Mayor Ellie's posture stiffened. "Councilwoman Holbrook, their business plan appears quite thorough."

"But not thorough enough for due diligence." Mavis smiled sweetly. "I move we table this proposal until our next meeting, giving us time to properly review all documentation."

Clara's jaw clenched so tight Maggie could see a muscle jumping in her cheek. Across the room, Francie's glare could have melted steel.

"All in favor?" Ellie asked, her voice tight.

Three hands rose. The bakery was officially tabled. For now.

The screen door slapped shut as Maggie trudged into Francie's kitchen, the last to arrive. Four women looked up from around the farmhouse table, each with a slice of pie already plated before them.

"There she is," Francie said, rising to pull out a chair. "I saved you the last slice of chocolate chess."

Maggie dropped her purse on the floor and sank into the seat. "I'm not sure even pie can fix this mess."

"Well, it sure can't hurt to try." Francie slid the plate in front of her and topped off everyone's sweet tea. "Eat up, sugar. Food before frettin' is what my mama always said."

Clara stabbed her fork into a mound of chocolate custard goodness. "I just don't understand it. Our paperwork was perfect. We answered every question. We've got the financing. What more does that woman want?"

"Blood sacrifice," Treva muttered, licking caramel from her thumb. "Or maybe just our souls."

Hattie shook her head. "I've known Mavis Holbrook for thirty years, and I swear she's gotten more ornery with each passing one. Used to be you could reason with her."

"Wonder what's got a burr under her saddle?" Francie asked, refilling Maggie's glass. "Seems like she's been extra prickly ever since George passed."

Maggie took her first bite, letting the rich chocolate melt on her tongue. For just a moment, the weight lifted from her shoulders.

"Three weeks," Treva said, her voice tight. "Three more weeks before they'll even look at our proposal again. That's three weeks of rent we're paying on an empty building."

"And three weeks closer to winter," Clara added. "We wanted to be open before the holiday rush."

"Seems like everything in this town is moving backwards these days," Hattie sighed. "First the factory closes, then the bank gets stingy with loans, now this."

Francie reached across the table to pat Maggie's hand. "Don't you worry. This ain't the first roadblock Willow Creek's faced, and it won't be the last. We'll figure something out."

The kitchen clock ticked relentlessly, marking time in the silent house. Maggie sat alone at her small table, the copied deed spread before her under the harsh overhead light. The boys had gone to bed hours ago, their bedtime prayers and goodnight kisses a temporary distraction from the weight pressing down on her chest.

Now there was nothing left but her and this terrible secret.

She traced the faded property line with her fingertip, the red mark dividing what Ben believed was his birthright. Half gone. Given away for a dollar by his own father.

"What am I supposed to do with this?" she whispered to the empty kitchen.

The refrigerator hummed. A tree branch scraped against the window. Somewhere down the street, a dog barked once, then fell silent.

Maggie pressed her palms against her eyes. "Why me, God? What did I do?" Her voice cracked. "I thought we were getting along better, You and I. I've been trying. Going to church again. Praying with the boys."

She looked up at the ceiling, as if she might find answers written there.

"Why would You put me in this position? How do I tell him his father betrayed him?"

She knew what betrayal felt like—the hollow ache that never quite healed, the way it changed how you saw the world. Roger had taken more than her marriage when he left. He'd stolen her trust, her confidence, her belief that life made sense.

Now she held the power to inflict that same wound on Ben.

The copied deed seemed to pulse under the light. Knowledge was supposed to be power, but this felt like a curse.

"I can't do this to him," she whispered. "But I can't keep lying either."

Through the thin walls, she heard Alan murmur something in his sleep. Her boys, innocent and trusting, unaware their mother sat wrestling with another man's demons.

Maggie folded the paper carefully, creasing it with her thumbnail. Then she folded it again. And again. Until it was small enough to slip into her Bible on the counter.

She didn't pray for a sign. Signs were for people who didn't know what to do. She knew what needed to be done—she just didn't know if she had the strength to do it.

"Just help me carry this," she whispered, her fingers lingering on the worn leather Bible cover. "Just until I figure out how to tell him."

Outside, clouds drifted across the moon, casting Willow Creek into deeper darkness. Another sleepless night stretched ahead.Paste your chapter text here...

ACT II

Planting Hope

Chapter 14 – Tree Fort Promises - Room to Soar

"God setteth the solitary in families: he bringeth out those which are bound with chains: but the rebellious dwell in a dry land." Psalms 68:6 (KJV)

The late afternoon sun filtered through the oak leaves, casting dappled shadows across the clearing where the Tree Fort stood. Three weeks of hard work had transformed the space into something magical. Ethan and Greg's sturdy picnic tables formed a horseshoe around the massive tree trunk, their cedar posts stretching skyward, now draped with twinkling fairy lights that would glow once dusk settled in.

Maggie arranged plates of brownies and lemon squares on the dessert table while Francie fussed with her signature pies—apple, chocolate chess, and pecan—cutting perfect slices and arranging them on paper plates. The sweet scent of sugar and butter wafted through the air, mingling with the earthy smell of the oak tree above them.

"You think we made enough?" Francie asked, wiping her hands on her apron, her brow creased with concern as she surveyed their handiwork.

"Lord, I hope so." Maggie laughed, tucking a strand of hair behind her ear. "Between twenty hungry foster kids and half the town showing up to welcome them, we might need to send for reinforcements. I've never seen children pack away sweets quite like teenagers who've been playing outdoors all day."

Across the clearing, Brittany flipped burgers on a portable grill, her chef's apron protecting her clothes. Beads of sweat dotted her forehead as she worked with practiced efficiency. Treva stood beside her, arranging hot dogs in neat rows, ready for the hungry crowd. The sizzle of meat on the grill punctuated their conversation as they worked in tandem.

"Buns need about five more minutes to warm," Treva called out, checking the foil-wrapped packages nestled near the grill. She adjusted her bandana and wiped her brow with the back of her hand, the afternoon heat making everyone's work just a little more challenging.

At the welcome table, Harry and Ava directed their crew with the precision of seasoned event planners. Noah and Ralph stuffed water bottles into the last of the backpacks while Alan and Emma Collins arranged them in neat rows.

"Remember, everybody gets one," Ava instructed, hands on her hips. "And make sure they know about the camp store coupons."

Anthony approached the table, his confidence growing after three weeks of training. "First van just pulled up at the main entrance. They'll be soon."

"Places, everyone!" Harry called out, straightening his camp counselor shirt.

The lights strung between the tables flickered to life as the sun dipped lower, casting a warm glow over the entire clearing. Clara and Ethan stood at the path entrance, ready to greet their first official campers.

A couple Maggie didn't recognize wandered into the clearing, looking slightly lost. The woman had kind eyes and a tentative smile, while the man beside her surveyed the setup with interest, his hands tucked into the pockets of pressed khaki pants.

"Welcome," Clara stepped forward, brushing a strand of hair from her face. "Are you here for the camp kickoff?"

"We weren't actually—" the woman began, adjusting the strap of her shoulder bag.

"We're the Dawsons," the man extended his hand, grip firm and friendly. "Edward and Sara. We're visiting from Nashville, thinking about relocating. Someone in town mentioned there was an event out here tonight. Said something about a retreat that's making quite a stir."

"Well, you picked the perfect night to stumble upon us," Clara smiled, warmth spreading across her features. "We're launching our first foster youth camp. I'm Clara Walker, and this is my husband Ethan. We started the Willow Creek Retreat just last year."

Sara's eyes brightened, a spark of genuine interest lighting them. "Foster youth? That's—" She exchanged a meaningful look with her husband, something unspoken passing between them. "Actually, we've been considering becoming foster parents for some time now. Just haven't taken the leap."

Sara felt a flutter in her chest as she watched the preparations around them. The colored lights, the eager children, the sense of community—it stirred something deep inside her that she'd tried to bury beneath years of disappointment.

Edward squeezed her hand, sensing her thoughts. They'd spent seven years trying to have a baby. Seven years of temperature charts and timed intimacy. Of hormone shots that left bruises on her stomach and hope that left bruises on her heart. Seven years of nurseries painted and then repurposed, of baby clothes purchased and then donated.

"You okay?" Edward whispered, his voice carrying the weight of their shared journey.

Sara nodded, blinking back unexpected tears. "Just thinking about how God closes doors but opens windows." She watched as a teenage girl with defensive posture stepped off a van, arms crossed tightly over her chest. "Maybe this is our window."

Edward followed her gaze. They'd finally stopped fertility treatments last Christmas after their third miscarriage. The doctor's words still echoed in Sara's mind: "I don't recommend you try again." That night, they'd held each other and cried until there were no tears left.

"Remember what Pastor Michaels said?" Edward murmured. "About how sometimes God's greatest blessings come wrapped in unexpected packages?"

Sara nodded. Their grief counselor had suggested they take a year before making any decisions about adoption or fostering. That year was almost up, and they'd begun researching options, attending informational sessions. But something had been missing—a sense of rightness, of being called.

"I never imagined we'd find direction in a random small town," Sara admitted. "But watching all this..." She gestured to the bustling activity, the careful preparations, the genuine care evident in every detail.

"Maybe we needed to see it in action," Edward said. "Not just hear about it in an office."

A child's laugh rang out—bright and uninhibited—and Sara felt something inside her shift. Not healing exactly, but realignment. The pain of what they'd lost would always be there, but perhaps God was showing them what they might gain.

"Then you're definitely in the right place," Ethan said, gesturing toward the tables laden with welcome packets and refreshments. "Why don't you join us? The kids will be here any minute, and we've got plenty to share. You might even meet some folks who can answer your questions about fostering."

The first van rumbled up the gravel drive, dust billowing behind it. Paul stood beside Clara and Ethan, clipboard in hand, his weathered face creased with anticipation.

"Here we go," he murmured.

The van doors slid open. One by one, teenagers spilled out, blinking in the afternoon light, their expressions ranging from suspicious to cautious to barely concealed excitement. Duffel bags and backpacks hung from slumped shoulders as they gathered in a loose cluster, whispering among themselves and stealing glances at the adults waiting to greet them.

A girl with braided hair stepped down from the van, her shoulders hunched forward like she was bracing against an invisible wind. She clutched a tattered backpack to her chest, fingers white-knuckled around the straps. Her eyes darted across the clearing, taking inventory of every adult, every exit, every potential threat. When Ethan smiled in her direction, she quickly looked away, her jaw clenched tight.

Behind her emerged a lanky boy with glasses too big for his face. Unlike the girl, he bounded down the steps with unexpected energy, his face split by a grin that seemed almost desperate in its brightness. His sneakers, worn nearly through at the toes, barely touched the ground as he bounced on the balls of his feet, head swiveling to take in the twinkling lights and the massive tree fort. His enthusiasm had the fragile quality of something that might shatter if challenged.

The last child to exit moved with deliberate slowness. A boy of about twelve with a close-cropped haircut and skin the color of burnished copper. His expression remained perfectly neutral, a practiced mask that revealed nothing. But his eyes—sharp, observant—missed nothing. His posture was military-straight, shoulders squared, chin lifted slightly. He carried no bag, just a small book clutched in one hand, pressed against his thigh as if to hide it. When Wade approached to welcome him, the boy's eyes widened just a fraction, the only crack in his carefully constructed facade.

A tall girl with dark braids twisted into a crown stepped off last, her chin tilted upward, arms crossed tightly over her chest. She surveyed the grounds with a practiced disinterest that didn't quite mask the wariness in her eyes. Her fingers drummed against her arm as she hung back from the others, taking in the sprawling trees, the weathered welcome sign, and the circle of adults whose smiles seemed a little too eager, a little too hopeful.

Maggie felt a tug of recognition watching her. That defensive posture, the careful assessment of every exit—she'd seen it in the mirror after Roger left. That girl had been let down more times than she could count.

Maggie watched the girl's calculated movements, feeling an echo of her own pain in that carefully constructed armor. She knew what it was like to build walls brick by brick, to fortify yourself against the next inevitable disappointment. The memory of Roger's abandonment flashed through her mind—his packed suitcases by the door, his hollow promises that he'd visit the boys, the finality of the door clicking shut behind him.

Five years later, and the wound still ached when pressed.

She placed the last brownie on the dessert tray, her hands suddenly unsteady. What was she doing here, trying to help these kids when she couldn't even sort out her own heart? What did she have to offer when she still woke some nights with that hollow feeling in her chest, that sense of not being enough?

Ben's face floated through her thoughts. The way he looked at her like she was something precious, something worth choosing. The gentle brush of his calloused fingers against hers when he'd helped her into his truck yesterday. The way his eyes crinkled at the corners when he smiled at her boys.

Hope and fear tangled in her chest, a painful knot she couldn't unravel. What if she let herself believe in this? In him? What if she opened that door again only to have it slammed in her face?

"You okay there?" Francie's gentle voice broke through her thoughts.

Maggie realized she'd been standing frozen, clutching an empty serving tray. "Just wool-gathering," she managed, forcing a smile.

But as she watched the girl with the braided crown scan the clearing for threats, Maggie recognized a kindred spirit. Someone else who'd learned the hard way that love wasn't always permanent, that promises were easily broken. She understood the exhaustion of constant vigilance, always waiting for the other shoe to drop.

"That one's gonna be a tough nut to crack," Francie murmured, following Maggie's gaze.

"Maybe," Maggie said softly. "Or maybe she just needs someone who understands what it's like when the people who should love you most walk away instead."

"Welcome to Willow Creek Retreat," Clara called out, her voice warm. "I'm Clara, this is my husband Ethan, and this is Mr. Paul, our camp director."

A smaller van pulled up behind the first. A social worker stepped out, then helped a group of younger children disembark. A small girl with beaded braids and bright eyes hopped down, clutching a worn backpack to her chest.

"That's Charnise Evans," Paul whispered, checking his list. "And the older one who got off first is Loquita Foreman."

Sheriff Wade approached from the parking area, his badge catching the sunlight. "Once you've all got your things, we'll head to the bunkhouses to get settled, then I'll go over some safety rules."

Loquita's eyes narrowed at the sight of the badge. She shifted her weight backward, almost imperceptibly.

Loquita stiffened at the sight of the sheriff's badge, her heart rate quickening. The last time she'd seen a badge that close, her entire world had collapsed. The memory flashed through her mind with painful clarity.

Mama screaming as they dragged Daddy away. The officer's hand heavy on my shoulder. "Your parents made their choices, honey. Now you gotta live with them."

She swallowed hard, fighting the familiar burn of anger. Three years in the system because some cop decided her parents' in-home meth lab made them unfit. Three years of different homes, different rules, different disappointments.

"You don't have to talk to him," she whispered to Charnise, who'd gravitated to her side. The younger girl had only been in the system for eight months, but they'd bonded instantly at the group home. Loquita had appointed herself Charnise's protector, a role she took seriously.

"But he looks nice," Charnise whispered back, her eyes wide as she watched Sheriff Wade help another child with a dropped duffel bag.

"They all look nice at first," Loquita muttered, her fingers unconsciously tightening around the strap of her backpack.

Wade approached them, his smile easy, his movements deliberately casual. "Welcome to Willow Creek," he said, keeping a respectful distance. "I'm Sheriff Beaumont, but you can call me Wade while you're at camp."

Loquita's chin lifted, defiance masking her fear. "We don't need any special attention, sir."

Something in Wade's eyes shifted—recognition, maybe understanding. He nodded once, no trace of offense in his expression. "Fair enough. The welcome table's that way when you're ready. No rush."

As he moved away, Loquita exhaled slowly. Maybe this place would be different. Maybe not. Either way, she'd keep her guard up. That's what survivors did.

"Don't worry," Wade said, catching her look. "I'm just here to make sure everyone knows how to stay safe in the woods. No badges, no rules except the ones that keep you from meeting our local poison ivy."

A few nervous laughs rippled through the group.

"Let's get your bags to your cabins," Ethan suggested. "Then we've got quite a welcome waiting for you at the end of the tour that winds up at the Tree Fort."

An hour later, the campers had settled into their bunks and completed Wade's safety tour. As Paul led the group toward the Tree Fort, the fairy lights twinkled against the deepening twilight, creating a magical glow that drew gasps from even the most stoic teenagers.

At the welcome table, Harry straightened the row of backpacks, his face serious with responsibility. "Remember," he whispered to Ralph, "smile big like Maggie always says when you're nervous."

Ava bounced on her toes, scanning the approaching group. "There she is!" She pointed toward Charnise, who trailed behind the others, taking in the lights with wide eyes.

As the campers approached, Emma stepped forward. "Welcome to Willow Creek! We've got SWAG bags for everyone."

"What's SWAG?" a lanky boy asked suspiciously.

"Stuff We All Get," Alan explained, handing him a backpack. "Camp shirts, water bottles, hats—all the good stuff."

Noah, usually quiet around strangers, held out a backpack to a younger boy. "There's sunscreen too. Mom says you'll need it by the lake."

Ava slipped away from the table and approached Charnise. "Hi! I'm Ava, remember? You want the purple backpack or the blue one?"

Charnise hesitated. "Purple, I guess."

"Good choice. Purple's the best color." Ava handed her the bag. "Do you like horses? We've got some at my grandpa's farm."

Charnise's face brightened. "For real? I've never touched a real horse before."

"Well, you will now. Apple Blossom is super gentle. She lets me brush her mane and everything." Ava reached into her pocket and pulled out a braided string bracelet. "Here. I made this. It's a friendship bracelet."

"For me?" Charnise looked stunned.

"Yep. We're gonna be friends. I can tell."

A school bus rumbled up the drive, and a dozen high school students piled out, carrying boxes and bags.

"More gifts!" Ralph announced. "The high school kids brought stuff too!"

The teenagers unloaded their cargo—shower shoes wrapped in cellophane, windbreakers with the camp logo, extra hygiene kits, and handmade cards.

"We wanted y'all to feel welcome," a girl in a cheerleading jacket explained. "Everyone needs the right gear to have fun at camp."

Loquita stared at the backpack thrust into her hands, confusion flickering across her face. She peeked inside, then looked up sharply at the teenage girl who'd given it to her.

"What's the catch?" she asked, voice low enough that only the cheerleader could hear.

The girl's smile faltered. "No catch. Just... welcome to camp."

Loquita's fingers tightened around the straps. In her three years bouncing between foster homes, she'd learned that nothing came without strings. The Hendersons had seemed generous at first too—until they started tallying every expense, reminding her that "charity cases should be grateful." The Millers had given her new clothes, then locked them away as punishment for imagined offenses.

"This is... mine? To keep?" She couldn't keep the suspicion from her voice.

"Of course," the cheerleader said, her expression softening with understanding. "Everything in there belongs to you now."

Across the clearing, Anthony Graves clutched his backpack to his chest, blinking rapidly. At eighteen, he'd aged out of the system just two months ago. His social worker had dropped him at a halfway house with nothing but a folder of paperwork and a "good luck." Now strangers were handing him brand-new things—a water bottle with his name already written on it, a hat that still had its tags, a journal with blank pages waiting to be filled.

"You okay, man?" one of the high school boys asked.

Anthony nodded, not trusting his voice. He'd spent years learning to want nothing, expect nothing, ask for nothing. This sudden abundance felt dangerous, like a trap he couldn't see.

Nearby, the boy with the military posture examined his backpack with methodical precision, removing each item and placing it in a neat row on the picnic table. His movements were economical, practiced—the habits of someone who'd learned that organization was the only control he had.

"There's a flashlight in there too," Noah offered shyly. "For reading under the covers after lights out."

The boy's hands stilled. He looked up, something vulnerable flickering in his eyes. "They let you read after lights out here?"

"Mom says books are friends that stay with you forever," Noah replied with a solemn nod.

The boy touched the book in his pocket—his one possession—and for the first time since arriving, his shoulders relaxed just a fraction.

Chapter 15 – Tree Fort Roots - Belonging Begins

"When my father and my mother forsake me, then the LORD will take me up."
Psalms 27:10 (KJV)

Brittany approached Loquita with a plate loaded with a perfectly grilled burger, the bun toasted just right. She'd seasoned the meat with her special blend of spices—the same ones that had impressed her culinary school instructors in Nashville. The smell wafted upward, rich and inviting.

"Made this one special," Brittany said, extending the plate. "Farm-to-table, literally from my brother's pasture to your hands."

Loquita eyed the burger suspiciously. "Thanks," she muttered, taking it without meeting Brittany's eyes.

Brittany's smile faltered. This wasn't the reaction she'd anticipated. In her vision for the farm-to-table café, she'd imagined grateful faces lighting up at first bites, the validation that would make losing everything in Nashville and returning home worthwhile. Not this wall of teenage wariness.

She stepped back, doubt creeping in. What was she doing here anyway? She'd failed at her attempt at a promising career in upscale restaurants to return to Willow Creek and chase some half-baked dream about local, sustainable food. Her former colleagues were probably laughing at her right now, imagining her slinging burgers for ungrateful teenagers.

Maybe they were right. Maybe I don't belong here anymore. Maybe I've outgrown this place.

She glanced around at the other chefs—Treva arranging pie slices, her mother setting out homemade pickles, Ben grilling more burgers. They all seemed so comfortable, so certain of their place in this community.

Brittany took a deep breath, straightening her shoulders. No. This was exactly where she needed to be. These kids deserved good food—real food—not processed cafeteria slop. They deserved to know that someone cared enough to make something special just for them.

"The secret's in the seasoning," she said, finding her voice again. "My grandma taught me how to blend them. Been perfecting it for years."

Loquita took a tentative bite. Her eyes widened slightly.

"This is... actually good," she admitted, surprise evident in her voice.

Brittany felt a warmth spread through her chest. "Wait till you try my apple-blackberry cobbler for dessert. The apples are from Ms. Francie's orchard, and the blackberries grow wild by the creek."

For the first time, Loquita's expression softened. "Never had homemade cobbler before."

"You cook?" Brittany asked, nodding toward the grill.

"Yeah." Loquita's answer was clipped, but she took a bite. Something flickered across her face—a hint of approval quickly masked.

"Kitchen's open to anyone who wants to learn," Brittany added. "I'm always looking for an extra pair of hands."

Loquita didn't smile, but she took another bite, larger this time.

Brittany watched as Loquita devoured the rest of her burger, a small sense of victory blooming in her chest. The girl's guard hadn't fully dropped, but food had created the tiniest crack in that wall—exactly what Brittany had hoped for.

This is why I came back, she thought, her earlier doubts receding. Not for fancy reviews or chef's awards, but for moments like this. God didn't lead me home to fail; He brought me back to feed people who need more than just a meal.

She gathered empty plates from a nearby table, nodding at Ben who gave her a thumbs-up from the grill. Her brother had believed in her vision for the farm-to-table café even when she'd doubted herself. The path forward wasn't clear yet, but the purpose was.

"Miss?" Anthony approached hesitantly, his empty plate clutched in his hands. "That was the best burger I've ever had."

Brittany smiled. "Thank you. There's plenty more if you're still hungry."

"Actually..." He shifted his weight. "I was wondering if you were serious about letting people help in the kitchen? I used to cook at one of my foster homes. Nothing fancy, but..."

"Absolutely serious," Brittany said, her smile widening. "We're making breakfast tomorrow at seven. Think you can handle cracking eggs?"

Anthony's face lit up. "Yes, ma'am. I can definitely do that."

As he walked away, Brittany felt a wave of certainty wash over her. The Nashville restaurant scene had nearly crushed her spirit with its cutthroat competition and superficial values. But here, food could be what it was meant to be—nourishment for body and soul, a bridge between strangers, a way to serve with love.

This is exactly where You wanted me, Lord, she thought, looking up at the twilight sky. Not climbing some fancy ladder, but right here, grounded in what matters.

Across the clearing, Noah approached Hector with a folded piece of paper clutched in his small hand. The teenager stood awkwardly at the edge of the gathering, watching.

"Made this for you," Noah said, thrusting the paper forward.

Hector unfolded it to find a crayon drawing of the Tree Fort with stick figures scattered beneath it. One tall figure wore what looked like a whistle around his neck.

"That's you," Noah pointed. "You're the coach."

Hector stared at the drawing, then at Noah. "I... thanks, little man." He carefully refolded the paper, sliding it into his pocket.

Charnise sat cross-legged beside Ava on one of the picnic blankets spread out around the area, admiring her new bracelet.

"Wish I had a place like this," she sighed, looking up at the wooden structure nestled in the branches.

Noah, who'd wandered over after his encounter with Hector, shrugged. "We built it together." He pointed to the weathered boards. "That part's old, from when Mom and Ethan were kids. But we fixed it up."

Sara and Edward Dawson lingered nearby, listening. Sara's hand found her husband's, squeezing gently.

"They're sweet together," she whispered.

Edward nodded, watching as Ralph joined the group, carrying a plate piled high with brownies.

"Best family vacation ever," Ralph declared, offering the plate around. "Way better than that time Mom tried to take us camping and the tent collapsed."

"Ralph!" Maggie called from across the clearing, but she was laughing.

Ava took a brownie, her eyes drifting toward Clara and Ethan, who stood side-by-side, watching the gathering.

"It's the first one that felt like family," she said softly.

Chapter 16 – Tree Fort - Between the Branches

"Turn thee unto me, and have mercy upon me; for I am desolate and afflicted. The troubles of my heart are enlarged: O bring thou me out of my distresses. Look upon mine affliction and my pain; and forgive all my sins." Psalms 25:16-18

The campfire crackled and spat embers toward the star-speckled sky. Shadows danced across eager faces as the teens and children huddled closer, marshmallows toasting on whittled sticks.

"My granddaddy swore it was true," Hector said, his voice dropping to a whisper. "Every full moon, you could hear chains rattling in the old Pearson hayloft. The farmer who owned it before disappeared one night. They say he haunts it still, looking for the gold he buried somewhere on the property."

A collective gasp rippled through the circle. One of the younger girls scooted closer to Rosita, who wrapped a protective arm around her shoulders.

"They say if you go there at midnight and call his name three times—" Hector leaned forward, eyes wide.

Noah suddenly popped up from his seat, flashlight beam illuminating his face from below, casting eerie shadows across his features.

"Knock knock," he announced.

A few campers groaned. Others giggled nervously, grateful for the interruption.

"Who's there?" Anthony played along, his smile encouraging.

"Boo."

"Boo who?"

Noah's face split into a wide grin. "Don't cry! It's just a story!"

Laughter erupted around the circle. Even Loquita, who'd maintained her careful distance all evening, cracked a smile before ducking her head to hide it.

"My turn," Ralph called out, jumping to his feet. "Once there was this kid who put Pop Rocks and soda in his mouth at the same time and his head exploded!"

"That's not even scary," Alan protested. "That's just gross."

The stories shifted then, from spooky to silly. Winona shared a tale about a haunted hairbrush that made everyone's hair turn green. Anthony told a joke about a ghost who couldn't find his "boo"-ts.

As the night deepened, the stories grew quieter, more personal. A boy with glasses and a faded T-shirt stared into the flames.

"Foster home I was in last year, they had this dog that howled all night," he said. "I used to pretend it was talking to me. Telling me stories about places I could go someday."

Silence settled over the group. The crackling fire filled the void, casting long shadows across their faces. No one seemed eager to break the spell that had fallen upon them, each lost in their own thoughts about a boy who found comfort in a howling dog's nighttime songs.

"I wish I had a place like this," he added, gesturing to the Tree Fort above them, fairy lights twinkling among the branches like earthbound stars caught in the oak's embrace.

Noah, who sat cross-legged nearby, looked up. His face glowed in the flickering firelight as he spoke. "We built it together," he said quietly, fingers tracing patterns in the dirt. "That part's old, from when Mom and dad were kids. But we fixed it. Added new boards and everything. Dad showed me how to use a hammer without smashing my thumb."

Maggie stood at the edge of the firelight, her fingers tracing the folded edges of the deed in her pocket. The weight of it felt heavier than paper had any right to be. She watched Ben across the circle, silhouetted against the flames, and her heart ached with the knowledge she couldn't share.

Maggie pressed her fingertips against the paper in her pocket, its edges worn from her constant touching. The deed felt like a burning coal—impossible to hold onto, yet impossible to drop. Each time she caught Ben's gaze across the fire, guilt twisted deeper in her stomach.

"Lord, what am I supposed to do with this?" she prayed silently. Show me the right path.

She watched Ben crouch down to ruffle Ms. Pickles' fur, his strong hands gentle against the dog's white coat. The firelight caught the lines of exhaustion around his eyes—a man fighting to hold onto his family legacy while it crumbled beneath his feet. And here she stood, holding a piece of paper that could shatter what little hope he had left.

Her chest tightened. The headaches had started three days ago, right after she'd found the deed in county records. Sharp, stabbing pain behind her eyes that aspirin barely touched. Sleep had become a distant memory, replaced by endless rehearsals of how to tell him the truth—that his father had sold half the farm years ago, that the land he was fighting for wasn't entirely his to save.

He'll hate me for keeping this from him, she thought, swallowing against the dryness in her throat. But he'll hate me more when I tell him.

The worst part wasn't the physical toll—though her body ached with tension—but the emotional chasm growing between them just as something beautiful had begun to take root. Every smile they shared now felt like theft, every moment of connection tainted by her silence.

She watched as Ben laughed at something Jake said, his entire face transforming. That rare, unguarded smile made her heart flutter and sink simultaneously.

I'm falling for a man whose world I'm about to break apart.

Maggie rubbed her temples, fighting another headache. The longer she waited, the worse it would be. But tonight—watching these children find a moment of peace around the fire—wasn't the time. Tomorrow, she promised herself. Tomorrow she would find the courage to tell him everything, even if it meant losing whatever chance they might have had.

Clara sidled up beside her, bumping her shoulder gently. "You're staring again."

"I'm not," Maggie whispered, but her eyes betrayed her, drifting back to Ben's tall frame as he gestured animatedly, moonlight catching the weathered lines around his eyes.

Clara's face softened. "What's wrong, Maggs? You look like you're carrying the whole world."

Maggie swallowed hard. "It's nothing." She fidgeted with the hem of her sweater, trying to ignore the familiar ache in her chest.

"That's the same nothing I saw when we were ten and you broke your mama's favorite vase. You've got that same guilty look—like you're holding something that weighs a ton but you're too stubborn to set it down." Clara tilted her head, studying her oldest friend with the kind of knowing that came from a lifetime of shared secrets.

From the opposite side of the flames, Brittany squinted suspiciously at their interaction. Throughout the night, she'd caught Maggie's extended looks toward her brother, how she'd retreat whenever he shifted nearer. Something seemed off about the situation. Ben was dealing with sufficient troubles without throwing romantic disappointment into the equation.

Brittany watched the exchange between Maggie and Clara with a mixture of concern and caution. The hushed conversation, the guilty glances toward Ben—it triggered memories she'd tried to leave behind in Nashville. She'd seen similar behavior before, and it had ended with betrayal.

Her business partner, Javier, had worn that same look in the weeks before she discovered he'd been systematically siphoning funds from their restaurant account. For months, he'd looked her in the eye, raised glasses to their success, all while secretly preparing to open his own place with her recipes, her investors, her dream.

"Everything okay?" she'd asked him once, catching that same furtive expression Maggie now wore.

"Just tired," he'd said. "Restaurant business, right?"

Two weeks later, she'd found herself locked out of their shared kitchen, her name scrubbed from the business license, and her signature forged on transfer documents.

Now, watching Maggie fidget and avoid Ben's gaze, that familiar knot formed in Brittany's stomach. But as she observed longer, she noticed something different in Maggie's expression—not calculation, but genuine distress. Unlike Javier's cold efficiency, Maggie's discomfort seemed to pain her.

Maybe I'm seeing ghosts where there aren't any, Brittany thought. Not everyone is Javier.

After all, Clara trusted Maggie completely. And Clara wasn't a fool—she'd survived her own betrayals. Perhaps whatever troubled Maggie wasn't malicious but just... complicated.

"You need help with those?" Brittany asked, approaching Maggie and Clara as they gathered leftover food containers.

"We're fine," Maggie answered quickly—too quickly.

Brittany managed a genuine smile. "Ben mentioned you might be helping with the farm stand this weekend."

"I—I'm not sure yet," Maggie stammered. "Things are complicated right now."

Complicated. The word gave Brittany pause, but she pushed down her instinctive suspicion. Maggie had been nothing but kind to her since she'd returned to Willow Creek. The woman volunteering at this camp had shown genuine care for these children—not the actions of someone plotting harm.

"Well," Brittany said, her tone softening, "if you can make it, we'd love the help. And if not..." She hesitated, then added, "Just let him know. My brother appreciates honesty more than anything."

Ben stood with Greg and Jake near the edge of the clearing, arms crossed over his chest.

"How's Dexter doing?" Ben asked, nodding toward Jake.

Jake's face fell slightly. "Hospice says it could be any day now. He's been asking for Mom more often."

"I'm sorry, man," Greg said, clapping Jake's shoulder. "He's a good one, Old Man Landry."

"How's it going, taking over the company?" Greg asked, changing the subject.

Jake shrugged. "Steep learning curve. Dad built something special, though."

A comfortable silence fell between them before Jake suddenly turned to Ben with a sly grin.

"So what's your plan for asking Maggie out? Because whatever it is, you're taking too long."

Ben choked on his sip of water. "What?"

"Come on," Jake laughed. "You've been watching her all night like a lovesick teenager. Every time she moves, your eyes follow her like she's the only person here."

"I haven't—" Ben stopped, rubbing the back of his neck. "Is it that obvious?"

Greg snorted. "To everyone except you two, apparently. Even Old Man Landry noticed, and he can barely see past his own nose these days. She smiles, you light up. It's like watching a high school dance where neither of you knows how to make the first move."

Ben's gaze drifted back to Maggie. The way the firelight caught in her hair, how she knelt to help Ralph with his marshmallow. His world might be crumbling around him, the farm slipping through his fingers, but watching her—watching these kids find joy in simple things—something shifted in his chest. A reminder of what really mattered.

Four generations of Reeves had worked that land. His great-grandfather's calloused hands had first turned that soil, his grandfather had expanded through the lean years, and his father had modernized what he could. Now it fell to Ben to either save it or be the one who lost it all. The weight of that responsibility had become a physical ache, settling into his bones alongside the day's labor.

But here, in this moment, with laughter rising toward the stars and Ms. Pickles warm against his leg, Ben felt something loosen in his chest. A knot he'd carried so long he'd forgotten it wasn't part of him.

Maggie tucked a strand of hair behind her ear, her smile gentle as she showed Ralph how to toast the marshmallow without burning it. Something about the patient way she guided his hands, the quiet confidence in her movements—it stirred something deep within Ben. Not just attraction, though Lord knew that was there too, but recognition. Here was someone who understood what it meant to fight for what mattered, to build something from broken pieces.

He'd spent so many nights alone in that farmhouse, surrounded by generations of ghosts and fading dreams, convinced that saving the land was all that mattered. The Reeves legacy. The family name. But watching these children—foster kids without roots, Maggie's boys healing from abandonment—Ben realized with startling clarity that legacy wasn't just about soil and crops and property lines.

Ben closed his eyes, suddenly transported back twenty-five years. He was nine, sitting beside a smaller campfire on the far edge of the eastern field. His father had taken him camping for his birthday—just the two of them and a pup tent pitched under the sprawling oak that marked the property line.

"This is where your great-granddaddy first camped when he bought this land," his father had said, voice reverent in the darkness. "He slept right here before there was even a house. Said he wanted to feel the soil breathe before he built anything on it."

Ben remembered how his father had taught him to build the fire, arranging the kindling in a careful tepee, showing him how to shield the match from the wind with cupped hands.

"Farming isn't just about growing things, son," his father had said, firelight dancing across his weathered face. "It's about knowing when to let things rest, too. Land needs to breathe same as people do."

They'd roasted hot dogs on whittled sticks and eaten beans straight from the can. His father had pointed out constellations, telling stories about how sailors used the stars to find their way home.

"You'll always know where home is," his father had promised, "long as you can see the stars."

That night, curled in his sleeping bag, Ben had listened to his father's steady breathing and the symphony of night sounds—crickets chirping, frogs calling, the distant hoot of an owl. He'd never felt so connected to anything as he had to that patch of earth beneath him, to the legacy stretching back through generations of Reeves men who had worked this soil.

Now, watching these children gathered around the campfire, Ben realized that his father had been teaching him something more important than farming that night. He'd been showing him how to create moments that mattered, memories that would outlast even the land itself.

It was about connection. About building something that outlasted you not in wood and stone but in hearts and lives. About creating a place where wounded souls could heal, where children could feel safe enough to laugh around a campfire and tell stories of their fears.

And maybe—just maybe—it was about finding someone to share that dream with. Someone whose smile made him believe tomorrow might be brighter than today.

The flames dipped lower as Ethan stepped into the circle, his face warm in the firelight. He lifted his hands, and the chatter settled into expectant silence.

"Before we head to our cabins, let's bow our heads together." His voice carried across the clearing, steady and sure. "Father God, we thank You for bringing us together tonight under Your stars. For the laughter we've shared, and for this place of refuge You've provided."

Ethan's gaze swept across the circle—over the foster kids with their careful eyes, the volunteers with their hopeful hearts, the families finding connection.

"Lord, we ask Your blessing on each person here. You know every story, every hurt, every dream. We thank You for second chances—" his voice caught slightly, "—even when we're scared to believe in them. Help us remember that Your mercies are new every morning, that no darkness is too deep for Your light. Amen."

"Amen," echoed across the clearing.

As the crowd began to disperse, a girl with braided hair bounced excitedly toward the bunkhouse. "This is the best! I wish I had a dad to take me camping all the time."

Harry, standing nearby, scuffed his shoe against the dirt. "I know what you mean."

Treva, who'd been gathering empty paper plates, froze at her son's words. The familiar knife of guilt twisted in her chest. She watched him stuff his hands in his pockets, his shoulders hunched against a weight no twelve-year-old should carry.

Across the clearing, Charnise leaned her head against Ava's shoulder, their matching purple friendship bracelets catching the fading firelight.

"I think I'll like it here," she said softly.

"Told you," Ava grinned. "Wait till tomorrow when we go riding."

Near the food table, Maggie and Brittany stacked containers of leftovers, working in awkward tandem.

"Did you see the way Ralph looked at that cow?" Brittany broke the silence, lips quirking upward. "Like he'd discovered aliens."

Maggie's tension eased slightly. "That boy's lived his whole life in town. A squirrel in the backyard is wildlife to him."

They shared a brief laugh, the ice between them thinning just a fraction.

Ben walked past with Ms. Pickles trotting at his side, her leash loose in his hand. He slowed as he approached Maggie, their eyes meeting across the table of leftovers.

He nodded once.

She nodded back.

No words passed between them, but something did—a current of understanding, of possibility, of questions yet unasked. Then he continued on, Ms. Pickles's tail wagging happily behind him.

Chapter 17 – Growing Things

"For as the earth bringeth forth her bud, and as the garden causeth the things that are sown in it to spring forth; so the Lord GOD will cause righteousness and praise to spring forth before all the nations." Isaiah 61:11 (KJV)

Morning dew still clung to the grass as campers spilled from the dining hall, their breakfast-filled bellies and chatter filling the air. Clara stood at the center of the pavilion, clipboard in hand, her hair pulled back in a practical ponytail.

"Alright, everyone! Circle up, please," she called, her teacher's voice carrying across the lawn.

The campers and counselors formed a loose ring around her. Maggie stood at the edge, watching Alan and Ralph jostle each other good-naturedly. They seemed lighter here, away from the empty spaces of their home where Roger's absence still echoed.

"We've got a busy morning ahead," Clara continued. "You'll be rotating through four stations—kitchen duty, garden prep, barn chores, and retreat cleaning. Each group will spend an hour at their station before moving to the next."

Brittany stepped forward, wooden skewer tucked behind her ear like a pencil. She clapped her hands and called, "Let's get to it, future chefs! Kitchen crew, follow me!" Her enthusiasm drew a few smiles as a handful of campers trailed after her toward the dining hall.

Ethan gathered his group for retreat cleaning, while Ben led the garden crew toward the freshly tilled plots behind the barn. Maggie found herself assigned to barn duty with Loquita and two younger boys.

She watched the orderly procession of groups heading to their stations. Everything ran with a precision that made her chest ache with longing. How long had it been since her own life had any semblance of structure? Since Roger left, she'd been patching holes in a sinking ship—mortgage payments, school lunches, broken appliances. Every day felt like waking up to a new emergency.

"Miss Maggie? We going?" Loquita's voice broke through her thoughts.

"Yes, sorry. Let's head to the barn."

As they walked, Maggie glanced back at the retreating groups—each with a purpose, a plan. She drew a deep breath of morning air, rich with the scent of soil and possibility.

"Lord," she whispered, too quiet for anyone to hear, "I need some of this in my life. Some order. Some help. I'm drowning trying to do it all myself." She swallowed hard. "Show me the way You've planned, because mine sure isn't working."

The morning sun warmed their backs as Ben led his group to the freshly tilled garden plots. Alan and Ralph hung toward the back, Alan's shoulders hunched slightly, uncertain in this unfamiliar territory.

"Alright, crew," Ben called, stopping at the edge of dark, rich soil. "Who here has ever grown anything before?"

A few hands went up, including Ralph's.

"I grew a bean in a cup at school," Ralph offered. "It got real tall, then died when I forgot to water it."

Ben nodded, a half-smile lifting his beard. "That's gardening in a nutshell. Life and death, all depending on care." He crouched down, scooping a handful of soil. "This here's where it all starts. Not in seed packets or garden centers. In the dirt."

He let the soil sift through his fingers, demonstrating its texture. "Feel this. Not too wet, not too dry. Just right for planting."

The teens gathered around, some eagerly digging their hands in, others more hesitant.

"We're spacing our rows eighteen inches apart," Ben explained, stretching a measuring string between two stakes. "Plants need room to breathe, just like people do. Crowd 'em too much, they'll fight each other for sunlight and nutrients."

He moved among them as they worked, showing Alan how to create a furrow at the proper depth, helping a girl named Jasmine untangle her string, demonstrating to Ralph how to gently place tomato seedlings into their holes.

"You've got good hands for this," Ben told Ralph quietly, watching the boy's careful movements. Ralph's face brightened with unexpected pride.

A lanky boy named Trevor wiped sweat from his forehead, frowning at the blisters forming on his palms. "Why do you still farm if it's this hard? Couldn't you just, like… get food from the store?"

Ben straightened up, stretched his back with a quiet groan, and gave a half-smile.

"Yeah, you can get food from a store," he said, brushing dirt from his hands. "But food from the ground hits different."

The other teens had paused, curious now.

"This land's been in the Landry family forever. My family's got a farm across town—been in the Reeves name for four generations. It's not easy. But that's kind of the point."

He crouched again beside a younger kid and helped him press seeds into the dirt. His tone was quieter now, more thoughtful.

"When you grow something yourself—watch it come up from nothing, take care of it, then eat it? You don't forget that. It sticks with you."

He looked over the rows they'd just planted, then back at Trevor. "Farming teaches you stuff. Like how to wait. How to trust the work when you can't see the results yet. How to keep showing up anyway."

Then, almost to himself, he added, "Sometimes… it reminds you why you started in the first place."

He stood again, nodding toward the field, voice steady. "And when the world feels like it's falling apart, it's kind of powerful to know you can still build something with your own two hands. That not everything worth keeping comes easy—but it's still worth it."

Ben has all the kids gather around him. "Jesus talks about the mustard seed in Matthew 13:32 "Which indeed is the least of all seeds: but when it is grown, it is the greatest among herbs, and becometh a tree, so that the birds of the air come and lodge in the branches thereof." He compares the Kingdom of God to a mustard seed. Back when Jesus walked the earth, mustard seeds were known for being tiny - you could barely see them in your palm. But He points out something amazing: this tiny seed grows into something much bigger than anyone would expect.

Let's think about how this might apply to us: Each of you might feel small sometimes. Maybe someone told you that you don't matter, or you maybe felt overlooked or underestimated. Jesus is saying appearances can be deceiving. Just like that tiny seed contains everything needed to become something huge and important, you have incredible potential inside you.

The mustard plant grows into something so big and strong that birds take shelter in its branches, hiding from predators, building their houses and growing their babies. That means it doesn't just grow big - it becomes useful to make life better for others.

That's the incredible thing about each of you. No matter what anyone's ever said about you, no matter what you've been through, you are able to grow into someone who makes a difference. Someone who shelters and supports others. You are able to nourish others just like these plants will nourish us. This is how the cycle of life works.

The seedlings we planted need water, sunlight, and good soil to grow and produce. That's what we're trying to create here at the Retreat. Be the people who believe in you, give you opportunities to learn, and a safe place to grow.

I want you to remember this the next time someone tries to make you feel small or insignificant: the mustard seed looks like nothing special, but it grows into a safe place for others. God made you to be just like the mustard seed."

Chapter 18 – Tending What's Broken

"He healeth the broken in heart, and bindeth up their wounds." – Psalm 147:3 (KJV)

Maggie led Loquita toward the barn, her steps slowing as they passed the garden area. Ben knelt in the rich soil beside a raised bed, his large calloused hands cupped like a bowl. A young boy—couldn't be more than nine—carefully sprinkled seeds into Ben's palm, his face a picture of concentration. Ben nodded encouragement, patient and steady as the earth itself.

Something twisted in Maggie's chest. The gentleness in Ben's weathered hands, the careful way he showed the boy how to space the seeds—it was beautiful and terrifying all at once.

"Why does that scare me more than the storm?" she whispered, not realizing she'd spoken aloud until Loquita glanced at her.

"What storm?"

"Nothing." Maggie shook her head and quickened her pace. "Let's get these chores started."

Inside the barn, the earthy scent of hay mingled with the muskier smell of animals. Ms. Pickles trotted up to greet them, her white coat gleaming in the barn's dim light.

"This is disgusting," Loquita complained, wrinkling her nose as Maggie handed her a pitchfork. "Why can't the animals clean up after themselves?"

"Because they're animals," Maggie replied, demonstrating how to muck out the first stall. "There's something honest about this work. These goats depend on us."

Loquita jabbed halfheartedly at the soiled hay. "Nobody depends on me."

"These animals do." Maggie paused, leaning on her pitchfork. "You know, when everything in my life was falling apart, taking care of something else kept me sane. Kept me showing up."

Ms. Pickles nudged Maggie's leg, demanding attention. She scratched behind the dog's ears.

"My foster parents change all the time," Loquita said suddenly, not looking up. "Seven homes in four years."

"Whoo-wee! How do you handle that much change?"

Loquita shrugged her shoulders.

Maggie nodded, letting the silence stretch comfortably between them. "My husband walked out on me and my boys five years ago. Signed away his rights to his own children."

Loquita's eyes widened. "That's messed up."

"Yeah. It is. Everybody's life changes all the time. Some more than others. You know what makes the difference?"

Loquita shook her head.

"What makes the difference is how you face all the changes and the challenges."

"When you have faith that you are not alone, you can more easily center yourself and find your peace and calm."

"When things out of your control overwhelm you, you can use that calm to control your emotions and make rational decisions."

"And you get bonus points if you learn to be grateful for what you have instead of lamenting what you think you're losing."

Loquita stood up straight, leaning on the pitchfork. "You really believe all that bovine scatt you just shoveled at me?"

Maggie cackled out loud. Not the reaction Loquita was expecting.

"Loquita, my friend, my ex-husband leaving me kicked the rug out from beneath my feet. I landed on my knees and all I had left was my babies and Jesus. We have clawed our way out of grief and are standing on our feet again. You bet your boots I believe every word. And sweet girl, make no mistake. Every time you get moved to another foster home, that's grief too - saying goodbye to what you knew, even if it wasn't perfect. You can't stop that from happening. But you can choose what you do when it happens."

Maggie let Loquita soak that all up in silence. They worked side by side, the rhythm of the chore building a bridge between them. Maggie noticed Loquita's posture softening, her movements becoming more confident as she realized Maggie wasn't hovering over her, was trusting her to do the job right.

A small black goat with budding horns pranced into the clean stall, eyeing Loquita mischievously before lowering his head and giving her a gentle butt against her leg.

"Hey!" Loquita laughed despite herself. The goat danced back, then forward again, clearly inviting play. After a moment's hesitation, Loquita set down her tools and mimicked the goat's stance, bending slightly at the waist.

The goat delightedly bumped his head against her outstretched hands. Ms. Pickles circled them, barking and jumping as if joining the game.

"He likes you," Maggie said, smiling.

The goat settled, allowing Loquita to scratch between his horns. His eyes half-closed in contentment.

When they finished the chores, Loquita's smile was real—small but genuine—as she gave the goat one final pat.

Not wanting to break the mood, Maggie said a silent prayer of thanks.

The kitchen buzzed with activity as Brittany directed her small crew. Stainless steel pots clanged against countertops, and the smell of fresh herbs filled the air. She tied her apron with practiced efficiency, surveying the motley group before her.

"Today we're making vegetable soup and homemade bread," she announced. "Everyone pick a station."

Rosita hesitated before taking a cutting board. Her knife hovered uncertainly over a carrot, her movements painfully slow.

Brittany noticed immediately. "Having trouble there?"

Rosita's cheeks flushed. "I've never really cooked before. Foster homes usually had rules about knives."

"Here, let me show you." Brittany moved beside her, gently repositioning Rosita's fingers. "Curl these under, like a bear claw. That way, you won't cut yourself." She guided Rosita's hand through a few strokes. "Rock the knife, don't saw. There you go."

Across the kitchen, Charnise stirred a pot of tomato base, her face pinched with concentration. As she turned to reach for salt, her elbow caught the wooden spoon. The pot tipped, sending a wave of red sauce cascading onto the counter and floor.

"I'm sorry!" Charnise froze, eyes wide with panic. "I didn't mean to—I'll clean it up!"

She dropped to her knees, frantically wiping at the spill with her bare hands, her breathing quick and shallow.

Brittany knelt beside her. "Hey, it's okay. Just a little spill."

"Ms. Diane would've—" Charnise stopped herself, hands trembling. "My third foster mom. She'd make me skip dinner if I spilled anything."

The kitchen fell quiet. Brittany gently took Charnise's sauce-covered hands in her own.

"Well, I'm not Ms. Diane." She helped Charnise to her feet. "And in my kitchen, mistakes are just part of the recipe."

She grabbed a towel and slowly took hold of Charnise's hands, looking them over for any injuries or burns. She gently wiped her hands clean and then reached for a clean spoon. Smiling, she asked, "You okay now? Or do you need a minute?

Charnise had stopped shaking but she still looked shook. Not yet able to talk, Charnise nodded her head telling Brittany she was fine. But Brittany could tell she wasn't.

"Tell you what. You go over there and wash your hands. Then grab yourself a drink out of that smaller refrigerator beside the door and take a seat over there at the table. Something with sugar in it."

Charnise started to turn but Brittany noticed she was still a little shaky. "Hey, look at me. You are okay. You're safe here. No one gets in trouble over mistakes at the Willow Creek Retreat. We're all about second chances here."

Charnise slowly looked, tears brimming her eyes, and took in a deep breath. "Thank you." she practically whispered as a tear rolled down her cheek.

Brittany couldn't help herself, she wrapped her arms around Charnise, a rogue tear falling down her face too. "Sweet child, you will never miss a meal here at the Retreat unless you choose to. I'm so sorry you have been treated so poorly. That shouldn't have happened." Leaning back enough to look her in the face, Brittany continued with "But the way you have handled yourself tells me you are going to be just fine. Because when things happen that are out of our control, the only thing we can do is control our emotions, control the way we react. You handled yourself like a champ today, Sis." One more squeeze to let Charnise know she meant everything she said. "Now, go get some sugar in you to counteract all that adrenaline racing through your veins. We'll start over when you're ready."

Brittany turned to get a handful of paper towels to start soaking up the liquid, wiping the tears from her face, grateful for the opportunity to be there in that moment, almost like she was meant to be there.

As the group resumed their work, Brittany leaned against the counter, watching them with a thoughtful expression.

"How's everyone doing? That bread in the oven smells so good it's making me hungry." "Our hour is almost up, so any questions before you change stations?" Rosita shyly asked "You ever mess up in the kitchen?"

Brittany laughed out loud. Not the reaction Rosita was expecting.

"I can't count the number of times I've messed up in the kitchen, my friend," she said, "cooking's not about being perfect. Some of my best dishes started out as mistakes. Cooking is about showing up hungry and leaving full." She smiled, tucking a strand of hair behind her ear. "Same goes for most things in life, I reckon."

Paul stood between the library shelves, surrounded by books pulled from various sections. Grace watched him from her desk, admiring the way he carefully studied each volume before adding it to his growing stack.

"Finding everything you need?" she asked, approaching with a fresh cup of coffee.

"Almost." He looked up, glasses perched on the end of his nose. "I'm putting together some devotionals for the retreat kids. Something that speaks to their experiences without talking down to them."

Grace set the mug beside him. "Black, two sugars. Just how you like it."

"You remembered." His smile crinkled the corners of his eyes.

"Hard to forget when you've been coming in here every Tuesday for fifteen years." She leaned against the shelf. "Have you looked at Psalms? David wrote a lot about feeling abandoned, afraid..."

"Good thinking." Paul reached for a concordance, his hand brushing against hers. They both paused, an unexpected current passing between them.

Grace cleared her throat. "I could help you compile these, if you'd like. I've got some downtime between the summer reading program and fall activities."

"I'd appreciate that." Paul adjusted his glasses. "Your insight would be most welcome. The kids need someone who understands..."

"How words can be a lifeline?" Grace finished.

"Exactly." He smiled again, longer this time.

Neither noticed how they'd moved closer together, or how their conversation had drifted from professional to personal. Neither recognized the gentle tug of something new beginning.

The morning sun filtered through the retreat chapel's windows, casting golden light across wooden benches filled with campers and counselors. The newly constructed building still smelled of sawdust and paint and had been transformed with simple beauty: wildflowers in mason jars, a cross made from reclaimed timber from some of the trees cut to make way for the retreat buildings.

Ethan stood at the front, Bible open in his hands. "Welcome to our first morning devotion at Willow Creek Retreat. This is a time for us to center ourselves, to remember why we're here, and to find strength for the day ahead."

Paul joined him, nodding to the group. "We thought we'd start with a story that might resonate with many of you—the time Jesus calmed a storm."

Paul and Ethan take turns sharing the story of Jesus calming the storm. (Mark 4:35-41) They talk about how even the disciples—men who walked beside Jesus—panicked when the waves crashed in. But Jesus? He was calm enough to sleep. And when they woke Him, scared and overwhelmed, He didn't shout or scramble. He simply stood up and said, "Peace, be still."

Paul closed the Bible and looked around the room.

"You ever feel like your life is a storm? Too loud, too messy, too much? I get that. Jesus gets that. But notice—He didn't face the storm in a panic. He stilled Himself first. Then He stilled the storm."

Ethan stepped forward. "That's your challenge this week. When something feels like too much—when a bunkmate is getting on your nerves, or a memory sneaks up and tries to steal your joy—pause. Be still first. Then face the storm. Breathe. Pray. Step back. Try it once, just once."

Paul added, with a smile: "On Friday night, we're gonna circle back and talk about how it went. What worked. What was hard. You don't have to be perfect. You just have to try."

The room fell silent. Sunlight caught dust motes drifting through the air, making them shimmer like tiny stars. A few campers nodded, others stared at their hands, processing the message in their own way. Then a hand rose hesitantly from the back row. It belonged to Anthony, his expression troubled, dark eyes reflecting both curiosity and pain.

"Why does God let us go through hard stuff?" he asked, voice barely audible. "If He can calm storms, why doesn't He stop them before they start?"

Paul nodded, acknowledging the weight of the question. His gaze swept across the room, taking in the faces of young people who'd weathered their own personal tempests. He let the question hang in the air for a moment before answering with gentle conviction.

"So we'll know how to help someone else through it."

The sun hung low in the western sky, casting long shadows across the retreat grounds. Maggie wiped sweat from her brow as she made her way to the barn, clipboard in hand. The day's activities were winding down, but she had one last task to complete before heading home.

Inside the barn, a section had been transformed into a makeshift greenhouse. Old windows salvaged from the renovation created walls of glass, capturing the day's warmth. Wooden shelves lined with seed trays created a patchwork of green against the weathered barn boards.

"Mom! Look what I found!" Ralph's voice echoed through the barn as he burst through the door, Alan trailing behind him.

Maggie set her clipboard down on a workbench. "Indoor voice, please. You'll get the goats all riled up again. What's got you so excited?"

Ralph skidded to a stop, his hands cupped together. Soil smudged his cheeks and caked under his fingernails. He carefully opened his palms to reveal a fat, pink earthworm wriggling against his skin.

"He was under the big rock by the creek," Ralph explained, his voice dropping to a whisper. "I named him Wiggles."

Alan rolled his eyes. "That's the most obvious name ever."

"Is not!"

"Is too!"

"Boys," Maggie said, her tone gentle but firm. "Let's focus on our greenhouse chores, okay? Those seedlings need water."

She handed Ralph a small watering can, watching as he carefully set the worm down in a tray of soil before taking it. His movements were deliberate, showing a tenderness that made her heart swell.

"Careful now," she instructed, filling another can for herself. "Just a little bit for each one."

Together, they moved along the shelves, giving each tray of tiny green sprouts a drink. Ralph worked with surprising patience, his tongue poking out the corner of his mouth in concentration.

"Look, Mom," he said suddenly, holding up the worm again. "He's slimy but strong. See how he pushes through the dirt?"

Maggie watched the worm flex and stretch in Ralph's small hand, it's simple existence somehow miraculous. The creature knew nothing of abandonment or heartbreak, only how to keep moving forward, how to transform what was broken into something new.

She smiled, reaching out to ruffle Ralph's hair. "Kinda like you, kiddo."

"Like you, kiddo."

Chapter 19 – Storm Shelter Prayers

"The Lord is good, a strong hold in the day of trouble; and he knoweth them that trust in him." Nahum 1:7 (KJV)

The air hung thick and heavy over Willow Creek Retreat, like a wool blanket draped across the sky. Maggie lifted her face, catching the metallic scent of approaching rain on the restless wind. The leaves on the old oak trees flipped their silver underbellies upward—a warning as clear as any weather report.

"We're in for a big one," Ben muttered beside her, squinting at the darkening western horizon.

Across the retreat grounds, people moved with urgent purpose. Clara and Ethan herded campers toward the main hall while Anthony and Rosita gathered scattered sports equipment. Even Pastor had arrived, helping Greg secure loose building materials by the half-finished cabins.

"Francine called from town," Wade announced, striding toward them with his phone in hand. "National Weather Service just upgraded to a severe thunderstorm warning. Possible tornado watch coming." His expression was calm but serious, the set of his shoulders betraying his concern.

Maggie glanced toward the dining hall where her boys were helping with indoor activities. The massive stone building was the safest structure on the property—they'd be fine there.

Ben followed her gaze. "They're good where they are." He turned toward the new barn, its freshly raised frame vulnerable against the gathering storm. "But we need to brace that barn roof. We haven't been able to set that last set of beams on the end. They only got one set of bolts set in. The goats at the other end should be okay."

Wade checked his watch. "I need to coordinate with Trent at the fire station. You two got this?"

Ben nodded, already moving toward the toolshed. Maggie hesitated only a moment before following him. The first fat raindrops began to fall, cold against her skin.

148

Inside the toolshed, Ben grabbed a hammer, nails, and extra support brackets. He hesitated when Maggie reached for the ladder.

"You sure about this?" His eyes narrowed with concern. "This isn't exactly what you signed up for when you volunteered at the retreat."

Maggie tugged work gloves from a peg on the wall and slipped them on. "No one else is available right now." She hoisted the ladder with surprising strength. "I'll hold the ladder. You'll swing the hammer."

Thunder rumbled closer as they hurried to the barn. The wind whipped Maggie's ponytail across her face, and she tasted rain on her lips. Ben climbed quickly, his movements efficient as he secured the first bracket.

"Hand me those three-inch nails," he called down.

Maggie passed them up, bracing the ladder against a sudden gust. While Ben hammered, she found her gaze drifting toward the tree line where ancient oaks swayed. Beyond them stood the old fort, barely visible through the branches.

"I helped build that tree fort back there," she said, almost to herself. "Summers felt endless then."

Ben paused mid-swing, looking down at her with genuine surprise. "You're a First and Forever?"

"Card carrying." A smile tugged at her lips. "Clara, Ethan, Wade, Greg, Harry, and me. We swore blood oaths and everything."

"The famous tree fort gang." Ben resumed hammering. "I heard stories about y'all growing up."

The memory softened her features—gathering wood scraps from Dexter Landry's construction sites, Clara sketching elaborate designs, Wade insisting on a trapdoor. For a moment, she felt like that girl again—fearless, believing in possibilities.

But the ache lingered too. How long since she'd felt that kind of belonging? That certainty?

Maggie steadied the ladder as Ben moved to the next section. Could Ben be the forever kind of friend? The thought fluttered through her mind unbidden, warming her despite the chill in the air.

Not with the secret I'm keeping from him.

A blinding flash split the sky, followed instantly by a deafening crack that shook the barn's frame. The lights flickered once, twice, then plunged them into darkness.

"Get down!" Ben shouted above the wind's howl. He scrambled down the ladder, nearly losing his footing as another gust slammed against the barn.

Maggie abandoned the tools, her heart hammering against her ribs as rain began to pour in sheets. They stumbled through the barn door, Ben's hand finding hers in the darkness, pulling her toward safety.

Inside, the storm's fury echoed against the metal roof like a thousand angry drummers. Ben flicked on a flashlight, its beam cutting through the shadows.

"Office is this way," he said, leading her past empty stalls. "There's a landline."

Maggie's fingers trembled as she dialed the dining hall. Through static and crackling, she heard Clara's voice.

"We're fine here," Maggie said, raising her voice over the storm. "Ben and I took shelter in the barn. The boys?"

"They're helping Rosita with the younger kids," Clara assured her. "Wade's here too. Stay put until it passes."

A violent bang against the barn's side made Maggie jump, nearly dropping the receiver.

"I'll check back when it's safe," she promised, hanging up.

Ben appeared in the doorway, rain dripping from his hair. "Goats are secure. Had to chase Houdini back to his stall—living up to his name."

The flashlight beam bounced wildly as another thunderclap rattled the windows. Debris slammed against the walls, each impact making Maggie flinch. The storm's ferocity reminded her too much of nights when Roger would come home in a rage, slamming doors, throwing things.

"Let's get away from these windows," Ben suggested, seemingly reading her discomfort.

He led her to an empty stall in the center of the barn, stacking hay bales against the wall to create a windbreak. With practiced hands, he spread a horse blanket across the clean straw, then grabbed a second blanket from a nearby shelf.

"It's not exactly the Percolating Grace," he said with a gentle smile, "but it'll keep us dry."

They sat close, shoulders touching, as Ben draped the second blanket across their laps. The air between them felt charged—not just from the storm outside, but from all the words they hadn't yet said to each other.

Ben shrugged out of his rain-soaked jacket, water droplets spattering the straw beneath their feet. He hung it carefully on a nearby stall divider, then removed his battered cap, running fingers through damp hair.

"You should get that wet coat off too," he said, nodding toward Maggie's jacket, dark patches spreading across the shoulders.

Maggie peeled off her sodden denim jacket, surprised at how heavy it had become. Ben took it from her hands, their fingers brushing momentarily, and hung it beside his own.

"Everybody okay up at the hall?" he asked, settling back down beside her.

Maggie nodded a little too fast, arms hugging herself as a shiver rattled through her. "Y-yeah—everyone else made it to the dining hall."

The tremor in her voice betrayed her. Ben's brow furrowed as he noticed her shoulders quaking, her lips taking on a bluish tint.

"You're freezing," he said, moving closer to lend her his body heat. "Okay if I sit close and wrap this blanket around us?"

Maggie nodded in the affirmative, unable to speak through her chattering teeth. Ben tucked the heavy horse blanket around them both, his arm settling cautiously across her shoulders. The warmth of him seeped through her damp clothes, chasing away the chill that had settled deep in her bones.

Outside, the storm continued its assault, but the violence seemed distant now, muffled by the solid barn walls and the rhythm of Ben's steady breathing beside her.

After several minutes, Maggie's shivering subsided. She relaxed against him, no longer rigid with cold.

"Thanks, Ben," she murmured. "It's been a while since I had anyone take care of me."

Ben's chest rumbled with a soft chuckle. "You're welcome, Pickles."

Maggie pulled back slightly, eyebrows raised. "Did you just call me Pickles?"

"Didn't like that one?" His eyes crinkled at the corners, teasing.

"It's been a while since a man flirted with me."

Ben shook his head slowly. "You've not been paying attention then, Sassafras."

Maggie tried not to smile, but failed. "I have no idea what you are talking about."

The lightness between them shifted as Ben's expression grew serious. "He really did a number on you, didn't he?"

Her breath caught in her throat and her eyes went wide as saucers as she tensed up. She couldn't stop the instant flood of tears and grief that burst from her soul like a dam breaking.

Ben stared, stunned by her reaction. She'd been hiding her pain so well. "I'm sorry, Maggie. I didn't mean to..."

He wrapped his arms around her and pulled her close, letting her cry out her grief as the storm raged on outside.

Maggie's tears fell hot and fast, soaking into Ben's flannel shirt. She hadn't cried like this in front of anyone since the day Roger walked out. Not even Clara had seen her completely break down.

"He didn't just leave me," she choked out, pulling back to wipe her face with the back of her hand. "He erased himself from their lives. Signed away his rights like they were... like they were a car he didn't want payments on anymore."

Ben kept one arm around her shoulders, steady and warm.

"I did everything right." Her voice cracked. "Waited until marriage. Built a home. Chose a man I thought would stay forever. I saved myself for a man who threw me away."

Lightning flashed, illuminating the barn in stark white for a heartbeat before plunging them back into shadow.

"You know what Alan asked me last Christmas?" Maggie stared at her hands. "He asked if Santa could bring Daddy back, just for one day, so he could find out why he wasn't good enough to keep."

Ben's jaw tightened, but he remained silent, letting her speak.

"And now I don't believe in happily-ever-after. I don't even believe in enough." She took a shuddering breath. "I keep thinking there must have been something I could've done differently. Something I missed."

"There wasn't," Ben said softly.

"The boys still wake up with nightmares. Ralph makes up these songs—these awful little songs about how daddies don't stay. And Alan..." She swallowed hard. "Alan's trying so hard to be the man of the house. He's nine years old, Ben. Nine."

The storm's fury seemed to match her own as she laid bare the wreckage Roger had left behind. The birthdays he'd missed. The promises broken. The Sunday mornings when her boys watched other fathers lead their families into church, their small faces tight with confusion and longing.

"I'm sorry," she whispered, suddenly embarrassed by her outburst, fingers twisting nervously in her lap. "I don't usually unload like this on anyone. Especially someone I barely know."

"Don't apologize." Ben's voice was gentle but firm, his eyes steady on hers. "Not for feeling what you feel. Not ever for that, Maggie."

Maggie nodded, surprised to discover that sharing her pain had lightened it, just a fraction. Like setting down a heavy load she'd been carrying too long. The weight hadn't disappeared, but her shoulders felt a little straighter, her breath coming easier than before.

"Thank you," she said. "For listening. Really listening." She smoothed her skirt with nervous fingers, unused to being heard so completely.

A comfortable silence settled between them as the storm continued its assault on the barn. The rain drummed against the metal roof, creating a strangely soothing rhythm that seemed to match the quieting of her heart. Ben stared at the flashlight beam cutting through the darkness, his face half-hidden in shadow, his expression thoughtful as though turning over everything she'd shared like precious stones in his palm.

"You know, I've never told anyone about the farm troubles," he said finally, his voice low. "Not even Brittany. My sister's got her own life in Nashville—fancy culinary school, big restaurant dreams. Don't want to burden her." He traced a finger through the condensation on the flashlight. "She left to chase something bigger than this place. Can't blame her for that. Sometimes I think she was the smart one, getting out when she did, before the roots grew too deep to pull up."

Maggie watched his profile, seeing how his jaw worked as he searched for words. The shadows played across the sharp angles of his face, highlighting the tension in his expression. She noticed the slight clench of his teeth, the way his Adam's apple bobbed when he swallowed hard. It was rare to see Ben this vulnerable, this open with his struggles, and something in her chest tightened at the sight.

"Truth is, I've been going it alone for a long time now." He absently twisted a piece of hay between his fingers. "After Mama passed, it was just me and the land. Farmers don't exactly have social lives—up before dawn, work till you can't see straight, fall into bed, do it all again."

"You must have friends," Maggie said softly, her eyes reflecting the dim flashlight glow.

Ben gave a short laugh that held little humor. "The Beaumont twins, I guess. But we talk tractors and feed prices, not..." He gestured vaguely between them. "Not this." He looked down at his calloused hands, as if suddenly aware of how rough they were. "Walt and Wes are good men, salt of the earth types. They'd give you the shirt off their backs if you needed it. But we don't sit around sharing our troubles or our feelings. That's just not how we were raised, I suppose."

Lightning flashed, briefly illuminating his face—open, vulnerable in a way she hadn't seen before. The sharp planes of his features softened in the momentary glow, revealing something raw and unguarded.

"You scare me, Maggie Cunningham," he confessed, the words tumbling out like water through a broken dam. "I've never been with anyone. Never even dated seriously." His voice dropped to nearly a whisper, rough with emotion. "I know how to talk about crop yields and feed prices, not..." He gestured vaguely between them. "Not this." He looked down at his calloused hands, as if suddenly aware of how rough they were. "Walt and Wes are good men, salt of the earth types. They'd give you the shirt off their backs if you needed it. But we don't sit around sharing our troubles or our feelings. That's just not how we were raised, I suppose."

Lightning flashed, briefly illuminating his face—open, vulnerable in a way she hadn't seen before. The sharp planes of his features softened in the momentary glow, revealing something raw and unguarded. Thunder rumbled in the distance, a low counterpoint to the hammering of his heart that he was certain she must be able to hear.

Maggie's eyes widened slightly, her lips parting in surprise. "Never?" She studied his profile, trying to reconcile this revelation with the capable man before her. The rain continued its rhythmic pattern against the windows, creating a gentle backdrop to this unexpected moment of vulnerability. Something about the soft confession in the storm's embrace made her see him differently—less the sturdy farmer with calloused hands and more the man underneath, with depths she hadn't thought to explore until now.

Ben shook his head. "Didn't have time. Too busy trying to fix what my daddy broke." His voice grew quieter. "The dreaming, the debts. By the time I buried him, there were ten projects half-done with only run-down equipment, some rusted through, and bills up to my eyeballs."

He looked down at his hands—strong, calloused from years of labor. The skin cracked at the knuckles, dirt embedded in lines that told stories of struggle better than words ever could.

"But sometimes," he whispered, "I still talk to Mama's old Bible like she's listening. Tell her about my day. Ask her what to do when I'm lost." A flush crept up his neck, spreading across his sun-weathered face. "Sounds foolish saying it out loud. Like a grown man playing pretend."

"It doesn't," Maggie said, reaching for his hand. Her fingers slipped between his, warm and certain. "It sounds like love. The kind that doesn't end, even when someone's gone."

The barn shuddered as another lightning bolt struck nearby, the thunder following almost immediately. Maggie flinched against Ben, her fingers tightening around his.

"That was close," she whispered, her voice small in the vast darkness of the barn.

Ben's arm tightened around her shoulders, and before he could think better of it, he pressed a gentle kiss to the top of her head. The gesture was so natural, so unplanned, that neither of them acknowledged it directly.

"Tell me about your boys," he said softly. "What makes Alan laugh? What's Ralph's favorite thing to do on Saturdays?"

Maggie's tension eased slightly at the mention of her sons. "Alan loves baseball. He's got this wicked curveball that surprises everyone because he's so small for his age." A smile crept into her voice. "And Ralph—that boy could climb before he could walk. He's never met a tree he didn't want to scale."

Ben listened, nodding as she described Alan's comic book collection and Ralph's silly made-up songs. The storm continued to rage outside, but here, in their makeshift shelter, something else was building—something fragile and new.

"Ben," Maggie said after a pause, her voice hesitant. "I feel something between us. Something I haven't felt in a long time." She took a deep breath. "But I'm not in a place to be anything more than friends right now. I don't know when I will be ready."

The confession hung between them, honest and raw.

Ben nodded, his eyes finding hers in the dim light. "I feel it too," he admitted. "And I understand. My life's not exactly stable right now either." He gave a small, rueful smile. "Friends, then. For now."

"For now," Maggie echoed. "Who knows what the future holds?"

Another crash of thunder made the barn walls creak and shudder. Maggie jumped, her breath catching in her throat, and Ben's hand found hers again, warm and steady against her trembling fingers.

"Would you... would you pray with me?" he asked, his voice barely audible above the storm's fury, a vulnerability in his tone she'd never heard before.

Maggie nodded, surprised by the request but deeply comforted by it too. Something settled in her chest as they bowed their heads together, fingers intertwined like they'd been meant to fit this way all along.

"Lord," Ben began simply, the farmer's usual gruffness giving way to gentle reverence, "keep us safe in this storm. All of us—Maggie's boys, Clara and Ethan, the kids at the retreat. And if..." his voice faltered slightly, a rough edge of emotion breaking through, "if Maggie and I are meant to happen, please show us the way."

"Amen," Maggie whispered, a tear slipping down her cheek, leaving a cool trail she didn't bother to wipe away.

No fancy words. No elaborate requests. Just two broken people, reaching out to God and to each other in the middle of a storm, asking for guidance and protection. The rain hammered against the roof, but somehow, the space between them felt like shelter.

For the first time in years, Maggie felt a flicker of hope that perhaps—just perhaps—second chances were possible after all.

Chapter 20 – Storms Bring the Good Stuff

"Remember ye not the former things, neither consider the things of old." Isaiah 43:18 (KJV)

The thunder receded to distant rumbles, leaving only the gentle patter of rain on the barn roof. Maggie's breathing had steadied, her tears dried, but neither she nor Ben seemed eager to break the comfortable silence that had settled between them. The shared vulnerability had created something fragile and precious—a connection that felt both new and somehow familiar.

"You know," Ben said softly, his voice barely above a whisper, "I remember you from high school."

Maggie turned to look at him, eyebrows raised in surprise. The rain continued its gentle rhythm overhead, creating a cocoon of intimacy around them in the dimly lit barn.

"You and the other forevers were ahead of me." He smiled, a touch of shyness crossing his features. "I had the biggest crush on you. Used to watch you in the hallways between classes, hoping you might notice me."

Maggie's lips parted in disbelief. "You did not." Her voice held a mixture of wonder and skepticism, as if she couldn't quite reconcile this revelation with her memories.

"Did too." Ben's eyes crinkled at the corners, the vulnerability in them making him look younger somehow. "Would get all tongue-tied whenever you came into Hattie's while I was stocking shelves after school. Being here with you like this is a dream come true for that awkwardly shy farm boy." He leaned forward and pressed a gentle kiss to her forehead, his lips warm against her skin, lingering just long enough to make his intention clear.

Maggie's heart fluttered at the contact, a warmth spreading through her chest that had nothing to do with the humid summer air. She didn't pull away, instead finding herself leaning slightly into his touch, surprised by how right it felt.

"I had no idea," she murmured, trying to remember Ben from those days. She could only recall a quiet boy who always sat in the back, who worked the family farm after school while she was busy with cheerleading practice. The memory of him stocking shelves at Hattie's was hazy at best—just a tall, lanky teenager with downcast eyes who seemed to vanish whenever she approached.

The rain lightened further, and moonlight began filtering through the barn's high windows, casting silver patterns across the hay-strewn floor. The storm's distant rumble had softened to a gentle percussion, nature's lullaby settling over the countryside.

"Maybe..." Ben's voice was hesitant, his fingers absently tracing circles in the hay between them, "maybe we can grab some coffee sometime? At Percolating Grace, perhaps? I hear they make a mean apple pie to go with their house blend." His eyes met hers with a hopeful vulnerability that made her breath catch.

Maggie felt a smile tug at her lips. "Maybe," she said. "We'll see." She met his eyes in the dim light. "I feel like I can say anything to you."

"You can," he replied simply.

Outside, the storm had passed. The violent winds had given way to a gentle breeze, and the moon peeked through parting clouds, casting silver light through the barn windows.

Maggie stood, stretching her stiff muscles. "I should probably head back to check on the boys." She looked down at Ben, still seated on the blanket. "I'm sorry for crying all over you last night, but thank you for listening."

Ben rose to his feet, towering over her. "Don't apologize. I meant what I said—you can tell me anything."

"I don't know why," she admitted, "but I feel I can open up to you."

Ben handed her the now-dry jacket, their fingers brushing as she took it. The touch lingered, neither pulling away too quickly.

Maggie slipped her arms into the sleeves, then leaned back against the stall wall, gazing out at the moonlit farm. The air smelled fresh and clean after the storm, and somewhere in the distance, a whippoorwill called.

"Maybe," she said softly, "maybe the good stuff grows after the rain."

Ben's eyes softened at her words. "I've always believed that," he said quietly. "Every farmer knows you need the storm before the harvest."

Maggie nodded, her smile not quite reaching her eyes. The weight of what she wasn't saying pressed against her chest like a physical thing.

I should tell him now, she thought, watching the moonlight play across his features. Just say it. Get it over with.

But the words wouldn't come. Not after the connection they'd just shared, the vulnerability he'd shown her. Not when she could still feel the gentle pressure of his lips against her forehead, the warmth of his hand in hers during their prayer.

Coward, she chided herself. You're just afraid of losing this... whatever this is.

She glanced at her watch, genuinely surprised by how late it had gotten. The boys would be wondering where she was, though she knew Clara would have everything under control. Clara always did.

"We should head back now," she said, though she made no move toward the door.

What would Ben think when he found out what she knew? That his land—half of it, at least—might not even be his anymore? That she'd seen the deed with her own eyes while organizing files at Town Hall last month, a document that showed his father had sold a significant portion of the Reeves property years ago? The very piece of land where Ben was planning to expand the farm's operations to save it from financial ruin.

The information would devastate him. She'd watched Roger walk away from their family without a backward glance. She couldn't bear to see the same hurt and betrayal in Ben's eyes when he learned she'd kept this from him.

Lord, she prayed silently, her eyes briefly closing, give me strength to tell him the truth. And when I do, please don't let him hate me for keeping it from him. I couldn't bear to lose his friendship now that I've found it. Help him understand why I waited, why I couldn't bring myself to break his heart tonight. And Lord... help me know when the time is right.

"Maybe the good stuff grows after the rain," she repeated softly, more to herself than to Ben, hoping with all her heart that their friendship would survive the storm that was coming.

Chapter 21 – Whispers & What-Ifs

"A time to rend, and a time to sew; a time to keep silence, and a time to speak."
Ecclesiastes 3:7 (KJV)

Morning broke over Willow Creek with gentle persistence, washing away the storm's fury. Puddles mirrored a cloudless sky as Maggie and Ben emerged from the barn, blinking in the sudden brightness.

"The boys," Maggie said, checking her watch. "They must be worried sick."

Ben nodded, falling into step beside her as they crossed the muddy yard toward the retreat. Their shoulders nearly touched, both careful not to close that final inch of space between them.

"Clara would've taken good care of them," Ben offered. "Probably made them hot chocolate and told ghost stories till they fell asleep."

Maggie smiled despite her worry. "That sounds like Clara."

The retreat kitchen hummed with activity when they arrived. Children's laughter spilled from the dining hall, mingling with the clatter of silverware and the smell of pancakes and bacon.

Maggie spotted her sons immediately. Alan sat at a table with Noah and Ava, cutting Ralph's pancakes into perfect triangles just the way he liked them. Relief flooded through her until Alan looked up and his expression shifted from joy to suspicion when he saw Ben standing beside her.

"Mom!" Ralph abandoned his breakfast and barreled into her legs. "We slept in sleeping bags! Miss Clara made s'mores in the microwave!"

Alan approached more cautiously, eyes narrowed at Ben. "Where were you all night?"

"The storm trapped us in the barn," Maggie explained, smoothing Alan's hair. "We couldn't get back safely."

"What were you doing with my mom?" Alan demanded, chin jutting toward Ben.

Ben crouched to Alan's level. "Keeping each other company while the storm passed. Your mama was really brave."

Ralph gave Ben a suspicious look that mirrored his brother's, small arms crossed over his chest.

Clara appeared with coffee mugs, her knowing smile making Maggie blush.

"Thanks for not panicking last night," Ben said quietly as they moved toward the buffet.

Maggie laughed softly. "I was. I just hid behind your calm."

Their eyes met, a current of understanding passing between them—something had changed, but neither knew exactly what shape it would take.

"Will I see you in Church Sunday?" Ben asked as they reached the food.

Maggie hesitated, feeling her sons' watchful eyes. "We'll see."

Maggie watched Ben talking with the boys, his patience evident as Ralph peppered him with questions about the farm animals. The scene blurred before her eyes as her mind slipped back to that rainy Tuesday afternoon at Town Hall last month.

She'd been researching the property they planned on housing their bakery. The deed had been tucked between property tax assessments instead of with the land deeds where it belonged.

"Reeves Farm, Parcel 14-87-A." The typed label had caught her eye immediately.

Her fingers had trembled as she'd opened it, curiosity rather than suspicion driving her. Inside lay a deed transfer, dated eight years ago. Half of the Reeves property—the eastern fields where Ben planned to expand his crops—had been sold to Ridgeline Development Group.

The signature at the bottom had stopped her heart. Samuel Reeves. Ben's father.

She'd stared at it for what felt like hours, tracing the signature with her fingertip, noting the notary stamp that made it official. Legal. Binding.

Ben didn't know. Couldn't know. He'd been talking about those expansion plans for weeks now—the salvation of his struggling farm.

Maggie had slipped the document into her purse before she could think better of it. Not stealing—borrowing. She needed time to figure out what to do, how to tell him.

But days had turned into weeks, and the right moment never seemed to come.

She hadn't told Clara, whose honest nature would have insisted on immediate disclosure. Not Brittany, whose business connections might have complicated things further. Not even her mother, whose wisdom she desperately needed.

The secret sat like a stone in her chest, growing heavier with each passing day, with each smile Ben gave her, with each moment they grew closer.

Tell him, her conscience screamed. He deserves to know.

You'll break him, her fear whispered back. You'll lose him before you even have him.

The farm wasn't just Ben's livelihood—it was his heritage, his identity. What would be left of him if he lost it?

The afternoon Bible study gathered under the sprawling oak behind the retreat. Children and counselors sat in a loose circle on picnic blankets, faces turned toward Principal Grayson. Maggie had volunteered to help supervise, though her mind kept drifting back to the barn, to Ben's gentle kiss on her forehead.

Paul opened his worn leather Bible, the pages ruffled by a gentle breeze. "Today we're talking about trust," he announced, his voice carrying across the circle. "Proverbs 3:5-6 tells us, 'Trust in the LORD with all thine heart; and lean not unto thine own understanding. In all thy ways acknowledge him, and he shall direct thy paths.'"

Maggie fidgeted with the hem of her shirt, feeling the weight of the deed hidden in her cabin.

"God's truth never changes," Paul continued, "even when people do. Even when circumstances do." His eyes swept across the circle, lingering momentarily on Maggie. "Our job isn't to understand everything, but to trust the One who does."

Alan, sitting cross-legged between Ralph and Noah, raised his hand. "Mr. Grayson? How do you know who you can trust?"

The question hung in the air. Several of the foster kids leaned forward, their faces reflecting the same uncertainty that haunted Alan's eyes.

Paul closed his Bible, considering the question with the gravity it deserved. "That's an excellent question, Alan." He smiled gently. "I think you start by being someone worth trusting."

Maggie's breath caught. She stared at her hands, unable to meet Paul's eyes.

"When we're honest, even when it's hard," Paul continued, "when we keep our promises, when we put others before ourselves—we're building trust. And when we're looking for people to trust, we look for those same qualities."

Ralph piped up, "Like Mom! She always tells us the truth, even when it's yucky stuff."

A few chuckles rippled through the group, but Maggie felt the words like a knife. Did she always tell the truth? The deed she kept hidden argued otherwise.

Her gut screamed *tell him*, the right thing was so painfully clear. But her fear whispered back, you'll break him. The thought of Ben's face when he learned the truth—learned that she'd kept it from him—made her physically ill.

She glanced at her sons, Alan's serious face and Ralph's trusting eyes. What example was she setting?

Later that afternoon, Kneadful Things Bakery buzzed with the usual mid-day crowd. Treva sliced pie behind the counter while Francine refilled coffee cups. The bell above the door jingled as Mavis Holbrook entered with Hattie Beaumont.

"Well I heard from my brother at the bank," Mavis said, voice pitched low but carrying in that peculiar way gossip always does. "Ben Reeves missed his last two loan payments."

Hattie frowned. "That farm's been in his family for generations."

"Won't be for much longer," Mavis replied, settling at a corner table. "Property taxes are due next month. No way he can swing it."

At the counter, Walt Beaumont leaned toward his twin. "If Ben loses that place, what happens to our arrangement at the Co-Op?"

Wes shrugged. "We'd have to find another supplier. Might not be local."

"And there goes the farmstand," Ophelia added from nearby. "That's half our summer produce right there."

The conversation rippled through the bakery, faces growing somber. Willow Creek couldn't afford another business closure, not after the factory shutdown.

The bell jangled again. Conversation died instantly.

Ben Reeves stood in the doorway, mud still caking his boots from morning chores. His eyes swept across the suddenly silent room, taking in the averted gazes and uncomfortable shifts.

Treva recovered first. "Morning, Ben! Coffee and peach pie?"

Ben's jaw tightened as he nodded, making his way to the counter. The whispers had ceased, but the damage was done. He'd heard enough.

He didn't say a word as Treva handed him his order, but his eyes had darkened to the color of storm clouds. The muscles in his neck stood out as he paid and turned to leave.

The bell's cheerful jingle mocked the heaviness in his chest as he stepped back onto Main Street.

Just what I need today. A bunch of gossiping ninnies.

Ben's truck smelled of hay and tractor grease as he slid behind the wheel, coffee and pie forgotten on the passenger seat. His knuckles whitened around the steering wheel.

What am I if I lose the family farm? The question hammered at him with each heartbeat. Four generations of Reeves men had worked that land, built it, bled for it. His great-grandfather's hands had laid the foundation stones of the barn where he'd sheltered with Maggie during the storm.

What kind of man can I be for Maggie and the boys if I can't provide for them?

The thought of Maggie's sons—their suspicious glances, their protective stance around their mother—twisted something in his chest. He wanted to be worthy of them, to offer stability after all they'd lost.

But how could he build a future for them when his own was crumbling beneath his feet?

Midnight found Maggie sitting cross-legged on her bed, the house quiet around her. Alan and Ralph had fallen asleep hours ago, exhausted from their night at the retreat and the excitement of the storm's aftermath.

The deed lay spread before her, illuminated by her bedside lamp. Next to it, her Bible sat open to Proverbs, the pages slightly dog-eared from years of seeking comfort in their wisdom.

Maggie traced Samuel Reeves' signature with her fingertip, feeling the slight indentation where the pen had pressed into the paper. A decision made eight years ago that would devastate his son today.

"Why?" she whispered to the silent document. "Why would you sell half your son's birthright without telling him?"

The signature offered no answers, just the cold, legal finality of what had been done. Ridgeline Development Group now owned the eastern fields—the very land Ben planned to plant next spring, the expansion that would save his farm.

Her stomach twisted as she remembered Ben's face that morning, the quiet determination in his eyes when he'd talked about the future. Their future, maybe. A future built on land he no longer fully owned.

Tell him, her conscience demanded. This secret will only hurt more the longer you keep it.

You'll break him, her fear countered. He'll lose everything—and you'll lose him.

Maggie closed her eyes, pressing her palms against her face. What kind of person was she becoming, keeping this from him? What would her boys think if they knew their mother was hiding something so important from someone they were growing to care about?

She glanced at her open Bible, words blurring through sudden tears.

"God," she whispered, voice breaking in the quiet room. "What do I do with this?"

Chapter 22 – Fences Mended, Seeds Planted

"And let us not be weary in well doing: for in due season we shall reap, if we faint not." Galatians 6:9 (KJV)

Morning sunlight streamed through the windows of Percolating Grace Café, catching dust motes that danced above steaming coffee mugs. The breakfast rush had faded, leaving a comfortable quiet broken only by the occasional clink of silverware and murmured conversations.

Jake Landry hunched over a stack of photographs spread across the corner table, his coffee cooling untouched beside him. Daisy Parks leaned in from the next chair, her lavender-streaked hair falling forward as she pointed to a faded image.

"This one's perfect for the cover," she said. "Your dad standing in front of the courthouse steps, right after they finished the rebuild."

Greg Whitlow nodded, sliding another photo into the arrangement. "The coffee table book's gonna be something special, Jake. Real tribute to what Landry and Son has meant to this town."

Jake ran his thumb over the edge of a black and white photograph—his father, decades younger, arm slung around his mother's shoulders, both grinning in front of a half-built structure. "Dad would hate all this fuss," he said, but his smile betrayed him.

"How's Old Man Landry doing these days?" Daisy asked, wrapping her hands around her mug. "Haven't seen him at Sunday service in a couple weeks."

The smile slipped from Jake's face. He stared down at the photos, his shoulders suddenly rigid. "Not good," he managed, voice dropping to just above a whisper. "Hospice says it's just a matter of days now."

Daisy reached across the table, her fingers light on his wrist. "Oh, Jake."

He swallowed hard, blinking rapidly. "Last night, he was talking about Mom like she was right there in the room with us. Telling her to make room, that he was coming home soon." Jake's voice cracked on the last word. "Kept asking if I'd take care of Princess for them."

Greg's weathered hand settled on Jake's shoulder. "Your daddy built half this town with his bare hands. Left his mark everywhere you look."

"Yeah." Jake drew a ragged breath, fingers tracing his father's face in the photograph. "Just didn't think I'd have to run the company without him so soon." He gestured vaguely toward the window, where the Landry and Son sign was visible on a truck parked outside. "All those years watching him work, and I still don't know if I'm ready. He had this way about him—could look at a building site and just know exactly what needed doing." Jake shook his head, a sad smile touching his lips. "Folks around here trusted him with their dreams, you know? Those aren't small shoes to fill."

At the café counter, Brittany Reeves leaned forward, her chef's notebook open to a page crowded with menu ideas and hasty calculations. Across from her, Treva Walker nursed a coffee, eyes narrowed with cautious interest.

"We'd start simple," Brittany said, tapping her pencil against a sketch of the farmstand layout. "Local produce transformed into grab-and-go meals for folks who don't have time to cook but still want something that didn't come from a freezer."

Treva raised an eyebrow. "And where do my pies fit in?"

"Everywhere." Brittany's eyes lit up. "Your baked goods would be the cornerstone. Think about it—your apple pie alongside my roasted chicken and vegetable dinner. Your sourdough bread with my seasonal soups."

"Sounds like you've thought this through."

"I've been dreaming about this since culinary school." Brittany's voice softened. "Coming home wasn't exactly in my five-year plan, but seeing Ben struggle with the farm..." She shrugged. "Maybe it's time to put down roots where they can actually grow."

Treva studied her over the rim of her mug. "You sure you're stayin' this time?"

The question hung between them, loaded with twelve years of hometown history.

Brittany's fingers stilled on her notebook. "I don't know what staying looks like yet. But I'm done running."

Treva nodded slowly, something shifting in her expression. "Harry's eating me out of house and home these days. Twelve years old and already putting away more food than a farmhand." A wry smile touched her lips. "Been looking for a side-hustle that works around his schedule."

"This would be perfect then. We could split the weekend shifts—you handle Sunday brunch after church, I'll take Saturday mornings."

"Could work," Treva admitted. She traced the rim of her mug, a faraway look in her eyes. "Sometimes I wonder what I'd be doing now if I hadn't come back home to raise Harry alone."

Brittany glanced up, surprised by the sudden vulnerability.

"Don't get me wrong," Treva added quickly. "I'd choose my boy every time. But watching you come back with all that training, all those experiences..." She shook her head. "Must be nice having options."

Brittany studied Treva's face, recognizing something familiar in her expression—the what-ifs that haunted so many who stayed behind in Willow Creek.

"Maybe we both needed to leave to figure out where we belong," Brittany said softly. "I learned a lot out there, but..." She gestured toward the window, where morning sunlight bathed Main Street in golden warmth. "There's something about this place that gets in your blood."

Treva's smile turned genuine. "That it does." She closed Brittany's notebook and slid it back across the counter. "Let's talk numbers next week. I've got some ideas of my own."

The café door jingled as Maggie Cunningham rushed in, hair windblown and cheeks flushed. She waved distractedly at the room before hurrying to the counter.

"Two coffees to go, please. Clara's waiting in the truck and we're already late." She drummed her fingers on the countertop, glancing at her watch. "The contractors are meeting us at the bakery site in ten minutes."

"Big day?" Brittany asked, sliding off her stool.

"Huge. The architect's bringing the final plans, and we're meeting with the plumber and electrician." Maggie's eyes sparkled with an excitement that transformed her face. "After all the delays, it's finally happening."

Five minutes later, Maggie hurried down Main Street, carefully balancing two steaming cups. Clara sat in the idling truck, phone pressed to her ear as she gestured animatedly. When she spotted Maggie, she ended the call and leaned across to push open the passenger door.

"That was Guy Nelson," Clara said as Maggie climbed in. "He can meet us now, but he's got another job at eleven."

The truck lurched forward, tires crunching on gravel as they pulled away from the curb. Maggie clutched her coffee, watching the storefronts blur past.

"Ready for this?" Clara asked, turning onto Elm Street where the old warehouse stood—soon to be Kneadful Things Bakery.

"As I'll ever be," Maggie replied, her stomach fluttering with a mixture of excitement and apprehension as the warehouse came into view.

The afternoon sun beat down on Main Street as Maggie stood outside the empty storefront that would soon become Kneadful Things Bakery. Her boots crunched on broken glass from the recently removed signage as she studied the electrician's quote.

"This seems high for rewiring just the kitchen area," she said, tapping the paper. "We're keeping most of the original circuits intact."

Guy Nelson scratched his beard. "Afraid those circuits won't handle your industrial mixers, Ms. Clara. Code requires separate lines for each major appliance."

Clara stepped in, her voice firm but friendly. "What if we phase the installation? Essential equipment first, then add circuits as we expand?"

"Could work," Guy conceded. "I'll rework the numbers."

Ellie Jernigan scribbled notes on her clipboard, her mayor's badge catching the sunlight. "The council will want to see cost-saving measures like that. Shows good stewardship."

Maggie's phone buzzed with a message from Hattie: JACKPOT! Won the auction. Six stainless steel prep tables for the price of two. Paddy's bringing them over tomorrow.

The image showed gleaming tables stacked in the back of Paddy's truck. Maggie felt a surge of gratitude—another piece falling into place.

"Hattie got the tables," she announced, showing Clara the photo.

Clara nodded, adding to her own list. "Perfect. And we need to call Luke. No way we can handle the bookkeeping ourselves with everything else."

Maggie watched the women around her—Clara negotiating, Ellie advocating, Hattie finding solutions. This is what strong women do, she thought. They build something from nothing. They don't quit.

A movement across the street caught her eye. A man in a charcoal suit stood beside a luxury sedan, clipboard in hand as he surveyed the empty hardware store. His polished shoes and crisp tie looked jarringly out of place on Willow Creek's dusty main street.

Something about his calculating gaze made her stomach clench. She'd seen that look before—investors who saw only numbers where locals saw history.

The man made a note, his expression betraying nothing but professional disinterest as he assessed another piece of Willow Creek's soul.

Maggie's throat tightened. The deed hidden in her dresser drawer suddenly felt heavier than ever.

Later that afternoon, golden light slanted through the gaps in the weathered barn boards at the Retreat. The scent of fresh hay and warm animals filled the air, a welcome change from the dust and construction plans of the bakery site.

Ben Reeves adjusted his worn Carhartt cap and hefted a large feed bucket in each hand. He'd just finished mending the back fence when he spotted two small figures darting between the paddocks.

"Mr. Ben! Mr. Ben!" Ralph's excited voice carried across the yard as he raced toward the barn, his brother Alan following more cautiously behind. "Mama said we could come see the animals while she talks to Ms. Clara!"

Ben set down the buckets, a smile warming his face. "Well now, that's perfect timing. I was just about to feed the critters." He gestured to the buckets. "You boys want to help? Got some hungry mouths waiting."

Alan hung back, hands in his pockets, eyes wary. "We won't mess anything up?"

"Not a chance," Ben said, crouching to meet the boy's eyes. "Farm animals need looking after, and extra hands make the work go faster." He lifted a smaller bucket. "Think you can carry this one? It's got grain for Houdini."

"The escape artist goat?" Alan's interest visibly sparked.

"The very same. Named him that 'cause he gets out more than he stays in."

Ralph bounced on his toes. "Can I help too?"

"Sure thing. You take this water pail for Beulah. She's our gentlest milk cow."

The boys followed Ben into the barn, Ralph chattering excitedly while Alan studied everything with quiet intensity. When Houdini bleated impatiently, pushing his head through the stall slats, Alan's serious expression finally broke into a smile.

"He's got a beard!" he exclaimed, reaching out hesitantly to touch the goat's coarse fur.

"Sure does. Thinks he's quite the gentleman too." Ben showed Alan how to hold his hand flat with grain, laughing when the goat's rough tongue tickled the boy's palm.

Meanwhile, Ralph had wandered to Beulah's stall, where the Jersey cow regarded him with liquid brown eyes. "She's so big!" he whispered, suddenly reverent.

"And gentle as a lamb," Ben assured him, guiding Ralph's small hand to stroke Beulah's warm flank. "That's it, nice and easy."

From the barn doorway, Maggie watched unnoticed, one hand pressed against her heart. The sight of her boys—so cautious around men since Roger left—slowly warming to Ben's patient guidance made her throat tighten. When Ben knelt to show Alan how to check Houdini's hooves, pointing out something that made both boys laugh, her heart did a funny lurch in her chest.

Alan watched intently as Ben examined Houdini's hooves, noticing how the man's hands moved with careful confidence. The goat squirmed and bleated indignantly, but Ben just chuckled, adjusting his hold without a hint of frustration.

"He sure gives you a lot of trouble," Alan observed, passing Ben a small brush when he pointed to it.

"That's just his nature," Ben replied, working methodically. "Goats are curious. They test boundaries. It's not 'cause they're bad—it's 'cause they're goats."

Alan chewed his bottom lip, his fingers worrying a loose thread on his sleeve. "Do you ever get mad when he keeps escaping? Even after you fix the fence?"

Ben paused, sensing the weight behind the question. He set the brush down and gave Alan his full attention. "No, I don't. Might get frustrated sometimes, but I'd never walk away from him just 'cause he's being who he is."

"You wouldn't?" Alan's voice was small, his eyes fixed on Houdini rather than Ben.

"Not a chance." Ben settled back on his heels. "And I can't think of a single reason I'd walk away from a young man like you either, Alan. Someone who takes care of his family, stands up for his mama the way you do."

Alan's head snapped up, eyes suddenly meeting Ben's, searching for any hint of dishonesty.

"I know it's hard to trust me, Alan. To trust that I will stay forever and take care of you, your mom, and Ralph." Ben's voice was steady, gentle. "I'll make a deal with you. I'm asking you to keep watching and asking questions about anything. I will answer your questions honestly and to the best of my ability, 'cause God knows there is a lot I don't know about this world. I'm giving you permission to call me out on my mistakes, respectfully, of course. I need you to help keep me accountable. Help me keep my promise. Is that a deal?"

Alan studied Ben's face for a long moment, his young features serious with consideration. Finally, he extended his hand. "Deal."

Ben's calloused palm engulfed the boy's smaller one, the handshake solemn and binding.

"Me too! Me too!" Ralph came bounding over from Beulah's stall, hay clinging to his shirt. "I want a deal too!"

Ben laughed, releasing Alan's hand to shake Ralph's with equal gravity. "Absolutely. Same deal for you, partner."

From her hidden spot by the barn door, Maggie pressed trembling fingers to her lips. Tears blurred her vision as she watched her sons—her brave, wounded boys—reach tentatively toward trust again. The sight of Ben's patient strength meeting their fragile courage filled her heart with something she'd almost forgotten how to feel: hope, wonder, and a quiet, expanding joy.

Behind the barn, the afternoon sun cast long shadows across freshly tilled earth. Sweat darkened Ben's shirt collar as he drove the last wooden stake into the ground, marking the final garden bed. Brittany knelt nearby, her chef's hands now dirt-stained as she nestled tomato seedlings into the rich soil.

"That's the last of them," she announced, sitting back on her heels and brushing hair from her face with her forearm. "Thirty-six tomato plants, twelve peppers, and enough squash to feed half the county."

Ben nodded, surveying their work with quiet satisfaction. The retreat's community garden had doubled in size since last year—row upon neat row of vegetables stretching toward the tree line.

"Weather holds, we'll have our first harvest by mid-June," he said, calculations already running in his head.

Brittany pulled a worn notebook from her back pocket and made a final entry. "Garden log's all updated. I'll leave the harvest calendar to you, though. My brain doesn't work in growing seasons like yours does."

She handed him the notebook, their fingers brushing briefly. Ben tucked it into his shirt pocket, a small smile playing at the corners of his mouth.

"We make a good team, Sis," he said, his voice full of brotherly love.

Across the garden, Ethan straightened from where he'd been helping Ralph plant carrot seeds. He checked his watch, then gave a short whistle that caught everyone's attention.

"Before we wrap up," he called, "let's gather round."

Alan and Ralph abandoned their watering cans. Maggie set down her trowel, wiping soil from her hands onto her jeans. Clara emerged from the toolshed carrying empty seed trays, while Brittany capped her pen and rose to her feet.

They formed a loose circle in the center of the garden, boots planted in the dark earth they'd spent the day preparing. Ethan removed his cap, and one by one, the others followed suit.

"Lord," Ethan began, his voice carrying clearly in the still afternoon air, "we thank You for this day of work and fellowship. For the soil beneath our feet and the hands that have prepared it."

The group bowed their heads, a gentle breeze stirring the leaves above them.

"Bless what we've sown today," Ethan continued. "And bless what we're still learning to grow—in this garden and in our hearts. Help us, Lord, to break up the fallow ground in our lives. Like it says in Hosea 10:12, 'Sow to yourselves in righteousness, reap in mercy; break up your fallow ground: for it is time to seek the Lord.' Let this place, and all of us in it, be good ground for You."

Chapter 23 – Forgiveness & Faith

"It is of the Lord's mercies that we are not consumed, because his compassions fail not. They are new every morning: great is thy faithfulness." Lamentations 3:22–23 (KJV)

The bell above the Co-Op door jingled as Wade pushed it open, his tall frame silhouetted against the golden light of sunset. Ben glanced up from behind the counter where he'd been tallying the day's meager receipts, surprised to see the sheriff this late.

"Thought you'd be off duty by now," Ben said, tucking his pencil behind his ear.

Wade shrugged, ambling toward the counter. "Just finished my rounds." He didn't ask about sales or comment on the empty aisles. Instead, he simply pulled up a stool and sat, his badge catching the last rays of sunlight through the dusty windows.

"Heard you're carrying more than seed and feed these days," Wade said quietly, his voice gentle but knowing.

Ben's shoulders stiffened before slumping in defeat. No point hiding from Wade—man had eyes like a hawk and ears in every corner of Willow Creek. He pushed the ledger aside and rubbed his calloused hands over his face.

"This drought is hurting everyone in town," Ben admitted, gesturing toward the window where brown fields stretched to the horizon. "Animal owners are selling off their livestock because no rain means no grass, which also means no need for Co-Op."

Wade nodded, patient and still.

"The Crop 'Til You Drop Farmstand business is doing okay because of the barter system in place," Ben continued, tapping his fingers against the worn counter. "Folks trading eggs for tomatoes, labor for corn. But bartering don't pay the bank."

"And Brittany's new venture?" Wade asked.

Ben shook his head. "I ain't sure her farm-to-table eatery is going to be the answer. She's got heart, but..." He trailed off, then met Wade's steady gaze. "The bank wants a piece of me. The town's losing faith. And I can't even pray without feelin' fake."

The words hung between them, raw and honest in the quiet store.

Ben leaned forward, forearms resting on the counter, staring at his work-worn hands. The words he'd kept locked inside tumbled out in a hoarse whisper.

"I go to church 'cause it's what my family always did. But I ain't felt God near me in years." He swallowed hard. "Not since Dad passed. I keep showing up, singing the hymns, nodding at the right parts of the sermon, but inside..." He tapped his chest. "Inside, it's just hollow."

Wade didn't interrupt, just watched him with those steady eyes.

"I've messed up, Wade. I kept pushing through, thinking I could fix everything on my own." Ben's voice cracked. "The farm, the business, the land—I thought if I just worked harder, longer, it would all come right. Pride, I guess. Stubborn pride."

A muscle worked in Ben's jaw as he fought to maintain his composure. "Now I'm about to lose everything my family built. Four generations of Reeves, ended with me."

Wade shifted on his stool, leaning in closer. "And yet here you are. Still standing." His voice was quiet but firm. "You want to know why? Because it ain't your strength that's been keeping you upright. It's His mercy."

Ben looked up, doubt etched across his features.

"He didn't let go—even when you did," Wade continued. "That's how faithful He is. Brand-new mercies every single morning, whether we deserve 'em or not."

The sheriff stood, his boots scuffing against the worn floorboards. "Come on," he said, nodding toward the back room. "Let's step away from this counter for a minute."

Ben hesitated, then followed Wade through the swinging door into the small stockroom. Bags of feed lined the walls, and the scent of grain hung in the air.

"I'd like to pray with you," Wade said simply. "Right here."

For a moment, Ben felt the urge to refuse, to make an excuse about locking up. But the weight on his shoulders was too heavy to carry another step.

"Alright," he said softly.

Wade removed his hat, set it on a stack of feed bags, and bowed his head. His voice, usually firm with authority, softened with reverence.

"Lord, we come before You tonight, two men who need Your strength. Ben here—" Wade's voice caught slightly. "He's carried a heavy load for too long. Restore his confidence, Lord. Remind him of Your strength when ours fails. Help him see that we all stumble, we all face hard times, but You never desert us, even when we can't feel You nearby."

The prayer hung in the air between them, mingling with the earthy scent of grain and soil. Wade looked up, his eyes meeting Ben's in silent invitation.

Ben swallowed hard, then bowed his head. His hands, calloused from years of working the land, gripped each other so tightly his knuckles whitened.

"Lord, I'm sorry I stopped trusting You." His voice was rough, barely above a whisper. "I've tried to fix everything by myself. And I'm tired." The last word broke, revealing the depth of his exhaustion. "Forgive me for my pride. For thinking I could do it all alone. For the silence between us—that was on me, not You."

He paused, drawing a shaky breath. "I need You now. More than ever."

When Ben fell silent, Wade placed a steady hand on his shoulder.

"You're not too far gone, brother. Not even close." Wade's voice was firm with conviction. "The good Lord doesn't count you out. His compassion doesn't fail. You woke up this morning, didn't you? That alone's proof enough His mercy's still working."

Ben lifted his head, meeting Wade's gaze.

"You've never been alone, brother," Wade said softly. "Not once."

The simple truth of those words washed over Ben like summer rain on parched earth. Something tight in his chest began to loosen—a knot of fear and loneliness he'd carried so long he'd forgotten it wasn't part of him. The weight he'd been bearing, seasons upon seasons of worry and isolation, started to dissolve beneath Wade's steady gaze and unwavering faith. For the first time in what felt like forever, Ben could draw a full breath, as if his lungs were finally remembering how to properly fill.

As Wade and Ben stepped back into the main area of the Co-Op, the evening shadows had lengthened across the wooden floor. The day's final light cast everything in amber and gold.

"Lock up," Wade said, retrieving his hat. "Whatever's left can wait till morning."

Ben nodded, something lighter in his expression now. "Thanks for stopping by, Sheriff."

Wade tipped his hat with a small smile and headed out, the bell jingling softly behind him.

Across town, Maggie folded the last of the clean towels and tucked them into the linen closet. The house smelled of fabric softener and pencil shavings—the comforting scent of ordinary life carrying on. Through the doorway, she could see Alan and Ralph at the kitchen table, homework spread before them.

Ralph's tongue poked out of the corner of his mouth as he concentrated on his math problems. Alan, finished with his own work, was doodling in his notebook, his expression unusually pensive.

"Mom?" Alan's voice broke the comfortable silence. "Do you think Mr. Reeves is in trouble?"

Maggie paused, a washcloth still in her hands. She moved to the kitchen doorway, leaning against the frame. "What makes you ask that, honey?"

Alan shrugged, not looking up from his drawing. "He looked sad at church. And I heard Ms. Hattie talking about the bank wanting his farm."

Maggie crossed to the table and sat down beside him. "He's having a hard time," she admitted gently. "But he's not a quitter."

Alan finally looked up, his eyes serious. "Is he having a hard time because he's bad?"

The question caught her off guard. "No, sweetheart. Why would you think that?"

"Dad always said bad things happen to bad people," Ralph piped up, his pencil still poised over his math worksheet.

Maggie's heart clenched. "That's not how it works," she said, reaching out to smooth Ralph's hair. "Everybody faces challenges in their life—good people included. Sometimes farms struggle, sometimes businesses close, sometimes people get sick. It doesn't mean they did anything wrong."

She took a deep breath, feeling every bit the hypocrite even as the words formed. "When hard times come, that's when we need to lean on Jesus the most. His mercies are new every morning, boys. That means no matter how tough yesterday was, God gives us fresh strength for today."

"Like a reset button?" Ralph asked.

Maggie smiled. "Something like that. His compassion never fails, even when everything else seems to."

Maggie closed the linen closet and turned to her boys. "Time to put away the homework. Alan, would you and Ralph set the table, please, while I figure out what we're having for dinner?"

Alan nodded, gathering his papers while Ralph slammed his math book shut with dramatic relief. Maggie smiled at their routine—Alan meticulously stacking his work, Ralph shoving everything into his backpack in a jumbled heap.

She headed to the kitchen, pulling open the pantry door and staring at the shelves. Pasta? No, they'd had that yesterday. Chicken? She frowned, trying to remember if she'd defrosted any. The mental inventory of her refrigerator wasn't promising.

"Looks like we might be having breakfast for dinner, boys," she called, pushing aside a box of cereal to see what lurked behind it.

The doorbell's sudden chime startled her.

"I've got it!" Ralph's feet thundered down the hallway before she could stop him. She winced, wondering which neighbor had come calling at dinnertime.

"Wait, Ralph—" she started, but he'd already yanked the door open.

"Hi, Mr. Reeves!" Ralph's voice carried clearly through the small house.

Maggie froze, one hand still on the pantry shelf. Her heart skipped, then raced to catch up.

"Mom, it's Mr. Reeves!" Alan's voice joined the chorus from the living room.

She stepped out of the kitchen just as Ben appeared in the entryway, Ralph bouncing beside him like an overexcited puppy, asking how Beulah and Houdini were doing. Ben stood awkwardly, holding a covered dish in one hand and a paper bag in the other. His smile was hesitant, soft around the edges in a way that made something flutter in her chest.

"I, uh, thought you all might be hungry," he said, lifting the dish slightly. "It's venison stew. And cornbread."

The rich aroma of slow-cooked meat and herbs wafted toward her, making her suddenly aware of her empty stomach. She hadn't realized how hungry she was until that moment.

Maggie stepped forward, wordlessly attempted to take the dish from his hands. Their fingers brushed, and she felt warmth spread up her arm that had nothing to do with the hot container. Ben stopped her, saying "I've got it. Just point the way to the table where I can set this down." He handed Ralph the bag of corn muffins. "You help me with this, Ralph?"

"Come in," she said simply, finding no other words adequate for the moment and led the way to the kitchen table. The small gesture—him arriving with food, thinking of her family—left her momentarily speechless. She tucked a strand of hair behind her ear as she moved through the narrow hallway, acutely aware of his presence behind her. The house suddenly felt different with Ben in it, as if the walls themselves were holding their breath, waiting to see what might happen next.

Ben settled the stew on the kitchen table, the delicious aroma filling the small room. Alan and Ralph took their usual seats, both boys unusually quiet as they watched Ben's every move. Ralph's legs swung beneath his chair while Alan sat perfectly still, his shoulders slightly tensed.

Maggie busied herself with plates and utensils for Ben, hyper aware of the strange new energy in her kitchen. She caught Alan's eye as she set a bowl in front of him—his expression guarded, assessing. It was the same look he'd worn when meeting his third-grade teacher for the first time, measuring whether this new adult could be trusted.

"This smells amazing," Maggie said, breaking the silence as she took her seat.

Ben nodded, standing awkwardly behind the empty chair. "My grandma's recipe. Slow-cooked all day."

Ralph reached for the ladle, but Alan caught his wrist with a subtle shake of his head. Both boys looked to their mother, then to Ben, waiting.

"Would it be alright if I say grace?" Ben asked, his voice soft.

Maggie nodded, folding her hands on the table. The boys followed suit, heads bowed, though Alan kept one eye cracked open, watching.

Ben cleared his throat. "Heavenly Father, we thank You for this food and the hands that prepared it. We thank You for bringing us together around this table tonight." His voice grew steadier as he continued. "Lord, we're especially grateful for second chances—for the opportunity to begin again when we falter. And for the people You place in our lives who help us recognize those chances when they come."

Maggie's chest tightened at his words. Each syllable landed like a stone in still water, sending ripples through her conscience. The secret deed hidden in her purse seemed to burn through the leather, a tangible reminder of her dishonesty.

"Thank You for Your mercy that's new every morning," Ben continued. "Amen."

"Amen," the boys echoed, Ralph's voice enthusiastic, Alan's barely audible.

Dinner passed with stories of Beulah's latest escape attempts and Ralph's enthusiastic questions about farm life. Ben answered each one patiently, his deep voice filling the kitchen with tales of stubborn goats and midnight calf deliveries. Alan remained quiet, pushing his stew around before finally taking a bite, then another, his shoulders gradually relaxing as the meal progressed.

When the last of the cornbread had been claimed and bowls sat empty, Ralph pushed his chair back with a screech against the linoleum floor.

"It's my turn to clear the table. Want to help me, Mr. Reeves?" he asked, already stacking his and Alan's bowls.

Ben looked surprised, then pleased. "I'd be honored to help, Ralph, if you'll show me what to do."

Maggie watched from her place at the table as Ralph carefully carried the dishes to the sink, his small face serious with concentration. Her gaze shifted to Alan, who remained seated, fingers tracing patterns on the wooden tabletop. She braced herself for him to excuse himself, to retreat to his room as he often did when visitors came. But he stayed, quiet and watchful, his eyes following Ben's movements.

Ben stood, gathering the remaining dishes. "My mama always made sure we did the dishes after a meal, so they are ready to go for the next one," he said, stacking bowls with careful hands.

Alan didn't speak. But he didn't leave either. Instead, he rose silently and collected the empty cornbread basket, carrying it to the counter where Ben stood.

Something warm and hopeful unfurled in Maggie's chest as she watched from the doorway. This wasn't forgiveness spoken aloud—not yet.

But it was something just as precious: a tiny seed of trust, planted in the fertile soil of a shared meal.

Ralph chattered away at the sink while Ben handed him dishes to dry. Alan stood nearby, not participating but not withdrawing either, his presence a quiet acknowledgement that perhaps—just perhaps—there was room at their table for someone new.

Maggie leaned against the doorframe, her heart thudding against her ribs. The deed in her purse still weighed heavy, but for this moment, watching her boys and Ben in her kitchen, she allowed herself to feel the first stirrings of hope.

Chapter 24 – Ghosts, Gossip & God's Plan

"Therefore to him that knoweth to do good, and doeth it not, to him it is sin."
James 4:17 (KJV)

Hector Rodriguez crouched behind the retreat's storage shed, his heart hammering against his ribs. "This is stupid, Rosita. We should go back."

Rosita Carter flashed him a grin, moonlight catching the determination in her eyes. "We've been cooped up for two weeks. Don't you want to see what this town's really like when all the do-gooders aren't watching?"

"We're supposed to be role models," Hector whispered, glancing back toward the cabins where their charges slept. "What if someone notices we're gone?"

"Everyone's asleep. We'll be back before sunrise." She tugged his arm. "Come on. You were the one talking about how suffocated you felt."

Hector hesitated. At nineteen, he was technically an adult, responsible for kids just a few years younger than himself. But tonight, the walls of responsibility had felt like they were closing in. One night of freedom couldn't hurt.

"Fine. One hour."

They slipped through the shadows, following the dirt path that led to town. The walk took twenty minutes, their footsteps crunching on gravel as Main Street came into view. Most storefronts were dark, but at the far end, neon lights hummed against the night sky.

"The Moon Shines," Rosita read aloud. "Sounds perfect."

The bass hit them before they reached the door—a steady thump that vibrated through the sidewalk. Inside, the small-town bar was alive with energy. A jukebox blared in the corner while locals clustered around pool tables.

"We shouldn't," Hector said, but his protest lacked conviction.

They didn't order drinks—neither had fake IDs or the courage to try—but they soaked in the atmosphere, playing darts and watching the locals. For an hour, they weren't former foster kids with responsibilities. They were just teenagers, laughing too loud and forgetting the weight on their shoulders.

Until someone recognized them.

"Ain't y'all from that retreat?" A red-faced man squinted at them. "Them troubled kids?"

Rosita stiffened. "We're counselors."

The man's eyes narrowed. "Don't look old enough. Hey, Marv! These kids sneak out from that camp?"

Heads turned. Whispers spread. Hector grabbed Rosita's arm. "We need to go."

They pushed through the door into the cool night air, but the damage was done. As they sat on the curb, trying to figure out how to get back without being seen, headlights swept across them.

The sheriff's cruiser pulled up, its light bar dark but its presence unmistakable. Sheriff Wade Beaumont stepped out, his expression unreadable in the shadows.

"Evening," he said, his deep voice carrying quiet authority. "Y'all are a long way from the retreat."

Hector and Rosita sat frozen on the curb, their momentary freedom evaporating like morning dew.

Sheriff Wade didn't reach for his handcuffs or his ticket book. Instead, he settled onto the curb beside them, his uniform creasing as he lowered his tall frame to their level.

"Mind if I join y'all for a minute?"

Hector swallowed hard. "No, sir."

Wade gazed out at the empty street, the neon lights of The Moon Shines reflecting in puddles from yesterday's rain. "First time I snuck out, I was fourteen. Made it all the way to Old Man Fletcher's apple orchard before my daddy caught me."

Rosita's shoulders relaxed slightly. "Did you get in trouble?"

"Grounded for a month." Wade chuckled. "But that wasn't the worst part. Worst part was seein' the disappointment in folks' eyes. People who believed in me."

He turned to face them fully. "Y'all made a mistake. One choice don't define you. But how you fix it? That will."

The words hung in the night air. No lecture followed, just silence that invited them to fill it.

"We just wanted..." Hector began, then faltered.

"To feel normal?" Wade suggested.

Rosita nodded, her eyes suddenly wet. "Everyone's always watching us at the retreat. Waiting for us to mess up or succeed. Sometimes I just want to breathe without feeling like I'm carrying the weight of everybody's expectations."

Wade nodded slowly. "I hear that. But running from responsibility doesn't make it disappear. Just means you gotta carry it twice as heavy when you pick it back up."

He stood, brushing off his uniform pants. "Come on. I'll drive y'all back."

The ride to the retreat was quiet at first. Then Wade spoke again, his voice gentle but firm.

"Part of growing up is learning that integrity means doing the right thing even when nobody's watching. And accountability means owning your mistakes, especially when they affect others."

Hector stared out the window at the passing trees. "Are you going to tell Ms. Clara?"

"No," Wade said. "You are."

As the retreat's lights came into view, Rosita whispered, "I'm not messing this up again." She clutched the edge of her seat, her knuckles white against the dark upholstery of Wade's patrol car. This place was her second chance—maybe her last one—and the weight of that knowledge pressed against her chest like a physical thing.

The next morning, Clara's coffee mug hit the kitchen table with a sharp crack.

"Have you seen this?" She thrust the latest edition of Creek Speak across the table to Ethan. The front page featured a bold headline: "Too Much, Too Fast? What's Really Happening Behind Willow Creek's Curtain."

Ethan's jaw tightened as he scanned the article. Mavis Holbrook's name appeared in the byline, her words sharp as broken glass.

"...while our community has always welcomed progress," the editorial read, "we must question the wisdom of throwing open our gates to troubled outsiders with no ties to our heritage. Last night's disturbance at a local establishment only confirms what some have feared—that this so-called 'retreat' brings more problems than solutions. With town finances already stretched thin, can we afford to support ventures that drain our resources and disrupt our peace?"

The article continued, casting shadows on everything from the retreat's mission to Kneadful Things' expansion plans.

"She's trying to turn the town against us," Clara whispered, her hands trembling slightly.

Ethan folded the paper with deliberate calm. "She's scared of change. And she's not alone."

Outside their window, the effects were already visible. Mrs. Fletcher crossed the street rather than pass directly by their house. At Hattie's, a cluster of women huddled near the register, their voices dropping to whispers when Tina approached.

By noon, the damage had spread like wildfire. Parents called to withdraw their teenagers from volunteer shifts at the retreat. Three foster families canceled their reservations for the following week's session.

At the Town Square Pavilion, Mavis held court among her followers, her voice carrying across the green. "I'm simply asking questions that need asking. If these new ventures are so beneficial, why all the secrecy? Why the midnight escapades?"

Sheriff Wade leaned against his cruiser nearby, his expression carefully neutral as he watched the crowd grow. When his eyes met Clara's across the square, he gave a slight nod—acknowledgment of the storm brewing and silent support in the face of it.

In her office at Town Hall, Mayor Ellie Jernigan fielded a dozen calls before lunch, each citizen "just concerned" about the town's direction. She rubbed her temples, the stack of messages growing by the hour.

"They're saying the retreat brings trouble," her assistant reported, adding another slip to the pile. "And that Kneadful Things is taking loans it can't repay."

Ellie stared out her window at the town she'd sworn to protect. The whispers and side-eyes had begun. Willow Creek was splitting at the seams.

At the retreat, Clara paced her office, crumpling Mavis's article in her fist. "I need to write a response. Set the record straight about what we're doing here."

"And feed right into her game?" Ethan leaned against the doorframe. "That's exactly what she wants—to drag us into a public fight."

"Then what do we do? Just let her tear everything down?"

"We pray." Ethan crossed the room and took her hands. "Remember what Pastor said last Sunday about fighting battles on our knees first?"

Clara's shoulders slumped. "I hate feeling helpless."

In the main hall, Paul shuffled papers at the volunteer desk, trying to patch the holes in next week's schedule. Three more cancellations had come in that morning.

"We're down to skeleton crew," he muttered, running a hand through his gray hair.

Clara knocked on Luke's door, finding her brother surrounded by spreadsheets and financial reports. "Got a minute?"

"Always for you, sis." He pushed back from the desk. "Though I'm neck-deep in these numbers."

"That's actually why I'm here. We need help with the books—both here and at Kneadful Things. I know you're heading home soon, but—"

"About that." Luke smiled, spinning his chair to face her fully. "I've been thinking. This town raised us right, taught us about faith and community. Maybe it's time I gave something back."

"What are you saying?"

"I've decided to move back home to Willow Creek. I'm staying. For good. These financial troubles? They're not just numbers to me—they're our neighbors' livelihoods. Our hometown's future." He tapped the papers on his desk. "And I think I can help."

Clara's eyes widened as Luke's words sank in. For a moment, she stood frozen, then flung herself at her brother with such force that his office chair rolled back against the wall.

"You're staying? For real?" Her voice cracked as she wrapped her arms around him.

Luke laughed, returning her embrace. "For real. Already called a realtor about that empty storefront on Elm."

Clara pulled back, her hands gripping his shoulders. "You have no idea what this means. The retreat needs you. The bakery needs you." She swallowed hard. "Your niece and nephew need you.I need you."

"Well, that settles it then." He grinned, the same crooked smile he'd had since they were kids building mud pies by the creek. "Can't have my big sister struggling when I've got perfectly good accounting skills gathering dust."

Clara perched on the edge of his desk, unwilling to move too far away. "Remember when we were kids and we'd plan our futures? You were always going to be the money man, and I was going to save the world."

"And look at us now." Luke's eyes crinkled at the corners. "You're actually doing it."

"We lost so much time," Clara said softly, reaching for his hand. "All those years I was... away. All the birthdays and Christmases."

"Hey." Luke squeezed her fingers. "We're here now. That's what matters."

Clara nodded, blinking back tears. "When Daddy gets wind of this, he's gonna throw the biggest welcome-home barbecue Willow Creek's ever seen."

"Lord help us all." Luke rolled his eyes, but his smile remained. "Burle Sharp with a reason to fire up that smoker? We'll be eating leftovers till Christmas."

They laughed together, the sound echoing in the small office—a bridge across the years they'd spent apart.

Outside at the retreat's garden patch, Maggie knelt in the dirt, pulling weeds with more force than necessary. The folded deed in her pocket felt like it weighed a hundred pounds. Every time she thought about Ben's farm—his father's secret sale, the looming disaster—her stomach twisted into knots.

She yanked another weed, dirt spraying across her jeans. The sun beat down on her neck as guilt pressed against her chest.

"I should just tell him," she muttered to herself. "Just say, 'Ben, I found something about your farm that you need to know.'"

The words formed on her lips, rehearsing for when she'd see him next. She'd tell him about the deed, about how his father had—

"Talking to the tomatoes, Sassafras?"

Maggie startled, nearly toppling sideways as Ben's voice came from behind her. He stood there, two glasses of lemonade sweating in his hands, his smile making her heart skip.

"I, uh—" The words died in her throat. She couldn't do it. Not here, not now, with his eyes crinkling at the corners and that easy smile she was growing to depend on. "Just garden therapy."

Ben handed her a glass, their fingers brushing. "You okay?"

She took a long sip, buying time. "I want to be."

"Anything I can help with?"

His simple offer hit her like a physical blow. If only he knew what she was hiding. Maggie looked away, focusing on a row of bell peppers.

"Not now," she said softly. "But thank you."

Ben settled beside her, his long legs stretching out in front of him. "I had a good time the other night. At dinner."

Maggie smiled despite herself. "Me too."

"It was nice," he said, his voice dropping lower, "having someone other than Ms. Pickles to share a meal with." He traced patterns in the dirt with his finger. "Felt like we were a family for a minute there. I've been thinking about that—what it might be like." He paused, then added quietly, "If only."

Something warm bloomed in Maggie's chest, pushing back against the weight of secrets. She looked at him—really looked—and saw the loneliness he usually kept hidden.

"If we had been a family back then," she said carefully, "I wouldn't have my Alan and Ralph. When he left us, he left behind the best part of himself." She touched the carved heart on the fence post, feeling its weathered grooves beneath her fingertips. "And as much as they drive me crazy sometimes, I can't imagine my life without those boys. They're the best parts of me, even on the hardest days." She touched his arm lightly. "But maybe we could all have dinner again sometime."

Ben's face brightened. "I'd like that. Why don't y'all come out to the farm some Sunday, after church? I could show the boys around, let them meet the animals."

The smell of grilled hot dogs wafted across the retreat grounds as Ben helped Ethan man the outdoor grill. Despite the tension in town, they'd decided to continue with the planned cookout for the campers. Maggie watched from her spot at the picnic table, her heart warming at the sight of Ben flipping burgers with the same careful attention he gave his crops.

"Food's up!" Ethan called, and a line of hungry teenagers formed, paper plates in hand.

Anthony, balancing a loaded hot dog on his plate, settled onto the bench next to Charnise, who was showing Ava a friendship bracelet she'd made.

"This is awesome," Anthony said between bites. "Haven't had a cookout since—"

A blur of white fur streaked across the lawn. Before anyone could react, Ms. Pickles executed a perfect leap, snatched the hot dog clean off Anthony's plate, and trotted away with her prize dangling from her mouth.

The look of shock on Anthony's face was priceless.

"Ms. Pickles!" Ben bellowed, his hands on his hips. "That's your third one this week!"

For a heartbeat, silence hung in the air—then Anthony burst out laughing. The sound was contagious, spreading through the group until even Sheriff Wade, who'd stopped by to check on things, was chuckling.

"Did you see that jump?" Rosita gasped between giggles. "Olympic-level theft!"

Ms. Pickles settled under a nearby oak tree, looking entirely too pleased with herself as she devoured her stolen goods.

Ben shook his head, fighting a smile. "I swear that dog thinks she's people." He handed Anthony a fresh hot dog. "Double condiments to make up for the trauma."

Maggie caught Ben's eye across the lawn and felt something loosen in her chest. For just a moment, the weight of secrets and town gossip lifted. The laughter continued as Ms. Pickles, finished with her snack, trotted back to the group and sat primly at Ben's feet as if nothing had happened.

"Shameless," Ben muttered, but he reached down to scratch behind her ears anyway.

As the cookout wound down, Maggie gathered empty paper plates, grateful for the simple task that kept her hands busy and her mind distracted. She'd been avoiding Ben's gaze since their conversation, afraid he might see the guilt written across her face.

"Need a hand with that?"

Maggie looked up to find Brittany, Ben's sister, holding out a trash bag. Her expression was friendly enough, but something in her eyes made Maggie pause.

"Thanks," Maggie said, dropping the plates into the bag. "I think we're about done here."

Brittany glanced around, then nodded toward the garden. "Got a minute? I'd like to show you something with the tomatoes."

Confused but curious, Maggie followed her away from the group. Once they were out of earshot, Brittany turned, her smile fading.

"Look, I'll cut to the chase. I know you're carrying something, and I don't need the details."

Maggie froze. "I don't know what—"

"Save it." Brittany's tone sharpened, though she kept her voice low. "I've seen that look before. On my daddy's face right before the bank came calling." She crossed her arms. "But if it affects Ben—you tell him."

Maggie stiffened, her defenses rising. "It's not that simple."

"It is when it's my brother." Brittany's eyes flashed. "You know what Daddy used to say? 'Knowing the right thing and not doing it is the worst kind of wrong.' That's practically scripture, and he was right."

She took a step closer. "Ben's given this town everything. His sweat, his time, pieces of his soul." Her voice wavered slightly. "Don't let him be the last one to know he's about to lose it."

Maggie's throat tightened. "How did you—"

"I don't need to know the specifics. But I know trouble when I see it." Brittany's gaze softened just a fraction. "He deserves the truth, Maggie. From someone who cares about him."

Without waiting for a response, Brittany turned and walked back toward the picnic area, leaving Maggie with a pounding heart and a truth she couldn't ignore any longer.

Dusk settled over the retreat grounds as the last of the day's visitors departed. Maggie lingered behind, helping Clara collect stray napkins that had blown across the lawn. Her mind raced with Brittany's words, the truth of them stinging like salt in an open wound.

"You heading home soon?" Clara asked, tying off a garbage bag.

Maggie glanced toward the small chapel at the edge of the property. Its wooden cross caught the last rays of sunlight, glowing warm against the darkening sky.

"In a bit. I think I need a minute first."

Clara followed her gaze and nodded with understanding. "Take all the time you need. I'll keep the boys distracted."

The chapel door creaked as Maggie pushed it open. Inside, the simple room held nothing more than a few wooden pews, a small altar, and a stained-glass window depicting a shepherd with his flock. Candles flickered in wall sconces, casting dancing shadows across the worn floorboards.

Maggie slipped into the front pew, then thought better of it and knelt on the floor. The wood was hard against her knees, but the discomfort felt right somehow—a physical reminder of the weight she carried.

"Lord," she whispered, her voice barely disturbing the silence, "I don't know what to do."

She closed her eyes, picturing Ben's face—the warmth in his eyes when he looked at her boys, the quiet strength in his hands as he worked his land. Land that might not be fully his.

"If I'm supposed to tell him, make it clear. If I'm supposed to wait, make me brave enough to hold it."

A soft evening breeze filtered through the open doorway, rustling the pages of the Bible that lay open on the altar. Maggie lifted her head, watching as the pages turned, then settled.

Curious, she rose and approached the altar. Her fingers traced the words on the open page: James, chapter four.

Her eyes fell on verse seventeen: "Therefore to him that knoweth to do good, and doeth it not, to him it is sin."

Maggie's breath caught. The words seemed to leap from the page, speaking directly to her heart.

She stood perfectly still, waiting for more—a sign, a voice, anything to tell her exactly what to do. But there was only silence. The candles continued their gentle dance, the chapel remained empty save for her, and the breeze died down to nothing.

Just stillness—and, surprisingly, peace.

In that moment, Maggie understood. God wasn't going to make this decision for her. He'd given her the wisdom to recognize right from wrong, and now He was leaving the choice to her.

To do what she knew was right.

ACT III

Reaping Redemption

Chapter 25 – Ben's Table

"Thou preparest a table before me in the presence of mine enemies: thou anointest my head with oil; my cup runneth over." Psalm 23:5 (KJV)

Ben hadn't planned to ask her. The words had tumbled out like seeds from a split bag—unintended but impossible to gather back up. They'd been standing by the retreat's garden fence, watching Ralph chase fireflies with Noah while Alan sat cross-legged under the oak tree, sketching something in his notebook.

"If you and the boys ever feel ready..." Ben had said, his voice low enough that only she could hear, "I'd be honored to cook y'all supper. Just us. My place."

The moment the invitation left his lips, he'd wanted to snatch it back. Too soon. Too much. The shadow that crossed her face told him everything.

"I'll think about it," was all she'd said before calling the boys to head home.

Three days passed without a word. Ben threw himself into work, fixing the chicken coop's roof, tilling the north field, anything to keep his mind off the silence. Ms. Pickles stayed close, sensing his unease, occasionally nudging his hand when he paused too long between tasks.

"Stupid," he muttered to the dog as they walked the property line at sunset. "Pushed too hard."

Wednesday morning found him at the feed store, loading fifty-pound bags into his truck when his phone buzzed. A text from Maggie asking if he'd be at the retreat that afternoon. Nothing more.

He wasn't scheduled to be, but he replied that he could stop by. She texted back that she's working at the vet clinic today. He texted back he would stop by after he finishes up at the Co-Op.

A short while later, Ben steered his vehicle into the Creekside Veterinary Clinic's gravel parking area. As his truck entered the lot, the side entrance swung open. Maggie emerged, dabbing her hands with a disposable towel. Her expression revealed nothing as she walked toward him.

"Got a minute?" she asked, tucking a strand of hair behind her ear.

Ben nodded, his throat suddenly dry. The late afternoon sun caught the highlights in her hair, making them shimmer like copper.

They walked toward the small bench under the maple tree, their footsteps crunching on the gravel path. Neither spoke until they sat down, the weathered wood creaking slightly beneath their weight.

"We'll come," Maggie said finally, "to dinner at your house." Her eyes fixed on the distant hills where shadows were beginning to lengthen across the valley. The late afternoon light painted the landscape in amber hues, a stark contrast to the tumult in her chest. She fidgeted with the hem of her scrub top, pinching the fabric between her thumb and forefinger. "But just dinner. Nothing more."

Ben's heart skipped, but he kept his expression neutral. "Of course."

"I don't want you getting your hopes up about anything," she added, finally turning to look at him. "The boys and I... we're still figuring things out."

"I understand," he said softly. "No expectations. Just food and company."

Maggie nodded, relief visible in the slight drop of her shoulders. "Friday? Around six?"

"Friday's perfect." He hesitated. "Anything I should know? Foods they don't like? Things that might make them uncomfortable?"

The question seemed to surprise her. She blinked, then offered a small smile. "They'll eat most anything. Ralph hates green beans though. And Alan... he gets nervous around loud noises."

Ben filed the information away carefully. "No green beans. No loud noises. Got it."

"I should get back," she said, standing.

"Maggie?" he called as she turned to go. "Thank you. For trusting me enough to try."

She paused, not quite looking back. "Don't make me regret it, Ben Reeves."

It wasn't a threat. It was a plea.

Friday evening arrived with a gentle breeze that rustled the leaves of the old oak trees lining Ben's driveway. Maggie's hands gripped the steering wheel tighter as she guided her car down the gravel path toward the farmhouse. In the rearview mirror, she caught glimpses of her boys—Alan staring out the window with feigned indifference, Ralph fidgeting with his seat belt.

"Remember what we talked about," she said softly. "Just dinner. We're being polite."

"Why are we even here?" Alan muttered, not meeting her eyes.

Maggie swallowed hard. "Because sometimes grown-ups need to... try new things."

The car rounded the final curve, and Ben's farmhouse came into view. It wasn't grand—just a two-story white clapboard structure with dark green shutters and a wraparound porch. Flowerbeds lined the walkway, bursting with late summer blooms. The place had character, the kind that spoke of generations who'd weathered storms and celebrated harvests within those walls.

And there was Ben, standing on the porch steps. No fancy clothes, just clean jeans and a button-down shirt with the sleeves rolled up. His hands were tucked in his pockets, his posture relaxed but attentive. He wasn't rushing toward them or waving eagerly—just waiting, giving them space to arrive on their own terms.

Ms. Pickles sat at his feet, tail sweeping the wooden boards in slow, patient arcs.

Maggie parked the car and turned to face her sons. "This is just dinner," she repeated, as much for herself as for them. "But I'd like you to be nice to Mr. Ben. He's been kind to us."

The weight of her secret pressed against her chest. The property deed hidden in her purse felt like a stone. Tonight wasn't the night to reveal it—she needed to see if there was even something worth protecting before she risked destroying it.

When the car doors opened, Ben let out the breath he hadn't known he'd been holding. He moved down the steps to greet his guests as southern hospitality demands.

"Welcome to my place," Ben said, his voice warm but careful. "Nothing fancy, but it's home."

Ms. Pickles trotted over to the boys, tail wagging with recognition. Ralph's hand instinctively reached out to scratch behind her ears.

"Can I pet her?" he asked, his voice small.

"Course you can. She's been waiting all day for y'all."

Ben led them up the porch steps and opened the heavy wooden door. The farmhouse interior opened before them—a living room that flowed into a dining area, with the kitchen visible beyond. The space was undeniably masculine but surprisingly tidy. A worn leather couch faced a stone fireplace where a quilt in faded blues and greens was folded neatly over one arm. Family photos lined the mantel—older folks with Ben's same strong jawline and kind eyes.

A wooden cross hung centered above the fireplace, simple and unadorned. No fancy decorations, just the essentials of a working man's home.

"Something smells amazing," Maggie said, inhaling deeply.

"My mama's pot roast recipe," Ben replied, leading them toward the dining room. "Only thing I can cook that's fit for company."

The table was already set with mismatched plates that somehow looked intentional rather than haphazard. Mason jars filled with sweet tea caught the evening light streaming through the windows.

"Y'all can sit wherever you like," Ben said, disappearing briefly into the kitchen.

Alan and Ralph slid into chairs, their eyes darting around the unfamiliar space. Maggie settled across from them, noting how Ben had placed cloth napkins at each setting.

When Ben returned with the pot roast, the rich aroma of slow-cooked beef, carrots, and onions filled the room. He served the boys first, careful not to give them too much.

"There's plenty more if you're still hungry," he assured them.

The first few minutes passed in awkward silence, broken only by the clink of silverware against plates. Maggie watched Ben's every move—the way he cut his food, how he looked at her boys with genuine interest but never stared, how he kept conversation light.

"This farm been in your family long?" she asked, desperate to break the silence.

"Four generations," Ben nodded. "My great-granddaddy built this house with his own two hands."

Ralph reached for his tea, his small hand misjudging the distance. The mason jar tipped, sending sweet tea spreading across the wooden tabletop, seeping between the planks and dripping onto the floor below.

"I'm sorry!" he blurted, eyes wide with alarm, his shoulders hunching as if bracing for angry words.

Ben simply reached for a napkin and handed it to him, his movements unhurried and gentle. No flash of irritation crossed his face, just a calm understanding as he passed the cloth across the table. His eyes held a reassuring warmth that seemed to say spills happened in every home, even his. "That table's seen worse. My daddy spilled an entire bowl of gravy on Thanksgiving when I was about your age." Ben's voice was gentle, his weathered hands moving efficiently to mop up the remaining droplets. "Mama liked to never let him hear the end of it, but that old wood just soaked it up and kept on servin' us for years after. A little sweet tea ain't nothin' to fret over, little dude."

Maggie felt her shoulders drop a fraction, tension easing from her spine as she watched Ben's calm response. Something about his steady presence soothed her—the way he handled the small mishap without flinching, treating Ralph's accident as just another moment in the day rather than a crisis. It reminded her of her daddy's patient ways, how he'd always said that getting worked up over spilled anything just made two messes instead of one.

As the meal progressed, Ben kept the conversation light, focusing on stories about the farm and its quirks.

"Y'all wouldn't believe what Ms. Pickles did last spring," he said, cutting another piece of pot roast. "Found her stuck headfirst in the chicken coop, rear end sticking out, barking at my best laying hen."

Ralph's fork paused halfway to his mouth. "What happened?"

"Well, seems she thought she'd help herself to some fresh eggs. Got in easy enough through the little door, but couldn't figure out how to turn around to get back out." Ben's eyes crinkled at the corners. "Had to take the whole front panel off the coop to free her. She wouldn't look me in the eye for days after that."

A small giggle escaped Ralph's throat. Even Alan's lips twitched upward.

Ben reached down and grabbed a handful of soil from a pot by the window. "Here, let me show you something my granddaddy taught me." He sprinkled some dirt onto a napkin. "You can tell what your soil needs just by feeling it. See how it crumbles?"

Alan leaned forward, forgetting himself for a moment. His fingers reached out to touch the soil, mimicking Ben's movements.

"That's good earth," Ben explained. "Perfect for growing just about anything."

Maggie watched the exchange, something warm unfurling in her chest. She caught movement under the table—Ralph sneaking pieces of carrot to Ms. Pickles, who took them gently from his fingers. The boy didn't even look down, just kept eating with one hand while feeding the dog with the other, as if he'd done it a hundred times before.

The scene before her shifted, softened. Suddenly it wasn't just dinner at Ben's house—it was something else. Something that felt natural, unforced. The way Alan's shoulders had relaxed, how Ralph's feet swung freely under his chair, the easy rhythm of Ben's voice as he explained about crop rotation and rainfall patterns.

For a moment, Maggie allowed herself to imagine. What if this wasn't just a one-time dinner? What if there could be more evenings like this—Ralph giggling at Ben's stories, Alan's quiet interest in farming knowledge, the easy rhythm of passing dishes across a shared table? She watched Ben explain something about crop cycles to Alan, his hands moving with the practiced grace of someone who knew the land like his own heartbeat.

How long had it been since she'd felt this? Not just the comfort of a meal with someone else, but the sense that maybe—just maybe—her boys could heal. That she could heal.

Roger had never been this patient. He'd demanded attention, commanded rooms, filled spaces with his loud opinions and larger-than-life presence. When he left, the silence had been deafening. But Ben's quiet strength felt different—like shelter rather than shadow.

Dangerous thoughts. She couldn't let herself fall into daydreams about family dinners and shared futures. Not when she carried secrets that could shatter whatever fragile trust they'd built tonight.

Still, watching her boys at this table, seeing them slowly unfold from their protective shells, Maggie couldn't help but wonder if God had plans she couldn't yet see.

After apple cobbler and more stories, the evening drew to its natural close. Ben walked them out to the car, Ms. Pickles trailing behind. The sun hung low on the horizon, painting the farmland in gold and amber. Fireflies had begun their nightly dance along the fence line, blinking like earthbound stars.

The boys climbed into the back seat, suddenly shy again as the spell of dinner faded.

Ben stood by Maggie's door, hands tucked in his pockets. "Thanks for trusting me with supper," he said softly, his voice barely carrying above the evening crickets.

Maggie nodded, keys clutched tight in her hand. "Don't read too much into it."

Ben smiled, the corners of his eyes crinkling. "I won't." He glanced toward the house, then back at her. "But I'll remember it."

The farmhouse grew smaller in her rearview mirror as Maggie drove down the gravel lane. The tires crunched against stone, a rhythmic sound that matched her racing heartbeat. In the backseat, both boys had drifted off, Ralph's head tilted against the window, Alan's chin tucked against his chest.

Dinner at Ben's had been... unexpected. Not the food—she'd figured a fourth-generation farmer would know his way around a kitchen. It was everything else. The easy way he'd handled Ralph's spilled tea. How he'd drawn Alan out with talk of soil and seasons. The way he'd served them first, making sure they had the best portions.

"A table prepared," she whispered, remembering Sunday School lessons from childhood. How God prepared a table even in the presence of enemies.

But who was the enemy here? Roger, with his betrayal? Her own fear? Or was it the secret she carried—the property deed folded in her purse that could change everything for Ben?

The night wrapped around her car like a blanket as she turned onto the main road. Stars scattered across the sky, countless and bright. Maggie's knuckles whitened on the steering wheel.

"Lord," she prayed silently, "I need Your wisdom here. Help me see the way. Help me see the truth. Help me see Ben for who he really is, not who I want him to be." Her throat tightened. "I can't be deceived again. I can't let my boys be hurt again."

The headlights cut through darkness, illuminating only the next few yards ahead—just like her life now. No seeing the whole path, just the next few steps.

"Don't fall too fast," she whispered to herself. "He's just a man."

But the memory of Ben's gentle hands serving cobbler, of his patient smile when Ralph asked for seconds, of the way he'd looked at her across the table like she was something precious—it all washed over her, filling something empty inside.

"But maybe..." she breathed, so softly she barely heard herself, "he's a truly good man." The road curved, and she slowed the car. "Maybe even good enough to forgive this betrayal."

In the quiet car, with her sleeping boys and her racing thoughts, Maggie felt something she hadn't experienced in years—a cup running over, not with fear or worry, but with possibility.

Chapter 26 – The Deed Revealed

"For nothing is secret, that shall not be made manifest; neither any thing hid, that shall not be known and come abroad." Luke 8:17 (KJV)

Maggie clutched the steering wheel, the manila folder burning a hole in her purse on the passenger seat. Her stomach twisted as she reversed out of her driveway.

"Where we going, Mama?" Ralph asked, buckling his seatbelt.

"To Mr. Ben's farm," she answered, voice steadier than she felt.

Alan's head snapped up from his comic book. "Again? We just had dinner there."

"I need to talk to him about something important." She met his eyes in the rearview mirror, hoping her smile looked genuine. "Y'all can visit with Ms. Pickles while we talk."

The boys exchanged glances but didn't question further. Small mercies.

As she drove, Maggie's thoughts tumbled over each other like clothes in a dryer. What would Ben think? Would he blame her? Would this shatter whatever fragile thing was growing between them?

"Lord, give me strength," she whispered, too low for the boys to hear. "He deserves the truth, no matter what it costs me."

The sunset painted the fields gold as they turned onto Ben's gravel drive. Her heart hammered against her ribs. This was it. No more hiding, no more pretending she didn't know.

She remembered Clara's words from Bible study: "The truth isn't always pretty, but it's always right."

Ben's truck sat in the driveway. The porch light glowed warm against the gathering dusk. Somewhere in the distance, a cow lowed.

"He deserves to know," she murmured, parking beside the barn. "Even if it ruins everything. It will be worth the cost of telling him the truth."

Her fingers trembled as she cut the engine. The folder seemed to pulse with its own heartbeat, the secret inside too big for such a small space.

"Mama?" Ralph's voice broke through her thoughts. "You okay?"

She turned, forcing a smile. "I'm fine, sweetie. Just thinking."

Ben stepped onto the porch as they approached, his face lighting up with surprise. Ms. Pickles bounded past him, her tail wagging furiously as she greeted the boys.

"Well, this is unexpected," he said, his smile warm but questioning. His eyes met Maggie's, and his expression shifted. Something in her face must have given her away because his smile faded, replaced by concern. "Everything alright?"

Maggie couldn't find her voice. She clutched the folder to her chest, her knuckles white.

Ben studied her for a moment, then turned to the boys. "Hey fellas, would y'all mind doing me a favor? I haven't collected eggs yet today. Think you could handle that important job?"

Ralph's eyes widened. "By ourselves?"

"Sure thing. Ms. Pickles knows the way. Just be gentle with those hens." Ben pointed toward the chicken coop. "Basket's hanging right inside the door."

Alan nodded, taking his brother's hand. "Come on, Ralph."

Maggie watched them go, Ms. Pickles trotting alongside, until they disappeared around the corner of the barn. The evening air hung heavy between them, filled with the weight of unspoken words.

"Whatever it is," Ben said quietly, "you can tell me."

Maggie's hands trembled as she extended the folder. "I found this at the town office. I wasn't snooping. I was researching something for the bakery... and this was in the same file."

Ben took it, his brow furrowed. "What is it?"

"Just... look."

He opened the folder and unfolded the paper inside. His eyes scanned the document, widening as they moved down the page. The color drained from his face.

"This can't be right," he whispered. His finger traced his father's name, then the property description—his property. "Where did you get this?"

"County records." Maggie wrapped her arms around herself. "It's a deed transfer for half your land, Ben. Signed by your father."

Ben shook his head, staring at his father's signature. Samuel Reeves. The handwriting was shaky but unmistakable.

"What is this?" he breathed, his voice hollow. "Is this actually real?"

"He wouldn't have sold that land." Ben's voice hardened as his fingers tightened on the paper. "He made me swear I'd never sell it. Said it was our legacy—the only thing worth passing down."

The porch boards creaked beneath his shifting weight. Twilight shadows lengthened across the yard, darkness creeping in like the truth that could no longer hide.

"I thought the same thing," Maggie said quietly. "But the date, Ben. Look at the date."

Ben's eyes flicked to the corner of the document. His jaw tightened. "Three months ago. After his stroke."

"When he couldn't speak clearly. When his right side was paralyzed."

Ben's breathing quickened. "Where exactly did you find this? And when?" His voice rose with each word, the paper trembling in his grip. "How long have you known about this?"

Maggie stepped back, defensive. "It was in the property record archives. I was researching permits for the bakery expansion. I saw your family name and..." She swallowed hard. "I've had it about a week."

"A week?" Ben's eyes flashed. "You've known for a week and said nothing? We sat at that table—" he jabbed his finger toward the house, "—breaking bread together, and you kept this buried?"

"I didn't know what to do with it!" Maggie's voice cracked. "I was trying to figure out what it meant, if it was even real. I didn't want to hurt you without cause."

"Without cause?" Ben laughed bitterly. "Half my farm might be gone, and you didn't think that was cause enough?"

A breeze stirred the leaves overhead, whispering like secrets finally coming to light. In the distance, they could hear Ralph's delighted laughter from the chicken coop.

"The truth always surfaces, Maggie," Ben said, his voice low and tight. "One way or another, what's hidden gets dragged into the light. I just didn't expect you'd be the one keeping me in the dark."

Ben paced the porch, the deed clutched in his fist. "You didn't trust me enough to tell me the truth?" His voice rose with each word. "You didn't think I could handle it?"

Maggie stood her ground despite the trembling in her knees. "That's not fair. I barely know you, Ben."

"You know me enough to sit at my table. Enough to let your boys run around my property." He gestured wildly toward the chicken coop. "But not enough to show me a document that affects everything I've worked for?"

"I was trying to protect you!" The words burst from her before she could stop them.

Ben's laugh was sharp as broken glass. "Protect me? By keeping me in the dark about my own land?" He stepped closer, eyes flashing. "What's your angle in all this, Maggie? What do you have to gain?"

"Gain? I'm not—"

"First you show up at my farm stand. Then you're suddenly interested in my property for the retreat. Now this deed appears, and you just happen to find it?" His voice dropped dangerously low. "Maybe you thought you..."

He stopped himself, jaw clenched tight. The accusation hung unfinished in the air between them.

Maggie felt the blood drain from her face. "Thought I what, Ben? Go ahead. Say it."

The sound of the boys' laughter floated across the yard, a jarring counterpoint to the tension crackling between them.

Chapter 27 – The Aftermath

"The sacrifices of God are a broken spirit: a broken and a contrite heart, O God, thou wilt not despise." Psalm 51:17 (KJV)

Maggie's spine straightened, her eyes flashing with a fire Ben hadn't seen before. Her hands balled into fists at her sides.

"My angle?" The words tore from her throat. "You think I get something out of this? You have no idea what secrets can do to a family. You know, like the one you fantasized about?" She jabbed a finger toward his chest. "You have no idea the scars it leaves behind. You haven't had to live through that kind of storm. You haven't had to bury the hurt to be able to survive just enough to make sure your kids are okay. This deed has nothing to do with me and mine. Don't go shootin' the messenger."

Ben stepped back as if she'd slapped him. "That's not fair—"

"Fair?" Maggie laughed, the sound sharp as a blade. "Was it fair when Roger walked out? Was it fair when he signed away his sons like they were furniture? Was it fair when I had to explain to my boys why Daddy wasn't coming home?" Her voice cracked. "Don't you dare talk to me about fair."

"This isn't about Roger," Ben growled, his shoulders hunching forward. "This is about you keeping secrets from me."

"Like your daddy kept secrets from you?" The words hung in the air between them.

Ben's face darkened. "Leave my father out of this."

"Why? He's the one who signed that paper. Not me." Maggie's voice rose. "I was trying to find the right time—"

"There is no right time to tell someone they're losing everything!" Ben slammed his palm against the porch railing. The old wood groaned in protest.

Maggie flinched but held her ground. "I know what it's like to have your world pulled out from under you. I was trying to spare you that feeling."

"By lying to me?" Ben's voice dropped dangerously low. "Just like Roger lied to you?"

The color drained from Maggie's face. "That's not the same thing."

"Isn't it? Keeping secrets? Deciding what I can and can't handle?" Ben's words tumbled out faster, sharper. "Maybe you're more like him than you think."

Maggie recoiled as if she'd been struck. The words hung between them, too cruel to take back, too painful to ignore.

"Maybe I was wrong," she whispered, her voice trembling with fury and hurt, "to believe what was between us was anything more than flirting. That it could maybe be a second chance."

Ben's jaw tightened, his eyes hard as flint. "Maybe I was wrong to believe someone could walk in and actually stay."

The silence that followed was deafening. In the distance, they could hear the boys' laughter fading as they approached with their basket of eggs.

"Alan! Ralph!" Maggie called, her voice cracking. "We're leaving. Now."

"But Mama, we just—" Alan appeared around the corner, his face falling when he saw her expression.

"Now." The word was final, brooking no argument.

The boys exchanged confused glances as Maggie hurried them toward the car, not even allowing them to say goodbye. Ben stood frozen on the porch, the crumpled deed still clutched in his fist, watching them go.

"Mama, why are we—" Ralph started.

"Not now," she cut him off, voice tight as she buckled them in.

The car engine roared to life. Maggie backed out of the drive without a backward glance, gravel spitting beneath her tires.

Ben watched until the taillights disappeared down the road. Then something inside him snapped. He tore across the yard toward the barn, the screen door slamming behind him.

Inside the barn's shadowy interior, he fell to his knees on the hay-strewn floor. His fingers dug into his scalp, a strangled sound escaping his throat.

"Why?" he demanded of the empty air. "What does this mean? What more are You going to throw at me, Father?"

Ms. Pickles appeared in the doorway, whining softly at the distress in her master's voice.

"Why dangle her in front of me?" Ben's voice broke as he looked up toward the rafters. "Why show me what a family could be, if they weren't meant to be mine?"

The barn offered no answers, only the soft rustling of hay and the distant call of crickets beginning their evening song.

Maggie's hands shook on the steering wheel the entire drive home. She didn't cry. Not yet. She spoke in clipped sentences to the boys, answering their confused questions with half-truths about Ben needing time alone.

"But we didn't even say goodbye," Ralph protested, his voice small in the backseat.

"Sometimes goodbyes have to wait," she managed, her throat tight.

She made it through dinner—frozen pizza that tasted like cardboard—and through bath time. She read their bedtime story with a mechanical voice that didn't rise and fall with the adventure like it usually did. Alan watched her with knowing eyes that were too old for his nine years, but he said nothing.

When the house finally fell silent, Maggie closed her bedroom door and sank to her knees beside the bed. The moonlight spilled through the curtains, illuminating her collection of butterfly figurines on the dresser—delicate creatures frozen mid-flight, free yet immobile.

Only then did she break.

The sobs came without warning, ripping from her chest with such force that she pressed her face into the quilt to muffle the sound. Her shoulders heaved as weeks of hope crumbled into dust.

"I knew," she gasped between sobs. "I knew this would happen."

She'd expected his anger, prepared for it even. But preparation hadn't dulled the pain. This cut deeper than Roger's betrayal—because with Ben, she'd started to believe again. Started to trust.

As her tears slowed, other emotions surfaced. Relief washed through her that the secret was finally out. Then guilt crashed down—she should have told him sooner. Shame burned her cheeks when she remembered the words she'd hurled at him, barbed and aimed to wound.

"He has every right not to forgive me," she whispered into the darkness. "I deserved his anger."

The burden of the secret was gone, but in its place sat the weight of regret. And beneath it all, a deep sadness that Ben now faced yet another storm alone.

Maggie wiped her face with trembling fingers and looked up toward the ceiling.

""God..." Her voice cracked. "I brought fear to that conversation. Not faith. I made him my enemy instead of my brother in Christ." Maggie's shoulders trembled with the weight of her confession. "I was so afraid of being hurt again, I couldn't see past my own scars. Instead of trusting You to guard my heart, I built walls that kept out the very blessing You were trying to give me." She pressed her palm against her chest, feeling the rapid beat of her heart beneath her fingertips. "How many times will I have to learn this lesson before it finally takes root?"

The words tumbled out in a broken prayer. She asked God to stand beside Ben, to walk with him through this storm, to guide his steps when the path seemed impossible to navigate. She thanked Him for the precious moments she and Ben had shared, however brief—those quiet conversations by the fence line, the warmth in his eyes when he looked at her children, the way his calloused hand had felt against hers when he'd helped her from the tractor. Each memory was a treasure she hadn't expected to find in her guarded heart.

"Bless him, Lord. Keep him," she whispered, her voice barely audible even to herself. "Even if he's not meant to be mine. Even if he can never forgive me. Guard his tender heart through whatever trials lie ahead." A tear slipped down her cheek as she clasped her hands tighter, the words flowing from someplace deep and vulnerable within her soul. "Watch over him when I cannot."

Her final prayer came as a whisper, born from the deepest part of her heart: "And I ask you Father, teach me to forgive Roger, for what he did to me and what he did to Alan and Ralph. Whether you meant Ben for me or not, I know I can't truly love another until I can forgive those who have trespassed against me. Teach me how to love without defense." The words trembled on her lips, fragile yet powerful, like a single flame in darkness. She hadn't meant to speak them aloud, but there they were—a confession of her greatest fear and deepest longing, offered up to the night sky and the God who had sustained her through every storm.

In the dimness of the barn, Ben's anger erupted. He grabbed a wrench from his workbench and hurled it across the space. It clattered against the far wall, sending a startled bird fluttering from the rafters. Ms. Pickles, unfazed by his outburst, padded over and rested her graying muzzle on his boot.

"What am I supposed to do now?" he asked the empty barn.

The loyal dog offered no answer, just steady companionship as she had through every hardship since he was eighteen.

Ben collapsed onto a three-legged stool, elbows on knees, head in hands. The fury that had propelled him here was draining away, leaving something worse in its wake—clarity.

"I forgot the boys were in the house," he whispered, shame washing over him. The memory of Alan's confused face as they were rushed to the car stabbed at his conscience. Those boys had already lost one man who was supposed to care for them. Now he'd given them a front-row seat to another man failing them. Another man losing control, throwing things, scaring them—just like their father had done before he walked out. Ben ran a hand over his face, the stubble rough against his calloused palm. Ms. Pickles nudged his ankle, as if sensing the weight of his regret.

And Maggie. The things he'd said to her.

"I compared her to Roger." The words hung in the musty air, their ugliness undeniable. "After everything she's been through. I threw her ex in her face like some kind of weapon." Ben's voice cracked with self-disgust. "The one person who hurt her most in this world, and I used him against her like we were cut from the same cloth."

Ms. Pickles nudged his hand, and he absently scratched behind her ears.

"She was trying to protect me. And I—" His voice caught. "I automatically assumed the worst. Just like I did with Dad." He ran a hand through his hair, a bitter laugh escaping him. "It's like I've got this talent for finding betrayal where there's only love. Some kind of twisted gift for turning good intentions into ammunition against the people who care about me most."

The realization settled heavy on his shoulders. He'd accused Maggie of keeping secrets when he'd been doing the same—hiding his fears, his doubts, his struggle to trust God's plan. For months, he'd been wrestling with his faith in silence, questioning why the Lord would let his family's legacy crumble after generations of faithful stewardship. He'd smiled through church services while inwardly begging for answers that never seemed to come, all while judging her for the very same protective instinct he'd been clinging to himself.

"I blamed her for not trusting me," he said softly, "but I didn't give her a safe place to speak." He ran his fingers through his hair, frustration etched in the lines around his eyes. "I was so quick to demand honesty while building walls around my own fears. How could I expect her to open up when I kept my own heart locked away behind all that pride? That's not how trust works—not how love works, either."

Ben rose and moved to lean against the nearest stall rail. His head bowed, shoulders slumped beneath the weight of his regret.

"Lord, I thought I could carry this alone. I thought I had to." The prayer came rough and unpracticed, the words stumbling from his heart rather than his lips. "I've been so focused on not losing this land that I couldn't see what You might be trying to give me instead. I've been holding on so tight to what was that I nearly missed the blessing of what could be."

He drew a shuddering breath.

"Father, bless Maggie. Watch over her and those boys. Keep them safe." His voice dropped to a whisper. "Even if they're not meant to be mine." He swallowed hard against the lump forming in his throat, fingers gripping the stall rail until his knuckles whitened. "And Lord... help me accept Your plan, whatever it might be. I'm tired of fighting this battle alone."

Ben stood in the barn for a long while, the silence broken only by Ms. Pickles' occasional whine. Eventually, he trudged back to the house. The dinner he'd prepared—a roast with vegetables from his garden—sat untouched on the counter untouched.

"A broken spirit," he murmured, remembering Sunday's sermon. "That's what I've got now, Lord. A broken and contrite heart."

He began clearing the table setting for one, methodically stacking the unused plate and silverware that had awaited a meal never to be shared. The lonely fork clinked against the ceramic as he gathered everything, his movements slow and deliberate in the quiet kitchen.

"I've been so proud, thinking I could handle everything myself." Ben stacked the dishes with careful hands. "But I can't. Not the farm, not my father's choices, not my feelings for Maggie."

He scraped the food into containers, methodically washing each pot and pan.

"Not my will, but Yours, Father." The words came easier now, humility replacing his earlier anger. "Help me forgive—my father, myself. Help me go back to her changed."

Across town, Maggie rose from her knees, feeling emptied yet somehow lighter. She padded down the hallway to check on her boys.

Ralph lay sprawled across his bed, one arm flung over his head. She gently tucked the blanket around him and brushed a kiss against his forehead.

In Alan's room, she found him curled on his side, clutching the sketch he'd made of Ms. Pickles. Maggie's heart squeezed painfully. She sat on the edge of his bed, stroking his hair.

"I've been so afraid," she whispered, though he couldn't hear. "So afraid of being hurt again that I couldn't see the gift God was offering."

She kissed his temple, inhaling the scent of shampoo and little boy.

"A broken spirit and a contrite heart," she murmured, remembering Pastor's words from weeks ago. "That's all I have to offer now, Lord. Take it and make something beautiful, if it be Your will."

She walked to the window, looking out at the night sky. Somewhere across town, Ben was under these same stars.

"Not my will but Yours," she prayed. "Help me forgive—Roger, myself. Help me go back changed."

The house settled into nighttime stillness. But in the quiet aftermath of their separate prayers, something sacred had begun to shift.

Chapter 28 – Table for Three

"A friend loveth at all times, and a brother is born for adversity." Proverbs 17:17 (KJV)

Maggie pressed her forehead against the breakroom window, watching a mockingbird hop across the clinic's back fence. The afternoon sun cast long shadows across the parking lot, but she barely registered the beauty of the late summer day.

"You've been staring at that same spot for ten minutes."

Maggie startled at WonderVet's voice. "Sorry. Just..." She gestured vaguely at the sink full of coffee mugs she'd meant to wash.

"Thinking about Reeves?" He leaned against the doorframe, concern etched across his tired face.

"That obvious, huh?" She managed a weak smile and turned back to the sink, mechanically rinsing a mug.

"Only to everyone who's walked through the door today" his voice was gentle. "Mrs. Peterson's cat is named Whiskers, not Pickles."

Maggie winced. "I called her cat Pickles?"

"Three times." Doc squeezed her shoulder. "Why don't you head out early? Lila can handle the front desk."

Alone again, Maggie dried her hands and pulled out her phone. She scrolled to Ben's name, thumb hovering over the call button. Three days since their fight, and the silence between them stretched like a chasm. She stared at his contact photo—Ben grinning beside Ms. Pickles, taken the day they'd fixed the chicken coop together.

Her finger slid away, scrolling up to Ginny's name instead.

"Hey Ginny..." Her voice came out shakier than intended. "Y'all eating supper at Mom's tonight? Mind if I crash?"

"Always, Magpie." Ginny's warm voice flowed through the speaker. "You bring the dessert, I'll cook up the comfort food."

Maggie twisted a loose thread on her sleeve, hesitating. "Can Martin come too?"

There was a brief pause, then Ginny's knowing reply: "Wouldn't be a sibling summit without him."

The Cunningham family home sat nestled among oak trees that had witnessed three generations grow up beneath their branches. Maggie pulled into the gravel driveway, the butterscotch pie she'd picked up from Kneadful Things test kitchen balanced carefully on her lap.

Lorraine Cunningham appeared on the porch before Maggie could even knock, arms already open wide.

"There's my girl," she said, enfolding Maggie in a hug that smelled of lavender and home. She pulled back, cupping Maggie's face between weathered hands. "You look tired around the eyes, sugar. Not sleeping?"

"I'm fine, Momma," Maggie murmured, surrendering the pie.

Inside, Alan and Ralph had already made themselves at home. Ralph sprawled on the living room floor with Grandpa Henry's collection of polished rocks, arranging them by color. Alan sat cross-legged at Henry's feet, listening intently as the older man explained the workings of an antique pocket watch.

"There's my butterfly," Henry called, his face lighting up at the sight of Maggie. He'd called her that since she was a toddler, flitting from one thing to the next, never still for long.

The kitchen smelled of roast chicken, sage, and fresh-baked biscuits. Ginny stood at the stove in a faded apron that read "Kiss the Cook—She Needs Encouragement," her dark hair twisted into a messy bun as she stirred gravy with focused intensity.

"Two more minutes," she announced without looking up. "Martin texted he's on his way."

As if summoned, the back door creaked open. Martin's heavy boots thumped against the mat as he brushed them off.

"Evenin', family," he called, hanging his cap on the hook by the door. His eyes found Maggie, and a teasing grin spread across his face. "How's it going with the new boyfriend? Is he treating my baby sister right?"

Maggie shot him a panicked look but said nothing, praying he got the message later.

Around the dinner table, conversation flowed easily between bites of tender chicken and fluffy biscuits. Lorraine asked carefully neutral questions about work and weather, clearly restraining herself from prying. Maggie pushed food around her plate, contributing little beyond "pass the salt" and "yes, it's delicious."

The boys, however, had no such reservations.

"Ben showed us how to fix a chicken coop," Ralph announced, mouth full of mashed potatoes.

"And Ms. Pickles knows how to high-five," Alan added, demonstrating with his hand.

"We were supposed to stay for dinner at his farm," Ralph continued, "but we left real quick instead."

Alan's fork paused halfway to his mouth. "I heard Momma crying in her room that night," he said quietly, eyes downcast. "After we got home from Ben's."

A weighted silence fell over the table. Lorraine's hand trembled slightly as she set down her water glass. Even Ralph, usually bursting with energy, seemed to shrink in his chair, his small fingers fidgeting with the edge of his napkin. No one seemed to know what to say, the only sound was the soft ticking of the kitchen clock and the occasional clink of silverware against china.

After dinner, Maggie slipped out to the back porch with a glass of sweet tea. The screen door closed behind her with a familiar creak as she settled into the old porch swing, its chains protesting softly. Her eyes drifted to the Whirly Flutterby standing sentinel in the yard—a metal garden spinner her father had installed when she was just a girl.

Once painted in cheerful pastels, now sun-faded and weather-worn, it whirred to life as the evening breeze stirred. Its butterfly wings caught the golden hour light, scattering shimmer across the weathered porch railings. Crickets began their nightly chorus from the tall grass beyond the yard. The mingled scents of freshly cut grass and honeysuckle hung heavy in the humid air as lightning bugs rose from the ground like slow-motion sparks, blinking their secret codes around and through the spinner's turning blades.

The screen door squeaked again. Ginny appeared with a patchwork quilt draped over her arm, Martin close behind balancing a plate of leftover biscuits.

"Thought you might need these." Ginny settled beside Maggie on the swing, draping the quilt across their laps despite the summer warmth.

Martin lowered himself onto the porch steps, setting the biscuits between them. "Remember when I named that thing?" He nodded toward the spinner. "Couldn't say 'butterfly' right."

"You were six," Ginny smiled. "Kept calling it the 'Whirly Flutterby' and it stuck."

Maggie's lips curved upward at the memory. The three siblings fell quiet, watching the spinner catch the last rays of sunlight. The swing creaked gently beneath their weight.

"So." Ginny's voice was soft but direct. "What happened?"

Maggie's fingers tightened around her glass. "I found something." The words came haltingly at first. "A deed. Ben's father sold half their land years ago." She described discovering the document, her panic, confronting Ben with it. "The second I handed it over, I saw it all unraveling. His face just... shut down."

"Did he explain?" Ginny asked, her tone gentle.

"He tried, but I—" Maggie's voice caught. "I didn't really listen."

Martin leaned forward, elbows on his knees. "What'd he say about the deed? Was it legit?"

"He seemed shocked. Said his dad never mentioned selling anything."

"So you bolted." Martin's bluntness made her wince.

"I panicked," she admitted. "I just grabbed the boys and left."

Martin shook his head, a wry smile forming. "You've been picking some winners lately, Maggs. First Roger, now this." He reached for a biscuit. "Never figured Ben to act like that. Maybe I should start picking your boyfriends."

Ginny snorted. "Right, because your love life's such a success story. Divorced, co-parenting with Julie, who still calls you 'the disappointment' to your face." She nudged Maggie. "Maybe we should find another matchmaker."

Despite everything, Maggie laughed through fresh tears. "Y'all are the worst. I came here for sympathy, and you're making jokes about my broken heart."

245

"Nah," Martin grinned, reaching up to squeeze her ankle. "You came because we love you, even with that stubborn streak of yours that other folks find endearing for some odd reason."

The laughter faded, leaving a comfortable silence. Martin's expression turned serious as he moved to sit beside Maggie on the steps.

"You're still carrying Roger around like he left yesterday," he said quietly. "Dragging that weight everywhere you go." He picked at a splinter on the porch rail. "Remember what you told me when Julie was sleeping with her yoga instructor and I couldn't figure out how to be a weekend dad?"

Maggie looked away. "That was different."

"Was it? You said I didn't have to prove I could handle everything alone." He caught her gaze. "When did you decide that advice was for everyone but you?" His voice softened. "Feels like you don't trust me enough to share your burdens, Maggs. I'd like to change that."

Ginny reached across the swing. "You've been in survival mode so long you've forgotten what it's like to share the load." She smiled gently. "Ben seemed ready to carry some of that weight with you."

Maggie's tears returned, hot and silent. "I wanted to believe in him so badly. I wanted to explore whatever this thing is between us." Her voice cracked. "But the second it started feeling real—"

"You ran," Martin finished. He moved to the swing, wrapping an arm around her shoulders and pulling her close. "That's not fear, Sis. That's grief." His voice was rough with emotion. "And you can't outrun grief. Lord knows I tried. You gotta walk through it. Ideally hand-in-hand with someone strong enough to pull you through when you're weary and thinking about stopping."

Ginny squeezed Maggie's hand. "We know you, Magpie. And we're proud of you." She brushed a strand of hair from Maggie's tear-stained face. "You don't have to earn love from anyone. Not from us, not from him."

Maggie leaned her head on Ginny's shoulder, watching the Whirly Flutterby catch the last light of day. "What if I broke things beyond fixing?" she whispered. "Is there any hope?"

Martin looked out across the darkening yard. "There's always hope. Especially if he's the man you think he is. And if God wills it to be."

After Ginny and Martin went inside, Maggie remained on the porch swing, its gentle creak keeping time with her thoughts. The night had deepened, stars pricking through the velvet darkness one by one. The moon hung low, casting silver light across the yard where fireflies still performed their lazy dance.

She pulled the quilt tighter around her shoulders. The boys had fallen asleep hours ago—Alan sprawled across his grandfather's lap in the recliner, Ralph curled up on the sofa with his collection of rocks still clutched in one small hand. She'd decided not to wake them. They'd be thrilled to wake up at Grandma's, helping make those famous buttermilk biscuits come morning.

The Whirly Flutterby caught a breeze, spinning lazily in the moonlight. Its metal wings reflected silver, creating a hypnotic pattern of light and shadow across the yard. Maggie watched, mesmerized by its constant, faithful motion—never stopping, never faltering, spinning through storms and sunshine alike.

Peace settled over her like dew, cooling the heated edges of her worries. The night sounds surrounded her—crickets chirping their steady rhythm, an owl's gentle hoot from the woods beyond, the rustle of leaves in the night breeze. They seemed to whisper reassurances, as if the whole night conspired to comfort her wounded heart.

"Thank you," she whispered, eyes lifting toward the star-strewn sky. "Thank you for family who tells the truth even when it hurts." Her voice caught. "For this place to turn to when everything falls apart. For people to lean on when I can't stand alone."

She closed her eyes, fingers tracing the worn pattern of the quilt—the same one that had covered her through childhood fevers and teenage heartbreaks.

"I want Ben to be that person too," she admitted softly, the words barely audible even to herself. "Someone I can turn to. Someone I can lean on." Her voice steadied with resolve. "Show me what to do, Lord. Show me how to make this right."

Chapter 29 – The Spaces Between

"To every thing there is a season, and a time to every purpose under the heaven."
Ecclesiastes 3:1 (KJV)

The bell above the door at Bless Your Hair! jingled as another customer entered, adding to the mid-morning chaos. Hair dryers whirred, the smell of perm solution hung in the air, and Daisy Parks moved between stations with practiced efficiency.

Mavis Holbrook sat rigid in the swivel chair, fanning herself with a church bulletin. Her freshly rolled curlers bobbed as she shook her head. "I'm just saying what everyone's thinking," she announced, voice pitched to carry over the salon noise. "My brother Vernon's done more for this town than anyone gives him credit for."

"That's the truth," agreed Pauline from under the dryer hood. "The man built this town's economy!"

Mavis nodded vigorously. "Without Tuttle Bank, half these businesses wouldn't exist. But does anyone thank him? No, they're too busy criticizing his foreclosure policies. Like it's his fault people can't manage their finances."

Letty Miller, waiting her turn in the next chair, leaned forward. "Speaking of poor financial choices, did y'all hear about Maggie Cunningham and that Reeves boy?"

"Lord have mercy." Mavis rolled her eyes dramatically. "Now she's got her sons tangled up with that Reeves boy. You'd think she'd learn after Roger. None of them Donahues are worth nothing."

"Didn't Roger run off with that notary gal from Vernon's office?" Letty snorted, adjusting her glasses.

"Trixie," Mavis confirmed, lowering her voice to a stage whisper. "Had that little star notary stamp she was so proud of. Carried it in her purse like it was a diamond ring."

"Hmm." Letty tapped her chin thoughtfully. "You know, I heard Frank Mercer lost his farm because of something to do with the notarization of his deed when his daddy went home to Glory." She tilted her head. "I wonder if Trixie was his notary."

A moment of silence fell across the salon before Mavis waved her hand dismissively. "Frank was probably behind on payments anyway. Vernon doesn't foreclose without reason."

Laughter rippled through the salon as Daisy moved to adjust Mavis's curlers. The clicking of curling irons resumed, but something darker lingered beneath the casual cruelty of their words—something that felt like secrets waiting to surface.

Sunlight streamed through the windows of Percolating Grace Café, catching dust motes in golden beams. The morning rush had dwindled to a comfortable hum of quiet conversations and the occasional clink of silverware against plates. In the corner booth by the window, Daisy, finished with her morning shift at the Bless Your Hair!, leaned forward, her lavender-streaked hair catching the light as she turned the page of a leather-bound notebook.

"Listen to this," she said, her eyes bright with admiration. "Dexter wrote this just last week." She cleared her throat and read in a reverent tone: "'A foundation isn't just poured in concrete—it's built on character, sacrifice, and prayer.'"

Treva Walker exhaled heavily, stirring her coffee without looking up. Dark circles shadowed her eyes, evidence of another night spent balancing books after Harry had gone to bed.

"That man wrote more wisdom than a seminary professor," she murmured. "Greg said he's been writing down everything for Jake to have when..." She let the sentence trail off, unwilling to finish it.

Brittany Reeves pushed a plate of lemon scones toward the center of the table. "Speaking of wisdom, I'm worried about Maggie. I think she's punishing herself for what happened with Ben."

"Aren't we all, in some way?" Treva rubbed her temple, where a headache had been threatening all morning. "Speaking of punishment—the new preacher's supposed to be introduced Sunday."

Brittany's eyebrows shot up, a smirk playing at the corners of her mouth. "What, you got preacher trauma?"

Treva lifted her mug to her lips, avoiding eye contact. She took a long, deliberate sip of her coffee, saying nothing.

Daisy reached across the table, patting Treva's hand with a gentle touch. Her voice softened, earnest and sweet. "Maybe God's putting people back where they belong."

Luke Sharp stood in the center of his Nashville apartment, surrounded by the ordered chaos of his life in boxes. The afternoon sun slanted through half-empty bookshelves, catching dust motes disturbed by his packing.

He uncapped a pen and drew a firm line through "Resign from firm" on his meticulous to-do list. The partners had been surprised—a senior position abandoned for small-town accounting seemed incomprehensible to them. They didn't understand that some callings ran deeper than career ambition.

Luke's gaze drifted to the framed photograph on his desk—the four Sharp kids sprawled on the porch steps of the family farm. Clara with her wild curls, Luke himself looking serious even then, Eli making rabbit ears behind Caleb's head. Taken the summer before Clara left for college, before everything changed.

"Time to go home," he murmured, carefully wrapping the frame in tissue paper before placing it in a box.

He settled at his desk, scrolling through spreadsheets of Willow Creek's economic data. His brow furrowed as he compared the figures from the past three years.

"That doesn't make sense."

The numbers told a story that contradicted what he'd been hearing. Population had remained stable. Farm revenue was actually up fifteen percent since the retreat opened. New businesses had launched—Brittany's farm-to-table venture, Mark's warehouse, expansions at Kneadful Things.

So why were foreclosures and bank liens climbing at such an alarming rate?

Luke pulled up the Tuttle Bank loan records he'd quietly obtained through a former classmate who worked there. He scratched notes in the margins of his printouts, circling interest rates, payment schedules, and dates.

"Something's off," he muttered, noting how many foreclosures happened within months of deed transfers or refinancing. All with the same notary stamp.

Working methodically, he copied the files to an encrypted drive and shut his laptop. "I'll find it."

Luke rifled through a stack of papers, searching for his phone. Finding it beneath his accounting journal, he dialed a familiar number.

"Sheriff's office, Wade speaking."

"Hey, Wade, got a few minutes?"

"I'm scarfing down lunch, but shoot." The sound of a sandwich wrapper crinkling came through the line.

Luke took a deep breath. "I've been checking out the financial scene in The Creek, and something doesn't add up..."

The porch swing creaked rhythmically as Jake settled beside his father, placing the tall glass of sweet tea within Dexter's reach. Late afternoon sunlight filtered through the oak branches, casting dappled shadows across the weathered boards.

"You shoulda seen Mavis's face when the town council approved Brittany's permit," Jake chuckled. "Looked like she'd swallowed a lemon whole. And get this—Clara caught Alan teaching Noah how to spit watermelon seeds off the retreat dock. Those boys were hittin' targets thirty feet out."

Dexter's laugh turned into a weak cough. He waved off Jake's concern, taking a careful sip of tea.

"Doc Sam stopped by the site yesterday," Jake continued. "Says Bettina's little one is growing right on schedule. She's hoping for a girl, but Jim's convinced it's another boy."

Jake fell silent, noticing how the evening light accentuated the hollows beneath his father's cheekbones. Dexter's weathered hands trembled slightly as he set down his glass.

"Feels like I'm fading just as the town's waking up again," Dexter murmured, his gaze fixed on the distant tree line.

Jake swallowed hard. "Business is solid, Dad. The crews are loyal as ever. Mark's running the warehouse expansion, and the retreat's thriving. Clara says they're booked solid through Christmas with camps for foster kids, and programs for abuse survivors."

Dexter nodded slowly, then gestured toward the side table. "Open that manila folder the lawyer brought over earlier. That shingle-hanger says the paperwork's all in order for the Retreat property." His voice softened. "Keep that handy for when I go home to be with your Mother and Princess."

Jake's fingers trembled as he opened the folder, skimming the legal documents without really seeing them. "Dad, I don't know if I can—" He paused, struggling to find words. "What if I can't fill your shoes? The company, the crews—they respect you. I'm just—"

"You're a Landry," Dexter interrupted, his voice suddenly stronger. "It's in the blood. You don't have to do it like I did, son. It's your turn to leave your mark. God won't lead you wrong. Trust in Him always." He reached for Jake's hand. "Landry and Son Construction was built for you, Son. That's why I brought you along with me, so you would be ready when my time comes."

Dexter's eyes, though tired, burned with conviction. "Sons never feel like they've had enough time with their father when the end nears. That's natural. But you are ready, Jacob Andrew Landry. Me and your Ma, we made sure you would be."

Jake blinked back tears as his father continued.

"Don't doubt yourself, Son. Just keep trying to be the best man you can be, every day of your life. When you make mistakes, fix 'em. When you wrong someone, make amends. Try your best not to lose your cool and curb your cussing. And you gotta keep going to church on the regular like I promised your Ma."

Jake clutched the folder to his chest. "I will, Dad. I promise."

They sat in silence as the sun dipped low behind the hills, casting long shadows across the porch. Neither spoke, but in the space between them hung a lifetime of love and the bittersweet knowledge that their time together in this world was drawing to a close.

Maggie stepped through the doorway of Cabin Mockingbird, where the sounds of teenage laughter mingled with the rustling of backpacks being stuffed with clothes and crafts. The scent of pine-scented cleaner hung in the air as counselors directed their charges in the cleanup before the last days at camp.

Hector, clipboard in hand, checked off rooms as they passed inspection. "Ms. Cunningham, Cabin Robin is all clear. Anthony's got the boys stacking up their fishing gear."

"Thanks, Hector. You've been a godsend this week." Maggie smiled, noticing how the young man stood taller at her praise.

She made her way to the small desk in the corner that had become her makeshift command center for the past week. A folded piece of construction paper sat propped against her mug of cold coffee. Opening it, she found a crayon drawing of two vibrant butterflies—one purple, one orange—soaring above a green hill. Beneath them, in careful block letters: "FROM ROSITA AND LOQUITA."

Maggie's throat tightened as she traced the butterflies with her fingertip. These girls had arrived at camp with downcast eyes and hunched shoulders. Now they drew themselves with wings.

"Do you like it?"

Maggie turned to find Loquita standing in the doorway, her usually guarded expression softened with hope.

"I love it," Maggie said, opening her arms as the teen crossed the room and wrapped her in a fierce hug.

"Thanks for letting us be brave here," Loquita whispered against Maggie's shoulder, her voice catching.

Maggie squeezed her tighter, remembering the girl's hesitation on the first day of camp, how she'd refused to join the swimming activities until Maggie sat with her on the dock, feet dangling in the water, talking about nothing and everything until Loquita was ready.

A small voice spoke up from behind them. "I don't wanna go home. I like who I am here."

Julian, a quiet ten-year-old who'd blossomed during the week, stood clutching his backpack straps, eyes fixed on the floor.

Maggie knelt down to his level, gently tilting his chin up. "You take that version of yourself with you. And you come back next year, okay?"

Julian nodded solemnly, the ghost of a smile touching his lips.

A harried voice called from the bathroom, breaking the moment. "Who has the mop? There's water everywhere!"

Twilight cast long shadows across the Crop 'Til You Drop Farmstand as Brittany tacked another blueprint to the wall. The wooden structure at the end of the structure hummed with potential—half-finished shelves lined the walls, sawdust still scattered across the floor. Carving out her own space, staking her ownership in building the Reeves family businesses, a long held dream come true. A gentle breeze carried the scent of freshly cut lumber through the open windows.

"The sandwiches need prime real estate." Brittany jabbed her finger at the blueprint. "Front and center, where customers first walk in."

Treva huffed, blowing a stray curl from her forehead. "Your fancy cucumber-watercress nonsense can go on the side wall. The mini-pies need the front counter—impulse buys."

"Impulse buys?" Brittany snorted, adjusting her bandana. "Like people just accidentally purchase pie?"

"They do when it's my pie." Treva crossed her arms, her flour-dusted apron evidence of a long day at Kneadful Things before coming to help. "Besides, we need space for the bread loaves, and the sweet tea jugs need their own section by the register."

"What about the pre-made salads? And the snack veggies?" Brittany countered, rearranging sticky notes on the counter layout. "People want healthy options."

"Put 'em by your fancy sandwiches," Treva said, waving her hand dismissively. "Health food corner."

Brittany's eyes narrowed playfully. "You're just mad 'cause I won't let you sell those pickled deviled eggs."

A beat of silence, then both women burst into laughter—the kind that comes after too many hours of work, when exhaustion transforms everything into hilarity.

"They're a delicacy!" Treva protested between giggles, wiping tears from her eyes.

"They're an abomination," Brittany countered, leaning against the counter to catch her breath.

Their laughter faded into comfortable silence. The last rays of sunlight filtered through the windows, painting golden stripes across the unfinished wood.

Treva ran her hand over the counter, feeling the grain beneath her fingertips. "I never thought I'd get to build something like this," she said softly. "I thought I forfeited all my dreams."

Brittany paused her blueprint adjustments, studying Treva's profile in the fading light. "You didn't," she replied, her voice gentle but firm. "You just found new ones."

Crickets chirped a nighttime symphony as Maggie settled into the porch swing, wrapping herself in the faded quilt her grandmother had made. The moon hung low and full, casting silver light across her backyard where the boys' bicycles lay abandoned from earlier adventures. Inside, Alan and Ralph slept peacefully, exhausted from a day of helping at the retreat.

Maggie's fingers hovered over Clara's name on her phone screen before she finally pressed call. Three rings later, Clara's warm voice answered.

"Hey, you. I was just thinking about you."

Maggie took a deep breath, the swing creaking beneath her as she pushed off gently with one foot. "I really messed up, Clara."

"With Ben?"

"With everything." Maggie's voice caught. "I thought I'd dealt with it all—Roger leaving, the cheating, the money problems. But seeing Ben with those land papers, something in me just... snapped." She brushed away a tear. "I said terrible things. Things he didn't deserve."

The night air felt cool against her damp cheeks as she continued. "I convinced myself I was protecting my heart, but I was just punishing him for what Roger did. Ben has never been anything but kind and honest with me."

Clara remained silent, listening.

"I keep waiting for men to leave," Maggie confessed, her voice barely above a whisper. "Even when they give me no reason to think they will. I can't stop expecting the worst. I ruined something good because I can't trust anymore."

The swing creaked rhythmically, filling the momentary silence.

"Ben isn't Roger," Clara said finally, her voice gentle but firm. "And you're not that same girl anymore, Maggie."

"I want to believe that."

"Then start by believing in Ben. He looks at you like you hung the moon."

They talked quietly for nearly an hour—about fear and faith, about learning to trust again, about the courage it takes to let someone new into a broken heart. Words flowed between them like they had when they were girls, soul-deep and healing.

"I should let you go," Maggie said eventually, noticing the time. "Ethan probably thinks I've kidnapped you by phone."

Clara laughed softly. "He's busy drawing up plans for the new counseling center. But Maggie?"

"Hmm?"

"Call Ben tomorrow. Just talk to him."

Maggie nodded, though Clara couldn't see her. "I'm so glad you finally came home. I really needed you, friend. Thank you for not giving up on me."

After they hung up, Maggie stayed on the swing, the gentle rocking soothing her troubled heart. She pulled her journal from beneath the quilt and opened it to a fresh page. The butterfly pen Clara had given her at the retreat glinted in the moonlight as she placed it on the open page.

"Lord," she whispered, "help me be brave enough to try again."

She wrote slowly, pouring her heart onto the page, working through her fears and hopes. When she finished, a sense of peace settled over her that had been missing for too long.

Maybe second chances don't always arrive at once, she thought. Maybe they unfold, one small moment of courage at a time.

Chapter 30 – The Boys' Prayer

"If we confess our sins, he is faithful and just to forgive us our sins, and to cleanse us from all unrighteousness." 1 John 1:9 (KJV)

Sometimes, the healing begins in silence.

Sometimes it begins in the prayers of little boys,

in dog-eared Bibles cracked open in barns,

in peace offerings left on porches,

and hands folded in the dark.

This is the grace that follows confession—

the space where God moves.

Maggie's alarm startled her from a fitful sleep. The red numbers glowed 5:30 AM—earlier than necessary, but sleep had abandoned her hours ago. She'd tossed and turned, replaying her harsh words to Ben, seeing the hurt flash across his face before anger replaced it.

She swung her legs over the side of the bed and sat there, Bible in hand. The leather was worn at the corners, pages dog-eared from years of seeking comfort between its covers. She turned to a passage her mother had underlined years ago.

"If we confess our sins, he is faithful and just to forgive us our sins, and to cleanse us from all unrighteousness."

Her finger traced the words. Confession. Forgiveness. Cleansing. Three steps that seemed so simple on paper, yet mountainous in practice.

The house creaked around her as she padded to the kitchen. She mixed pancake batter mechanically, her mind elsewhere. The heaviness in her chest had nothing to do with lack of sleep.

"Morning, Mama." Alan appeared in the doorway, hair mussed, eyes watchful. He'd been doing that lately—studying her face for clues, as if trying to gauge the emotional weather of the day.

"Morning, sunshine." She forced brightness into her voice. "Pancakes okay?"

He nodded, pulling plates from the cabinet without being asked. Such a little man already.

Ralph thundered down the stairs moments later, energy crackling around him despite the early hour. He climbed onto his chair, immediately reaching for the syrup.

"Are we still going to see Mr. Reeves again?" Ralph asked, cutting through the careful quiet Maggie had constructed.

The question hung in the air. Alan's hands stilled, his eyes darting between his mother and brother.

Maggie set the spatula down and took a deep breath. "I hope so. But only when we're ready—and kind."

"You mean when you're ready?" Alan's voice was soft but direct, making Maggie wince.

"Yes," she admitted, confession settling heavy on her tongue. "I said some things I shouldn't have. I need to make it right first."

"Like when I broke Ms. Pickles' toy and had to say sorry?" Ralph asked, pancake halfway to his mouth.

"Exactly like that." Maggie nodded, throat tight. "God forgives us when we're truly sorry, but we still need to fix what we broke if we can."

After breakfast, Maggie sent the boys off to play at the Sharps' farm for the afternoon. Burle had promised to teach them how to fix a tractor, and Francine had pie-making planned afterward. The arrangement gave Maggie the space she needed—both to think and to act.

She'd spent the morning at work, mechanically filing charts and answering phones at the veterinary clinic. Doc had noticed her distraction but kindly said nothing beyond offering her an early departure. "Sometimes the heart needs tending more than paperwork," he'd said, patting her shoulder.

Now, driving down the winding country road toward Ben's farm, Maggie's hands gripped the steering wheel tightly. The afternoon sun filtered through the trees, dappling the road ahead with shifting patterns of light and shadow. She'd made this drive countless times over the past months, usually with anticipation bubbling in her chest. Today, there was only the heavy weight of regret.

She slowed as she approached the gravel drive, heart hammering. Ben's truck was nowhere in sight—likely he was out working the back fields. A small mercy. She wasn't ready to face him yet, not until she'd sorted through the tangle of emotions that had erupted during their argument.

Maggie parked behind the barn, out of view from the main road. She grabbed the brown paper bag from the passenger seat and walked the familiar path to the farmhouse porch, gravel crunching beneath her boots.

Ms. Pickles appeared from around the corner, her white coat gleaming in the sunlight. The dog paused, head tilted, before trotting over with her characteristic dignified gait.

"Hey, girl," Maggie whispered, kneeling to scratch behind the dog's ears. "I've missed you."

The porch steps creaked as Maggie climbed them. She placed the paper bag carefully by the door, making sure it wouldn't blow away. Inside was a bright blue rope toy—sturdier than the one that had sparked their first real conversation months ago—and a homemade dog biscuit shaped like a pickle, a private joke between her and Ben.

She tucked a folded note beneath the bag: "For Ms. Pickles. Tell her I'm sorry too."

Ms. Pickles watched Maggie drive away, her tail slowing to a thoughtful wag as the car disappeared down the lane. The dog settled on the porch beside the paper bag, assuming her self-appointed role as guardian of this unexpected delivery.

Ben trudged up from the back pasture, boots caked with mud and shoulders aching from mending fences since dawn. The morning sun had climbed high, promising another scorcher of a day. He wiped sweat from his brow with his forearm and squinted toward the house.

"Pickles, you still breathing?" he called out, spotting his faithful companion's white form on the porch.

The dog's ears perked up at his voice. She rose to her feet, tail sweeping in wide, excited arcs as she pawed at something near the door.

"What you got there, girl? Better not be another possum." Ben climbed the steps, noticing the brown paper bag. His pace slowed. He hadn't ordered anything, and deliveries usually went to the mailbox at the end of the drive.

Ms. Pickles nudged the bag with her nose, looking up at him with expectant eyes.

"Alright, alright." He crouched down, his knees popping in protest. The bag was light in his calloused hands. No name on it, just a folded note tucked underneath. His heart gave a peculiar lurch when he recognized the handwriting.

Ben unfolded the note, reading the simple message twice. "For Ms. Pickles. Tell her I'm sorry too."

He opened the bag slowly, pulling out the blue rope toy and the pickle-shaped dog treat. Ms. Pickles danced in place, her excitement palpable as she eyed the offerings.

Something tight in Ben's chest loosened. He ran a thumb over the careful stitching of the toy, remembering how Maggie had laughed the day Pickles destroyed her old one. How she'd promised to replace it someday.

She had remembered. Even after everything.

Ben exhaled slowly through his nose, a sound somewhere between resignation and relief. "She meant it," he whispered, more to himself than to Ms. Pickles, who was now gently taking the treat from his open palm. His calloused fingers brushed against the dog's soft muzzle, and he felt something inside him shift—like a door that had been jammed shut for years suddenly creaking open. The evening breeze ruffled through the porch screens, carrying with it the scent of approaching rain and possibilities he hadn't dared consider before.

After Ms. Pickles finished her treat, Ben sat on the porch steps for a long while, watching the horizon where storm clouds gathered in the distance. The air felt different—charged with something beyond the coming rain. He rubbed his jaw, feeling the stubble there, and made a decision.

Morning came with the scent of damp earth and possibility. Ben rose before dawn, pulled on his work clothes, and headed to the garden plots behind the house. The vegetables glistened with dew as he carefully selected the best of his harvest—plump tomatoes still warm from yesterday's sun, tender yellow squash, crisp greens that Brittany had taught him to grow in the shadier patch.

He worked methodically, filling a wicker basket that had belonged to his mother. Near the back door, he paused, then reached for a jar of his grandmother's pickle relish recipe that Brittany had helped him perfect last summer. He nestled it among the vegetables, a peace offering wrapped in memories.

In the kitchen, Brittany leaned against the counter, coffee mug in hand, watching him arrange and rearrange the contents of the basket. She'd arrived early to help with the farmers' market preparations, but found her brother already busy with this unexpected project.

"You're not grumbling today," she observed, head tilted. "You sick?"

Ben straightened, adjusting the checkered cloth over the basket's contents. The corner of his mouth twitched—not quite a smile, but the closest thing to it she'd seen in days.

"Nah," he said, voice rough from disuse. "Just... done wasting time with anger."

Brittany raised an eyebrow but said nothing, hiding her surprise behind her coffee mug. This was new territory—Ben voluntarily stepping away from his stubborn standoff.

The Percolating Grace Café hummed with morning activity. Steam hissed from the espresso machine as Darla, the owner, called out orders with practiced efficiency. The mismatched chairs scraped against worn wooden floors as the breakfast crowd settled in, trading gossip as freely as they passed cream and sugar.

Clara pushed through the door, balancing a large cardboard box from Kneadful Things. Francie followed behind with another, the scent of fresh-baked cinnamon rolls and apple turnovers announcing their arrival before they'd even reached the counter.

"Morning blessing has arrived," Clara called out, setting her box down with a small grunt.

Darla's face brightened. "Right on time! My regulars have been eyeing that empty pastry case something fierce."

As Clara helped arrange the pastries in the display case, she caught fragments of conversation from a nearby table.

"...saw her car leaving his place yesterday, driving like the devil himself was after her."

"Mmm-hmm. And he wasn't at the co-op meeting last night either. First time in months."

"Guess that farm boy and the vet's office girl are off again."

"Shame, really. Thought those two might actually make it."

Clara's hands stilled over a raspberry danish. She glanced toward the voices—two older women she recognized from church, their heads bent close together over steaming mugs.

Francie finished wiping flour from her hands and moved beside Clara, eyebrows raised in silent question.

Clara nodded toward the gossiping pair and murmured, "Let's get some coffee." She guided Francie to a quiet corner table.

"You heard that?" Clara asked once they were seated.

Francie nodded, stirring sugar into her coffee. "About Maggie and Ben? Lorraine mentioned something in passing yesterday when she dropped off eggs. Nothing of substance, mind you. Just that they'd had some kind of disagreement."

"Did she say what about?"

"No details. You know how it is with those two. Who can tell what sets them off?" Francie shook her head. "One minute they're thick as thieves, next minute they're avoiding the same aisle at Hattie's."

Clara sighed, wrapping her hands around her warm mug. "I've never seen such stubborn mules when it comes to each other. Ah, but then, I guess Maggie's got a valid reason for being a bit persnickety."

"After what Roger put her through?" Francie nodded. "That kind of hurt doesn't heal overnight."

They sat in companionable silence, watching the café fill with the morning crowd. Without speaking, both women closed their eyes briefly, heads bowed slightly over their coffee cups.

Help them remember why they started. And help them see Your hand still at work.

Evening settled over the Cunningham house like a heavy blanket. Maggie moved through the rooms, turning on lamps against the gathering darkness. The boys had been quieter than usual during dinner, pushing food around their plates and exchanging glances when they thought she wasn't looking.

Bath time passed without the usual splashing contests. Even Ralph's dinosaur toothbrush battle was subdued, lacking his typical roaring commentary. Now, as Maggie tucked the blankets around their small bodies, the weight of unspoken questions filled the bedroom.

"Mama?" Alan's voice broke the silence. His fingers twisted the edge of his quilt, eyes serious in the glow of the nightlight.

"Yes, baby?" She perched on the edge of his bed, smoothing his cowlick with gentle fingers.

"Does God get mad at us when grown-ups fight?"

The question caught her off-guard. Maggie's breath hitched as she looked between her sons' expectant faces. Ralph had rolled to face them, clutching his stuffed cow against his chest.

"No, sweetheart." She took Alan's hand in hers. "God doesn't get mad at us for that. He understands that sometimes people disagree, even people who care about each other."

"But you're sad," Ralph observed, his voice small. "And Mr. Reeves is sad too, probably."

Maggie swallowed hard. "Yes, we are. But that doesn't mean God is mad. Actually, it's times like these when God stays especially close to us."

"Like how you stay close when we're sick?" Alan asked.

"Exactly like that." She nodded, blinking back tears. "God loves us no matter what, even when we misbehave or make mistakes. He never walks away."

Ralph sat up suddenly, folding his small hands together. "Then we better pray for Mr. Reeves too."

"What?" Maggie whispered.

"For bedtime prayers," Ralph explained patiently. "We always pray for people who are sad or sick. Mr. Reeves is sad, so we should pray for him too."

Alan nodded in agreement, already folding his hands.

A tear escaped, trailing down Maggie's cheek as she bowed her head beside her sons. Ralph's small voice filled the room, earnest and clear.

"Dear God, please help Mama not be sad anymore. And help Mr. Reeves too. And Ms. Pickles. And help Mama and Mr. Reeves be friends again 'cause we miss him, Ms. Pickles, the cow, the chickens, and the farm. Amen."

"Amen," Alan echoed. "And help them remember that forgiveness is important, like Pastor Ethan said."

Maggie wiped away another tear, adding her own silent prayer.

Thank you, Lord, for these boys. For their tender hearts and simple wisdom. Help me be worthy of them.

The farmhouse creaked and settled in the darkness, its familiar sounds a backdrop to Ben's restless thoughts. He sat at the kitchen table, a single lamp casting long shadows across the worn wood. Ms. Pickles dozed at his feet, occasionally twitching in her sleep.

The blue rope toy lay on the table beside a mug of cold coffee and the deed—that damned piece of paper that had upended everything. Ben ran his fingers over the faded ink, studying his father's signature with new eyes.

"Something's not right here," he murmured.

Ms. Pickles lifted her head, ears perked at the sound of his voice.

Ben leaned back in his chair, rubbing his jaw. The anger that had consumed him for days had ebbed, leaving behind a hollow space where questions now took root. He wondered if Maggie had found the basket he'd left on her porch before dawn—wondered if she understood what it meant, that he was trying to reach across the chasm between them.

"I should've listened," he told the empty kitchen. "She was just trying to help."

The memory of her face when he'd lashed out made him wince. Fear, hurt, disappointment—emotions he'd been too blind with rage to recognize at the time. Now they haunted him.

He glanced at the clock: 11:42 PM. Too late to call, too late to drive over. Too late for a lot of things, maybe.

"What were you doing, old man?" Ben whispered, turning back to the deed. His father's signature looked right at first glance—the familiar slant, the looping 'R' in Reeves—but something about it nagged at him. The pressure of the pen strokes seemed off, like his father had been hesitant or...

Ben pushed back from the table abruptly. He moved to the old rolltop desk in the corner, yanking open drawers and rifling through folders. Tax records, equipment manuals, seed catalogs—he pulled them all out, searching for anything with his father's handwriting.

In the bottom drawer, beneath a stack of yellowed receipts, he found it—a leather portfolio containing the original deed to the property, along with his parents' will and birth certificates. Ben's hands trembled slightly as he spread the documents across the table, comparing signatures.

The difference was subtle but unmistakable. The signature on the newer deed lacked the distinctive hook at the end of the 's' that appeared on every other document his father had signed.

Ben stood still, processing what this might mean. Not anger now, but a cold clarity washed over him. He glanced at the clock again, then reached for his boots by the door.

"Come on, Pickles," he said, voice steady with purpose. "We're going to see Sheriff Wade."

The sheriff's office sat quiet on the edge of town, a single light glowing from the window. Wade Beaumont had drawn the short straw this week, covering night shifts while Deputy Collins enjoyed his first vacation in three years. He didn't mind the quiet—gave him time to catch up on paperwork and think through the strange pattern of incidents around town.

The sharp rap on the door startled him. Midnight visitors usually meant trouble.

"Ben?" Wade's eyebrows shot up as he opened the door to find Ben Reeves standing there, Ms. Pickles at his heels. "Everything alright at the farm?"

"Need your eyes on something." Ben's voice was tight, controlled. He clutched a folder in his hand, knuckles white against the manila.

Wade stepped aside. "Come on in."

Ben strode to the desk, Ms. Pickles padding faithfully behind him. He spread the documents out under the desk lamp, pointing to the signatures.

"Look here. This deed—the one Maggie found—it's got my father's signature, but something's off." His finger traced the letters. "Dad always finished his 's' with this hook. Every document he ever signed has it. But this one doesn't."

Wade leaned in, eyes narrowing as he studied the papers. "How'd you come to have this copy anyway?"

Ben ran a hand through his hair. "Maggie brought it by. Found it in some records in the town archives when she was researching stuff for the bakery. I didn't... I didn't take it well when she gave it to me." He swallowed hard. "But after she left, I started thinking. Dad would never sell off land without telling me. He made me swear not to sell not one inch. So I dug through his files tonight and found these papers he signed over the years, all at different times."

Wade listened quietly, reviewing each document. Something flagged in the back of his mind—a connection he couldn't quite place. He flipped through the papers again, verifying details on the copy of the deed.

"There's definitely something off about this," he muttered. "Let me look into this."

Ben watched him, hope and uncertainty warring in his expression. "You'll help me then? Really help me get to the truth?"

Wade clapped a hand on his shoulder. "That's what brothers do for other brothers, even when they make our sister cry."

Chagrined, head down, toe of his boot scraping the floor, hands in his pockets, Ben mumbled, "Heard about that, huh? I'm working on it."

Wade gripped his shoulder a little harder. "Work on it harder."

The night wrapped Maggie's house in silence, broken only by the ticking of the grandfather clock in the hallway. She stood by the kitchen window, staring into the darkness, her fingers tracing the edge of the wicker basket Ben had left on her porch. The vegetables had been washed and put away, but she kept the empty basket close, a tangible reminder that maybe all wasn't lost.

"I was so stubborn," she whispered to the empty room. "I just wanted to help, but I should've..."

Should've what? Given him time? Approached it differently? The truth was, she'd crossed a line without realizing how deep his wounds ran. Land wasn't just property to Ben—it was legacy, identity, promise.

Maggie moved to the small desk in the corner where her Bible lay open, the pages illuminated by a single lamp. Her fingers found 1 John, the familiar words blurring slightly as tears gathered.

"If we confess our sins, he is faithful and just to forgive us our sins..."

The verse settled in her chest like a balm. How simple it sounded. How difficult it felt.

Miles away, Ben knelt on the dusty floor of the barn, his father's old Bible open before him. The leather was cracked with age and use, the pages dog-eared from years of searching. Ms. Pickles lay beside him, her warm presence a comfort in the cool night air.

"I was wrong," he admitted aloud, the words hanging in the stillness. "Pride. That's what it was. Plain and simple."

His finger traced the same verse Maggie read across town, words worn smooth by generations of Reeves men seeking guidance.

"...and to cleanse us from all unrighteousness."

Cleansing. That's what he needed. The anger had poisoned him, made him lash out at the one person who'd been trying to stand beside him through it all.

Both closed their eyes, hands folded, hearts open.

"Lord," Maggie prayed, "I want to do this right."

"Lord," Ben whispered in his barn, "I want to do this right."

The night held their prayers, identical and earnest, carrying them upward like twin flames reaching for the same stars.

Chapter 31 – Porchlight Apologies

"He that covereth his sins shall not prosper: but whoso confesseth and forsaketh them shall have mercy." (KJV)

The evening sky burned orange and pink as Ben's truck rumbled up Maggie's gravel driveway. He cut the engine but sat there, hands gripping the wheel, heart hammering against his ribs. Ms. Pickles whined from the passenger seat, nudging his arm with her nose.

"I know, girl. Can't sit here all night."

Ben grabbed the tin of blondies from the dash and his hat from the seat. The walk to Maggie's front door felt longer than the trek across his south pasture. Each step carried the weight of his pride, his fear, his hope.

Light spilled from the kitchen window. He caught a glimpse of Ralph setting dishes in the sink while Maggie wiped down the table. The sight of their simple routine—the life he'd pushed away—made his throat tighten.

Before he could lose his nerve, Ben climbed the porch steps and knocked. The sound echoed like thunder in his ears.

Footsteps approached. The door swung open, and there she stood—Maggie, her hair pulled back in a loose ponytail, eyes widening at the sight of him.

"Ben." Not a question, not quite a greeting. Just his name, hanging between them.

"Evening, Maggie." He twisted his hat in his hands, the brim already showing wear from his nervous fingers. "I, uh—I came to apologize. If you'll let me."

Maggie wrapped her arms around herself, a shield against hurt that might come. But she nodded, her eyes never leaving his face.

"I brought these." He held out the tin. "Brittany's blondies. Not that I think sweets can fix what I broke, but..." He shrugged, feeling foolish now. "Figured it couldn't hurt my chances."

"You didn't have to bring anything."

"I know. But I wanted to. I wanted to say I'm sorry, Maggie. For how I reacted, for what I said. For letting you walk away." He swallowed hard. "I'd like a second chance, if you think I deserve one."

Maggie gestured to the porch swing. "Would you like to sit?"

Ben sank onto the wooden seat, but Maggie remained standing, arms crossed, the porch light casting long shadows across her face.

"I let fear speak for me," Ben admitted, turning his hat in endless circles. His eyes fixed on a knot in the porch boards. "When you showed me that deed, everything I thought I knew just... collapsed. My whole life's been about keeping that land safe, and finding out my father might've—" He shook his head. "I lashed out. I'm not proud of it."

"I wasn't exactly kind myself," Maggie said, her voice soft but firm. "I used my words like weapons, trying to protect myself. I'm not proud of the way I behaved either."

The night sounds filled the silence between them—crickets chirping, a distant owl, the creak of the swing as Ben shifted his weight.

"The worst part," Ben finally said, "was watching you walk away. That hurt more than anything else. Made me realize I want this—us—even when it's hard." His voice cracked on the last word.

Something in Maggie's posture changed. She moved to the swing, sitting at the far end, a careful distance between them.

"It hurt somethin' awful to walk away from you, to upset the boys that way. But I was expecting your reaction. I've been in those shoes. I've walked miles in 'em. Heck, I'm still wearin' 'em." She took a deep breath. "I knew the truth would wreck you, Ben." She moved closer, taking his hand in hers. "And I struggled with whether to do that to you or not. I'm sorry it took me so long to figure out which was worse, the knowin' or the not knowin'. I was selfish. I was enjoying myself, prideful as it was. I was doing things on my own, in my own time, my heart telling me I was right to hold onto the information."

Ben opened his mouth to speak, but Maggie raised her hand.

"Please, let me finish. I opened my Bible for the first time in a long time, searching for answers, and the page opened to Jeremiah 17. Verse 9 practically leapt off the page at me. 'The heart is deceitful above all things, and desperately wicked...' I knew in my gut that telling you was the right thing to do, but my heart said don't do it. And I ended up hurting all of us." Her voice trembled. "My only explanation is that I'm still learning how to trust you, or anyone, with my story. Will you ever be able to forgive me?"

Ben nodded, reaching to pull her close, wrapping his arms around her as tears of relief sprang forth. "You were forgiven as soon as I was able to calm myself down, Sunbeam."

She choked out a laugh through her tears, leaning back to see his face, finally meeting his eyes. "I'm so sorry, Ben. I missed you so much. I thought I lost my second chance."

Ben cupped her face, his thumbs gently wiping away her tears, his eyes shining with unspoken emotion. "Sweet Maggie. Carrying such a load all on your own. You, my Sunbeam, can have all the chances you need to fly like the butterfly." He leaned forward, pressing his lips to hers. The kiss deepened as thousands of colorful butterflies seemed to explode around them in a weightless dance of color. Just as he moved to change their position, the screen door squeaked, and they jumped apart.

Alan stood in the doorway, a small silhouette backlit by the kitchen light. His thin shoulders were squared, arms crossed tightly over his chest. The screen door banged shut behind him.

"Momma, you okay?" His voice cracked slightly, but his stance was unmistakable—protective, wary.

"Alan..." Maggie began, shifting away from Ben on the swing, her cheeks flushed.

Ben raised his hand gently. "Maggie, he's just doing what the man of the house does." He stood up, hat back in his hands, showing Alan respect by meeting him at eye level.

Maggie tried again, smoothing her hair back with nervous fingers. "We're just talking, baby. Everything's fine."

Alan's eyes never left Ben's face. The boy's jaw tightened, and when he spoke, his voice was steady despite his youth. "You made her cry last time." The accusation hung in the night air, simple but powerful. His eyes were stormy, holding more hurt than anger—the look of someone who'd seen too many tears already in his young life.

Ben didn't flinch from the boy's gaze. The truth in those words stung worse than any shout could have. This wasn't just about winning Maggie back. There were two young hearts here who'd already learned to expect disappointment from men.

The cicadas filled the silence between them, their endless chorus the only sound besides the creak of the porch boards beneath Ben's boots as he shifted his weight.

"Alan..." Maggie's voice sharpened with the tone mothers use when children overstep. Her posture straightened, ready to defend both Ben and her authority.

Ben lifted his hand, palm out toward Maggie. "It's alright, Maggie. He's doing what he's supposed to do, holding me accountable, making sure you are treated right." His voice softened as he met her eyes. "I'd like to answer his challenge if you don't mind."

Maggie hesitated, caught between maternal instinct and recognizing the importance of this moment between her son and Ben. She pressed her lips together, then nodded silently.

Ben turned back to Alan, squaring his shoulders but keeping his stance open. No crossed arms, no defensive posture. Just honesty.

"You're right, son. I made myself cry too." Ben's voice remained steady, though the admission cost him. "I came over tonight to apologize like a man should. I didn't abandon her or you. We just needed some time to cool off, calm down, so we could think rationally."

The porch light caught the moisture in Ben's eyes. "I realized I made a mistake letting y'all leave as soon as you pulled out of the driveway. I just didn't know what to say to get you to come back." He swallowed hard. "I'm more sorry than you'll ever know that I hurt your Mom and you and your brother. You all deserve better than I gave. That wasn't how a man is supposed to act."

Ben knelt down, bringing himself to Alan's level, his hat still clutched in his hands. "I'm trying to do better. Not just for her, but for y'all too."

Alan stood perfectly still, his young face solemn as he studied Ben. The boy's eyes moved over Ben's face with an intensity beyond his years, searching for any hint of deception. The seconds stretched between them like taffy, neither male breaking the silence.

Finally, Alan gave a single, decisive nod. Without a word, he turned and walked back inside, the screen door closing behind him with a soft click.

Chapter 32 – Sunday Dinner Proposal

"Therefore if any man be in Christ, he is a new creature: old things are passed away; behold, all things are become new." 2 Corinthians 5:17 (KJV)

The screen door creaked again, and a smaller head poked out from behind Alan's shoulder. Ralph's curious eyes darted between the adults, then widened with hope when they landed on Ben.

"Mr. Ben, did you bring Ms. Pickles with ya?" Ralph stepped fully onto the porch, his pajama top slightly askew, one sock bunched around his ankle.

The tension in Ben's shoulders eased slightly at the boy's eager expression. He chuckled, grateful for the innocent interruption.

"Just dropping off some of Britt's blondies tonight, buddy. Ms. Pickles is waiting in the truck."

Ralph's face fell momentarily before he straightened up, crossing his arms in a miniature imitation of his older brother. He shook his head with such solemn disapproval that Ben had to bite the inside of his cheek to keep from smiling.

"Momma likes pickles when she's sad," Ralph announced with the certainty of someone sharing profound wisdom.

Maggie's face flushed crimson. She choked on a surprised laugh, her hand flying to cover her mouth.

"That's... not wrong," she admitted, shooting Ben a sheepish glance.

Ben's eyes softened as he looked at her. "Is that right?"

Ralph nodded emphatically. "She says Pickles reminds her of sunshine and they counterfact the sweet."

"Counteract" Maggie chuckles.

Alan nudged his brother with his elbow, but Ralph continued undeterred.

"When Momma's happy, she makes pancakes shaped like animals. We ain't had animal pancakes in five whole days." He held up one hand, fingers splayed wide to illustrate the gravity of the pancake drought.

"Ralph Edward," Maggie sputtered, caught between mortification and amusement.

Ben knelt down to Ralph's level, his voice gentle. "Well now, that's a real shame about those pancakes. Think Ms. Pickles might help with that situation if she came to visit tomorrow?"

Ralph's entire face lit up. "She could sit right next to me! I saved a special drawing of her eating ice cream!"

Alan's expression softened at his brother's enthusiasm. He glanced between his mother and Ben, then tugged at Ralph's pajama sleeve.

"C'mon, Ralphie. Let's go finish reading that comic before bed." He steered his younger brother toward the door, pausing just long enough to give Ben a look that clearly said their conversation wasn't over.

The screen door closed behind them with a gentle slap against the frame. Silence settled between Maggie and Ben, broken only by the symphony of night insects and the distant hoot of an owl.

"Walk me to my truck?" Ben asked, offering his hand.

Maggie hesitated before slipping her fingers into his. The simple touch sent warmth spiraling through him as they descended the porch steps and moved across the moonlit yard.

The gravel crunched beneath their feet. Ms. Pickles spotted them through the truck window and wagged her tail furiously, her silhouette bouncing with excitement.

When they reached the gate, Ben turned to face Maggie, still holding her hand. Moonlight silvered her hair and softened the worry lines around her eyes.

"I'm not asking you to forget what happened," Ben said, his voice low and earnest. "Lord knows I won't. But I am asking for a chance to replace those memories with better ones." He squeezed her fingers gently. "I want to be a better man than I was last week. Than I've ever been."

Maggie looked up at him, her eyes reflecting starlight and uncertainty. "You're asking me to risk more than my heart, Ben. You're asking me to risk theirs." She glanced back toward the house where two small shadows moved behind the curtains. "Those boys have already lost one man who was supposed to love them forever."

Ben followed her gaze, understanding the weight of what she was saying. When he looked back at her, his expression was solemn.

"Then I'll treat that risk like holy ground," he whispered, voice rough with emotion. "Because that's what it is, Maggie. Sacred trust."

The night breeze stirred the leaves above them. In that moment, Ben felt something shifting inside him—as if old, brittle parts were falling away, making room for something new to grow.

Maggie studied his face for a long moment. Then she nodded once. Not a yes—but not a no. A willingness to try.

"Come back tomorrow," she said finally. "Bring the pickles."

Ben's lips curved into a smile as he raised her hand to his lips and brushed a butterfly soft kiss on it before releasing it, stepped back. He settled his hat on his head, tipping the brim slightly.

"I'll be here."

Ben lingered at the gate, his hand resting on the weathered wood. He couldn't tear his gaze away from Maggie, the moonlight catching in her hair, turning ordinary brown to something magical. Time seemed suspended between them, neither willing to break the fragile moment.

"I should go," he said, not moving an inch.

"You should," she agreed, making no move to turn away.

The corner of his mouth lifted in a half-smile. "Ralph's gonna expect those animal pancakes tomorrow."

"He'll hold me to it." Maggie tucked a strand of hair behind her ear, her eyes never leaving his. "Ben?"

"Hmm?"

"Thank you for coming back."

Something passed between them then—unspoken but as real as the ground beneath their feet. A recognition that some broken things, when mended, could be stronger at the seams.

Ms. Pickles gave an impatient woof from the truck, breaking the spell. Ben chuckled, finally taking a reluctant step back.

"I reckon that's my cue."

Maggie nodded, wrapping her arms around herself as the night air cooled. "Goodnight, Ben."

"Goodnight, Sunbeam." The endearment slipped out naturally, warming the space between them.

He forced himself to turn away, each step toward his truck feeling like it stretched across miles. He climbed in beside Ms. Pickles, who immediately pressed her nose against his arm in greeting. The engine rumbled to life, headlights cutting through the darkness.

Ben glanced back one last time. Maggie still stood by the gate, a silhouette against the porch light behind her. She raised her hand in a small wave.

As he drove down the long driveway, the rearview mirror showed her figure growing smaller until she disappeared from view. But the feeling in his chest—that expanding lightness—only grew. For the first time in years, Ben felt the stirring of something he'd almost forgotten: hope. Not just for his land or his future, but for his heart.

Ms. Pickles settled her head on his lap with a contented sigh.

"Yeah," Ben whispered, patting her head. "I think we might get our second chance too."

Chapter 33 – When the Rain Falls

"And he prayed again, and the heaven gave rain, and the earth brought forth her fruit." James 5:18 (KJV)

Ben woke before his alarm, pulled from sleep by a restlessness he couldn't name. The farmhouse sat quiet around him, save for Ms. Pickles' soft snoring from her bed in the corner. He padded to the kitchen, bare feet against cool floorboards, and started the coffee pot with practiced movements.

Something felt different this morning. The air held a weight, a promise.

While the coffee brewed, Ben leaned against the counter and closed his eyes. His mind drifted to Maggie's porch, to Alan's stern face and Ralph's innocent questions about pancakes. Those boys had more backbone than most grown men he knew. Alan especially—standing there like a sentinel, protecting his mama's heart.

"Can't fault him for that," Ben murmured, pouring the fresh coffee into his favorite chipped mug.

Coffee in hand, he stepped onto the front porch just as dawn broke across the eastern sky. Ms. Pickles followed, stretching her front legs before padding to his side. The parched fields stretched before them, the crops hanging limp and desperate after weeks without rain.

A soft breeze stirred the air—different from the hot, dry gusts of recent days. This one carried moisture. Ms. Pickles lifted her head, ears perked forward, nostrils flaring.

Ben chuckled, imagining Ralph at Maggie's kitchen table right about now, squealing over pancakes shaped like dogs and horses. That boy's smile could light up the darkest corners.

"What do you think, girl? Will she make Ms. Pickles pancakes too?" He scratched behind his dog's ears, heart warming at the thought of Maggie in her kitchen, flour on her cheek, boys chattering around her.

Something wet touched his hand. Ben looked down, thinking Ms. Pickles had licked him, but she sat perfectly still, eyes trained on the sky.

Another drop hit the porch rail. Then another. Within seconds, more droplets pattered around them, creating tiny dark circles on the weathered wood. The sweet, earthy scent of rain on parched ground began to rise, a promise fulfilled after weeks of waiting.

Ben froze, coffee forgotten in his hand. The drops came faster now, pattering against the tin roof in a rhythm he'd prayed for weeks to hear. His parched fields flashed through his mind—withered corn stalks, dusty bean rows, the cattle gathered listlessly around nearly empty watering troughs. This rain might not save everything, but it was hope falling from the heavens, each droplet a tiny answered prayer.

Then it hit—a steady, drenching rain falling in silver sheets across his land. Ben spread his arms wide, face tilted upward as the cool droplets washed over him. The parched soil seemed to sigh beneath his feet, drinking in the blessed moisture after weeks of cruel drought. In the distance, lightning flickered silently, illuminating the far edges of his fields where withered crops now stood in the path of salvation.

Without a second thought, Ben set his coffee mug on the porch rail and stepped off the covered porch. The rain instantly soaked through his thin t-shirt and sleep pants, plastering them to his skin. Ms. Pickles whined from the safety of the dry porch, but Ben paid her no mind. Each step across the yard pressed his bare feet into earth that seemed to pulse beneath him—drinking, awakening, reviving.

He walked farther into the downpour, arms spread wide as if to embrace the storm itself. Water streamed down his face, catching in his eyelashes and dripping from his chin. The sensation was glorious—cool and cleansing after weeks of suffocating heat and dust.

"Thank You, Father," he whispered, the words catching in his throat. "Thank You."

He turned his palms upward, letting the rain pool in his cupped hands before spilling over. All around him, the parched landscape transformed. Blades of grass that had lain flat and yellow began to straighten. The leaves on his mother's old oak tree seemed to unfurl, their dusty surfaces rinsed clean and glistening. Even the air itself felt different—alive with possibility and the promise of renewal.

Ben closed his eyes, raindrops mingling with tears of relief on his cheeks.

"Thank You, Father," he repeated, louder this time. "Thank You for not forgetting us."

Lightning flashed in the distance, followed by a low rumble of thunder that Ben felt in his chest. The storm was building, not fading—a blessing that might last for hours. His mind raced with calculations—how many inches they'd need to save the corn, to replenish the pond, to keep the cattle watered through August.

But those thoughts faded as quickly as they came. For now, Ben simply stood in the middle of his yard, face tilted toward heaven, receiving the gift with humble gratitude. This wasn't just water falling from the sky. This was mercy. This was grace. This was God's hand reaching down to touch his weary land.

"Thank You, Father," he whispered once more. "Thank You."

Across town at the Willow Creek Retreat, Ethan stepped onto the wide covered porch of the main lodge, his coffee mug warm in his hands. He froze mid-sip, eyes widening as the first fat raindrops splashed against the dusty ground.

"Clara!" he called over his shoulder, voice cracking with emotion. "Come quick!"

Clara appeared in the doorway, wiping her hands on a dish towel. "What is it?" Then she saw it—the rain coming down in earnest now, a silver curtain descending on their parched land. "Oh, thank the Lord," she whispered, stepping beside him.

Inside the lodge, Ava spotted the rain through the window and let out a whoop that startled everyone at the breakfast tables. "It's raining! God heard us!"

The reaction was instantaneous. Chairs scraped across the floor as children and counselors alike abandoned half-eaten breakfasts and raced for the doors. Loquita was the first one down the steps, arms outstretched as she tilted her face to the sky.

"I can't believe it!" she laughed, spinning in a circle as water darkened her t-shirt. "It's actually raining!"

Rosita kicked off her sandals and joined her, dark hair quickly plastered to her cheeks as she twirled with abandoned joy. "This is what freedom feels like!" she shouted, grabbing Charnise's hands and spinning her around.

Anthony hung back on the porch steps, uncertainty written across his face until Hector clapped him on the shoulder. "First time dancing in the rain?"

Anthony nodded, watching the others splash through puddles forming in the yard.

"Mine too," Hector admitted. "Guess we better learn." He grabbed Anthony's arm and pulled him into the downpour.

Ethan wrapped his arm around Clara's shoulders as they watched from beneath the porch eaves. "Look at them," he murmured against her hair. "Some of these kids have never celebrated rain before."

Noah and Ava organized an impromptu splash contest, jumping into puddles with all their might, measuring whose splash went highest. Winona held little Oscar above her head, his chubby legs kicking with delight as raindrops tickled his face.

Principal Paul appeared beside them, his eyes misty as he watched the joyful chaos. "It's more than weather," he said quietly. "It's provision."

Clara nodded, leaning into Ethan's embrace. "God's timing is perfect."

At the Cunningham house, Maggie stood at the kitchen window, coffee forgotten in her hands as the first drops splattered against the glass. Her heart leapt at the sound—a sound she'd prayed for every night alongside her boys.

"Alan! Ralph!" she called, voice trembling with excitement. "Come quick!"

Alan appeared first, sleep still heavy in his eyes. "What's wrong, Mama?"

"Look!" She pointed out the window where rain now fell in earnest, creating rivulets down the glass.

Ralph barreled into the kitchen, hair sticking up in all directions. "Is that—" His eyes widened. "RAIN!"

Before Maggie could stop them, both boys bolted for the back door, flinging it open and racing into the yard in their pajamas. Ralph hit a slick patch and his feet flew out from under him. He landed with a splat in a rapidly forming mud puddle, his shocked expression melting into pure delight.

"Look at me!" he cackled, smearing mud across his cheeks like war paint. "I'm a mud monster!"

Alan stood with his arms outstretched, face tilted toward the heavens. "It feels so good!" he shouted, spinning in circles. "Mama, come out here!"

Maggie hesitated only a moment before setting her mug on the counter. She kicked off her slippers and stepped onto the back porch, then down into the wet grass. The cool mud squished between her toes, a sensation she hadn't felt since childhood.

She closed her eyes and lifted her face to the sky, letting the rain wash over her. Water trickled down her neck, soaking her nightshirt, plastering her hair to her cheeks. For weeks, the world had felt brittle and desperate—but now, with each passing minute, life seemed to surge back into everything around them.

The steady downpour continued for hours, a gentle, persistent blessing. From her porch, Maggie watched the transformation unfold. The grass in her yard, once flat and yellowed, gradually straightened, standing tall once more. The drooping leaves on her maple tree perked up, their dusty surfaces rinsed clean until they gleamed.

Down the street, she could hear the rush of water in the creek—no longer a trickle but a proper flow, washing away weeks of stagnation. The whole town smelled different—clean and new, as if the rain had rinsed away more than just dust and heat.

Maggie's heart raced as she herded her mud-covered boys back inside. "Alright, mud monsters, shower time. Clean clothes for everybody."

Ralph protested, holding up his brown-streaked arms. "But Mama, I just got my war paint perfect!"

"And you can put it back on another day. Right now, we've got somewhere to be." She gently steered him toward the bathroom, her mind already made up.

Twenty minutes later, with both boys scrubbed clean and dressed in fresh clothes, Maggie stood at the kitchen window again. The rain continued its steady rhythm, drumming against the roof and streaming down the glass. She pressed her palm against her heart, feeling it beat beneath her fingers.

"I gotta see Ben," she whispered, the words forming before she could question them. The thought repeated, stronger this time, like a voice she couldn't ignore. Not her own voice—something deeper, more certain.

This wasn't just about her feelings anymore. This was about something bigger than herself.

"This means everything to him." The rain, the salvation of his crops, the answer to weeks of desperate prayers. And she needed to be there, to stand beside him in this moment of grace.

Maggie turned from the window, decision made. "Boys! Put your boots on. And grab your raincoats."

Alan appeared in the doorway, eyebrows raised. "We going somewhere? In this?"

"We're going to Mr. Ben's farm."

Ralph whooped, already racing for his boots. "Are we gonna splash in his puddles too?"

"Maybe." Maggie smiled, reaching for her own raincoat. "But mostly, we're going to be with him while God answers his prayers."

They piled into the car, raincoats zipped and boots squeaking. The windshield wipers fought valiantly against the downpour as Maggie navigated the familiar road to Ben's farm. Fields on either side glistened, thirsty soil drinking in the blessing.

Alan sat quietly in the passenger seat, watching the rain-washed landscape. "Do you think he's okay?" he finally asked, his voice small but steady.

Maggie glanced at her eldest, this boy who carried the weight of protecting her heart. She reached over and squeezed his hand.

"I think he's finer than frog's hair today," she said, the old saying bringing a smile to both their faces. "And I think maybe we all will be."

The Reeves farmhouse came into view as Maggie rounded the final bend. Even through the rain-streaked windshield, she could see the transformation already beginning across Ben's land. Rivulets of water carved paths through parched soil, and the entire landscape seemed to shimmer with renewed hope.

"Look!" Ralph pointed through the side window. "There's Ms. Pickles!"

Maggie slowed the car, squinting through the downpour. The faithful Kuvasz darted across the yard, splashing through puddles and barking at the sky as if challenging the clouds themselves.

And there, standing motionless in the middle of his field, was Ben.

He hadn't bothered with a raincoat or boots. His t-shirt clung to his broad shoulders, soaked completely through. His face was tilted skyward, arms slightly outstretched at his sides, receiving the blessing that poured down upon him.

Maggie's breath caught in her throat. "He looks like he's praying," she whispered.

Alan studied the farmer through the rain-streaked window. "He is."

She parked near the house and turned to her boys. "Ready to get wet again?"

Ralph was already unbuckling his seatbelt. "Race you!"

They tumbled from the car into the downpour, raincoats doing little to keep them dry as the deluge continued. Ms. Pickles spotted them immediately, bounding over with excited barks.

Ralph broke away first, splashing through puddles toward Ben, calling his name. The farmer turned slowly, as if waking from a dream. His eyes widened when he saw them—first the boys, then Maggie, standing in his field in the pouring rain.

"Mister Ben!" Ralph crashed into his legs, wrapping his arms around Ben's waist. "God sent the rain! You asked Him and He did it!"

Ben's hand came down gently on Ralph's head, but his eyes never left Maggie's. Something passed between them—understanding, recognition, faith.

Alan hung back, watching the scene unfold with cautious eyes. Ben noticed, giving the older boy a respectful nod that acknowledged his protective stance.

Maggie walked slowly across the soaked field, mud clinging to her boots with each step. Water streamed down her face, plastering her hair to her cheeks, but she barely noticed.

"We thought you might want some company," she said softly when she reached him, voice nearly lost in the drumming rain.

Ben's eyes shimmered with emotion. "I've never wanted anything more."

No grand gestures followed. No dramatic declarations of feelings too new and tender to name. Instead, Ben simply opened his arms, and Maggie stepped into them.

They stood together in the pouring rain, arms wrapped around each other in a long, reverent embrace—bodies soaked, hearts still mending, but moving forward in faith. Ralph hugged them both from the side, his small arms barely reaching around their waists.

Alan watched from a few paces away, uncertainty written across his young face.

Ben looked up, meeting the boy's eyes over Maggie's shoulder. He extended one arm, an invitation without pressure.

"Pretty amazing what God can do when we ask, isn't it?" Ben said quietly.

Back at the farmhouse, Ben toweled his hair dry while watching through the kitchen window as Maggie's car disappeared down the long driveway. The boys had waved frantically from the back seat, Ralph's face pressed against the glass until they rounded the bend and vanished from sight.

The rain continued its steady rhythm against the roof, a percussive reminder of grace. Ms. Pickles shook herself vigorously by the door, sending water droplets flying across the worn linoleum. Ben couldn't even bring himself to scold her.

"Some days just change everything, don't they, girl?" he murmured, scratching behind her ears.

He glanced at the clock on the stove—nearly noon. The morning had slipped away in a blur of rain and unexpected company. For the first time in weeks, the knot of anxiety in his chest had loosened. He could breathe again.

Ben's gaze fell on his phone, abandoned on the counter since before dawn. He picked it up, surprised to see the screen lit up with notifications—three missed calls from Walt, two from Wes, and a string of text messages from both.

He tapped on the first message from Walt: Ben! Answer your damn phone! Rain's changing everything. Calls coming in.

The second, from Wes: Grain contracts! Feed orders! Where are you?

Ben scrolled through the rest, piecing together their broken, excited messages. The Co-Op had received more calls this morning than in the past two weeks combined. Farmers from three counties over were reaching out, looking to lock in contracts now that the drought was breaking.

Walt's final message made Ben's breath catch: Miller's Feed just called. Want to talk exclusive supply. This could save us all.

Ben looked up at the tin roof above the phone desk, listening to the steady drumming of raindrops. A smile spread slowly across his face, warm and genuine, reaching all the way to his eyes for the first time in months.

"Thank You," he whispered, the words carrying all the weight of his gratitude—for the rain, for Maggie and her boys showing up when he needed them most, for this unexpected chance at salvation. "Thank You for the abundance."

Ms. Pickles nudged his hand with her wet nose, and Ben scratched her head absentmindedly, his thoughts already racing toward possibilities that had seemed impossible just hours ago.

As evening fell, the rain gentled to a soft patter against leaves and soil. Ben stepped out onto his back porch, breathing deeply of the transformed world. The air hung heavy with the scent of wet earth and green things awakening. Even in the fading light, he could see how his fields had changed—no longer brittle and desperate, but softened, receptive, alive again.

"Come on, girl," he called to Ms. Pickles. "Let's check the south pasture."

The Kuvasz bounded ahead, her white coat still damp from earlier adventures. Ben followed at an unhurried pace, boots squelching in mud that no longer cracked beneath his feet. Water pooled in the furrows between crop rows, reflecting the pink-gold light of sunset breaking through thinning clouds.

He reached the fence line where his property met the old creek bed. The water flowed strong now, no longer the anemic trickle of recent weeks. It gurgled and splashed over rocks, carrying away months of dust and debris.

Ms. Pickles trotted to the edge of the pasture and stopped suddenly, ears perked forward. A breeze rustled through the trees, bending branches still heavy with rainwater. She barked once, twice, as if challenging the wind itself to leave their newly blessed land.

Ben laughed, the sound surprising him with its ease. "You telling that wind to stay put?" He scratched behind her ears. "Today was a Butterfly day, girl. Flying high and purty as Maggie when she smiles."

He leaned against the fence post, watching as the last rays of sunlight gilded puddles across his land. Something caught his eye in the nearest field—a flash of green where yesterday there had been only brown. He walked closer, crouching down to examine the soil.

There, pushing up through mud, were tiny green shoots—seeds awakening after their long dormancy, reaching for light and life.

Ben touched one gently with his fingertip. "And the earth brought forth her fruit," he whispered, remembering the verse Pastor had shared during last Sunday's sermon.

He straightened, looking out over his fields as twilight settled across them. In the distance, the lights of Willow Creek winked on, one by one.

Ben bowed his head, raindrops from his hat brim falling to join those already soaking the earth. "Thank You for the rain," he prayed softly. "And thank You for sending Maggie today. I think maybe You're growing something there too."

Chapter 34 – A Sunday Kind of Love

"Two are better than one; because they have a good reward for their labour. For if they fall, the one will lift up his fellow: but woe to him that is alone when he falleth; for he hath not another to help him up." Ecclesiastes 4:9–10 (KJV)

The morning broke over Willow Creek like God Himself had washed the world clean. Sunlight sparkled off raindrops clinging to leaves and fence posts, turning ordinary things into jewels. Birds called from every direction, their songs a celebration of life renewed.

Ben Reeves stood before his bathroom mirror, studying his reflection with uncommon scrutiny. He'd shaved twice, combed his hair three times, and changed his shirt once already. His best jeans—the dark ones without a single work stain—felt stiff against his skin. His boots were polished to a shine that would make his grandfather proud.

"Lord," he whispered, "I've been carrying everything alone for too long. Today I'm stepping out in faith."

The drive to Maggie's took less time than usual. His truck hummed along roads still puddled from yesterday's downpour, tires splashing through water that reflected a perfect blue sky. He rehearsed his words, changed them, then settled on simple truth.

When he pulled into her driveway, his heart hammered against his ribs. This wasn't just about church. This was about declaring something to the whole town—that Margaret Mary Cunningham and her boys were worth falling for, worth lifting up, worth building a life alongside.

He walked up her porch steps, Sunday hat in hand, and knocked. The wait stretched like taffy until the door swung open.

Maggie stood there in a yellow dress that caught the morning light, her hair loose around her shoulders. Her eyes widened at the sight of him.

"You're here early," she said, surprise coloring her voice.

Ben shifted his weight, suddenly aware of his hands, his height, the way his heart refused to slow. "Wanted to ask if I could escort y'all to church. All four of us, together."

From behind Maggie, two faces appeared. Alan narrowed his eyes, suspicion written across his features. Ralph beamed, gap-toothed and hopeful.

Maggie studied Ben's face, understanding dawning in her eyes. "You do know what will happen if we all show up to church together, right?"

Ben's smile grew as his cheeks turned pink. "Yes, ma'am, I do. I'm ready for it if you are."

Maggie considered for a brief minute, knowing the time was right. "Well, folks are already talkin', let's at least give them something true to gossip about." She nodded. "We'll be ready in ten."

The church parking lot bustled with Sunday morning activity when Maggie's sedan pulled in. Ben spotted familiar faces.

Ben slid out first, circling around to Maggie's door before she could reach for the handle. He opened it with a steady hand, offering his arm as she stepped out. The boys tumbled from the backseat, their church shoes already scuffed despite Maggie's best efforts.

"You boys stay close now," Maggie whispered, smoothing Alan's cowlick one last time.

Ben held his hat against his chest, his other hand finding the small of Maggie's back. The touch was gentle but deliberate—a silent claim that sent a clear message to anyone watching. And everyone was watching.

"Mom, why's everybody staring?" Ralph stage-whispered, his eyes darting around.

"Just keep walking, sugar," Maggie murmured, her cheeks warming.

Ben held the heavy wooden door, nodding at Pastor who stood greeting folks at the entrance. His eyes widened slightly before a knowing smile spread across his face.

"Beautiful morning, isn't it?" Pastor said, clapping Ben's shoulder.

Inside, the sanctuary hummed with pre-service chatter. Ben guided them past his usual spot—back row, easy escape—and continued forward. His heart thumped harder with each step toward the third pew where Henry and Lorraine Cunningham sat.

Henry spotted them first, his weathered face registering surprise before settling into something more guarded. Lorraine turned, her smile blooming like spring flowers.

The boys slid in first, settling next to their grandmother who reached out to squeeze their hands. Her smile stretched ear to ear, eyes bright with approval.

Ben guided Maggie in next, his hand still at her lower back. Henry's gaze locked onto that hand like a hawk spotting movement in a field. When Ben leaned across to shake Henry's hand, the older man raised a questioning eyebrow.

"Morning, Mr. Cunningham. Mrs. Cunningham, Ma'am. Good to see you," Ben said, his voice steady despite the scrutiny.

Lorraine beamed. "It's good to see you all, Ben, here in church, together." She turned to Maggie with that universal mother look—part "I told you so," part "about time," all wrapped in love.

"Morning, Momma, Daddy. Y'all get enough rain out your way?" Maggie asked with a cheeky grin that didn't quite hide her nervousness.

Ben caught the silent conversation passing between mother and daughter and wisely chose not to interpret. He settled beside Maggie, their shoulders touching. Henry's "harumph" carried down the pew like distant thunder.

Throughout the sanctuary, the ripple effect of Ben and Maggie sitting together spread like wildfire. Across the aisle, Mayor Ellie Jernigan tilted her head, lips curving into a knowing smile. Three rows back, Sheriff

Wade caught Ben's eye and gave a subtle nod of approval. Had Francie Sharp been there instead of home nursing Burle through a summer cold, she'd have clasped her hands and whispered, "Praise the Lord," loud enough for the choir to hear.

The piano began the opening notes of "Amazing Grace," and the congregation rose. Ben found himself standing straighter, his voice stronger than it had been in years. The familiar words washed over him—I once was lost, but now am found—and he felt their truth deep in his bones.

When they sat for the sermon, Ben's hand moved of its own accord, finding Maggie's where it rested on the hymnal. Her fingers were cool against his calloused palm, hesitating only a moment before interlacing with his. Something settled in his chest, like the final piece of a puzzle sliding into place.

In Willow Creek, sitting together in church wasn't just sitting together. It was a declaration. More binding than a Facebook status, more telling than town gossip. When a man and woman shared a pew, shoulders touching, hands linked—it meant family. It meant forever.

Pastor's sermon on Ecclesiastes seemed written just for them. "Two are better than one; because they have a good reward for their labour." Ben squeezed Maggie's hand, feeling her gentle pressure in return.

After the final hymn and benediction, they filed out with the boys between them. The usual post-service chatter swelled around them, punctuated by meaningful glances and not-so-subtle smiles.

At the bottom of the church steps, Henry Cunningham intercepted them. His handshake was firm enough to make Ben's knuckles ache.

"We'll see you at home for Sunday dinner," Henry said, his tone making it clear this wasn't a request.

Ben met the older man's gaze, understanding dawning. This wasn't an invitation—it was a summons from the father of the woman he loved.

She wasn't truly his until he asked for and received Henry's blessing. The bones in his hand ground together under Henry's grip.

"Yes, sir. I'll be there," Ben replied, swallowing hard.

Time to face the music. Time to humbly beg to take Henry Cunningham's daughter from him.

Can't wait.

The Cunningham house buzzed with Sunday dinner chaos. Steam billowed from pots, the sizzle of chicken in cast iron punctuated conversations, and the scent of buttermilk biscuits filled every corner. Ben stood in the doorway of Lorraine's kitchen, momentarily forgotten in the flurry of activity.

Lorraine wielded her wooden spoon like a conductor's baton, turning chicken pieces with practiced precision. "Maggie, sugar, those potatoes need more butter. Can't have dry potatoes at Sunday dinner."

Maggie and her sister Ginny worked elbow-to-elbow at the counter, a choreographed dance they'd performed since childhood. Maggie mashed potatoes while Ginny rolled out biscuit dough, flour dusting her cheeks.

"Remember when Maggie tried making gravy that Christmas?" Ginny said, cutting perfect circles with the rim of a glass. "Daddy called it 'wallpaper paste' and Momma nearly fainted."

"I was twelve!" Maggie protested, but her eyes crinkled with laughter. "Besides, Martin's the one who put salt in the peach cobbler thinking it was sugar."

Lorraine shook her head. "Lord help me, I raised a bunch of kitchen disasters."

In the dining room, Martin supervised the teenagers setting the table. Julie, his sixteen-year-old daughter, arranged silverware while her brother Tim and Ralph carried in water glasses.

"Uncle Martin, where does this fork go?" Ralph asked, holding it up like a treasure.

Before Martin could answer, Tim flicked a green bean across the table. It hit Alan square in the forehead.

"Bull's-eye!" Tim crowed.

Alan's eyes narrowed. He grabbed a handful from the serving bowl and launched a counterattack.

"Boys!" Martin barked, but his stern face cracked when a stray bean landed in his shirt pocket. "That's not—" He plucked it out, aimed, and sent it sailing toward Tim.

Brittany swept in with a pitcher of sweet tea, dodging the crossfire. "Really, Martin? You're supposed to be the adult."

"Just showing them proper green bean trajectory," Martin said, ducking another volley.

"Martin Cunningham!" Lorraine called from the kitchen. "Don't make me come in there!"

The green bean war ceased immediately.

Ginny sidled up to Brittany as she arranged glasses. "So, any special someone these days? That new deputy's been asking about you."

"The cute one with the accent?" Lorraine chimed in, suddenly interested.

Brittany rolled her eyes. "I'm just here for the fried chicken, ladies. Nothing more to report."

Ben noticed Henry slip away after washing up. The older man caught his eye with a subtle nod toward the hallway. Understanding the unspoken summons, Ben excused himself from the chaotic dining room preparations.

He followed Henry down the hall to a small study. The room smelled of leather and pipe tobacco, walls lined with well-worn books and family photographs. A worn leather chair sat behind a desk cluttered with papers and fishing magazines.

Henry closed the door behind them, muting the cheerful din from the kitchen. He gestured to a chair across from his desk before settling into his own with a creak of springs.

"You're a good man, Ben. I can see that." Henry's voice was measured, his weathered hands folded on the desk. "But I won't make the same mistake I made with Roger—assuming without asking." He leaned forward slightly, the leather chair creaking beneath his weight. His eyes, kind but searching, studied Ben's face with the careful assessment of a father who'd been burned before. "Maggie and those boys deserve someone who'll stand by them through whatever comes. That's not something I take lightly anymore."

Ben sat straighter, his throat suddenly dry.

"How's your walk with the Lord these days?" Henry asked, eyes never leaving Ben's face. "Haven't seen you in church much until recently." His weathered hands remained folded on the desk, but his gaze was penetrating, the kind that seemed to look straight through to a man's soul rather than just at him. It was the same look Ben had seen him give Maggie's boys when they'd tried fibbing about who ate the last cookie.

"No sir, you haven't," Ben admitted. "After Dad died, I let my faith slip. Figured God and I had an understanding—I'd handle the farm, He'd handle everything else." Ben shook his head. "Wasn't much of a partnership." He rubbed his calloused palm against his jeans, feeling the weight of Henry's gaze. "Truth is, I've been so busy trying to keep everything from falling apart that I forgot who was holding it all together in the first place. Been praying more lately, though. Starting to remember what that feels like."

"And your intentions toward my daughter? Those boys?"

Ben met the older man's gaze steadily. "I love them, sir. All three of them." Ben's voice was steady, his gaze unwavering. "I know it hasn't been long, but there's something about Maggie and those boys that feels like... like coming home. They've filled empty spaces in my life I didn't even know were there. I want to be the man they can count on, the one who shows up every day, no matter what."

He took a deep breath, his calloused fingers fidgeting slightly with the hem of his worn flannel shirt. "I can't promise I'll never make mistakes—Lord knows I've made plenty already—but I can promise to put them first. To be there when they need me, to listen when they speak, and to show up every single day, not just when it's easy."

"Love's easy to claim on sunny days," Henry countered.

"Yes sir, it is." Ben leaned forward, elbows on his knees. "I own my mistakes. I've been distant from God, doubting His plan. I've failed to lead like a man should." His voice grew stronger. "But I know now—I was never meant to carry it all. God's teaching me to kneel before I try to stand." Ben's voice cracked slightly with emotion as he looked up, meeting Henry's weathered gaze. "Like a stubborn mule, I kept trying to pull the whole farm by myself, thinking that's what strength meant. But real strength? It's knowing when to bow your head and ask for help—from the Lord above and the good folks He puts in your path."

Henry studied him, eyes searching. After a long moment, he nodded slowly. "Fear thou not; for I am with thee: be not dismayed; for I am thy God: I will strengthen thee; yea, I will help thee; yea, I will uphold thee with the right hand of my righteousness."

Ben's eyes grew damp. "Isaiah 41:10," he whispered. "That's the word I needed."

"Maggie needs a man who'll stand with God beside him," Henry said quietly. "Not behind, not ahead. Beside."

Ben nodded, swallowing hard. "Mr. Cunningham, I'd like your permission to ask Maggie to marry me. To become a father to Alan and Ralph." Ben's voice trembled slightly, but his gaze remained steady. "I know I'm not perfect, sir. My farm needs work, and I've got plenty to learn about being a husband and father. But I promise you this—I'll love them with everything I have, every day God grants me on this earth."

Henry rose, circling the desk. He gripped Ben's shoulder, his hand strong despite his years, calloused from decades of honest work. His eyes, wise with the weight of experience, held Ben's gaze steadily.

"Make it count, son," he said, the simple words carrying the gravity of generations of love and commitment. "Every dang day."

"And you can quit with the Mr. Cunningham bit. Call me Henry, or Dad, if Maggie will have you."

Henry emerged from his study, a quiet satisfaction settling over his weathered features. His steps were lighter than when he'd entered, as if a burden had been lifted from his shoulders. The protective father in him had seen what he needed to see—a man who would cherish his daughter and grandsons, who understood that love wasn't just sweet words but daily choices.

Ben followed a moment later, tugging at his collar like it had suddenly tightened. His face had taken on a peculiar shade somewhere between seasick and terrified. The blessing he'd sought—and received—

now left him with the most important question of his life to ask. And not tomorrow or next week, but today. Right now.

Why wait? The thought settled in his chest with surprising clarity. He loved Maggie. He loved her boys. God had led them to each other, and every moment spent hesitating was a moment wasted.

His hand slipped into his pocket, fingers brushing against the small velvet box he'd carried for days. His mother's ring. Simple but elegant, just like Maggie. He'd retrieved it from the lockbox in his closet the morning after their first real date, knowing with a certainty that defied logic that she was the one.

The dining room hummed with post-dinner contentment. Lorraine was passing around a second helping of peach cobbler while Martin told a story about Tim's baseball game that had everyone chuckling. Ralph was building a small fort with his leftover biscuit, while Alan explained something to his grandfather with animated hands.

And there was Maggie, laughing at her brother's story, her eyes crinkling at the corners in that way that made Ben's heart stutter. A shaft of afternoon sunlight through the window caught in her hair, turning the brown strands to honey-gold.

Ben took a deep breath and stepped into the room.

The table had fallen into that comfortable post-dinner lull. Empty plates scattered with crumbs of cobbler, tea glasses sweating in the afternoon heat. Alan and Ralph were whispering about something that made them giggle, while the adults traded stories about town happenings.

Ben set his napkin beside his plate and cleared his throat. The sound rippled through the conversation, drawing all eyes to him. He shifted slightly under their collective gaze, feeling the weight of the moment press against his chest like a physical thing. The late afternoon sunlight streaming through the window caught the dust motes dancing in the air around them, making the pause seem somehow golden and suspended in time.

"If I could... I've got something I'd like to say."

The room quieted, forks pausing mid-air. Henry caught Ben's eye and gave an almost imperceptible nod.

"First, I want to thank y'all for welcoming me today." Ben's voice was steady despite the hammering in his chest. "The Cunninghams have always been the heart of this town, and now I understand why."

He turned to Lorraine. "Ma'am, that was the finest meal I've had since my mama passed. Thank you for sharing your table with me."

Lorraine dabbed at her eyes with a corner of her napkin.

Ben shifted his attention to Alan and Ralph, who stared back with wide eyes. "And thank you boys, for letting me spend time with your mama these past few weeks. You two are the bravest, smartest young men I know."

Ralph beamed while Alan straightened his shoulders, suddenly looking older than his nine years.

Finally, Ben turned to Maggie. Her cheeks flushed pink under his gaze, her eyes questioning. She clutched her napkin a little tighter in her lap, the simple white cotton crumpling between her fingers as something unspoken passed between them. The kitchen suddenly felt warmer, more intimate, despite the children's presence.

"Maggie," he said, his voice softening. "You've helped me find my faith again. Showed me what love rooted in God looks like." His voice caught on the word 'love,' and he saw her eyes widen. "Yes, I said love. I'm in love with you, Margaret Mary. Probably always have been, if I'm being honest with myself. I was just never brave enough to say it out loud before now."

He rose from his chair and, to Maggie's visible shock, dropped to one knee beside her. The room collectively gasped as he pulled a small velvet box from his pocket. The worn navy fabric had clearly been treasured for some time, its edges softened with age. Around them, time seemed to stand still as even little Ralph, who could rarely sit still for more than a minute, froze with his fork halfway to his mouth, eyes wide with wonder.

"The Bible says two are better than one, because they have a good reward for their labor. For if they fall, one will lift up his fellow." Ben's voice grew stronger, steadier. "I've been falling for too long, Maggie, with no one to help me up. And I've watched you carry burdens no one should shoulder alone."

He opened the box, revealing a modest diamond ring that caught the afternoon light streaming through the window. The simple gold band held a small stone that sparkled with quiet dignity—nothing flashy or extravagant, but beautiful in its sincerity, much like the man who offered it. Its gentle gleam seemed to embody all the unspoken promises between them, promises that until now had remained safely tucked away in their hearts.

"Margaret Mary Cunningham, will you do me the honor of being my bride? Will you allow me to become father to your children? Will you share your big, loud family with me? Will you let me help you carry the load you've shouldered by yourself for too long? Will you become my helpmate, my best friend, my lover?" His voice broke slightly. "Marry me, Maggie?"

Maggie gasped, her hand flying to her mouth. The room fell utterly silent, the only sound the gentle ticking of the grandfather clock in the corner and the distant chirp of cicadas through the open window. Time seemed suspended as tears welled in her eyes, reflecting the afternoon sunlight like tiny diamonds.

But instead of answering, she turned to her sons, her voice thick with emotion, her eyes still glistening with unshed tears. The weight of Ben's proposal hung in the air between them, as tangible as the afternoon sunlight streaming through the windows.

"I love him," she said softly. "But I won't say yes unless you're ready too. This isn't just about me—it's about us. All three of us."

Alan looked at Ben with serious eyes, his small face a mirror of his mother's determination. The weight of the question seemed to settle on his young shoulders as he held Ben's gaze. "Does that mean he'd be our dad?"

Ben swallowed hard, still on one knee, his gaze shifting between the boys. "If you'll let me be," he answered, his voice choked with emotion. "I'd be honored to be your dad. Not to replace your father, but to be here for you. Every day."

Alan considered this, his young face solemn with the weight of the decision. "Can I still drive the farm truck?"

Ralph bounced in his seat. "Can I be your farm hand?"

Ben's face broke into a wide grin, relief washing over him. "Only if you help me grow your momma all the pickles she can eat." He winked at Maggie, whose tears were now flowing freely down her cheeks.

The boys exchanged glances. Alan smiled first, a slow, careful smile that transformed his face. The wariness in his eyes melted away like morning frost in sunshine, replaced by something tentative yet hopeful. "Okay."

Ralph nodded vigorously. "Me too. Yes!"

Maggie turned back to Ben, her eyes shining with a mixture of joy and disbelief. The weight that had settled on her shoulders for so long seemed to lift, replaced by something lighter, something hopeful. "Then yes. Thank you for loving me, and helping me find hope again. Thank you for wanting us, for staying." Her voice broke. "Yes, Ben Reeves, I will marry you. We will marry you. You and God... you light up my life. You brought sunshine to the darkest corners of my soul when I thought I'd never feel warmth again. Every time I look at you, I see His grace reflected in your eyes—a miracle I never thought I'd be blessed enough to witness. Together, you've given me something to believe in again."

Ben slipped the ring onto her finger with trembling hands before pulling her into an embrace. Around them, the family erupted in cheers and applause. Brittany wiped away tears while Ginny hugged her husband. Henry stood tall, his eyes suspiciously bright.

"Two are better than one," Lorraine whispered, squeezing her husband's hand.

The kitchen erupted into a flurry of activity. Lorraine dabbed at her eyes with her napkin while Ginny hugged her husband, whispering something that made him smile. Ralph bounded from his chair to throw his arms around Ben's waist while Alan approached more cautiously, offering a solemn handshake that Ben turned into a gentle hug.

Martin rose from his seat, circling the table with measured steps. The room quieted as he approached, his expression unreadable beneath his beard. He towered over Ben, arms crossed over his chest, the sleeves of his work shirt rolled up to reveal forearms corded with muscle from years of working on engines.

"So," Martin said, his voice low and gravelly. "You're fixin' to be my brother-in-law."

Ben straightened, standing tall, meeting Martin's gaze directly. "Appears so."

Martin's serious expression held for another heartbeat before cracking into a broad grin. He clapped Ben on the shoulder with enough force to make him stumble. "Welcome to the family, bro. Lord help you—you'll need it with this bunch."

The tension in the room dissolved into laughter as Martin pulled Ben into a rough embrace, thumping him on the back. When he pulled away, however, his eyes had hardened slightly, his voice dropping so only Ben could hear.

"My sister's been through hell," he said quietly. "Those boys too. I watched her put herself back together piece by piece after that sorry excuse for a man left them high and dry." He glanced at Maggie, who was showing her ring to Ginny, her face alight with joy. "She deserves the world, Ben. And those nephews of mine? They're the best things God ever put on this earth."

Martin's grip on Ben's shoulder tightened. "You take care of them, you hear? All three of 'em. Or we're gonna have ourselves a real problem." His voice was calm, matter-of-fact, but the steel beneath it was unmistakable.

Ben nodded, meeting Martin's gaze without flinching. "I understand. And I thank you for taking care of them until I could get my head outta my, well, you know. I swear to you, on everything I hold sacred, I'll spend every day making sure they know how loved they are."

Martin studied him for a long moment before nodding once, satisfied. "Alright then." He extended his hand. "Welcome to the family, brother."

"Five," corrected Ralph, counting on his fingers. "Momma, Ben, Alan, me, and Ms. Pickles."

"Six," Ben added softly, looking at Maggie. "Don't forget God. He's the one who brought us together."

The Cunningham house slowly emptied as evening approached. Lorraine insisted on packing leftovers for Ben to take home. Martin offered to help with fence repairs that weekend. Ginny hugged Maggie so tightly she could barely breathe, whispering plans for a simple autumn wedding that made Maggie's heart flutter.

By twilight, Ben's truck was parked in front of Maggie's modest house. The porch swing creaked gently as they swayed back and forth, Maggie's head resting against Ben's shoulder. Ms. Pickles lounged contentedly at their feet, occasionally lifting her head to watch the boys race through the yard, their bare feet slapping against the cool grass.

"I'm gonna be faster than you when Ben teaches me to run like a real farmer," Ralph called, his small legs pumping furiously as he chased his brother.

"Nuh-uh," Alan shot back, grinning. "But maybe he'll teach us both to drive the tractor!"

"You think he'll build us a tree house like Mr. Ethan did for Noah and Ava?" Ralph asked, stopping to catch his breath.

Ben squeezed Maggie's hand, his heart swelling at the boys' excited chatter. "Listen to them," he whispered. "Already planning our whole life together."

Maggie smiled, watching the golden sunset light dance across her sons' faces. A monarch butterfly drifted lazily through the yard before settling briefly on her shoulder, its orange wings catching the fading light.

"We're not just building a life," she whispered, turning to Ben. "We're adding on to the Reeves Family legacy."

Ben's eyes glistened as he brought her hand to his lips, kissing the ring that now adorned her finger.

"Alright, boys," Maggie called. "Time to get ready for bed."

"Aw, Mom!" Alan protested, while Ralph flopped dramatically onto the grass.

"Five more minutes!" Ralph pleaded, rolling onto his stomach and propping his chin in his hands.

"No, sir. I have work tomorrow and you are going to the Retreat with Ava and Noah," Maggie answered firmly, rising from the swing.

Ralph scrambled to his feet, a hopeful expression crossing his face. "Can Mr. Ben and Ms. Pickles read tonight's story and tuck us in?"

Ben's breath caught in his throat, the simple request touching him more deeply than he'd expected. He looked at Maggie, uncertain.

"If that's alright with your mama," he said softly.

Maggie nodded, relief washing over her face at her sons' easy acceptance. "I think that's a wonderful idea."

Soon they were all crowded into the boys' small bedroom. Ralph snuggled under his cow-print comforter while Alan sat cross-legged on his own bed, watching Ben carefully. Ms. Pickles settled on the rug between them, her watchful eyes moving between the boys as if she'd already claimed them as her pack.

"This one," Ralph insisted, pushing a well-worn picture book about farm animals into Ben's hands. "It's got cows. I love cows."

Ben settled into the small chair between their beds, Maggie perched on the edge of Alan's mattress. As Ben began to read, his deep voice giving each animal its own distinct sound, Alan slowly relaxed. By the third page, he'd scooted closer to his mother, his eyes fixed on Ben's animated face.

When Ben mooed particularly loudly, Alan laughed—a full, unguarded sound that made Maggie's heart soar. For the first time, he fully joined in, secure in the knowledge that Ben would be taking care of his mother from now on.

After the third story, Ralph's eyelids had grown heavy, his small body curled around his favorite stuffed cow. Alan had lasted through one more book before his own eyes drifted closed, though he fought sleep valiantly, determined to stay awake as long as possible.

"Good night, sweet boys," Maggie whispered, kissing each forehead. She lingered a moment, watching their peaceful faces in the soft glow of the nightlight.

Ben stood in the doorway, his heart full. "Sleep tight, little farmers," he murmured, his voice thick with emotion.

Ms. Pickles circled twice before settling at the foot of Ralph's bed, her watchful eyes meeting Ben's as if to say, "I've got this shift."

They tiptoed from the room, leaving the door cracked just enough for the hallway light to spill through. Maggie's fingers found Ben's as they made their way back to the porch, the evening air warm and sweet with the scent of honeysuckle.

The porch swing creaked softly as they settled into it, the rhythm of their gentle rocking matching the chorus of crickets in the yard. Stars winked into existence above them, painting the night sky with silver light.

"I can't believe this is real," Maggie whispered, her fingers tracing the outline of the ring on her finger. "That you're here. That you want us."

Ben turned to face her, his calloused palm cupping her cheek. "I've wanted you since the first day I saw you in high school, hair all wild from the wind, cheeks flushed pink." His thumb brushed across her bottom lip. "But I was afraid. Afraid I wasn't good enough. Afraid I couldn't be what you needed."

"And now?" Maggie asked, her breath catching as she leaned into his touch.

"Now I know that with God's help, I can be the man you deserve. The father those boys need." His eyes shone in the porch light. "I love you, Maggie. All of you."

"I love you too," she whispered.

Ben leaned forward, finally free to kiss her the way he'd dreamed about for months. His lips met hers, gentle at first, then deepening as her arms wound around his neck. The kiss held all the promise of their future—tender, passionate, and built on something stronger than either of them alone.

When they finally broke apart, both breathless, Maggie rested her forehead against his. "I never thought I'd feel this way again."

Ben reluctantly releases her and says "I'd better go, before I forget my manners. I want you so much, Sunbeam. But I want to do this right. I want God's blessings for us. So I'd better get to the house, so I can make sure we start our marriage within the covenant as God decreed."

Ben stands and takes Maggie's hand to help her up with him. She walks him to his truck, where he kisses her a bit more, hand on the back of her neck, claiming her as his. "I love you, Maggie. Forever. Goodnight, Sunbeam. I'll drive away when you are inside."

Maggie brushed his brow and his cheek, amazed that he was really hers. "Goodnight, Ben. I'll call or text you in the morning. It depends on what kind of morning the boys are having."

One more kiss then he was in his truck, waiting until Maggie closed her front door behind her to drive away from his heart.

Chapter 35 – Butterfly Moments

"Be still, and know that I am God. I will be exhalted among the heathen. I will be exhalted in the earth." Psalm 46:10

Maggie woke before the sun had fully risen, her eyes opening to the soft gray light filtering through her bedroom curtains. For a moment, she lay perfectly still, letting the events of yesterday wash over her. The proposal. The ring. The yes that had changed everything.

She slipped from beneath the covers, careful not to wake the house. The floorboards creaked softly beneath her bare feet as she padded down the hallway, pausing to peek in on her boys. Alan lay sprawled across his bed, one arm flung over his head. Ralph had somehow turned completely sideways, his feet dangling off the edge. Both breathed the deep, even breaths of childhood dreams.

The morning air carried a hint of summer storms when she stepped onto the porch, wrapping her cardigan tighter around her shoulders. Dew sparkled on the grass like scattered diamonds. Maggie settled into the porch swing, tucking her feet beneath her as she placed her worn Bible in her lap. The leather was soft from years of handling, the pages marked with underlined verses and notes in the margins.

Her fingers traced the gold band on her left hand, the small diamond catching the first rays of sunlight. She couldn't stop looking at it, this tangible proof that she was loved, chosen, wanted.

Maggie reached for her phone and typed a quick message to Ben: "Good morning. It wasn't a dream, was it?"

She smiled at his immediate response: "Not unless we're having the same one, Sunbeam. I love you."

Opening her camera, she angled her hand just so, capturing the ring against the backdrop of her Bible. She sent the image to Clara without comment, knowing her friend would understand everything the picture didn't say.

Clara's response came moments later: "!!!!!!! FINALLY!!!! Call me after my shift ends! So happy for you, sweet friend. ♥ ♥ ♥ "

Maggie set her phone aside and opened her Bible to Psalm 46, the verses she'd been meditating on all week. As she read, a flash of orange caught her eye. A monarch butterfly drifted down from the sky, its wings like stained glass in the morning light. It hovered for a moment before settling on the porch railing, wings opening and closing slowly.

Tears welled in Maggie's eyes, not the desperate tears she'd cried so many times after Roger left, but tears of profound gratitude. The butterfly seemed like a sign, a reminder of transformation, of beauty emerging from darkness.

"We made it through," she whispered, her voice barely disturbing the morning stillness. "Thank You, Father."

By mid-morning, news of Ben and Maggie's engagement swept through Willow Creek faster than a summer thunderstorm. The town hummed with excitement, conversations shifting from weather forecasts to wedding dates at every corner.

Sheriff Wade Beaumont leaned against the counter at Percolating Grace Café, his voice low as he slid a folder across to Mayor Ellie.

"Take a look at these deed transfers. Something's off with the notary stamp—it's similar to what we found on Ben's property papers, but the registration number doesn't check out."

Ellie flipped through the documents, her brow furrowing. "How many properties are we talking about?"

"Five so far, all foreclosures." Wade tapped the paper. "All with the same stamp issue."

"Keep digging, but quietly." Ellie closed the folder. "Last thing we need is panic. Report directly to me, no one else."

The café door jingled as Lorraine Cunningham entered with Ginny, both talking animatedly.

"After Maggie and Ben confirm the date, we'll have to check with the florist to see what flowers will be available for their wedding"

Wade caught Ellie's eye across the table. "Told you," he said, a hint of smugness in his voice.

Ellie just smirked, sipping her tea. "You're not as observant as you think, Sheriff. I had them pegged at the church picnic.

At the Crop 'Til You Drop farmstand, Brittany arranged colorful summer squash while customers buzzed around her.

"Congratulations," Treva said, setting down a fresh pie. "Your brother finally worked up the courage."

"Took him long enough," Brittany replied, straightening a basket of tomatoes.

Treva raised an eyebrow. "Next it'll be you," she teased, nodding toward the bakery truck where Harry Jr. was unloading bread.

Brittany rolled her eyes. "I'm just here for the squash. Some of us have restaurants to run."

Over at Hattie's General Store, Tina rang up Mrs. Fletcher's groceries, leaning forward conspiratorially.

"Did you hear about Ben Reeves and Maggie Cunningham? Engaged last night!"

Hattie looked up from her inventory sheet. "Well, praise the Lord. That farm needs a woman's touch—and those boys need a daddy."

At Bless Your Hair!, Daisy worked lavender streaks into Grace's bob, her comb never stopping as she shared the news.

"He used his mama's ring, can you believe it? Maggie texted Clara this morning with a picture."

Grace smiled, watching Daisy's reflection in the mirror. "That's what this town needs—a little more love story and a little less hardship."

The afternoon sun beat down on Main Street as shop owners swept their storefronts and townsfolk gathered in small clusters, exchanging the day's news. The excitement over Maggie and Ben's engagement had mellowed into a pleasant hum, making way for the next item of gossip: the end of the Retreat's first summer camp.

Outside the Percolating Grace Café, Clara checked her watch. "The buses should be there soon," she said to Ethan, who nodded as he loaded the last of the donated supplies into his truck.

"God's timing is perfect," he replied, kissing her cheek. "Let's head over."

At the Retreat, organized chaos reigned. Duffel bags and backpacks littered the grassy area between the bunkhouses and the waiting buses. Counselors darted between buildings, arms full of forgotten sweatshirts and water bottles.

"Anthony, did you check under all the bunks?" Clara called, clipboard in hand.

The young man nodded, wiping sweat from his brow. "All clear, Mrs. Clara."

Loquita hugged Ava fiercely, both girls with tears streaming down their faces. "I'm gonna miss you so much."

"You'll be back next year," Ava promised. "And I'll write you letters. Real ones, with stamps."

Maggie knelt beside a small girl with braids, helping her zip an overstuffed backpack. "You've got everything now, Charnise?"

The child nodded, then threw her arms around Maggie's neck. "Thank you for teaching me to swim, Miss Maggie."

Ben stood nearby, helping load suitcases into the bus's storage compartment, his strong arms making quick work of the task. Ralph and Alan darted between the adults, collecting last-minute high-fives and fist bumps from their new friends.

Winona clutched baby Oscar to her chest, waving his tiny hand at the departing campers. "Say bye-bye," she cooed.

Wade checked his watch. "Five minutes, folks. Final boarding call."

The board members—Clara, Ethan, Maggie, Wade, Francie, Ellie, and Principal Paul—formed an impromptu receiving line, hugging each child as they boarded.

"You are loved," Clara whispered to each one. "Remember that."

Finally, the last camper climbed aboard. The bus doors folded shut with a hydraulic sigh. Engines rumbled to life, and slowly, the caravan of buses pulled away down the gravel drive.

Everyone waved until the last bus disappeared around the bend, dust settling in its wake. Then, stillness descended—a profound quiet after days of laughter and activity.

No one spoke. They simply stood, breathing in the silence, feeling the weight of what they'd accomplished and the emptiness left behind.

Rosita wiped her eyes. "Did we do good?"

"We did," Ethan answered, his voice thick. "God was here."

Clara squeezed his hand. "Is here. Still."

One by one, the counselors and staff members drifted away—some to clean cabins, others heading home for much-needed rest. Plans were made to meet in three days for a proper debrief.

Maggie found Ben's hand with her own. "Walk with me for a bit?"

Ben and Maggie led the boys down the winding garden path that Clara had designed at the Retreat. Summer blooms spilled over the edges, creating a riot of color against the weathered stone walkway. Butterflies—real ones this time—danced between the flowers, their wings catching the afternoon light.

"Remember Clara's wedding?" Maggie asked softly as they rounded the corner near the small meditation pond. "Just twenty people, right here at the chapel."

Ben nodded, his thumb tracing circles on the back of her hand. "She wore that simple dress with the lace sleeves."

"And wildflowers in her hair," Maggie added. "No fuss, no extravagance. Just love and promises."

They paused at the wooden bench looking out at the field of wildflowers. Alan and Ralph had run ahead, chasing each other around the perimeter of the path, their laughter carrying on the breeze.

"Is that what you want?" Ben asked, his voice gentle. "Something small like Clara's?"

Maggie turned to face him, the question settling in her heart. "I think so. Or maybe..." She glanced toward the small white chapel at the edge of the property. "Maybe at the church? Where we stood together and you called us a family for the first time."

Ben's eyes softened. "I'd marry you anywhere, Maggie. In a courthouse, in a field, under the stars." He lifted her hand to his lips, pressing a kiss to her knuckles just above the ring. "All that matters is that we're together—you, me, and those two wild boys of yours."

"Ours," she corrected, tears welling. "They're ours now."

Ben nodded, his throat working. He wrapped his arm around her shoulders, drawing her close against his side. They sat in comfortable silence, watching the boys play, feeling the gentle rhythm of each other's breathing.

"Be still," Maggie whispered, "and know that I am God."

"The verse you were reading this morning?"

She nodded. "Sometimes I think we spend so much time running—from pain, from the past—that we forget to just be still and let God work." She leaned her head against his shoulder. "I'm learning to be still now."

The afternoon sun beat down on Ben's back as he hefted the post-hole digger, sweat trickling down his temples. The old fence post had rotted through at the base, leaving the gate hanging crookedly. Alan and Ralph flanked him on either side, their small faces serious with concentration.

"Hold it steady now," Ben instructed, guiding Alan's hands to the wooden post. "That's it."

Ralph scooped dirt into the hole, his tongue poking out between his teeth as he worked. "When's the wedding?" he asked suddenly, patting the soil with his small hands.

Ben smiled, tamping down the earth around the new post. "Soon, if I have any say in the matter. But weddin's are for the women folk, and sometimes they take a while with the plannin'. We want you guys to be part of everything, if you'd like."

Alan looked up, his eyes suddenly anxious. "Even if I mess up? Like at baseball when I dropped that fly ball?"

Ben set his tools aside and knelt in the dirt, bringing himself eye-level with the boys. The sun caught the gold flecks in Alan's worried eyes—eyes so like Maggie's it made Ben's chest tighten.

"Especially then," he said softly. "That's what families are for. We stick together, no matter what."

Ralph edged closer, picking at a scab on his elbow. "You're gonna be our dad?"

"If that's okay with you fellas."

Alan studied Ben's face with a solemn intensity that seemed beyond his nine years. "Our real dad—Roger—he yelled a lot. And then he just...left."

"He didn't even say goodbye," Ralph added, his voice small. "He promised to take us fishing, but he never did."

Ben swallowed hard, letting the boys' words settle in the space between them. "I won't promise that I won't get upset, because I'm just as human as the next person. Just like you can't promise you won't get upset.," he said carefully. "But I can promise I'll never leave. I can promise that if I do get upset, you can always count on me to stay around and work things out. That is how God wants us men to handle our problems. And I hope I can count on the same from you young men. I always keep my promises."

"We know," Alan said simply. "You're not like him, our daddy who left us. You help us with homework and you taught me how to fix the tractor and you make Mom laugh again."

"And you make the best pancakes," Ralph chimed in, his face brightening. "He never made us pancakes. He never did much of anything with us. And you read books with us and make the funny animal voices. Oh, and you gots cows and goats."

Something shifted in Ben's chest—a loosening, an opening. These boys, with their simple observations and unguarded hearts, had just handed him the most profound gift: their trust.

He looked across the pasture, where the late afternoon sun gilded the tops of the trees. The world seemed to still around them, the constant chatter in his mind quieting to a whisper.

Be still, and know that I am God.

In this moment—dirt on his knees, two boys looking at him with hope in their eyes—Ben felt the presence of something greater than himself. A divine hand guiding them all toward healing, toward family.

The boys' breathing had deepened into the steady rhythm of sleep, their small bodies curled beneath quilts Lorraine had stitched years ago. Maggie closed their bedroom door softly and padded down the hallway to her own room, Ben's goodnight kiss still warming her lips.

Before long, she wouldn't have to watch him walk away after their goodnight kisses. She anticipated feeling a husband's warmth beside her through the night once more. Yet beyond that physical comfort, she eagerly awaited sharing herself with Ben—the man whose mere glance or soft murmur of "Sunbeam" sent flutters through her stomach. Though she might have more past experience, everything with Ben would feel like the first time, because their union had been divinely orchestrated.

The house settled around her with familiar creaks and sighs. She sat on the edge of her bed, the weight of the day—of all that had happened—pressing on her in the gentlest way. Not a burden, but a fullness.

From beneath her bed, she pulled out a cedar box, its lid worn smooth from years of handling. The brass hinges protested slightly as she opened it, releasing the scent of dried flowers and old paper.

Her fingers brushed past childhood treasures: a ribbon from her first spelling bee, a polished stone from the creek bed, a faded photograph of her parents on their front porch swing. Then she found it—the pressed butterfly, its wings still vibrant despite the years, preserved between sheets of wax paper.

Clara had given it to her the summer they turned sixteen. They'd been lying in the tall grass behind the Sharp farm, watching clouds drift overhead, dreaming of futures that seemed impossibly distant.

"Look," Clara had whispered as a monarch settled on a nearby wildflower. "It's a miracle."

They'd watched, breathless, as it opened and closed its wings, sunlight filtering through the delicate orange patterns.

Later, they'd found it on the ground, its brief life complete. Clara had carefully pressed it between the pages of her Bible, and weeks later, presented it to Maggie.

"To remind you," Clara had said, "that beautiful things come from dark places."

Maggie traced the butterfly's outline now, remembering how lost she'd felt after Roger left—cocoon-wrapped in grief and betrayal, unable to imagine transformation.

Beside the butterfly, she placed Ben's mother's ring box and a photo Alan had taken that afternoon: Ben with his arms around her and the boys, all four faces alight with joy.

"This is our chrysalis," she whispered into the quiet room. "Every broken piece, every tear, every moment of doubt."

She closed her eyes, feeling the stillness descend like a blanket around her shoulders. The verse she'd read that morning returned, settling deep in her spirit: "Be still, and know that I am God. I will be exalted among the heathen, I will be exalted in the earth."

In the stillness, she understood. God hadn't wasted a single tear, a single heartbreak. He'd been weaving something beautiful all along—this new family, this second chance—out of what had seemed like only endings.

Across town at the Reeves Farm, the evening light cast long shadows across freshly tilled earth. Ben wiped sweat from his brow, surveying the new patch behind the barn with satisfaction. The rich soil would soon yield crops for Brittany's farm-to-table eatery—a venture that had surprised everyone with its success. His sister's passion for local ingredients had transformed the modest farmstand into something remarkable, bringing new life to land that had been in their family for generations.

Ms. Pickles trotted alongside him as he made his way back to the house, her white coat tinged golden in the sunset. Ben pulled his cell phone from his pocket, dialing a familiar number.

"Ethan? Got a minute?" He leaned against the porch railing. "I've been thinking about a wedding gift for Maggie. Remember that butterfly bench at the retreat? Could you build something like that? Something special where she could sit and watch the boys play." He nodded, smiling at Ethan's enthusiastic response. "Perfect. I appreciate it, brother."

Next, he dialed another number, his heart quickening slightly.

"Mr. Cunningham? Henry? It's Ben Reeves." He cleared his throat. "I was wondering about that Whirly Flutterby thing Maggie's always talking about. The one from the county fair when she was little?" He listened intently, nodding. "You think Fletcher might know how to recreate one? That'd be perfect. Thank you, sir."

After hanging up, Ben settled onto the porch swing, the evening breeze cooling his skin. Ms. Pickles curled at his feet with a contented sigh.

The memory of Maggie's goodnight kiss lingered on his lips, sweet as summer honey. Soon, he wouldn't have to leave her doorstep each night. Soon, they'd build a life together under one roof—he, Maggie, and those two remarkable boys.

His heart swelled at the thought of claiming Maggie as his wife. The way her eyes crinkled when she laughed, how she hummed hymns while kneading bread dough, the gentle strength with which she mothered her sons—all of it enchanted him beyond measure.

Ben closed his eyes, breathing deeply of the night air. The verse Maggie had shared that morning echoed in his mind: "Be still, and know that I am God."

In the quiet, with a cricket song rising around him, Ben felt the truth of those words settle into his bones. God had been working all along—through drought and foreclosure notices, through loneliness and doubt. All those years of struggle had been preparing him for this: a family to love, land to tend, purpose renewed.

Ben rocked gently on the porch swing, Ms. Pickles snoring softly at his feet. The memory of earlier that evening washed over him with comforting warmth.

They'd been sitting just like this, but on Maggie's front porch, the boys chasing fireflies in the yard. The evening air had been thick with summer heat and the scent of Maggie's roses climbing the trellis. Their hands had found each other naturally, fingers intertwining without thought.

"Look at that," Maggie had whispered, going perfectly still.

A monarch butterfly, its wings a stained-glass masterpiece of orange and black, had landed on her shoulder. It perched there, wings opening and closing with unhurried grace.

"Don't move," Ben had breathed, watching in wonder as the creature stayed, seemingly content on its human perch.

Maggie's eyes had sparkled with delight. "It's a sign," she'd murmured after nearly a full minute. The butterfly finally took flight, spiraling upward into the darkening sky.

"A sign of what?" Ben had asked, mesmerized by the joy on her face.

"That beautiful things come from dark places." Her smile had turned thoughtful. "Oh, I almost forgot to tell you—the new preacher, Harry something-or-other, is giving his first sermon this Sunday."

Ben had replied. "Ethan mentioned him."

Maggie had turned toward him, her eyes suddenly bright with possibility. "What do you think about asking him to do our wedding? After service?"

"Yes," Ben had answered without hesitation. "I don't want to wait long, Maggie. I don't need anything fancy."

"Me neither. Just us, the boys, our families." She'd squeezed his hand. "Soon."

He'd leaned in then, drawn by the moonlight in her hair and the promise in her eyes. Their kiss had been long, slow, and sweet—just a hint of heat simmering beneath, a promise of more to come.

"Have I told you I love you today, soon-to-be Mrs. Reeves?" he murmured against her lips.

"Why, no, you haven't, sir." Her smile had been playful, her eyes holding his. "Kiss me again before the boys interrupt us."

He'd wrapped his arms around her, pulled her close, tilted his head, and done exactly as he was told.

In that moment, with Maggie in his arms and the boys' laughter carrying across the yard, Ben had felt it—that holy stillness, that perfect peace. The verse had whispered through his mind, settling into his soul: "Be still, and know that I am God."

Ben shook away the memory, but the smile and heat remained. "Come'on Ms. Pickles. Time for bed. The sooner we sleep, the sooner we get to talk to my Sunbeam again.

Epilogue – The Treehouse and the Promise

"Through wisdom is an house builded; and by understanding it is established:"
Proverbs 24:3 (KJV)

Maggie sat at her kitchen table, pen tapping against the yellow legal pad. Her wedding list had grown from a few simple items to two full pages. Ralph sprawled across from her, tongue caught between his teeth as he colored what appeared to be a family portrait—complete with Ms. Pickles wearing a bow tie.

Alan hunched over the counter, methodically sharpening pencils and arranging them by length.

"For the big meeting," he explained when Maggie raised an eyebrow. "Gotta be prepared."

The knock at the door came right on schedule. Ben never rang the bell this early, knowing the boys might still be sleeping. Maggie opened the door to find him already halfway back to his truck, a paper sack on the welcome mat. She scooped it up, breathing in the smell of fresh biscuits and scrambled eggs.

Inside was a folded note in Ben's neat handwriting: "One week engaged, forever to go. Love you."

Maggie pressed the paper to her chest, warmth spreading through her. Following God wasn't always easy, especially when His Word seemed to contradict what the world called normal. The world said live together first, see if it works out. God's plan looked different. She knew plenty of folks who'd laugh at the idea of waiting, of building a marriage on faith rather than a trial run. But something about Ben's old-fashioned ways felt right to her soul, like coming home to a place she'd never been but somehow always belonged.

She and Ben had agreed from the start—they wanted to honor the Lord in their relationship. Honor the covenant of marriage God has decreed. That meant separate homes until wedding vows were spoken, no matter how inconvenient. Planning a life together while living apart wasn't simple, but they were determined to start on the right foot. A life blessed by God, built on his will, was worth the wait, work, and effort.

"Ben say if the new preacher agreed?" Alan called from the kitchen.

Maggie returned, unloading breakfast onto plates. "I asked him yesterday. He thinks Preacher Spinnaker will say yes to officiating."

"Spinnaker?" Ralph looked up from his coloring. "Like a boat sail?"

"Seems like a good man," Maggie said, pouring orange juice. "Ben says he grew up here in Willow Creek but's been away a long time."

She paused, spatula mid-air. Something about that name tugged at her memory. Spinnaker. The name felt familiar, like a song she'd once known but couldn't quite recall. Had she met him before? Was he connected to someone she knew?

Her overtired brain refused to make the connection. Between wedding planning, the boys' summer activities, and helping with the retreat, she barely had time to breathe, let alone solve mysteries from the past.

"Maybe it'll come to me later," she murmured, setting plates before her hungry sons.

The Shepherds Gather

The scent of fresh coffee filled the retreat's dining hall as Willow Creek's business leaders settled into mismatched chairs. Summer sunlight streamed through newly installed windows, casting golden rectangles across the polished floor where children's laughter had echoed just days before.

The first foster kids camp had wrapped up with tearful goodbyes and promises to return. Clara and Ethan had opened the retreat's common spaces to the community while keeping the residential areas private—a balance of hospitality and protection that suited Willow Creek's needs perfectly.

Maggie slipped into a seat beside Ben, their shoulders brushing. His presence steadied her in a way she was still getting used to. Around them, familiar faces gathered—Wade checking his phone for messages from dispatch, Jake sketching something on a notepad, Paul arranging handouts with military precision. Greg and Daisy arrived together, her purple-streaked hair bright against his faded flannel shirt.

"Looks like we've got almost everyone," Ben whispered, his breath warm against her ear.

"Treva and the others are knee-deep in pie crust at Kneadful Things," Maggie replied. "Last-minute Nashville order. Hundred pies by morning."

Ben whistled low. "Bet those gals are in their element."

Mayor Ellie tapped her water glass with a pen, bringing the chatter to a gentle halt. "Folks, let's begin with a word of prayer."

They bowed their heads as Ellie thanked the Lord for community, for new beginnings, and for guiding hands through troubled times. When the soft chorus of "amens" faded, she straightened her papers and smiled.

"Before we begin, I'd like to introduce the new Preacher at Willow Creek Baptist. A Willow Creek son returning home to lead the same church he grew up in... Harry Spinnaker."

The room went utterly still.

Clara drops her pen. It rolls across the table and tumbles to the floor, the only sound in the suddenly silent room. Greg's head jerks up, coffee sloshing dangerously close to the rim of his mug. Maggie's eyes widen as recognition floods her face.

"No. Way." Wade pushed back his chair and stood, shaking his head in disbelief. "Harold 'Harry' Spinnaker, the prodigal son, a card carrying member of the First and Forever Friends, finally came home." He crossed the room in three long strides and wrapped Harry in a bear hug that lifted the new preacher's feet clean off the ground, a reunion years in the making.

When Wade finally released him, Ethan was next, grinning as he reached out to shake his long lost best friend's hand. "Harry James Spinnaker—you've got some explaining to do."

Harry chuckled, hands raised in surrender. His eyes crinkled at the corners, older but unmistakably the same boy who'd climbed trees and skipped rocks with them decades ago. "I've been home a while, settling in at the Church. There's more to it than you might think. Figured this was as good a time as any to show my face."

Clara pushed past the others, tears welling in her eyes as she threw her arms around him. "You were our brother before my parents gave me three of 'em. We've missed you so much, Harry!"

The room buzzed with whispers as others recognized the name from old stories, the legend of the First and Forever Friends—the tight-knit group that had once been inseparable.

Greg grinned, running a hand through his salt-and-pepper hair. "We thought you ran off to be a cowboy or something."

Harry smiled softly, his expression holding something deeper than mere homecoming joy. "Turns out God had other plans."

The Shepherds meeting stretched well into the afternoon, plans laid out for Willow Creek's revival. Harry's unexpected return dominated conversation even after Ellie adjourned the official business. Old friends clustered around him, years melting away as they reconnected.

"You're staying for good this time?" Clara asked, her hand on Harry's arm.

He nodded, something unreadable flickering across his face. "God brought me home for a reason."

Sheriff Wade settled back into his chair, still grinning from Harry's return, when his gaze snagged on a figure near the back of the room. A man in a crisp gray suit stood apart from the group, his grin sharp enough to slice pie and twice a cold. The Suit's eyes flicked toward Harry, then Wade, before settling on the window overlooking the Retreat's grounds. Something about him felt… off—like a city slicker at a barn dance. Wade's instincts prickled, the same way they had when he'd first spotted that Landry and Son truck on the county road months back. He made a mental note to keep an eye on the stranger, his hand absently brushing the folder of deed transfers on the table.

As twilight approached, they gradually dispersed—Wade back to his patrol, Clara and Ethan to check on their children, Ellie to review town permits. Ben kissed Maggie's cheek and whispered, "Taking the boys to fix that treehouse roof tomorrow. Might be good for them."

"I think it might be good for all of you," she replied.

The Treehouse – Restoration, Not Nostalgia

The next day dawned clear and bright. Summer heat settled over the retreat as Ben's truck rumbled up the gravel drive, Alan and Ralph bouncing in the back seat. Ms. Pickles sat between them, her tail thumping against the upholstery.

"I still don't understand why we gotta bring the dog, she can't even climb up the ladder," Alan grumbled, though his hand never stopped petting her white fur.

Ben chuckled as he parked near the trailhead. "Every good construction site needs a supervisor."

They unloaded tools from the truck bed—hammers, nails, fresh shingles, and lengths of lumber to replace what the storm had torn away. The boys carried what they could, trudging up the path toward the massive oak that had sheltered generations of Willow Creek children.

The treehouse looked worse in daylight. One corner of the roof had completely collapsed, and rain had warped the wooden floor beneath.

"This is gonna take all day," Alan sighed, dropping his tool belt.

"Then we better get started." Ben ruffled his hair. "Ralph, you and Ms. Pickles clear away those broken branches. Alan, let's sort these shingles."

They worked steadily, the sound of hammering punctuating their conversation. Ralph carefully stacked debris while Ben showed Alan how to measure and cut replacement boards.

"Can we make a flag?" Ralph asked suddenly, looking up from his task. "Every fort needs a flag."

Ben grinned. "Only if you let Ms. Pickles be our lookout."

"She'd make a terrible lookout," Alan snorted. "She falls asleep in the sun."

"I dunno," Ralph countered, scratching behind the dog's ears. "She barks at squirrels. That's like enemy soldiers."

"Enemy soldiers?" Ben raised an eyebrow. "What kind of fort are we building here?"

The boys dissolved into giggles as Ms. Pickles flopped onto her back, paws in the air, completely undermining her potential as a guard dog.

From the retreat trailhead, Maggie watched the scene unfold. Ben's patient instructions, the boys' eager responses, the way they worked together without tension or fear. Six months ago, she couldn't have imagined this—her sons comfortable with a man who wasn't their father, her heart open enough to let someone in.

She smiled, no longer afraid of what tomorrow might bring.

A Quiet Moment – Paul's Prayer

The afternoon sun filtered through the oak leaves, casting dappled shadows across the half-repaired treehouse. Ben stood back to survey their progress, wiping sweat from his brow with his forearm. The boys had fallen into a rhythm—Ralph handing nails to Alan, who carefully positioned them for Ben to hammer into place.

"Y'all hear that?" Ben paused, hammer suspended mid-swing.

Footsteps crunched along the path, and Paul Grayson emerged from the tree line, a wicker picnic basket swinging from one hand. His weathered face broke into a smile at the sight of their construction project.

"Thought you folks might need some sustenance," he called, setting the basket down at the base of the tree. "They packed up enough to feed an army at the Percolating Grace."

Ralph scrambled down the ladder. "Did they make those oatmeal cookies? The ones with the raisins that look like bugs?"

Paul chuckled. "Two dozen. And said to tell you they're definitely not bugs."

As the boys dove into the basket, Paul moved closer to Ben, reaching into his shirt pocket. He withdrew a folded piece of paper, cream-colored and slightly worn at the edges.

"This is for you," he said quietly, pressing the note into Ben's palm. "Been carrying it around for a few days, waiting for the right moment."

Ben unfolded it carefully. In Paul's neat handwriting were the words: "For the ones who nearly missed each other. And the God who made sure they didn't."

Something tightened in Ben's chest as he read it, a fullness he couldn't quite name.

Paul glanced toward the retreat, where Maggie had started walking their way. "Been watching you two find your way to each other. Reminds me of another story I know well."

He placed a hand on Ben's shoulder. "Mind if I say a blessing over all this?"

Ben nodded, suddenly unable to speak past the lump in his throat.

Paul removed his hat and bowed his head just as Maggie joined them. The boys, sensing the shift in mood, set down their cookies and gathered close.

"Lord," Paul began, his voice steady and sure, "bless the hands that build. Bless the hearts that heal. We thank You for second chances and for the courage to take them."

Ms. Pickles sat perfectly still, as if she too understood the gravity of the moment.

Clara's Keepsake – A Butterfly Reborn

The kitchen timer chimed just as Maggie pulled the last batch of blueberry muffins from the oven. The scent of warm berries and butter filled the small kitchen, mingling with the breeze drifting through the open window. She'd been baking all day—a habit from her childhood that still calmed her racing thoughts.

A gentle knock at the screen door pulled her attention from the cooling rack.

"It's open!" she called, wiping flour-dusted hands on her apron.

Clara stepped inside, her sundress bright against the muted kitchen walls. She carried a small paper bag, carefully folded at the top. Her eyes sparkled with something like excitement.

"You're up early," Maggie said, offering her oldest friend a still-warm muffin.

Clara shook her head. "Can't stay. The kids are waiting at the retreat for a nature hike." She held out the paper bag. "But I wanted to give you this before the wedding madness takes over everything."

Maggie set down her spatula and accepted the small package. Inside, nestled in tissue paper, was a wooden butterfly no larger than her palm. The craftsmanship was exquisite—each delicate wing carved with intricate patterns, the body slender and graceful. The wood had been sanded smooth, then stained a rich honey color that caught the morning light.

"Ethan made this?" Maggie whispered, running her fingertip along the edge of one wing.

Clara nodded. "I asked him to make it for you to always remind you that no matter how ugly life gets, when you have faith in God, trust him with your entire being, you will always be like the butterflies you have always loved, free and able to rise above it all."

Tears pricked at Maggie's eyes. She closed her fingers around the butterfly, feeling its solid weight against her palm. She drew a deep breath—steady and whole.

Evening on the Porch – A Porch, a Ring, and a Prayer

Crickets sang their evening chorus as Maggie rocked gently on the front porch swing, the wooden slats creaking a familiar rhythm beneath her. The scent of late summer honeysuckle drifted on the breeze, mingling with the earthy smell of freshly watered grass. Inside, the boys had finally surrendered to sleep after a day of treehouse repairs and excited wedding talk.

The crunch of gravel announced Ben's arrival before his truck's headlights swept across the yard. Ms. Pickles' ears perked up from her spot by the screen door, tail thumping against the porch boards in anticipation.

Ben climbed the steps, a wicker basket of late tomatoes in one hand, moonlight catching on his tired smile. Ms. Pickles rose to greet him, circling once before settling at the top of the steps, her watchful gaze scanning the darkness beyond.

"Evening, Sunbeam," Ben murmured, setting the basket down and easing onto the swing beside her.

His arm found its way around her shoulders, drawing her close enough that she could feel his breath warm against her cheek. The swing rocked gently as he took her hand in his, pressing a reverent kiss to her knuckles.

"One more week," he said softly, his thumb tracing the simple engagement ring on her finger.

Maggie nodded, leaning into his solid warmth. "And then I'll be Mrs. Reeves."

Ben's chest rumbled with a low chuckle. "No more kissing goodnight on your porch or mine. Just mornings beside you—with God in the middle." His eyes crinkled at the corners. "Well, maybe not always in the middle. I gotta admit I'm looking forward to seeing how the other half lives."

The swing creaked as Maggie shifted, her expression growing serious. "Ben, I still get scared sometimes." Her voice dropped to barely above a whisper. "The scars Roger left... they may never fully heal. I'm trying to stay present, to be grateful for you and this second chance. I just don't want you caught in the crossfire when I backslide."

Ben's arm tightened around her. "Jitters are normal, Mags. Been having them myself." He turned to face her. "Not because of you, but because marriage is a big, permanent life choice for anyone. Living within the covenant of marriage as God has decreed is a sacred undertaking."

His calloused fingers gently tilted her chin up. "It's okay to have missteps. God knows we aren't perfect, but He continues to give us grace every day anyway. We just keep communication open and honest, own our shortcomings, ask for forgiveness, and strive to do better next time."

His voice deepened with emotion. "That's a love that stays, Sunbeam. That's a love that outlives our earthly journey. That's how I love you, my Maggie."

As if summoned by their words, a butterfly—rarely seen at night—fluttered down and landed on their joined hands. It lingered there, wings opening and closing in the moonlight, as if offering a blessing.

They exchanged a smile, recognizing God's gentle reminder in this small miracle. The butterfly's delicate presence seemed to affirm everything they'd just shared—a living testament to beauty emerging from transformation, to hope taking flight even in darkness. In that perfect moment, neither needed words to understand the blessing they'd been given.

Maggie's whispered prayer rose into the night air: "Thank You, Lord, for teaching us how to wait—and for giving us something worth waiting for. For showing us that sometimes the longest roads lead to the sweetest destinations, and that Your timing, though mysterious, is always perfect."

Coming Soon: Book 3 – Truth Begets Light

You've just walked with Maggie through heartbreak, survival, and surrender—and with Ben through loss, longing, and quiet faith. *Harvest of the Heart* isn't just a love story. It's a testimony to what happens when we choose to believe again… in hope, in healing, and in a God who never lets go, even when we do.

Thank you for taking this journey through Willow Creek. The story continues in *Truth Begets Light*.

At Maggie and Ben's wedding, Willow Creek is buzzing with laughter, reunion, and celebration. The First and Forever Friends are finally together again, swapping memories and teasing old scars with easy affection.

One friend, however, remains conspicuously absent—Treva Walker. She's helping Maggie get ready, avoiding the crowd… and avoiding the new preacher she hasn't yet met.

But fate has a different plan. As Preacher Harold Spinnaker steps into the chapel to officiate, Treva finally looks up from her camera—and the world shifts.

Twelve years vanish in an instant. Recognition burns.

She's looking at the father of her son.

And he has no idea.

Neither does their son.

Where It All Began: An Excerpt from Book 1 of the Willow Creek Second Chances Series Tennessee

Before Maggie and Ben... before Treva and Harry Sr.... there was Clara and Ethan. The story that started it all in a town full of faith, second chances, and hope... begins here.

Second Chances in Middle Tennessee

Book 1 of the Willow Creek Second Chances Christian Romance Series

Chapter 1: No Place Like Home

"God is our refuge and strength, an ever-present help in trouble." – Psalms 46:1

Clara white-knuckled the steering wheel of her weathered SUV, a faithful old Nissan Pathfinder she'd nicknamed "Old Trusty," its motor droning a deep, constant melody as she steered toward the drowsy dot on the map in Middle Tennessee she'd left behind. The dreary February heavens loomed, a steel-colored blanket stretched above land now populated with real estate markers instead of crops, their "For Sale" signs dotting the countryside like lost sheep. The question nagged at her thoughts - that tired phrase about the impossibility of returning home - while the radio softly played an old country tune she remembered from high school dances. Yet remaining put wasn't feasible, not with all those memories haunting every street corner back in Memphis. Her former spouse, Truman, languished in a psychiatric prison, serving a lifetime sentence for holding up businesses - a sterile legal summary that didn't begin to capture the nightmare he'd created in their little family's world. The truth resided in her hidden wounds, in their daughter's suspicious looks at age ten, in their son's subtle recoils at seven whenever a door slammed too hard or voices raised above a whisper. That emergency room visit - following his brutal assault while their children looked on from behind the kitchen counter - had marked the end, leaving her with three cracked ribs and a resolve harder than Tennessee limestone. The speedy trial preceded a swift divorce, cutting all connections between them and their father like a sharp knife through butter. They'd achieved genuine freedom, though the price had been steep as a mountain holler. She'd arranged shipment of their belongings to their future residence, crammed what remained into her SUV, and escaped to the sole place offering sanctuary: Willow Creek, a fading community where men like Truman had no place among its weathered barns and honest folk who still left their doors unlocked at night.

The placard welcomed them as their vehicle rumbled along the unpaved entrance, memories of youth flooding her consciousness. She gestured toward familiar spots for her children—Ava, listening through headphones, brightened at the ancient tree she'd once scaled, while Noah pressed against the window, softly exclaiming "Cows!" with an innocence his father couldn't extinguish. Clara steered into the lot at Hattie's General Store, its aging signboard gently swinging, and switched off the car. She just needed fuel and provisions until morning. Yet ascending the squeaking stairway, familiar aromas drifted past: boot leather, crispy fried chicken from the counter, a comforting blend of hometown scents that pulled at her frayed emotions. She doubted her place here after her extended absence. The media had exposed Truman's offenses, yet nobody comprehended the full extent—her family, Maggie, Ethan, unaware of the violence, the terror. How will they react to reality? Will they condemn my failure to shield us? Reject us like others did? Perhaps they should have chosen an unfamiliar community where nobody knew them.

Clara inhaled deeply and entered. The overhead chime resonated, a remembered sound that coursed through her like a forgotten melody. The store stretched ahead, timeworn but intact—orderly merchandise, footwear and headwear section, coolers humming by the food counter. The mingled scents embraced her, coaxing a slight grin despite her burden. Tina Edwards complained from her scratched station, "Business is slow," in a weary tone. Their gazes met, and Tina brightened. "Nice to have company. You visiting? Where from?"

Clara smiled, approaching with extended hand across years of worn flooring. "I'm Clara Jennings. We're relocating to my parents' property." Tina beamed, clasping firmly. "I'm Tina. Returning home? Which folks are yours?" Before responding, the acrid coffee scent behind Tina struck her-triggering memories of Truman's violent outburst, shattering ceramic, searing pain on her face. She stiffened, breathless, until someone called from within. "Those would be Burle and Francie Sharp." Hattie Beaumont emerged, embracing, her genuine smile piercing the fog. "Clara, you're a blessing to see. Come here."

Clara released her anxiety, melting into Hattie's nurturing embrace, feeling truly home-until spotting him beyond. Ethan Walker. Her former love. More muscular now, carpenter's debris on his shirt, his gentle eyes meeting hers warmly before turning cautious. His distinctive cedar fragrance-natural, reliable-struck like buried remembrance: closest companion, first romance, the one abandoned. Her soul yearned for him, but she remained still, unprepared for this early encounter. That woodsy essence calmed her, despite internal turmoil-sweet memories of youth with Ethan and Maggs, Wade and Greg, conflicting with the pain of departure, especially leaving him.

Ethan shook himself alert, muttering, "I'll finish Landry's cart before the cabinet, Hattie. I'll give you a call." He moved doorward, acknowledging, "Ladies." His sleeve brushed her, a gentle touch, scent of cedar, whispering, "It's real good to see you, Clara," barely audible above the bell's departure ring. The atmosphere thickened with his lingering presence, echoing past connections.

Clara composed herself, facing Hattie, who gestured outside saying, "In case you was wondering, he's unattached," then continued, "Welcome back, Clara. Tell your parents I'll see them Sunday." Clara genuinely laughed, presenting her children. "Meet Ms. Hattie, kids." Hattie glowed, offering sweets-"A homecoming gift!"- as Sheriff Wade Beaumont approached, purchasing lunch, winking at his favorite aunt. "Look who's here," Hattie announced, indicating. Wade brightened, grinning broadly. "NoBoots!" Noticing her footwear, he added, "You're gonna need some proper boots, city girl- them ain't farm-worthy." She embraced his robust hug, soothing after Ethan's impact. "Wade, hey. Who thought it was a good idea having the fox guard the hen house?" He squeezed back, laughing, then addressed her children. "Your mother once walked home from the creek barefoot -lost her shoes in muck. Always refused to wear her boots, preferred her sandals, thus earning her the nickname NoBoots."

Maggie Cunningham entered, catching Clara's response-"There ain't no Fashionable boots!"-both exclaiming simultaneously, echoing childhood. Clara embraced Maggie, her dearest friend, feeling divinely blessed-both Ethan and Maggie, her foundations, appearing instantly. The burden lightened slightly. It was like the Holy Spirit was showing her the instinct to come home was on target.

Providence had guided her toward healing, love, and protection. After farewells and future plans, Clara gathered the kids and the supplies, heading toward Old Trusty, their farmhouse destination-continuing this uncertain journey.

Chapter 2: Refuge Found

"Thou art my hiding place and my shield: I hope in thy word." Psalms 119:114

Clara guided her old SUV along the gravel path toward her childhood home, anxiety building in her stomach like a tightening knot. She'd kept Truman's darkest deeds from her parents—protecting them with her silence—but reality would surface now, impossible to hide behind careful phone calls and cheerful holiday cards. Worry and guilt began to surface, threatening to overwhelm her. Mother will weep. Father will feel let down. They'll blame themselves. She forced a cheerful expression, checking her children's reflection in the rearview mirror. "Here at last! See—your grandparents are waiting outside. I bet Hattie gave them a heads-up from town." Ava wriggled free of her seatbelt for a better view, excitement shining in her face like morning sunshine, as Noah followed her lead after a thoughtful pause, his innocent faith touching something deep inside Clara's wounded heart. The vehicle crawled to a halt in the familiar yard, and her children darted toward Burle and Francine Sharp, who descended their worn front steps with outstretched arms and beaming faces. Clara's feigned happiness transformed into genuine warmth at their radiant welcome and time-worn expressions, etched with love and worry. It felt like ages since she'd seen her parents' faces, though every line and wrinkle felt achingly familiar. Burle lifted Noah skyward with surprising strength, murmuring grateful words, his rough voice soothing: "Lord above, You've delivered them safely home." Francie embraced Ava, tears welling up and spilling freely, her cotton apron dancing in the spring wind. This perfect instant held everything—protected children, sheltered Clara, sanctuary found at last.

Strong embrace enveloped her, familiar scents of cologne and mint overwhelming her senses—Father, solid and unchanging as the mountains themselves. She melted into his protective hold, emotions warring behind her dampening eyes—solace, guilt, possibility, shame. Burle hummed a childhood melody, dabbed at his "allergies" with a weathered handkerchief, and murmured, "All's well now, Sweet girl. You're home with Daddy now. You and your little ones are protected here—that villain's harm ends here. Here you will only find peace. Let the Lord restore you for your children, Child." She tensed against him—realization dawns that he's aware, he knows. Humiliation scorched through her like wildfire, questions racing: What details does he know? What's his opinion? Does Mom know too? Will they ever look at me the same? Burle gentled his grip, voice dropping lower, "Your mother's unaware and I've kept quiet. This stays between us until you're ready to talk. You chose right coming here, darling. Let your mom care for you. Pie always makes things better." She released a steadying breath, inclining her head as the tension eased from her shoulders. "We'll unload the truck while Grandma loves on her grandbabies."

***

Later, after unloading under a sky bruising purple and gold like a fresh peach, after heaping helpings of Francie's chicken-n-dumplin's warmed their bellies and her apple pie—tart with memories of the orchard and sweet as summer sunshine—sweetened the ache, baths done and prayers said, Ava and Noah were tucked in snugly upstairs with grandparents' love. The old quilts smelled of sunshine and lavender, just like Clara remembered from her childhood summers spent chasing fireflies and catching june bugs in mason jars. She showered alone in her old bathroom, steam curling around her like a sigh from an old friend, her forehead pressed against the shower wall in surrender and submission, water droplets running down her face like tiny rivers seeking the sea. Tears came, unbidden as spring rain, and a presence wrapped around her like a warm embrace from someone long missed. She had been so lost for so long she was rusty when it came to talking with God, her prayers forgotten like old friends she'd left behind in the dust of her past, scattered like cotton balls after a storm.

She prayed, raw and halting: "God, thank You for bringing us through. I'm so lost and tired—too much chaos swirling like leaves in an autumn storm. Help me, Father in Heaven. Help my kids find their way back to joy. Show me how to have faith in you again. Grant us peace and calm the madness that's been chasing us like a hungry hound. In Jesus' name, Amen." The water cleansed, a baptism of sorts, giving her clarity and peace like morning dew on grass, and she decided it is time to tell them everything, every last painful detail, bitter as green persimmons.

Dressed in comfy pajamas, the soft cotton worn and familiar against her skin like an old friend's embrace, she joined them in the den, fire roaring against the cool spring night like a guard dog keeping watch. Mom's tea waited for her, chamomile and honey, its steam mingling with woodsmoke—smells of home that wrapped around her like a familiar blanket worn soft with age and love. Clara settled on the couch and sighed, "Guess it's story time, huh?" They waited, patient as farmers watching crops grow, firelight dancing on their faces, casting shadows that seemed to hold secrets of their own, dark as molasses in wintertime.

"Y'all might want to settle in for this one," she started, her voice soft as a church whisper, then spilled it all—Truman's isolation, verbal venom that stung worse than yellow jackets on a hot August day, thrown plates, backhands, drugs, abandonment. The hardest thing, telling them about the night he left her broken, with the kids as witnesses, and she ended up in the hospital with three cracked ribs and a concussion that had her head spinning like a tornado in tornado alley. That was the same night he got caught committing armed robbery at the convenience store on Fifth Street, desperate as a long-tailed cat in a room full of rocking chairs. "He robbed stores for his fix, then left us for days at a time, sometimes without food in the house, not even a biscuit to share between us and nothing left in the bank account, cleaned out slicker than a whistle. Our divorce came fast, as fast as his trial. He walked away from everything, quick as a summer storm, and left me with a mortgage to pay and kids to raise on my own. So, we sold the house, packed up our lives tighter than Mom's canning jars, and here we are, worn out as old shoes but still walking."

Tears flowed like creek water after a spring rain—Burle remained silent, his weathered hands clenched tight as bark on an old oak, wrestling with a father's guilt and regret deeper than a well; Francie weeping, "My baby," her voice thick with a mother's pain, sweet as molasses and just as heavy, sticking to their hearts like pine sap. She vowed to provide the "Mom remedy" of care for the body and soul—church, therapists, time and space to heal, and lots of homemade pie, saying "There's nothing can't be fixed with some time with God, good home cookin' and plenty of love, sweet as blackberry cobbler fresh from the oven." Burle prayed out loud for peace, wisdom, courage, his voice steady as a plow horse despite the emotion: "Lord, heal their hearts, minds, bodies, and spirits. Provide us the wisdom to know the next steps. Grant them peace and comfort, Lord. Help us with forgiveness, Father and guide us along the way, straight as a corn row. In Jesus name, we pray Amen."

Small smiles bloomed like spring flowers, hope flickering like the dying embers in the fireplace. Clara slept deep that night, her psyche sensing safety in her childhood bed, and she dreamed of sunshine, cedar trees among the pines, their branches reaching toward heaven like faithful hands in prayer, swaying, gentle as a mother's lullaby. The next morning, fully rested and ready to face the day like a rooster greeting dawn, the scent of cedar lingered in the periphery lingering like a promise of what's to come, a whispered assurance that healing would follow, sure as seasons change and creeks run downhill.

Chapter 3: Unfinished Business

Cast all your anxiety on Him because He cares for you - 1 Peter 5:7

The coffee cup crashed to the gravel, Ethan's notebook tumbling after it as he fumbled the key to his truck's lock. Hot liquid splashed his boots, and he growled "Good grief, what in thunderation!" under his breath, bending to snatch the cup, notebook, and keys—only to thwack his forehead on the door's edge. His worn ball cap spun off, landing in the dust. A groan rumbled out as he straightened, massaging the throbbing spot. Planting his hands on his hips he spoke out loud "Just great! Ain't this the way my whole week's been goin'!" The cool March air bit his lungs, sharp and clean, and he sucked in a deep, steadying breath, sawdust drifting from his flannel like a faint cloud. Lord, help me, he prayed silently, eyes tracing the horizon where the sun crept over Willow Creek's hills. Push these Clara thoughts away—I can't do this today, not with everything else on my plate. It had been a week since she'd walked into Hattie's, all sunshine in weary skin, and Ethan Walker still couldn't unsee her changed appearance. She'd still managed to take his breath, that earthy scent—wildflowers and soil—clouding his senses as it had at fifteen, when she'd shifted from friend to something more precious than gold. He hadn't seen her in seven whole days. He wasn't hiding, at least that's what he told himself and his sister Treva, he was just swamped with work. But the lie gnawed at him like termites on fresh wood: she'd undone him and he didn't know how to handle it.

Seven nights of tossing and turning had left him addlebrained and hollow-eyed, raw as a fresh-scraped knee. Seeing Clara had ripped open scars he'd thought healed—love buried deeper than a well when she'd fled for college, guilt stitched tight after Justine's breast cancer stole her two years back. His past lives were colliding like two runaway trains, the life before Clara left him waging war with his life since. Sleep dodged him worse than a cat avoiding bath time, and his focus was frayed as old rope. Today's youth project demanded better. The Baptist Church youth group's barn-raising at the old Stout place—now the Masons' farm—needed him at 100%. He'd pushed hard for these service projects since taking over as Youth Pastor, and the church had agreed to foot half the bill twice a year, praise the Lord. The High School had agreed to count some of the projects that fit the curriculum requirements as a final project grade for Juniors and Seniors. So, the Junior and Senior High kids had voted to tear down the rotting barn, salvage what they could, and build a new barn for the Mason's. Some of these kids had never gripped a hammer, but the Masons said they'd provide the lumber, the high school loaned them the tools since this was an approved final project, and Greg, the Shop Teacher, was going to be onsite to both mentor and grade the final product. Ethan's carpentry skills and leadership had to shine brighter than a new penny. There is no room for distraction.

He couldn't let old demons lick at his heels—Clara's abandonment, watching Justine fade away unable to stop death, that renewed spark he felt he didn't deserve flickering to life again like a stubborn ember. "Jesus, take the wheel," he murmured, eyes drifting shut. "Keep us safe today, Lord. Set my mind on this barn, not her. Make my mind calm and sharp as Mama's good scissors, focused on the project. I need You today and always, Jesus." Calm seeped in like morning dew and the chaos in his mind went still, a quiet tide over churning waters. He scooped up his cap, brushing it clean as a whistle, gathered the cup that had not emptied completely, and the project notebook—ink smudged but legible as Sunday's sermon—and climbed into the truck. The engine growled to life, rumbling toward the old Stout place. Time to lock it down tighter than his nephew Harry's curfew.

The Willow Creek Second Chances Series (Christian Romance)

- Book 1: Second Chances in Middle Tennessee [Clara & Ethan] – Available now
- Book 2: Harvest of the Heart [Maggie & Ben] – You just finished it!
- Book 3: Truth Begets Light [Treva & Harry Sr.] – Coming soon
- Book 4: [Jake & Tina] – Coming soon
- Book 5: [Grace & Paul] – Coming soon
- Book 6: [Hannah & Wade] – Coming soon
- Book 7: [Ellie & Mark] – Coming soon

Get your copy of The Willow Creek Second Chances Series books at Amazon.com

About the Author

Les Dupuy writes heartwarming stories about second chances, small towns, and the grace that finds us when we least expect it. She lives just outside Nashville and believes in the healing power of sweet tea, buttered biscuits, porch swings, and a well-placed "Bless your heart." Come visit Willow Creek—a town where hope always has a home, and God walks beside the tree fort and whispers through the creek beds.

To learn more about the author and upcoming books in the Willow Creek Second Chances series, visit the official author page on Amazon.

☞ https://amzn.to/4j8bWfm

Be sure to follow the author to get notifications when new titles release!

Made in the USA
Columbia, SC
02 June 2025